Poppy Shakespeare

Poppy Shakespeare

CLARE ALLAN

BOND
STREET
BOOKS
DOUBLEDAY
CANADA

Copyright © 2006 Clare Allan

Doubleday Canada and colophon are trademarks.

LIBRARY AND ARCHIVES CANADA CATALOGUING IN PUBLICATION

Allan, Clare, 1968–
Poppy Shakespeare / Clare Allan

ISBN-13: 978-0385-66214-7
ISBN-10: 0-385-66214-9

I. Title.

PR6101.L43P66 2006   823'.92   C2005-907608-9

Typeset by Hewer Text UK Ltd, Edinburgh
Printed and bound in the USA

Published in Canada by Bond Street Books
an imprint of Doubleday Canada
a division of Random House of Canada Limited

Visit Random House of Canada Limited's website:
www.randomhouse.ca

BVG   10 9 8 7 6 5 4 3 2 1

For Bernadette
An insufficient tribute

'Since prisons and madhouses exist, why, somebody is bound to sit in them' *Anton Chekhov*

1. How it all begun

I'm not being funny, but you can't blame me for what happened. All I done was try and help Poppy out. Same as I would of anyone, ain't my fault is it, do you know what I'm saying, not making like Mother Teresa, but that's how I am.

It weren't like you realised anyway, not at the time, not that first Monday morning. It weren't like you seen it all then and there when Poppy come stropping in them doors with her six-inch skirt and her twelve-inch heels; it weren't like you seen it all laid out, the whole fucking shit of the next six months, like a trailer, do you know what I'm saying, the whole fucking shit of *the rest of our lives*, which the way I'm feeling, do you know what I'm saying, most probably come down to the same.

Poppy Shakespeare, that was her name. She got long shiny hair like an advert. 'Shakespeare?' I said when Tony told me. 'Fuckin'ell bet she's smart.'

Tony smiled at the carpet, like this flicker of a smile, like a lighter running low on fluid.

'So what am I s'posed to *show* her?' I said. '*I* don't know nothing, do I,' I said.

'Just show her around the place,' he said. 'Introduce her to people, that sort of thing.'

'Nah,' I said and I shaken my head. 'Ain't up to it, Tony.

Sorry; I'm not. Does my head in, that sort of thing. What you asking *me* for?' I said.

But Jesus, if you'd of heard him go on! Weren't nobody else would do, he said. Weren't nobody else in the world, he said, not Astrid Arsewipe – couldn't argue with that – not Middle-Class Michael, not no one at all, alive or dead or both or neither, known as much about dribbling as I did.

2. How Tony Balaclava got a point

Fact is I been dribbling since before I was even born. My mum was a dribbler and her mum as well, 'cept she never seen her hardly, grown up in a home while they scooped out bits of her mother's brain, like a tater, taken the bad bits out, till she never even knew she *got* a daughter no more and all she could do was dribble and shit, and one time I seen her, went with my mum, and it done my head in a bit to be honest, all humps and hollows and whispy white hair but afterwards Mum said what the fuck. 'Come on, N,' she said, 'let's what the fuck!' and we gone to this massive like stately home except it weren't it was a hotel, but that's what you'd think, you'd think, *Brideshead Refuckingvisited*, which my mum loved that programme, give her ideas, and she gets us this room like the size of a church, starts ordering salmon and champagne and shit and dancing around in her underwear, which I don't know why she was down to that but she was, I remember it certain. And then I remember the knock at the door, she was twirling her tights round her head at the time, and policemen and handcuffs and, 'You come with me, love. Your mum will be fine; she's just not very well.' Like news to me, do you know what I'm saying, and I give her 'Fuck off!' and wriggled her arm off my shoulders.

When Mum weren't twirling her tights round her head,

s hanging off bridges and slashing her arms and swallowing pills by the bottle and shit, till one Tuesday evening 6.15, Mill Hill East station, not that it matters, she jumped in front of a train and that was the end of it.

When I weren't living with Mum I got fostered out, or I stayed down Sunshine House which was better 'cause none of the staff give a fuck, and you done what you wanted. Back then we was into sniffing glue and the longer you sniffed, like the harder you was, and this one time it's me against Nasser the Nose and everyone's cheering, do you know what I'm saying, and the next thing I know I come round six months later playing pool on the caged-in balcony of this unit for fucked-up kids.

After that it was like I never looked back. By thirteen I been diagnosed with everything in the book. They had to start making up new disorders, just to have me covered, then three days before I turned seventeen, they shipped me up to the Abaddon to start my first six-month section.

Don't get me wrong. I ain't after the sympathy vote. The only reason I'm telling you this is just to prove how for once in his life Tony weren't talking out of his arse; he got a point and a fair enough point and in the end I had to admit, weren't no one better qualified to show Poppy round than me.

3. A bit about the Dorothy Fish and the Abaddon and stuff like that you can skip if you been there already

At the time all this happened I was going to the Dorothy Fish, which in case you don't know is a day hospital, and in case you don't know what one of *them* is, it's this place where you go there every day and when it shuts at half-four you go back down the hill to your flat on the Darkwoods Estate.

Most probably you's wanting the history as well, like why did they call it the Dorothy Fish, but I ain't going into none of that on account of I don't know. Middle-Class Michael said they called it after this lady or something, 'The widow of Thompson Fish,' he said, 'the haulage man,' like you ought to know, who give all her money to dribblers when she fallen out with her daughter. Rosetta said she'd heard they'd called it after this nurse, like a tribute. But Astrid said bollocks to both of them. *Everyone* knew Dot Fish, she said, she was manageress down the Kwik Kleen launderette, got stabbed to death and stuffed in the spin drier when a customer mistaken her for a tiger. Sue thought it must be an anagram and she used to get Verna to try and crack it, but they never got further than 'history' and some shit that didn't work out.

The Dorothy Fish was on the first floor of the Abaddon – that's *Abba*-don's how you say it. And the Abaddon Unit was this huge red tower as tall as the sky, stood on top of

5

this enormous hill. Above the Dorothy Fish you got in-patient wards, stacked up like a chest of drawers. No one even known how many; the lift stopped at seven but there was loads more than that. If you looked from the bottom of Abaddon Hill, the tower was so tall you couldn't even make out the top of it. It gone up so high you couldn't see the windows and it kept going up until all you could see was this faint red line disappearing into the clouds. Professor Max McSpiegel said that even if you could see all the floors, you'd run out of numbers to count them with before you got halfway up. Said the tower was so tall if you got to the top you'd see right around the world and back in through the windows behind you.

The way it worked at the Abaddon was the madder you was, the higher you gone, then they move you down through the floors as you get better. And as you moved down you could do more things. On the seventh you couldn't do practically nothing, you couldn't even take a piss in private 'cause the toilets hadn't got no doors on them. On the fourth they'd let you have a bath though you had to use your foot for a plug and they checked you every three minutes. When you reached the second you was allowed to go out, like round to the Gatehouse or Paradise Park, so long as you come back in time for your meds and didn't take the Michael. It was all meant to get you to lay off the mad stuff and start acting normal, like showing a dog a treat to make it sit.

From the eighth floor up it was one-way traffic and that's about all I can tell you. If you gone up the eighth floor you never come back, just disappeared like crap up the hose of a hoover. In the Dorothy Fish we used to call it 'The Floor of

No Return' 'cause even with all the bragging and bollocks what pours out of mouth of your average dribbler as thick as the clouds of cheap fag smoke, you never met no one who'd claim they been there, or no one aside of Candid Headphones which just proves my point that I'm saying.

The Dorothy Fish was the best of both worlds: you was getting the help but you done what the fuck you wanted. All day long we sat in the first-floor common room, with its wall of windows looking down over London: St Paul's the size of a teenager's tit, Canary Wharf, the London Eye, the Thames twisting through like the width of a worm, fuck knows how many flats and streets and shops and offices and shit, and all those millions of sniffs, crossing the windows every day and back again each evening, all shrunk into ten panes of reinforced glass. Us day dribblers sat across the back with our feet on the tables smoking our fags and flicking our ash in the brown metal bins at our sides. The flops, what was allowed off the wards, they sat in two rows under the windows, smoking their fag butts and flicking their ash on the carpet. The carpet was the filthiest carpet you ever seen in your life. You couldn't even tell what colour it was on account of it was so fucking filthy. The walls was a pale shitty brown from the smoke and across the back wall above our heads was this line of yellow rectangles where there'd used to be pictures but they'd took them down 'cause the flops kept throwing their cups at them and breaking the glass. You could still see the splashes where the coffee exploded and run down the shitty brown walls. In one of the rectangles Zubin drawn this picture of Tony Balaclava, with his beaky nose and his purdy hair and triangular fangs like his teeth had been sharpened with a nail file.

The reason the flops kept throwing their cups was on account of the fact they was jealous. What they said was we clogged up the system, like stopped them from getting moved down. The flops said we eaten their cake or whatever, and we didn't *want* to leave. Which was bollocks, and even if it *weren't*, if we wanted to stay then that *proved* we was mad and if we was mad we weren't ready to leave. It was Zubin worked that out and Zubin was smart; you couldn't even tell if he was joking half the time.

4. How Brian the Butcher was late for his break and how he broke us the news about Pollyanna

Everyone talks like it started with Poppy, but really it started before she arrived. The first thing was Manic Pollyanna and this is what happened.

We was all sat in the common room one morning completely like usual, when Sue glanced up at the clock with no hands and noticed how Brian was late. 'He's late for his break,' she said. 'I wonder what's happened.' So we all had a look and seen it was true: Brian the Butcher was nearly three minutes late.

Well just as we's sat there puzzling and wondering what could of happened, there's this huge crashing boom as Brian bursts in, sending the swing-doors flying either side, hurries across without checking the carpet and sits in his chair bolt upright with his hands in his lap.

'Is everything alright?' said Middle-Class Michael.

And Brian he give this quick look round and he rubbed his hands on his trousers. Behind him the double swing-doors still flapping, open and shut like the gills of a fish. 'Pollyanna's been discharged,' he said.

No one said nothing. No one moved even, just froze how we was, with our fags halfway to our mouths.

'She's *what?*' said Astrid, had to be Astrid. Then everyone jumped in. And we asked Brian that many questions he panicked and sat there just shooking his head, and saying, 'Very much so.'

So after that Rosetta took charge 'cause Rosetta and Pollyanna was like best friends. And Brian he taken a few deep breaths and rubbed his hands on his trousers. And his hands made a sound like sandpaper scratching and bits of skin floated down to the carpet like sawdust. Then he told us how he'd seen Pollyanna when he come out the toilets for his break, and he never even known it was *her*, he said, on account of she looked so different, and he said she weren't manic no more, not at all. 'In fact, quite the reverse,' he said. And she looked all kind of deflated, he said, like someone had let half the air out. Then he said what she'd told him about being discharged, and we got him to tell it us three times over on account of we couldn't believe it. But the fourth time we asked he said he had to get going, 'cause his break was up and he needed to wash his hands.

5. How everyone reacted different, accorded to how self-centred they was, and how secure in theirselves

Well there weren't a dribbler amongst us could make no sense of it.

Rosetta just sat there shooking her head, staring across at the empty brown vinyl with the foam poking up through the holes in the seat and the red letter 'P' wrote in marker pen on the back. 'Just can't believe it,' she kept on saying. 'She wasn't normal last night, Lord knows! She was high as the sky last night,' she said. 'How's she turned normal all of a sudden . . . Must be the counselling,' she said, 'and the medication.' Must be that. Must be the Lord done a miracle! Let's hope he'll be helping the rest of us soon . . .

'Just can't believe it,' she kept on saying. Her fag-burnt fingers played with the bracelet she got off Pollyanna for her fiftieth birthday, with a gold–link necklace and a pair of studs, all out of Littlewoods, two pound a week for the next five hundred years.

'They're no fools, those doctors,' Rosetta said. 'You got to admit they know their business.'

'Well I'm glad someone thinks so,' said Sue the Sticks, formerly known as Slasher Sue before she give up self-harming. 'Ain't that right, Vern. I'm glad someone thinks so.'

'Just like that!' Rosetta said. 'They'll be curing us all and shipping us out.'

'Speak for yourself!' said Astrid Arsewipe, taken the hump like usual.

Weren't every dribbler was so convinced the doctors knew their business, but the more Rosetta kept saying they did, the more the doubts crawled in. And the flops as well, you could see in their faces, even the ones what was so drugged up they looked like they been whizzed in a blender and poured back into their bodies; you seen their eyebrows twist into frowns as one by one they realised what had happened.

'You'd think they'd be happy about it,' said Astrid. 'This is what they've been waiting for: us lot to get discharged so they can move down!'

'Nah,' said Zubin. 'They're shitting theirselves.'

'They look quite *excited*,' said Middle-Class Michael.

'Shitting theirselves,' said Zubin, again. 'If there's one thing flops can't stand,' he said, 'even worse than nothing not changing, it's anything changing at all.

'Just take a look at him,' he said, and he jerked his head to the corner beside him and everyone turned to look, but all you could see was the plant in the corner, a 'weeping fig', which I known 'cause it said so, still got the label tied round its trunk like a tag on the toe of a corpse. Then we spotted him. Second-Floor Paolo; he'd curled hisself up like a wintering hedgehog under the scaly dead branches, half of him covered in crispy brown leaves and his dark hair stood up in spikes.

'Who's that?' said Dawn.

'Him?' I said 'Second-Floor Paolo. They'll be moving him down 'cause of Pollyanna.'

'Oh!' she said. She thought for a bit. 'Who's Pollyanna?' she said.

It weren't Dawn's fault she couldn't remember, they'd give her too much ECT. It was years before, on the wards, they done it. They got her all wired up on the bed, and all of these students stood around, who was s'posed to be learning how to do it – loads of them, I mean, all squashed round – and this one he leant on the thing by mistake, and they hadn't set the dial or nothing, so Dawn she got this massive electric shock. It was so fucking massive it blown every fuse in the Abaddon, and all the lights gone out and all the tellies gone off, and all the flops started rioting and hurling their slippers. And it blown all the memory out of Dawn's brain as well.

But every cloud got a silver lining, 'cause Dawn was brilliant at making tables. The Dorothy Fish got this wood workshop. No one gone in there except for Dawn but Dawn gone in there pretty much all the time. She made that many tables you couldn't give them away but she never got bored 'cause she couldn't remember she'd ever made one before. We'd all took about six hundred home each. Every flat on the Darkwoods was full of them and the drop-in was so packed you couldn't get in through the door. And we still had about a thousand left over for the common room.

'Who's Pollyanna?' she said again. She always picked me on account I was patient.

'She's gone,' I said. 'Don't worry about it.'

'Who's gone?' she said.

'Pollyanna!' I said.

'Who's Pollyanna?' she said.

Then Rosetta stood up and everyone gone silent. Rosetta got skin like deep-polished wood. The light from the windows shone off of her face as she stood there besides me, hands spotted black with fag burns. 'I'll go and ask Tony what happened,' she said. 'I'll ask him how come she got cured so sudden.' She glanced along the line of dribblers, Verna and Middle-Class Michael and Astrid, picking their letters and paring their nails and scratching their arse respective. I never even thought – it was that automatic – just leant down and tightened the lace on my Nikes, and Rosetta she passed right over my head and straight on to Elliot, two seats down, who dived underneath his chair.

6. How Middle-Class Michael done my fucking head in

Lunch at the Abaddon was always fatty lamb, 'cept for Fridays, you got flabby fish instead. Sometimes the lamb was curried, and sometimes it come in chops, and either way you ate it with a plastic knife and fork what melted into the curry sauce leaving trails like a couple of slugs. Canteen Coral ladled out the dinner plate by plate. She never looked up on account of she couldn't stand dribblers, and when it's got to you she gone, 'Peas or carrots,' like with no question mark on the end, and if you said 'Both' she gone, 'Peas *or* carrots,' like you was totally stupid. That was Canteen Coral.

The flops lined up first 'cause they got fed at quarter to twelve in the morning and by quarter to ten there was always like six of them, shuffling side to side in their slippers and sucking their fingers in front of the bolted doors. By eleven o'clock the queue gone over the landing and round to the lifts, where nurses herded them down like cows in batches of eight from the wards. The flops already sat in the common room eyed each other to see who was going to move first, then suddenly they'd all charge forward, all at once and all together, all of them forward and into the queue what grumbled and shuffled and grumbled some more as it stretched to fit them in.

Canteen Coral opened the doors at quarter to twelve and

not one second before. Sometimes they started to hammer on the glass but Canteen Coral never heard nothing, just sat on her stool by the fire escape, smoking her Superkings, resting her back and thinking about how in Abaddon Tower weren't nobody who'd suffered as bad as what she had. One time the van broke down with the food but Canteen Coral never explained or nothing, just sat on her tight arse smoking her fags, and outside the flops, who know the time like cows know it's time for milking, they got a bit restless and started to twitch, and then they begun to stamp their slippers, then suddenly there's tables flying and panic alarms going crazy, and Curry Bob, he butts the door and cracks the glass with his head, and the nurses grab him as everyone cheers, and then the police rush in and everything's batons and helmets and shields till they've got them all rounded up in a pen, then in come the crash team in rubber gloves and give them all jabs up the arse. And all the time it's kicking off there's Canteen Coral, sat on her stool and smoking her fag and flicking her ash out the door of the fire escape.

We never seen sight nor sound of a flop three days after that, just lain on their beds from A to Z like slaughtered carcasses. Curry Bob needed that many stitches, his head looked like one of them patchwork blankets everyone knits a square of, and Fat Cath got trampled and sprained her wrist, and Gunga Din broke three ribs, he said, and one nearly punctured his lung, he said; doctors never seen nothing so close in their lives, and even in textbooks, he said they said. He was full of it, Gunga Din.

Us day dribblers ate at twelve-fifteen. As the last of the flops gone shuffling through we followed on behind. And sometimes we give them a bit of a shove, on account of twelve-thirty the hatch come down and Canteen Coral stopped serving. And even in the middle, if she'd give you your lamb but not done your peas and potato, the hatch come down and what you got was all what you was getting.

Dinner time come and Rosetta still weren't back. The rest of us, we all lined up. Astrid and Tina and Brian the Butcher, and Middle-Class Michael who only ate peas, then me and then Wesley, give Big Nose Jase two fags for his morning meds. And Middle-Class Michael kept going on about this fucking petition, and I ain't saying it was a *bad* idea, not as such, but he just gone *on*. And everyone he'd send it to and everyone who'd sign it and so on, and on and on and on and on and the queue shuffled forward that slow it was doing my head in.

'I'm not going to bother with Tony,' he said. Like total waste of time. 'You need to go straight to the top,' he said. 'If there's one thing I've learned in this business,' he said, 'it's not to waste time on people with no authority.'

'I thought he did,' I said . . . 'Tony?!' I said.

'He's a puppet,' said Michael. 'Just has to do what other people tell him. No genuine *authority*.' He give his nose a pull. 'You need to go straight to the top with these things, get to the people who make the decisions.'

'Like who,' I says, 'Dr Diabolus? He don't even *talk* to dribblers!' I says.

'Not *Derek*!' he says, like *I'm* half backwards! 'Not *Derek*! Someone with *influence*.'

I give a shrug, like who gives a fuck anyway. 'Like who?' I said.

'Do you know what I'm going to do?' he said. He was that hopped up, his pale blue eyes was watering over the edge. 'Strictly between you and me,' he said. 'I have a contact at the Ministry.'

The queue shuffled forward that slow, it was going backwards.

'The *Ministry*,' says Middle-Class Michael and he raises his eyebrows and nods, like get where I'm headed.

'You what?' I says.

'The *Ministry*! You know!' he says. 'The Ministry? The Ministry for Madness?'

'Oh, right,' I says.

'Friend of my brother's,' said Middle-Class Michael. 'Chap he was at school with. Works in the press department, I think, or public relations, that sort of thing. Knows everyone from Veronica down.'

'Oh right,' I said.

'Veronica Salmon . . . You know *her*,' he said.

'Not personal,' I said.

'The Minister for Madness? The new Mad Tsar? They appointed her a few months ago.'

'I know who she *is*,' I said. 'What you said's did I *know* her!'

'Poisoned chalice, if you ask me,' says Michael. 'Give me Northern Ireland,' he said. 'Give me Transport, any day!' like waving his hand like they's fucking asking *him*.

'I ain't political,' I said, 'to tell you the honest truth.'

'Give me *Education*!' he said. 'Anything but the MAD portfolio! I heard her on the *Today* programme! She said what was needed was a comprehensive cost/benefit analysis . . .'

'Peas or carrots' said Canteen Coral, 'cause we'd reached the front of the queue and even though Michael only ate peas and even though that's all he'd ate in seventeen years and Canteen Coral knew it, she give him a ladle of stew just the same and wiped her nose on the palm of her hand when he said how he didn't want it. Then she slammed the plate back on the clean white stack and the gravy dribbled over the edge and down the side and all the way down to the bottom. 'Well you don't get no more peas,' she said, 'just 'cause you ain't having stew.' And Middle-Class Michael said that was fine and she give him a spoonful of peas in a saucer and tutted a bit and said how she hadn't got time to 'mess about' and Middle-Class Michael taken the peas and a sachet of salt and put them on his tray, then he slid it along for his orange squash and gone to join Brian the Butcher at his table.

7. How I gone to the toilet and heard someone crying in the cubicle next door

Sometimes I sat with Rosetta and Pollyanna, sometimes I sat with Elliot and Dawn and sometimes I sat by myself. I weren't one of those dribblers who has to have like a best friend, do you know what I'm saying. Even as a kid I weren't into that stuff. I used to sit where I felt like mostly and if I didn't feel like nothing I sat by myself and I kept my eyes fixed firm on my plate, so no one couldn't catch me a glance and ask to sit down.

I had my eyes fixed so firm that day, I couldn't tell you nothing 'cept the food on my plate and in less than the time it'd take to describe it ('The Shovel', my mum used to call me) I'd swallowed it down and gone back out to the common room. It was almost empty, just a couple of nurses rounding up the last few flops and prodding them back to the wards for their midday meds, and I reckoned I'd just like use the toilets, on account of once Verna the Vomit come through we'd be queuing up all afternoon. So out I gone through the double swing doors, on to the landing, round to the left and into the cold blue glare of the ladies' toilets.

There was three cubicles and two of them already taken. The one on the far end weren't never free 'cause that was where Fifth-Floor Fran lived. Fifth-Floor Fran was a funny sort of dribbler, should of made her a hermit or something instead 'cause all she'd ever wanted was a bit of peace and quiet, she said, and she couldn't get *that*. She done up the inside of the cubicle and everything, with photos of her childhood all black and white, 'cause she must of been over a hundred easy, and her all in frills and her dad like as stiff as a post. There was this little china spaniel on top of the cistern and a coronation mug and a crucifix hung from the door lock. I know 'cause this one time I climbed up next door and had a snoop over the top. Fifth-Floor Fran was sat there on the toilet, knitting up her jumper with a little pair of plastic knitting needles. A lot of the older dribblers done that, the ones as was allowed the needles anyway. They'd knit up their jumpers and then when they'd finished, they'd unravel them and knit them up again.

The middle one was empty so that's where I gone, but I'd hardly sat down before I heard this sobbing, or that's what it sounded like, come from my left-hand side. At first I'm like hoping my ears is playing tricks and really the sobbing sound come from my right and all it was was Fifth-Floor Fran upset herself over her photos. I could still hear her needles like click–click–click and I'm sat there like hoping and praying it's her but I never been one for fudging the facts and sooner or later I got to admit I'm hearing stereo.

So what I done was I sat for a second and Weighed Up the Pros and Cons. 'Cause Weighing Up the Pros and Cons was this thing we got taught in Life Skills. What Rhona done was she drawn these scales on the flip board, and everyone had to say a dilemma which was something they weren't sure whether to do or not. Then she gone round us all in turn 'cept Brian the Butcher, who felt too anxious on account of not washing his hands, and we had to give all the reasons for doing it and all of the reasons for not doing and she wrote them down on either side and the side which come out heavier, that side won. Course we soon worked out that the way to swing it was just to give more reasons for what you wanted. Like I done whether to clear out my cupboard, and the truth was I knew I just couldn't be arsed so I come up with that many reasons she gone off the paper, like all the things I might find in there and it raking up the past and shit, and needing somewhere to put stuff first, and not being too hard on myself (she loved that), and waiting till the time was right, and by the end of the third sheet there weren't no question and clearing it out seemed the stupidest thing in the world. I could say more about that group 'cause it turned out pretty lively once we got hold of it, and Middle-Class Michael done his dilemma 'bout politics or something and Astrid got the hump and walked out and said how he'd done it deliberate to make her feel stupid, but I won't 'cause I got to get on.

It didn't took me more than a second to spot how the scales was tilted. And the side they was tilted said GET OUT QUICK! And that is precisely what I done; still pulling up my tracksuit bottoms, I unbolted the door and out I run and the crash of the scale pan bashing the floor behind me.

But just as I grabbed the door to the landing, this voice come blaring from down the far end. ''Ere!' it gone, 'cut out the racket can't ya! Some of us is trying to get a bit of peace and quiet!' And as I turned back to give it 'Fuck off!', the door of the cubicle nearest me opened and there was Rosetta with eyes like marshmallers and I knew I hadn't made it in time.

'I thought the tower had fallen down! Are you alright?' she said.

'I'm fine,' I said.

'Hold on!' she said. 'I'll just wash my face.'

So I stood and waited like I got to, innit, with one hand still on the door. Her fag-scarred hands kept scooping up water and splashing it over her face. She splashed it all over her throat as well and round the back of her neck. A few of the droplets stuck to her hair like little sparkling jewels. When she'd finished she gone for a paper towel but there weren't none left.

'Alright?' I said. I started to open the door.

'You don't have a tissue, do you?' she said.

She was rubbing her face with this black woollen glove, must of took about five layers of skin off. 'I'm sorry,' she said. There was tears in her eyes.

'I'll leave you, if you want,' I said.

'It's just . . .' she said, and she started crying again. And she carried on crying louder and louder, one hand on the sink just to hold herself up. And I got the door but I can't just go, but I can't stay neither, do you know what I'm saying, so I keep on moving it backwards and forwards like I'm trying to fan her or something.

' 'Ere!' shouts Fran. 'Can't you go somewhere else?' And she rapped on the door of her cubicle like three sharp raps and her knuckles sounded like steel.

'Thinks she fucking owns the place.' I tapped my head. 'Fucking mental,' I said.

' 'Ere,' said Fran. 'I heard that, you know!'

'I'm just being selfish,' Rosetta said. 'I should be happy to know she's better. But I can't help worrying,' she said. 'I mean what if they made a *mistake*, what then? But they don't make mistakes, do they, N?' she said. 'Not after all that studying. Doctors don't make mistakes,' she said.

'She'll be fine,' I said, still holding the door.

'I should have more trust,' Rosetta said. She started crying *again*.

'You going to be out there all day?' shrieked Fran.

'It's just Tony, he wasn't himself at all. He was really strange . . .'

'Always is,' I said. 'Look I'm not being funny, Rosetta,' I said. 'But . . .' The door swung towards me suddenly, Wham!, winding me in the chest, as Verna the Vomit pushed her way past, slamming the door of the cubicle behind her. And even though that's the rudest behaviour I ever seen in my life, I couldn't of been much more gratefuller if Gabriel hisself had come and saved me.

8. How Elliot grabbed Tony's leg by mistake and we practically pissed ourselves laughing

Tina and me was always the first ones in. It gone Tina and me, then Manic Pollyanna, then Astrid and Middle-Class Michael neck and neck, then Rosetta then Dawn and finally Brian the Butcher, who had to climb up the hill seventeen times, else the tower would fall like a tree in a storm, killing us all and clearing a path through the Darkwoods to Armageddon.

When Tina and me reached the common room, Elliot would still be sleeping under the chairs, his sweatshirt rolled under his head like a pillow and one sleeve over his eyes to block out the light. 'Seems a shame to wake him,' Tina would say, and she'd fetch him his coffee, milk with six sugars, and put it beside him and tap him on the shoulder. Well the morning after I told you about, she give him his coffee like normal, but her hand shook a bit as she put the cup down and a bit of the coffee, it slopped over on to the carpet. And Tina being Tina she picked up the cup and taken it back to her handbag to fetch a tissue. And she's just heading back to mop up the splash when Tony Balaclava appears through the double swing-doors.

There's two things you should know right off 'bout Tony Balaclava. The first is he was a genius. What Tony didn't know about dribblers and dribbling weren't worth wiping your arse on. And he weren't just smart, he was psychic on top: he could read what you was thinking. Fact half the time he could tell what you thought before you'd even thought of it yourself. The second thing is he was the most thinnest person you ever seen in your life, anorexics included. His legs was as thin as a skinny old pigeon's and his shoulder-blades stuck out that far he could pick things up with them. His face weren't no more than a great bony beak come shooting out his forehead and down to his chin, with these tiny black eyes set one either side what never blinked in case they missed something.

So in comes Tony starts walking towards us, and what happened next is like science. You remember that coffee Tina spilled, it started evaporation. And as Tony opened the double swing-doors, it sent this gust of wind across what drove that coffee smell up Elliot's nose. And Elliot, still fast asleep, with his sweatshirt rolled under his head like a pillow and one sleeve over his eyes, he smelled that milky sugary coffee come drifting up his nostrils, and very very slowly right it started to wake him up. And it weren't like he was properly awake, but just sort of meds-like drowsy and he reached his hand out from under the chairs to take his cup like he always done but instead of his cup he found he was grasping at nothing. So his hand's kind of waving backwards and forwards trying to find his coffee, and me and Tina stood there frozen, and Tina with the coffee cup still in her hand and the packet of tissues to mop up the spill, when, without no more noise than a sparrow would make, crossing the carpet on tiptoe, Tony Balaclava reaches the chairs.

I seen it coming a mile off, but I still couldn't never believe how perfect he done it! Elliot's hand come from under the chairs and grabbed Tony's leg round the ankle. And without even realising what he done, on account of his still being half-asleep and half-doped up to the eyeballs, he started trying to pull the ankle towards him. I'm not sure what give the game away, maybe the fact the cup didn't feel right, being no more thicker than a blade of grass, or maybe the way it pulled as he tugged, 'stead of coming towards him full of sweet coffee, but suddenly this terrible shriek come from under the vinyl cushions and the hand shot back with a crack and a yelp as he whacked his elbow hard on the leg of the chair.

Well I was just pissing myself; I couldn't help it, and before very long I'd set Tina off too and the more we tried not to the more it just seemed even funnier and every time one of us managed to stop, the other one would set them off again and I never seen Tina so out of herself, and the coffee cup shooking so bad it was flowing down the sides.

But Tony Balaclava never said nothing. Just straightened his trouser leg, took the cup off her and put it on the table. And Tina and me we stopped laughing then, like instantly like turning off a tap. And that's when Tony turned to me and said how he wanted a word.

9. What Tony said

As I followed Tony down the corridor, all I could think of
was what it could be he wanted. Rational speaking I knew
they weren't going to discharge me. I might not of been the
most maddest dribbler attended the Dorothy Fish (though
speaking objective I ain't saying I weren't) but I weren't the
most *normalest*, not by a very long margin. And even despite
of all my anxieties, I knew even then no one in his right
mind would of worried for half of one second, 'bout
getting discharged. The fact of it was though, I *weren't*
in my right mind, and no matter how hard I tried, I
couldn't *help* worrying, and the more I worried the more
I got certain, I *was* going to get discharged. And I got so
certain, tears come in my eyes, and the floor started
swimming, and Tony in front like Jesus walking on the
water.

Well I needed to get a grip of myself, so what I done was
I started to count off the doors as we gone past. There was
the staff room and the locker room and two rooms for
doing one-to-ones in and the room where they held the
weekly meeting, and each time we gone past a door I give it
a number and said what it was for and that way I distracted
myself and I started to feel a bit better. There was the
woodwork room where Dawn done her tables and the art
room as well for making candles, 'cept the woman been off

sick for about ten years. Then after that the Quiet Room and the large group room like for Life Skills and stuff, then a couple of small group rooms and after that . . . the doors they just gone on forever and I begun to wish I'd wore my other Nikes 'cause the ones I had on was rubbing the side of my toe.

We walked on and on past door after door but Tony never stopped outside none of them. And he never spoke neither, but every so often he'd spin round his head like a bird without moving his shoulders, and give me a quick look just to make sure I was there.

Then suddenly Tony stopped, so sharp I jarred my knees with trying not to walk in the back of him. And he unhooked his keys and opened the door, and as he waved me in front of him, I seen we was outside the interview room, where I come every week for my one-to-one and I couldn't see how it had took us so long to get there.

The dirty-pink chairs was a step up from those in the common room, with cloth-covered seats what itched your arse through your trousers. Between the chairs was this small square table, chipped on one corner, and on top of that an empty box of tissues. I seen it all in detail like a camera done close-up.

Tony sat crouched forward with his elbows on his knees and his leg muscles twitching inside of his skinny black jeans. He didn't say nothing for maybe a minute and all you could hear was the rain outside tap-tapping against the window. Then suddenly he clasped his hands. 'So how *are* you, N?' he said.

I give a shrug, I weren't going to say nothing more till I

knew what he wanted. Now we'd stopped walking my fears had woke up and begun to wriggle about like a pile of puppies.

'Well I won't beat about the bush,' he said, and he rubbed his hands like a football rattle; I practically shat my load. 'How would you like to do a job for me, N?'

It was like coming round, the nurse's face, then the rails, and the curtains, and the drip and the lights and I started to realise I weren't being discharged after all.

'Shakespeare?' I said when Tony told me. 'Fuckin'ell! Bet she's smart!'

He smiled at the carpet, like this flicker of a smile, like a lighter running low on fluid.

'So what am I s'posed to *show* her?' I said, ('Careful, girl' I says to myself. 'You ain't out of this one yet.') '*I* don't know nothing, do I,' I said.

'Just show her around the place,' he said. 'Introduce her to people; that sort of thing.'

'Nah,' I said, and I shaken my head. 'Ain't up to it, Tony. Sorry; I'm not. Does my head in, that sort of thing.' (Like still looking for the trap, do you know what I'm saying.) 'What you asking *me* for?' I said.

'Because,' he said, 'we think it might help. You need to connect with people, N . . . And for Poppy as well. She's new to all this. Imagine how she must feel,' he said. 'She needs someone in the know . . .'

'Don't trust no one though, do I,' I said. 'Not after . . .'

'You know you can always ask for time. That's what we're here for, N,' he said. 'I know it might seem like we're always busy, but we *are* here to help; you just have to ask.' And he gone on and on about how much they cared and how it might seem like they didn't but they did, and on and on and on till he done my head in.

'Alright!' I said. 'Alright, I'll do it!'

'I'm sorry?' he said.

'I'll show her around.'

'Oh right,' he said. 'Yes, thank you, N.' It was like he'd forgot all about it. Then he give me the info, like when she was coming and where to meet and stuff.

10. How I never got a chance to say on account of Pollyanna

The corridor shrunk like a concertina and in less than no time I was back through the doors to the common room. I knew right away Tina must of told them 'cause it all gone hush and the only sound was the double swing-doors flap-flapping behind my back.

The flops was slumped in their chairs like usual, bug-eyed with meds and madness, but as I gone past their heads turned to follow, like dogs looking after a biscuit, and as I sat down, I seen them all shifting to make sure they got a good view. The day patients tried to act normal like nothing had happened, and even though they was burning to know, so I reckoned I'd wind them up a bit, not nasty or nothing but just for a laugh, so without saying a word I lit up a fag and sticking my feet on the edge of the table I sat back and puffed like I didn't got a care in the world. And next to me Astrid, who'd made up her mind they'd kicked me out already, she started to look a bit huffy at that, like I done her down or something.

I give a great yawn, so open and wide, the furthest flop seen straight down my throat to the breakfast still sat in my stomach. Then I slouched myself sideways, like right towards Astrid, with my head on my hand and my elbow on the arm of the chair, and very slowly, *very* slowly, I let my eyes close, like I just couldn't help it, I couldn't stay awake another second.

I sometimes think life would be more easier if I weren't so sensitive to people's feelings. I don't know if I was born that way or if it's because of all stuff that's happened but sometimes, do you know what I'm saying, it's like I got fucking radar! I mean, I hadn't hardly shut my eyes before I knew something was wrong. It weren't the fact that Astrid tutted, or the fact that nobody spoke, or the fact I could feel them all sat there staring and there's me grunting and grumbling away like fast asleep in the middle, it was more I just suddenly tuned in that something weren't right.

'What?' I said.

They're like, 'Ain't you heard?'

'Heard what?' I said.

They're like, 'Pollyanna!'

'Heard *what*?' I said.

'Last night,' they said.

'At two in the morning,' said Middle-Class Michael. 'Suicide Bridge, so we understand. Apparently, a cyclist found her . . .'

'Called on his mobile,' Astrid said.

'Lucky she didn't hit him,' said Wesley.

'Shut up, Wesley!' said everyone. Except for Rosetta. Rosetta didn't say nothing.

'Can't believe you just sat there,' said Astrid.

'Fuck off!' I said. 'I didn't know, did I!'

'So what did Tony want?' she said.

'Nothing,' I said and I rolled my eyes, like who'd give a fuck about *that* at a time like *this*.

'Rosetta's got a letter,' whispered Tina.

'She was going to read it when you came in,' said Astrid Arsewipe, pardon me for breathing.

So everyone's like, 'Go on, Rosetta! Read it! We want to hear!'

Then the flops joined in. 'Go on, Rosetta!', the ones that could shout did anyway, and the ones what couldn't mouthed the words and Schizo Safid drummed on the arm of his chair.

'I'll read it if you like,' said Middle-Class Michael.

So Rosetta unzipped her handbag and got out the letter. Weren't much, just a page from a spiral-bound notebook, folded in half with her name on and underlined. She stood up holding it out in front like reading in church or something.

'Get on with it!' I says to myself. It's not that I weren't *upset*, upset me as much as anyone, more I should think, with all of *my* issues; I mean, not just my mum but my dad as well before I was even born, and my nan, and Mandy down Sunshine House, who I found as well, do you know what I'm saying. It was more just her timing could of been better, the one time *I* got something to say, but that's rappers all over, got to be centre stage.

So Rosetta read the note out and everyone listened. She done it alright, never cracking or nothing and I looked at the empty chair as she read with the 'P' on the back wrote in red marker pen and the fag-burnt arms and the stuffing come through and I give it a bit of a stare.

My friend when you receive this letter
I will be gone. I think you know
How much you mean to me, Rosetta,
But also that I have to go.
My hope has died, not merely faded;

My light extinguished, not just shaded.
I feel completely unprepared
For life outside. I'm old and scared.
I feel no pain, nor even sorrow,
But rather one enormous blank.
As fish thrown out the goldfish tank
Know only that there's no tomorrow.
Goodbye my friend, don't grieve for me;
I'm going to where I want to be.

11. What everyone said about the note and how they started rowing about the rhyme

When Rosetta had finished she bowed her head and stood there for a moment and the flops all bowed their heads as well and us day dribblers too, except for Dawn, who'd come in for her coffee break somewhere around the middle, and forgot Pollyanna ever existed anyway. Then Rosetta sat down, refolded the note, and zipped it back in her handbag and she sat there quiet for a bit with the bag on her lap.

'She post it through your door last night?' said Astrid.

Rosetta nodded.

'I should have called round,' whispered Tina. 'I knew I should have.'

'There weren't nothing none of *us* could do,' said Astrid. 'It's down to *them!*'

'I called round last night,' Rosetta said. 'When I left here I went straight round. I knocked and knocked but there wasn't any answer. I was thinking she must have gone round to her sister's. I never thought for a second . . .'

'It's down to *them*,' said Astrid. 'Ain't that right, Brian?' But Brian didn't answer, being outside washing his hands.

'Excuse me,' says this whiny voice, and we all looked up and there was Professor McSpiegel.

He was stood by the pillar behind Pollyanna's chair, with this black bin-liner all stuffed full of papers and more papers under each arm as well, all covered in writing and all in a jumble and upside down and back to front, not that that made no difference to him, being happy to read however it come, left to right and right to left and diagonal and foreign languages too.

'Excuse me,' he said. 'I wonder, could I see it?'

'See what?' said Astrid.

'The note,' said Rosetta. Rosetta got respect for Professor McSpiegel. 'You want to see the note?' she said.

'If you don't mind,' he said. 'I'll be very careful. I just want to look at the rhyme scheme.'

White Wesley cracked up. 'You hear that man?'

Rosetta unzipped her bag and took the note out. She handed it to Professor McSpiegel across the empty chair.

'It weren't even rhyming anyway,' said Astrid folding her arms.

'I think it was,' said Middle-Class Michael.

'Not *rhyming*,' said Astrid.

'I think so,' said Michael.

'Don't hassle,' said Wesley. 'What difference it make?'

'I'm sorry,' said Dawn. 'What difference does *what* make?'

'The *rhyming*,' said Astrid, never spoken to Dawn, or not unless she was making a point. 'He wants to see the *rhyme* scheme,' she said. 'And I said to him, said it weren't even rhyming.'

'What wasn't?' said Dawn.

'The note,' said Elliot, peeped out from under his chair.

'I thought she had!' said Professor McSpiegel. 'She's modelled it on Pushkin!'

'She *hasn't*!' said Michael. He got up to see.

Rosetta stood waiting.

'It weren't even rhyming,' said Astrid.

'Look here,' said McSpiegel. He shown Rosetta. 'You see the endings?'

Rosetta nodded. 'Why did she do that?' she said.

'It's a sonnet you see,' said Professor McSpiegel, which actually I knew without being told or I did once I'd remembered. Fact is I written a poem myself, must of been nine or ten at the time, 'bout this fox in the garden of Sunshine House, not that I never seen a fox, not that we had a garden neither, more just a yard full of pig bins. But my teacher, Mr Pettifer, said it was one of the best poems he'd ever read by a kid my age, or something like that, and he sent it in for this competition and it come back highly commended. 'There's a poet in you,' Mr Pettifer said, 'bout the only nice thing any teacher said ever; he was alright, Mr Pettifer. My mum was fucking over-the-moon, decided we got to celebrate. 'I always knew you were gifted,' she said. 'Come on, you choose, what shall we do?!' I'd only been home about five minutes. Last time I'd seen her she was laying on a stretcher with an oxygen mask clamped over her mouth and her skin like the colour of Blu-Tack. We gone for a Mexican I think; they had this place they stuck sparklers in your pudding and sung you 'Happy Birthday'. We taken it in turns, me and Mum, like every time we gone there, but they never realised, or if they did they never *said* nothing anyway.

Professor McSpiegel finished his bit and give the note back to Rosetta. I can't remember what he said on account I weren't paying attention but I know it was all big words and bollocks, like how many beats you got to have, which *I* never knew none of that when I wrote my fox poem. Then he smiled and give her a pat on the arm and walked out the common room dragging his bin-bag behind him.

'He's off his fucking head,' said Astrid. 'It weren't even rhyming anyway.'

'It's a sonnet,' Rosetta said. 'Some of it rhymes.'

'I *thought* it was a sonnet,' said Verna, who done a year of college or something, or reckoned she knew anyway.

'Some of it!' said Astrid Arsewipe. 'Either it does or it doesn't.'

'Do you know,' said Dawn, 'the strangest thing; I fancy making a table!'

'Some of it rhymed,' Rosetta said.

'Do you think I could make one?' Dawn asked Wesley.

'Yeah, man,' said Wesley. 'Do one for my bruvver.'

'I don't *know*,' said Dawn.

'It weren't even rhyming!' Astrid said. 'Not *rhyming*,' she said. 'Not like she normally done.'

12. How Tony Balaclava come through and landed me right in it

Well I kept myself out of the rhyming row, what carried on all through the morning and dinner time too when we filed in the canteen to eat our fish and peas. 'Just show her the *note*,' said Sue the Sticks, formerly known as Slasher Sue, before she give up self-harming. 'Just show her the *note*. She's giving me a headache.' But Rosetta wouldn't show her the note, and she kept her handbag under her arm holding the straps with both hands.

It was right after dinner and we'd gone back out to the common room, and we's sat in our chairs with our feet on the tables smoking our fags and finishing our coffee. And it's still pretty tense with the row, but relaxing a bit, 'cept for Astrid who's still got the hump 'cause of what Sue the Sticks said. When suddenly the doors swing open and in comes Tony Balaclava.

'Uh-oh!' I says to myself. 'That's me in the soup.' I hadn't forgot about the new girl of course, just 'cause I hadn't said nothing. But the fact of it was with all of their rowing there hadn't been no chance to tell them. And now Tony come in, do you know what I'm saying, and I still hadn't said and I weren't sure how they'd like take it.

The moment he come in, the room gone quiet and the flops all turned to look at Second-Floor Paolo. Now I got to admit that up to then I'd never *noticed* Paolo, being more took up with Rosetta and that and how she must be feeling, but as the flops all turned to look, we turned to see where they was looking, and there he was with St Paul's by his ear and Canary Wharf just a bit to his right, and Fat Florence wedged in the chair to his left with her hand round his like he'd stuffed it into a Café Diana sponge pudding. He looked so different I had to look twice to be sure it was even him, same Second-Floor Paolo been curled up under the dead plant the day before. But that's who it was.

Second-Floor Paolo always worn pyjamas, or if he didn't these scaggy old jeans so worn and faded they looked like pyjamas anyway. But today he had on this crisp white shirt, all clean and ironed, like fuck knows where from, and these shiny black trousers, creased down the front, and his hair like slicked back and I couldn't see his shoes but I'll bet they was shining too. He weren't looking over-comfortable, kept glancing up at the clock with no hands, and his lips was moving but no sound come out and I reckoned he must be praying to hisself, else going through his lines of what he had to say.

'He's got a nerve,' said Astrid Arsewipe, perking up like instant. 'She ain't hardly cold, and he's eyeing her chair!' And they all joined in how bad it was and how insensitive and that and there's me thinking *any second now* . . . as Tony Balaclava walks over our end and he goes right past Paolo without even stopping, and all the flops are like 'Eh?' all at once, and they turn their heads to follow Tony, then they turn back to check on Paolo; then they turn to look at each other, like gobsmacked, and then they turn back to Tony, and all of these heads turning this way and that like some giant machine gone mad.

Tony come and stood between our two rows of chairs and he kept sort of nodding and trying to be friendly and not meeting nobody's eye. And he crossed his legs so one foot was over the other, then he crossed them again so his legs was like in a plait. And he tried to stick his hands in the pockets of his jeans 'cept they wouldn't go in further than the tips of his fingers on account of his jeans was so tight. And once they was in he couldn't get them back out. So he's stuck with his elbows bent outwards like wings sort of flapping and trying to get free.

'I gather you've heard about Pollyanna,' he said. 'I just want to say that if anyone needs time, you only have to knock on the staff-room door. I realise it must have raised difficult issues for many of you.' His arms flapped again. 'And we want to support you as much as we can.'

'So why d'you kick her out?' said Sue. Astrid rolled her eyes.

'I can't discuss Pollyanna,' he said. 'It's not appropriate.' And he give such a tug I thought his fingers come off, but they stayed where they was anyway.

'We do our best to help,' he said, 'but we can only do so much. Sometimes, tragically, that's not enough.' I looked at Rosetta. She didn't say nothing. Tony gone red, but that could of been his fingers.

'On a happier note,' he said, looking down at the carpet. 'A decision has been taken to admit a new patient.' Well that was it with the flops, I tell you. All fucking hell broke loose. Above our heads started raining fag butts, dirty old slippers, *anything* they could get their fag-burnt hands on. But Tony didn't move, just carried on talking like he never even noticed, and the weird thing was, crap flying all sides, not a single piece ever hit him. Not a MAD money form, not a screwed-up Coke can; nothing even come within six inches. It was like he had this invisible body and everything just bounced off of it. And it *did* as well: this bottle of Lonzadine bounced off what would of been his shoulder. And I reached out my left hand and caught it like that and I downed them quick before anybody seen me.

White Wesley started throwing things back and Rosetta told him to stop but he just thrown harder, and he tried to get Elliot into it too but he'd hid underneath the chairs, reckoned the snipers might see their chance to take a shot at him.

Verna, down the other end, was going for it full throttle. Every time she thrown something, she shouted, 'Get that! Yeah!' Candid started lobbing CDs, and even Sue the Sticks joined in till she thrown her crutches and had to sit down again.

And through it all Tony kept on talking, how Poppy was starting on Monday and stuff and how he was sure we'd make her feel welcome and I'm bracing myself for the bit about me but just *exactly* as he said it, like you couldn't of *timed* it more perfect, this filthy great trainer come flying past my ear and hit the panic alarm. And I know I said my luck's been bad, but you know what I'm saying, I'm like maybe there *is* a God.

I ain't into violence, however it calls itself, and general speaking I'm pretty much a pacific. But there's violence and *violence*, you got to admit, and some of it has its uses. That riot, I tell you, by the time Tony left us, the last few flops was just being injected and stacked to go back to the wards.

And instead of us dribblers all scrapping and fighting, the sun come out and the birds started singing and we weren't even sat in the common room no more, but lounged in the park in deckchairs and we felt like we'd had a few beers as well, least *I* did anyway, on account of all that Lonzadine begun buzzing around my system.

And as the sun come out all the frostiness melted. Astrid and Sue made up and was friends and Sue said she never even *meant* it like that, but just that she *did* have a bit of a headache on account of her meds and nothing to do with Astrid; and Astrid give her a pill out her handbag and Sue the Sticks took it, said thanks very much. Verna the Vomit was on such a high she never even bothered with throwing up her lunch, and Elliot crawled out from under the chairs, sat laughing and smiling as Wesley described him all of the flops he'd knocked out. And then, I couldn't believe I was seeing it, Astrid, right, she turned to Rosetta and said how she could of been wrong. She said maybe the letter *did* rhyme after all, just not what she'd *thought* of as rhyming, and Rosetta reached over and give her her hand and Astrid took it and give it a squeeze, like right in front of my nose. Even Brian the Butcher was happy, going around tidying up. Said some ways it worked even better than washing his hands.

It was Michael said about Poppy first, and just for a second I felt a chill as a cloud come over the sun, but I needn't of worried. Turned out there wasn't a single dribbler hadn't run into Poppy before, and no one had a word to say against her.

Middle-Class Michael met Poppy at the MAD symposium. Said she'd come up to him in the bar and told him how much she'd enjoyed his speech and how well it gone down. 'She said I'd have made a politician,' he said and his ears gone red, then he coughed, said of course he knew she was just being kind.

Rosetta said Poppy had shown up at church and she'd been in a terrible state. And she didn't have no support at all. And it just shown how Good could come out of Evil and the Dorothy Fish was a sheepfold or something like that.

Elliot reckoned he known her at school. 'I'm sure she was called that,' he said. And he said how everyone picked on her and taken the piss and that, but he'd got them all to stop and they'd been like friends. And when he was up on the ward, he said, she visited every day and brought him presents and stuff. But then he begun to worry he'd got her name wrong, and maybe it weren't Poppy after all, and he must of got confused with his medication.

Astrid reckoned he must of done, 'cause *she'd* met Poppy up on the wards and she was far too old to of been with Elliot at school. Said she couldn't remember that much about her, on account of she'd been so ill at the time, she couldn't remember nothing; and she started on about how ill she'd been and she gone on and on and on; and she gone on so long they all fallen asleep, on and on about how ill she'd been and everyone round her sleeping like corpses till I was the only one *wasn't* asleep on account of all that Lonzadine still buzzing around my insides.

But she could of been talking to herself s'far as I was concerned. All I could think of was Poppy Shakespeare and how we was going to be friends. 'Cause I'm not being funny, I knew even then, I known all along we was going

to be friends; it was like a premonition. And all down the
hill I was showing her things and cracking jokes and stuff,
and beside me White Wesley, who'd just woken up,
rattling on how she'd fancied him, but he'd had to say
no 'case his girlfriend got jealous, 'cept he couldn't remember if maybe he'd dreamt it, he said.

14. A bit about the weekend
you can skip if you want,
and what happened Monday morning

Unbefuckinglievable! I finally get there and look where I am with my chapters! Now I'm not being funny, but d'you know what I'm saying, that ain't coincidence. When I started writing about me and Poppy, I reckoned I'd do it all in one go. I made up a cafetière of coffee, taken some Penguins from out the cupboard and sat myself down with an exercise book and an old *Marie Claire* to lean on. But that weren't how it happened 'cause once I'd begun, it was like it just kept on coming. It was like – I'll tell you what it was like – it was like Fifth-Floor Fran, right, sat in the toilet, she drops her ball of wool. And it rolls out from under the cubicle door, and she can't go and get it on account of she's sworn she ain't never leaving her toilet again, or not this side of paradise, and she ain't even going to open the door till the priest comes to give her her ticket. So she just got to keep on pulling her end, but the more she pulls, it just keeps on coming and she's wrapping it round and around her hand and the wool just keeps coming and coming.

I didn't choose the chapters, that's just how it come; all *I* done was keep on winding and hoping like Poppy'd show up in the end. Which finally, do you know what I'm saying, I can *see* her under the door, maybe two, maybe three loops maximum, and that's when I realise: chapter★★; I mean what are the chances of that! It give me a shiver, right through my insides, which if you think I'm being paranoid you ain't heard *nothing* yet! By the time I finished you'll be too scared to *think*, case they've planted bugs in your brain.

Poppy never stood a chance. But I ain't making things no worse by starting her off in a chapter like that. Fact thinking about it the least I can do . . .

15. A bit about the weekend you can skip if you want, and what happened Monday morning

At the time this all happened, I was living on the Dark-woods at the bottom of Abaddon Hill. It weren't such a bad estate to be honest, packed full of dribblers on account of being so handy for the Abaddon, and sanity-free 'cause no sniff in his right mind would take a flat so close to a mental hospital. It weren't exactly what you'd call peaceful. There was always music thumping away, and tellies blaring so loud the windows rattled. You had schizos on balconies hurling plates whilst beneath them old ladies pissed in the gutter and alkies threw beer cans at passing cars as naked rappers tried to direct the traffic. In fact the only time the noise stopped was at night and then it stopped altogether, and the whole of the Darkwoods gone quiet, I mean really kind of spooky kind of quiet, 'cause everyone was zonked with medication.

Personally I never minded the noise. I liked the feeling of all of them people around me. And even at ten when it all gone quiet, it weren't like you felt on your own, 'cause you knew all around to your right and your left, and above and below and behind your back wall, there was all of these dribblers just a few feet away, laying there like you was, waiting for their meds to kick in.

The only thing I *would* say about was the numbering system. They must of had dribblers design it, I reckon, 'cause it definitely didn't make no sense. I lived in 17B Rowan Walk, which was in between 66D and 17F. Above me was 36DD and the whole of the Darkwoods was numbered like that, like they ordered it flat-packed and screwed it together all wrong. The thing with the Darkwoods was you just had to trust your instincts. You couldn't afford to stop and think, 'cause the moment you thought was when you gone wrong, and once you gone wrong it taken forever to find your way back where you was. Like Rapper Rashid upstairs from me, he gone for a can of Tennent's and didn't come back till two years later and he never even got the drink anyway, on account of the offy was shut by the time he got there.

That weekend, it seemed like it gone on forever. I mean, dribblers always hate weekends; bank holidays is extra bad and Christmas and Easter is worst of all, you can wind up with four fucking days on the trot and nothing to do 'side of laying in bed or watching TV till your eyes start to melt in their sockets. Sometimes I gone up Paradise Park with a couple of cans, seen the ducks and stuff, and Sundays I gone down Café Diana; I always gone down Café Diana (Sunday Special £3.95, meat, roast potatoes, veg *and* pudding) but it still seemed to leave like a million hours to fill up with doing nothing. Even the Darkwoods' drop-in was closed, used to be open eight till eight, but now 'cause of staffing they only done two to five-thirty Saturdays, and the queue stretched right down on to Borderline Road, circling around the estate like a giant 'No Entry' sign.

But that weekend before Poppy arrived, it felt like the longest ever. I even thought of going up the tower, score some Minozine off of Banker Bill to knock me out for a bit, but in the end I couldn't be arsed. I couldn't be arsed with doing nothing at all, 'cept for sit on the sofa and wait for Monday morning.

By the time Monday morning finally come I felt so fucking shattered, was all I could do to light up a fag and drag myself through to the bathroom. And what I seen in the mirror when I did, it didn't look much like a guide at all, not even a mentally ill one, but I give my face a bit of a splash and checked again and splashed some more and the thing in the mirror, it grown a nose and a couple of ears and a pair of eyes blinked roughly in time with my own.

I gone through, put the telly on and made a cup of tea. The only thing was now I'd woke myself up, I'd woke up my nerves as well. I sat there watching the GMTV, staring at the numbers in the corner of the screen as they marched through the minutes to the time when I'd have to go out. If you've ever watched GMTV, you'll know how it keeps going round. And they give you the news every fifteen minutes and it's always the same unless something's happened – like *exactly* the same I mean, word for word – so even if you ain't really watching, you start to know it by heart. Well I'm sure they had something on that morning about that Mad Tsar woman, Veronica Salmon. She was stood outside of this hospital and all these reporters asking her stuff, and as soon as they said like 'Veronica Salmon' I remembered what Middle-Class Michael said. I'm like, '*I* know her! Ain't she Minister for Madness!' And two seconds later they said it theirselves, and when they did, I felt pretty smart, I can tell you.

★   ★   ★

I got to the Abaddon ten past nine. Sharon was sat at his desk by the entrance. 'You're early,' he said, and he give me my pass. He never looked up on account of he didn't, just carried on reading his fitness mag, turning the pages with his huge right hand while his left one pumped a dumb-bell up and down above his glistening black head.

The lobby weren't big, maybe twenty foot long with double sliding-doors either end. The only place to sit was this black leather sofa with a trailing plant beside it on a stand. It weren't the sort of sofa you sat on easy. With its smooth leather cushions and its soft leather arms, there was dribblers I could think of I'd of sat on more easy, but there weren't nowhere else so in the end I just gone ahead and done it.

Well as I sat down it done this fart, ain't no nicer way I can say it. And I swear I seen Sharon smirk to hisself, but he never looked up and he never said nothing, just tossed the dumb-bell over his head, caught it like a rattle in his huge right hand and carried on reading his mag. And it didn't stop there, do you know what I'm saying, 'cause every time I moved it done another. And I sat so still I weren't even *breathing*, but each time the sliding-doors slid open, I just couldn't help it, it give me a jump, and each time I jumped, it let off a thumping stunker. So then all I could do was like look at the floor and sit and hope and pray it wouldn't be Poppy.

I don't know how long I stayed sat in that lobby, but I seen Sharon's hair grow from bald to a number four. I tried counting nurses to pass the time, but with so many of them, they all seemed to merge, till I couldn't no more count them than counting the drops in the Thames. Dr Clootie gone past and Dr Azazel, and Dr Neutral, wheeling his

bike, with the veins in his legs stood out like thin blue
worms. I even thought, being sat there so long, I might get
to see Dr Diabolus, 'cause I only ever seen him twice and
that was from a distance. Some dribblers never seen him at
all, reckoned he must have a separate entrance, either that
or he never gone home at night but covered hisself in MAD
money forms and slept on his desk with a pile of psychiatry
journals for a pillow. I seen Rhona the Moaner, looked
suicidal, and Malvin Fowler, red in the face, with his fat
pink fingers wedged down the back of his trousers. I seen
the day dribblers coming in too, all of them in order, and,
after Tina gone through, I wondered if Poppy might come
next, in the gap where Pollyanna should of been, but there
wasn't no one. As the dribblers gone past me, I nodded and
said 'Morning', and most of them give me a 'Morning'
back, and Middle-Class Michael wished me luck, and
Astrid as well, though you seen how much it cost her.

What I couldn't get was how Sharon knew who was
who. He never looked up, just reached out his hand and
give them a pass, red, purple or green, depending on what
they was. And he never once made a single mistake. He
never give a doctor a dribbler's pass or a dribbler a nurse's
pass or nothing like that, and I couldn't work out how he
done it.

So after that Dawn come in with her son – he walked her
right into the lobby – and she kept trying to tip him 'cause
she thought he was a cab and he kept going 'Mum!' and
giving it back. And after Dawn the flow begun to slow
down.

So after Brian the Butcher come in for his seventeenth
time that morning and taken his pass off Security Sharon

and pinned it on, and taken it off and pinned it on, and taken it off so many times I lost count, after he'd finally disappeared on his final climb up the stairs I begun to worry. I started to think I should go up and check, 'cause maybe I'd missed Poppy somehow. Or maybe I'd just imagined it all, do you know what I'm saying, just made it up, 'cause I weren't uncapable. And the more I thought, the more it seemed weird that *Sharon* didn't know nothing. 'Cause Poppy's name should of been on the list, and I couldn't believe I didn't check. So then I thought I'd better ask Sharon, but just as I was about to get up he tossed the dumb-bell over his head and started again with his left arm, and I made up my mind I'd wait till he finished his set.

It was then this shouting starts up outside, like swearing and crashing around and stuff. 'What the fuck *is* this fucking place! Don't tell me I know!' and other voices, low so I couldn't hear them. Then the shouting again, 'I'm telling you, mate, you lay a finger on me, I'll sock you!' And I reckoned it must be some dribbler lost it and heading for The Floor of No Return. I seen Sharon prick up his ears as well, and he spun round the dumb-bell, like twirling a pencil, psyching hisself for action.

Then the doors slid open and in come these nurses, one male, one female, gone up to the desk. 'Visiting's not till six,' said Sharon, without looking up from his mag.

'We're not visiting,' the male nurse said. He weren't so much fat but his sides bulged over his belt top. 'I'm bringing in a new patient,' he said. Outside the noise had all gone quiet, must of give her a shot up the arse.

'So who are *you*?' Sharon said to the woman, dragging his eyes up from off of his mag. 'I'll have to see some ID.'

The woman was stood, arms folded, leant on one hip. She worn this little black suit, a lacy white blouse, black tights and snakeskin heels. Maybe she *ain't* a nurse, I thought. Maybe she's an executive. I'd never met an executive but I reckoned they might look like that.

'You don't understand,' the male nurse said. He got curly fair hair, didn't like him. 'This *is* the patient. I'm bringing her here.'

Sharon put the dumb-bell back on the stand, picked up a towel and mopped his head, then slung it around his shoulders. He looked at the nurse. 'OK,' he said. He pointed at the woman. 'You're telling me *she* is a psychiatric patient?'

'Thank you!' said the woman. 'Do you know what I'm saying!'

The male nurse nodded.

Sharon thought for a minute, then he shrugged like what can you do? 'I'll have to check upstairs,' he said; the phone disappeared inside of his fist. 'What's the name?' he said.

'Poppy Shakespeare,' says Goldilocks.

I don't know when the sofa stopped farting, but I reckon it must of been saving them up for half an hour at least. 'Cause now as I jumped up, it let rip a stunker. The loudest, smelliest, most inignorable stunker you heard in your life! And Poppy and the male nurse, they spun round like the sofa exploded behind them.

I couldn't of told you what I said. It all come tumbling out so fast. All jumbled together and tangled so bad Professor McSpiegel couldn't of made no sense of it. I know I told them I was her guide, and I must of said it like seventeen times, if not seventeen times seven, and the three of them stood there staring at me, least Poppy and the nurse was stood; Sharon sat like a mountain behind them. And each time I said it I kicked myself, but almost straightaway I said it again.

Later when we was friends and remembered about it, Poppy said I didn't come over too bad. She said maybe I'd seemed a bit hyper and that but it weren't like I said nothing stupid. I kept holding out this leaflet, she said, then pulling it back and shooking it up and down like a leaf of lettuce ('Welcome to the Dorothy Fish', the leaflet was called; I'd got it off Tony). But apart from that I come over alright. And she said, 'cause I asked her, it didn't even show how this was my first time guiding. But she weren't really focused on me, she said, being as how she was having a stressful morning.

I don't remember shooking the leaflet, maybe I did; I know I give it to her. And she held it up, like to have a quick look and I noticed the skin on her hands was as smooth as butterscotch Angel Delight, and her nails wasn't chewed but filed to perfection and painted to match her lips. And I'm stood there staring at her hands, one either side of the 'Dorothy Fish' on the leaflet, and I'm thinking this must be some strange sort of dribbler when all of a sudden, that perfect right hand it takes the leaflet, scrumples it up and lobs it at the bin beside the sofa.

I thought it was going to miss it at first, but it caught the far side and balanced right on the edge, and all four of us staring; it balanced for maybe a minute, sometimes leaning a little bit one way, sometimes leaning the other, but balancing all the time like a pair of scales, till suddenly it give up and fallen inside, and we heard it bounce off the empty metal bottom.

We was halfway up the stairs to the first-floor landing. The fag smoke funnelling down from the common room, it made like this tunnel around us and in the tunnel everything seemed echoey and louder. I could hear Poppy's breathing next to me, and the tap-tap-tap of her snakeskin heels on the stairs.

'It ain't much further now,' I said. But Poppy didn't say nothing.

'I'll take you to meet Tony first,' I said. 'He's the manager. Then probably you'll see the doctors.'

'I don't care who I see,' said Poppy. 'I've just got to get this sorted! I've got a fucking kid, do you know what I'm saying!'

'You got a kid?' I said.

'I just said so, didn't I?'

'Alright,' I said. We gone on a bit in silence.

'So you neurotic, psychotic or what?' I said, like just making conversation. Ask most dribblers what's wrong, they's that fucking grateful, they'll talk till their throats is raw, but Poppy just stopped where she was, head down, not moving so much as a muscle and she didn't say nothing for maybe a minute then, I can't describe it like anything else, she turned to me and she give me this look like I'd pissed on her mother's grave. 'Let's just get one thing straight,' she said. 'I Am Not A Nutter. There Is Nothing Whatever Wrong With My Head! Alright?' She spelled out the words like I was foreign or stupid, tapping her head to make sure I got the point. Then she pulled out her Bensons, lit up a fag and carried on climbing the stairs.

Now it weren't like I hadn't met dribblers before made out there was nothing the matter, but they made sure everyone realised it was just on account they was mad. Like Candid Headphones said she was normal then got so worried case someone believed her, she slashed her throat with a sweet-pickle jar; took thirteen stitches to sew her back up, left a scar like a great jagged grin. There was plenty like that, do you know what I'm saying, but this was something different. I mean, the clothes she got on, the whole way she come over; not being funny but you couldn't help thinking, like watching her striding up the stairs with her shoulders pushed back and her tits stuck out, you couldn't help thinking unless this Poppy got something like *mental* hid up her sleeve, the most yours truly be showing her was the way back down Abaddon Hill.

I ain't sure if I was more relieved or more disappointed to tell you the honest truth. She was arsey as fuck, no doubt about that; weren't going to be no walk in the park showing this dribbler round but, at the same time, there was something about her you just sort of felt you'd be missing out if she left.

You never seen nobody smoke a fag as fast as Poppy Shakespeare. Seemed like she sucked them straight down to the butt with a single drag of her perfectly lipsticked lips. And before the one butt had hit the stairs, she'd lit up again and was halfway down through her next. By the time we reached the first-floor landing she was on to her second pack, and as we turned into the corridor, where if anything she begun to speed up, I reckoned I got to say something.

'I'm not being funny, Poppy,' I said. 'But you's not

s'posed to smoke down here. I'm not being funny; it's just staff don't like it.

'You can smoke in the common room,' I said. 'I'll show you after. You can smoke in there.

'Everyone smokes in there,' I said. I kept on saying 'cause it was like she hadn't heard. Every time I opened my mouth another butt hit the floor. 'I'm not being funny,' I said. 'I'm just saying.' And I kept on till I ground to a halt like a car run out of petrol.

Poppy waited a bit, then she started laughing. 'So what you going to do?' she said. 'Chuck me out?' She lit up another, smoked it down in one long drag then crushed it under her heel.

'*I* don't know,' I said. 'I'm just saying.'

She stopped laughing then, stood and frowned at the floor. A molehill of fag butts appeared by her shoe. 'Hang on,' she said. '*Who* was it you said you were?'

So I told her again about me being a guide. And how Tony had asked me special. And I told her how Astrid weren't even a guide, and neither was Middle-Class Michael. And I said how they'd thought it would do me good and help me with some of my issues and stuff, which I weren't going into I said, but they weren't nothing minor. 'Cause I'd been a dribbler all my life, I said, since before I was even born, and as I begun to tell her about it, I seen her face clear like the frown just melted. And by the time I'd finished she was smiling ear to ear.

'I'm sorry,' she said, and she shaken her head. 'I thought you were one of the *staff!*' she said and she carried on smiling and shooking her head like ain't *I* got shit for brains.

'The what?' I said. I didn't get it. I'm stood there staring back at her, shooking my head and smiling like a reflection.

'I'm sorry,' she said. 'I didn't realise. I thought you were one of the *staff*!'

'What, *me*?' I said. 'Like a *nurse*,' I said. 'You thought I was a *nurse*?' I said.

'I'm sorry,' she said.

'It's alright,' I said. 'I don't take the hump *that* easy.'

'Shit!' she said suddenly. 'That thing I said on the stairs? I'm really sorry.' I stared at her. 'About not being a nutter? I didn't realise; that's all.'

'You thought I was a *nurse*?' I said.

'Well maybe not a nurse,' she said. 'Maybe some sort of assistant or something.'

'Fuckin'ell!' I said.

Then suddenly Poppy started laughing and before I know it *I* was laughing and both of us stood there just laughing and laughing like we'd known each other for years.

'*You* can talk,' I said.

'How d'you mean?' she said.

'Well,' I said, but I couldn't think how to put it.

'It's not that I've got a problem with mental illness,' Poppy said. 'It's just there's nothing the matter with *me*. Do you know what I'm saying?'

'I wouldn't worry 'bout that,' I said. '*They* must think you's mad or you wouldn't be here. Candid Headphones don't reckon *she's* mad. Never stopped her,' I said. 'Schizo Safid don't reckon *he's* mad – *Schizo Safid*, do you know what I'm saying! At the end of the day it don't matter,' I said. 'It's what *they* think that matters,' I said. 'Least you's here,' I said. 'That's a start.'

60

We set off walking again in silence. A couple of times she glanced at me and taken a breath like to speak but she changed her mind.

'Poppy?' I said, 'cause I got to say it. Be like watching a blind man walk under a bus. 'You know what you said 'bout not thinking you's mad?'

'Yes,' she said, like what of it?

'Well I wouldn't say nothing to them about that,' I told her. 'Not at the moment. I mean, don't get me wrong, I ain't *saying* nothing. It's just the doctors, you never know. They might decide to pick up on it. I mean, it's up to you, do you know what I'm saying, but maybe if you stick to your other symptoms.'

'Alright,' she said.

'Not being funny,' I said. 'I just thought I should warn you, that's all. They're really weird, the doctors here.'

'No,' she said. 'Thank you. That's useful to know.' And I seen she was grateful I'd told her.

'Anyway,' I says to her, and I give her a nudge with my elbow. 'You must be pretty mad,' I says, 'if you reckoned I was a *nurse!*'

It was then we reached the end of the corridor; I'd seen it coming and everything. I knew as the staff-room door gone past I was going to have to turn us around but the fact is I'd been enjoying myself and I couldn't help thinking this might be the last I'd be seeing of Poppy Shakespeare. 'Cause even with what I'd warned her about I didn't hold much optimistic. I'd only ever met one dribbler ever could pull off a look as glossy as that and that was my mum which, like I say, my mum was in a class of her own.

'In here?' said Poppy and she reached for this door and

almost walked straight in the doctor's room without even knocking or nothing.

So then I had to explain how we'd come too far. 'Least we had a good chat,' I said. And Poppy said yes, least we'd had a good chat, but now she'd best get to Tony 'cause she'd got some stuff to sort out.

As I gone back to the common room, I gathered Poppy's butts up. And they filled my backpack right to the top and the pockets too and the pack was so heavy I couldn't hardly walk.

16. How Middle-Class Michael should of got in the *Guinness Book of Records*

I hadn't been sat in my chair ten minutes, and all of them burning to know what had happened, and what Poppy looked like and what was her problem and was she the same one who fancied White Wesley or the black girl Rosetta had seen down the church who needed the help so desperate, when suddenly the doors burst open shooking the room like a cardboard box, and the cups on the tables slopped over their sides, and one of the windows gone CRACK!, right across, snapped Canary Wharf like a twig.

You never seen nobody move so quick as Elliot, reckoned the snipers had started. Inside of a half a millisecond he was under his chair and didn't come out for a fortnight. The rest of us, we all looked up and everyone gasped, all exactly together as we seen Security Sharon come in, ducking his huge head to fit through the doll's house doorway. And there on his shoulder this tiny speck like a flea on the coat of a dog, and as he come closer I seen the speck got legs and the legs was kicking, and closer still and I seen the legs got snakeskin heels on the end.

Security Sharon come over our end and he set Poppy down and give her her bag, what he'd stuffed in the pocket of his jeans. Then without saying nothing he turned and gone out and everything trembling behind. There was total silence.

To say she weren't looking best pleased is putting it mild. Where her eyes should of been was balls of flame and the smoke come puffing out her perfect ears in rings. As we sat there staring, Poppy fished in her bag and pulled out a packet of Bensons. She ripped off the wrapper with one angry swipe, taken one, lit it, and started to pace in circles. Round and round and round she paced in front of the canteen doors, fag after fag sucked down to the butt. Round and round the small group of flops already stood waiting for dinner, and they huddled together like nervous sheep, as Poppy kept pacing and smoking and it was like the pack didn't got no bottom as fag after fag come out of it, and soon the sheep was stood in a pen of butts.

Well I weren't sure what to do, to be honest, like go and say 'Hi' or leave it or what. I couldn't work out what the fuck had happened and why was Poppy so pissed off and was it something to do with me, which I didn't see how but I felt a bit sick all the same. All I could think was they must of said she wasn't mad enough, which at least I'd warned her, do you know what I'm saying. But then what was Sharon doing fetching her through? It didn't make sense, nothing didn't make sense; and the more I thought the less sense it made, till in the end I got so confused, my mind just crashed like a DSS computer. 'Poppy!' I said.

Now every head in the common room been following Poppy round. But the moment I spoke, it was like a hypnotist snapped his fingers or something. 'Cause they all spun back and stared at me and you heard like this gasp as the bolt gone home: 'You're telling us *that* is *Poppy!*'

'Funny sort of dribbler,' said Astrid, and Sue the Sticks giggled and so did Candid, and Wesley as well though he sworn he never; I *seen* him, stupid wanker. And Omar Bombing laughed so hard a mouthful of half-chewed pic 'n' mix come flying out his mouth and stuck upside down on the ceiling.

'Hadn't you better introduce her?' Middle-Class Michael said. And he got to his feet like *he* was going to, fucking cheek of it, so that's when I got up and gone over, almost trod on Elliot's head, peeping out from under the chairs.

Now either Poppy was so took up with being pissed off she never seen me or else she was one of the rudest dribblers you ever met in your life. Either way she just keeps walking and all I can do is like follow behind, asking her how it gone with the doctors and whether she's alright and stuff and she never even replies or nothing, just keeps on walking round and round like we never known each other. And I ain't even looking where everyone's sat but that don't mean I can't hear them sniggering and one time Astrid catches my eye and gives me a wink and a thumbs-up.

Then Middle-Class Michael cleared his throat – you'd of known him a mile off, weren't nobody cleared his throat like Middle-Class Michael. 'Ladies and Gentlemen, fellow patients, service users, comrades in the struggle . . .' He done it so professional, you couldn't help but stop, even *Poppy* stopped and turned and I had to step round and stand next to her on account she was blocking my view.

Middle-Class Michael had stood hisself on one of Dawn's coffee tables. Though you'd hardly of known it was one of Dawn's tables 'cause all the crap been cleared off, and he'd covered it in this red tablecloth and that was what he was stood on. I'd never seen he was wearing a suit, but he was and a waistcoat and tie, and in his hands he was holding this stack of white cards. And as he finished reading a card he'd put it to the back and start on the next one and I kept on thinking this must be the last but then he begun on another. And it seemed like the speech never ended, just kept on going round. But this is what he said anyway 'cause he published it after in *Abaddon Patients' News*.

'It gives me great pleasure to welcome Poppy on behalf of the Patients' Council.' I glanced across; I couldn't resist it. Fat Florence was shooking her head so hard her chins swayed side to side like sailors' hammocks, and beside her sat Paolo with his arms tightly folded, scowling down at the carpet. Michael coughed and started to clap, holding the cards in one hand. I seen the top one was covered in tiny black writing. Some of the dribblers begun clapping too, slowly at first, then more and more till pretty soon everyone was clapping – everyone except for Fat Florence and Paolo – and even the flops too out of it to know why they was clapping, and some of the flops kept missing their hands so they stamped their feet instead. Made a fucking racket.

When he reckoned they'd clapped enough, Middle-Class Michael raised his hand like a copper holding up traffic, but everyone just carried on, they was all enjoying it so much, and Schizo Safid was up on his feet clapping away and whooping, and it taken about ten minutes of shushing to get them to quieten down, and after that each time Michael paused, just to take a breath or start the next card or something, Schizo Safid would jump to his feet and set them all going again. Even Paolo had to sit on his hands, 'cause he kept forgetting and joining in, earning hisself a nudge in the ribs from Fat Florence.

'I'd like to take this opportunity to welcome Poppy on behalf of the Patients' Council. However long your stay with us, I hope you will find it a useful and beneficial one. I don't know how much you already know about the Abaddon Unit. The date of the building is uncertain, but it seems highly probable that even before this splendid structure which houses the unit today, there were earlier buildings standing on the site. Victorian patients speak of a ballroom where weekly dances were held, though, sadly perhaps, no trace of this remains. The land now covered by the Darkwoods Estate used to be cultivated by Abaddon patients growing vegetables for the hospital. It may be hard to imagine beneath all the concrete today! [*pause*] There was also a farm producing eggs and milk the excess of which was sold to provide an important source of income. The Gatehouse pub next door occupies what used to be the hospital laundry where patients were put to work washing and mending for their fellow inmates and also the public at large. Indeed the Abaddon was much admired as a model of Moral Management, a self-sufficient community, restoring the mad through a combination of discipline and productive employment. Treatment of the insane was seen as a measure of the new, enlightened society and Londoners would come out from the city specially to visit the Abaddon and observe the patients at work and leisure. Charles Dickens attended an Abaddon Ball, who knows perhaps on this very spot where we find ourselves now assembled! [*pause*]

'In previous eras the focus was more upon physical

restraint and containment. Before the relatively recent advent of anti-psychotic medication, many were shackled and held in chains to prevent them committing acts of violence towards themselves and others. Strait-jackets were frequently used, the arms crossed over in front and secured behind.' (Middle-Class Michael shown us how.) 'Patients were muzzled and locked into chairs; whips and chains were frequently used to beat them into submission. Treatment was often punitive: bleeding, purging, half-drowning patients whose conditions failed to improve. Diagnoses were often arbitrary, reflecting the patient's social background and gender more than anything else, but of course things have moved on! [*pause*]

'I shan't go further into our history now, but if you are interested I would warmly recommend the work of my good friend, the medical historian Professor Max McSpiegel, currently occupying the 'M' bed on the second floor. Max is in the process of researching his definitive history of the Abaddon, in which, he tells me, the name of every patient past and present will be listed with diagnosis, physical description/photograph where possible, and brief biographical details, in his exhaustive "Appendix C", which is expected to run to seventeen volumes alone. [*long pause*]

'The Dorothy Fish is a somewhat newer institution. For indeed it is only relatively recently that patients have been encouraged out of the asylums and with the help of medication, community-based resources and day hospitals such as this one, enabled to live as part of a wider society. Established in 1983, seven years before the MAD act of 1990, the Dorothy Fish very much sets the standard for a client-centred, user-led approach to psychiatric treatment.

[*pause*] We have twenty-five patients, from Astrid to Zubin (the "X" chair is currently vacant) drawn from every sector of society and representing a broad cross-section of the multi-cultural community from which our client group is drawn.

'Day patients at the Dorothy Fish have often moved down from the wards. And the day hospital forms part of a programme of rehabilitation and reintegration back into the community. This can take time, especially for those who may have spent much of their lives in institutions. For others, the day hospital represents a move in the opposite direction. People who find themselves shipwrecks in the storm of life, washed up on a desert island perhaps or drifting aimlessly across an unresponsive sea. For such as these the Dorothy Fish provides much-needed rest and water, an opportunity to rebuild one's ship, to catch up the log books and take on fresh supplies for the voyage ahead.' ('That'll be peas then,' said Astrid and everyone laughed. Middle-Class Michael been doing pretty well but he gone a bit red in the ears at that, and he pulled at his nose and coughed and looked down, and Schizo Safid leapt to his feet, begun, 'Three cheers for Middle-Class Michael.' 'Please,' said Michael. 'Please!' and he held up his hand but they just give him three cheers more. 'Please,' he said, coughing. 'I'm really . . . I'm just doing my job.')

'However you use your time here, there's one thing of which I am certain. And that is that we will all do our best to make you feel a valued part of our therapeutic family. [*pause*] And the Patients' Council, of which I am an elected representative, sits very much at the heart of that family. [*pause*] Our sole and exclusive purpose is to represent the interests of every Abaddon patient. [*pause*] And as a patient you are automatically entitled to have your views and opinions respectfully expressed at a twice-yearly forum of Patients' Council members, members of staff and representatives from the medical profession. We also provide an award-winning patients' advice service, Abaddon Patients' Rights, which is staffed entirely by users and can offer help and advice on all practical matters from housing to benefits as well as referring patients where necessary for legal representation. Your guide will I'm sure be more than happy to show you to our office.' (The flops was all clapping and cheering again; I couldn't help smiling a bit.)

'On the subject of the Patients' Council, I have an announcement to make. You have all heard, I know, of the tragic death of Pollyanna Pleasance. Not only was Pollyanna a close friend of mine and a much-loved member of our community, her premature discharge offers a warning to us all. [*long pause*]

'We are witnessing a critical time, a decisive time, a dangerous time for all psychiatric patients, a time in which the role of the Patients' Council has never been more crucial. [*pause*] You will be aware from reports in the press and perhaps on television, of government proposals to privatise our mental health services. Veronica Salmon, the Minister for Madness, has commissioned a number of feasibility studies, and at least two of our largest pharmaceuticals companies have already expressed an interest. The treatment and care of the mentally ill, a yardstick by which, as has sometimes been noted, a civilisation may measure itself, is now to be viewed as nothing more than a commercial enterprise. Already evidence suggests that hospitals are feeling the pressure and being forced to improve their discharge figures or withdraw from the marketplace. The message is simple: Madness Must Pay and anything which stands in the way of Profit must be dispensed with!

'As patients we have an obligation to fight these proposals with every resource we can muster. [*pause*] We have the right to demand the services we need, services based on our requirements and not on the greed of avaricious shareholders!!!! [*pause*] Madness is our heritage, our cultural identity, our bond, our common struggle. [*pause*] It is not to be traded on the stock exchange by men in suits commuting from the home counties! It belongs to us, the service users; [*pause*] it belongs to us, the underclass; [*pause*] it belongs to us, the madmen. [*very long pause*]

'I hope that Poppy will not object to my using this speech to express such concerns, affecting us all as they do. As a new member of our community no less than our older patients, some of whom have been at the Abaddon sixty years or more, [*pause*] Poppy needs to know that her concerns will be properly represented, and therefore . . . *da capo senza fine* . . .'

Well every time Michael done his speech he got himself more and more worked up, especially with all the politics and that 'bout Veronica Salmon, and he kept on getting his hanky out and wiping his forehead and the back of his neck and I reckoned you could of wrung out that hanky and filled a bath with it easy. So like I say the flops gone wild and Schizo Safid was having the time of his life, and the day dribblers too got well into it, and the way Michael spoke, do you know what I'm saying, none of the flops could of spoke like that in a million years, so I reckon they felt pretty proud. Even Dawn, I ain't saying she knew what was going on exactly but she sat there clapping with everyone else and cheering him on and it never crossed her mind to make a table.

Rosetta didn't seem to be enjoying it so much. I looked when he said about Pollyanna. She was slumped like a sack just staring across at the empty brown chair opposite, and her skin was as dull as a dusty old shelf and I seen this tear trickle down her cheek and left a line in the dust.

As for Poppy, there's only one word can describe what she looked like: 'gobsmacked'. But 'gobsmacked' don't *begin* to describe how totally gobsmacked she looked. I tell you if fucking St Paul's Cathedral had picked itself up from behind Paolo's shoulder, walked all through the Dark-woods, up Abaddon Hill, got a pass off of Sharon, walked in through the doors, sat down next to Jacko, lit up a fag, and begun singing 'Hallelujah!', the look on her face still wouldn't of come nothing close. She weren't even smoking, that's how stunned she was; she'd forgot she was even a smoker. Just stood there gawping at Middle-Class Michael, reading his cards and punching the air and wiping the sweat off his forehead. And if Curry Bob had exploded behind her, she wouldn't of flinched, I reckon, she was that fucking gobsmacked.

So Middle-Class Michael gone on and on and like I say it seemed like he weren't never going to finish. And every time he reached the end I knew he kept turning the cards and doing it again but I never could get the point where he done it exact. And like I say, the flops was enjoying it, kept jumping up and clapping and stamping and three cheers for Middle-Class Michael, but after a time, I mean quite a long time, I noticed even *they* begun to get restless. Seemed to me them cheers sounded more and more empty, and the clapping sounded like kind of distracted; they didn't come in so quick or go on so long.

Well flops ain't hard to read, do you know what I'm saying, and all it is is you just got to know how to read them. So as soon as I heard the flops dying down, I had a look up at the clock with no hands, seen it was only a half-hour till dinner, and didn't need to look no further. But Middle-Class Michael, he weren't going to give in easy. And it was like he could feel them wandering off and he just got more worked up so's to try and keep them, and he kept on adding in these bits he hadn't done last time round, like stuff about medication and that and MAD money forms, being the two things what gets dribblers going. And the poor fucking flops, it was like they was ripping in two. And instead of the cheering all you could hear was cries like being tortured and the clapping sounded like bones being pulled apart, 'cause half of them needed to get in the queue what was already gone out the doors and the other half needed to hear the end of the speech so as not to miss it. And half of each flop I mean, not half of them total.

So in the end, it was really weird. Nobody said nothing, nobody looked, there weren't no signal, like firing a gun or blowing a whistle or nothing, but they all got up *exactly* together and all of them, they rushed at Middle-Class Michael. And all you seen was this huge crowd of flops, like surging forwards any way they could. And it was like they was ants or something; every crack, the tiniest gap between two chairs, the space behind the dead plant, they found it. And as soon as one gone through the others followed, like streams and streams of them pouring in, round the ends and between the chairs, in and out and around the tables, not even thinking, do you know what I'm saying, like ants just streaming forward. And Fat Cath said it was Jacko the Penguin and Jacko the Penguin said it was Curry Bob, but *somebody* upset the empty 'P' chair, and it lain on its back with its legs sticking forwards and after that they poured in even faster. And when they got to Middle-Class Michael, still stood on the table, still *shouting*, still stood on the table, they picked him up, I mean not with their hands but just with the force of them moving, and they carried him off, still punching the air and shouting Veronica Salmon, and they moved off, all the mass of them, back across the common room and out through the double swing-doors and the last thing I seen was this fist waving high above their heads and the last thing I heard was 'Minister for Mad . . .' as they gone round the corner and into the corridor.

17. How everyone turned to Poppy
and what Poppy said

Well once the flops had took Michael out and gone off to join the dinner queue, they left a bit of an empty space behind them. And the day dribblers sat there twiddling their thumbs and wondering what to do next. Candid put her headphones on and turned the volume up so loud you could see her head vibrating in time to the beat.

'I was enjoying that,' said Astrid. 'What they have to carry him out for?'

'Turn it down, Candid,' said Sue the Sticks, but Candid didn't hear her. Up the other end of the row, Wesley drummed on the arm of his chair.

'He weren't even talking to *them*,' said Astrid.

'Do you think it's true about privatisation?' said Verna. Sue the Sticks shrugged.

'Yeah man,' said White Wesley, though it weren't too clear if he was answering Verna or not.

'He weren't even talking to *them*,' said Astrid.

Tina nodded and gone a bit pink. 'He was welcoming Poppy,' she said, so quiet she hardly said it at all. But just the name, do you know what I'm saying, it was like someone pressing a switch. Every one of them – 'cept for Rosetta, who was still on a bit of a downer – every one of them lit up like that, and turned their heads to where we was standing, me and Poppy, next to the mountain of fag butts. 'Speech!' they shouted. 'Speech! Speech! Speech!'

We'd been stood there ever since Michael gone out. I knew how we should of been chatting and stuff but I couldn't think how to get started. And it didn't help each time I looked at her, like just to say 'Alright', or something, she never even met my eye but stood arms folded, leant on one hip, staring across through the safety-glass windows, like blanking the whole of London.

'Speech!' they shouted. 'Poppy! Speech!' She glanced down and seen two rows of dribblers clapping and stamping the carpet.

'Don't worry,' I said. 'You don't have to say much.' She looked at me. 'You alright?' I said.

'Speech!' they gone. 'Poppy! Speech!'

'I've been better,' she said. 'I saw the doctors . . .'

'Yeah?' I said.

White Wesley whistled.

'They say I've got to stay a month!'

'That's alright!' I said, which I know it ain't science but every cell in my body sighed with relief. 'They say that to *everyone*,' I said. 'It's like a probation. Don't worry about it. They're bound to extend it; they always do! Fuckin'ell, Poppy!' I said.

She frowned.

'I thought they'd turned you *away*!' I said. 'Reckoned you wasn't mad enough.' I knew that was tactless as soon as I said it but I was just so relieved do you know what I'm saying, like for *her* I mean, fact she hadn't been kicked out. 'You'll be fine!' I said. She was staring at me. 'Play your cards right, you could be here for years.'

'I'm not being rude,' she said, 'but are you fucking *stupid*?!'

She knew she was out of order alright. She looked away and taken a big deep breath. But then she just kind of waved her hand, like 'Fuck it! I can't be arsed.' And she walked off and stood between the two rows of dribblers, kept shouting 'Speech! Poppy. Speech!' And I had to sort of squeeze around behind her to get down the row to my chair, but I never said 'Excuse me' or nothing and I shown her the back of my head.

I don't know why Poppy decided on Tina, maybe because she was done up so nice with her skirt clean and ironed and her hair all turned under, but she seemed to reckon she was her likeliest option. So most of what she got to say, she said it like talking to Tina, and Tina was so embarrassed being picked she knotted her fingers together, and she kept on glancing across at Astrid, and wriggling her fingers about and trying to get free.

'I need to get out of here,' said Poppy.

'Get *out*?' said Astrid. 'You've just arrived!'

' 'Cause there's nothing wrong with me,' said Poppy.

'So why you here?' said Sue the Sticks.

'Look at me!' said Poppy. 'Do you know what I'm saying?!' Tina blushed, stared down at her lap. 'Do I *look* like I'm mentally ill?' said Poppy. Tina nodded then shaken her head. She glanced over at Astrid like desperate. 'What's the procedure for getting out? I've *told* them there's nothing the matter with me! They're saying I've got to stay a month. I mean, Jesus Christ, I can't stay here a month!'

'So what did you come for?' Astrid said and everyone said yeah. You could see not one of them weren't convinced; she might look as normal as a Sniff Street sniff but any second she'd whip out her ace and trump them.

'So what did you come for?' said Astrid, again.

Poppy shrugged. 'I didn't have a choice.'

'You always got a choice,' said Sue. 'It might not feel like you have, but you do. I'm not saying it's easy but there's always a choice. I mean, personally, I used to self-harm . . .'

'But I *don't* have a choice,' said Poppy. 'That's the point.' She give up on Tina. 'It's compulsory!'

'Compulsory?' said Sue the Sticks. 'I never heard of that before.'

'*I'm* compulsory,' Candid said. But nobody paid no attention.

'Day patients aren't compulsory,' said Astrid. 'There's no such thing.'

'Compulsive maybe,' Zubin said, 'but not compulsory.'

'But I *am* compulsory,' Poppy said. 'They say if I don't come every day they'll have to admit me as an in-patient.'

Well no one knew *what* to say to that; it didn't make no sense at all, but you had to admit she seemed genuine stressed; it was hard to just dismiss it as dribbler bragging.

All morning Rosetta been slumped in her chair, staring across at the empty brown vinyl, but now she looked up at Poppy. 'If that's what they told you,' she said, 'they must have a reason . . .'

'I *said* there was nothing the matter,' said Poppy. 'They wouldn't listen!'

'They're *doctors*,' said Zubin.

'It's just generally speaking,' Rosetta said, 'day patients aren't compulsory, we're here on a voluntary basis.'

'You mean you *choose* to come!' said Poppy – thought *I* was slow on the uptake.

'We come 'cause we need to,' Rosetta said.

'They say I've got to stay a month,' said Poppy. 'So they can work out what's wrong. I told them there *wasn't* anything wrong! I can't stay a month, do you know what I'm saying!'

'Why can't she stay a month?' asked Sue, but Verna just shook her head.

'So did what they say?' Rosetta asked.

Poppy blinked. For one awful second I thought she was going to start crying. 'Well that's when they said about having me admitted.'

'Who?' said Rosetta.

'I don't know,' said Poppy. 'That blonde woman I think it was.'

'Dr Clootie,' said Rosetta.

'And everyone agreed,' said Poppy. '*Everyone*! Sat nodding their heads. So that's when I walked out.'

'You what!' they gone.

Poppy shrugged. 'I walked out. I told you; I don't need to be here. Whatshisname, Tony?, must have followed me out. I could hear him shouting at me to come back, so I legged it, killed my fucking feet in these heels. I almost made it but that bloke downstairs, that security bloke, he locked the doors.' She had them now. They was well impressed.

'What did Tony say to *you*, N?' Rosetta suddenly asked. 'When he asked you to guide, did he *say* anything?' I shrugged. I weren't even listening. Had my head turned away gazing out through the windows, watching a plane glide across the glass. To be honest I just thought the whole thing was fucking stupid.

Now ever since his morning break, Brian the Butcher been outside washing his hands. So the way it worked out he'd missed everything. He hadn't seen Poppy and he hadn't seen Michael and he hadn't seen the flops taking Michael out; fact he hadn't seen nothing at all. Course he'd *heard* all about it from the flops in the toilets, all the highs and lows of the morning, each one right after it happened. He'd heard as they surfed in on every wave, buzzed up or harping, depending, but either way full of it. And of course he'd wanted to see for hisself, but he knew how he had to finish his washing or the tower was going to fall over.

At five to twelve Middle-Class Michael come in and give him a run through his speech on account of he'd missed it. And Middle-Class Michael stood on the seat of a toilet and done it proper and Brian the Butcher tried to listen, but he had to keep counting till he'd finished his washing, 'cause if he didn't we'd all be killed and half of London too most probably and everything dust and rubble.

So it weren't till twelve-fifteen exactly, Brian the Butcher turned off the taps, and on and off and on and off, seven times till he was happy. And he shaken his hands 'cause there weren't no paper to dry them properly with, and he felt a bit anxious on account of the paper and he hoped it would be alright. And exactly the same time Brian turned off the taps, Middle-Class Michael started to think about peas. And he couldn't see his cards no more 'cause all he could see was peas, and he couldn't speak his speech no more 'cause all he could taste was peas, and all he could smell was sweet green peas and all he could hear was frozen Birds Eye pouring into the pan. So Middle-Class Michael stepped off of the seat and he broke off his speech mid-sentence, and he put the cards in his jacket pocket, ready to file them later down Patients' Council. Then Brian the Butcher and Middle-Class Michael they stepped out the door and on to the first-floor landing.

Well us day dribblers should of been queued up already, waiting for dinner, but like I say the flops got behind on account of Middle-Class Michael. And on top of which a scrap had broke out in the ruins of the fag-butt sheep pen. Like not content with starving us, the flops had been cramming their pockets with butts and stuffing their slippers and anywhere else they could think of to squeeze them into. So the flops stood behind seen the butts disappear and they reckoned it wasn't fair, and it weren't democratic neither they said 'cause they should of got shared out equal. And they all pushed forward to grab their butts and the flops behind them pushed forward as well and just as Brian and Michael come in, the whole thing collapsed like dominoes and everywhere's flops on top of each other all kicking and fighting and scratching and biting and Brian he turned white as a sheet, grabbed a hold of his chest and fallen on to the floor.

'Press the alarm!' called Middle-Class Michael. 'Astrid! Press the alarm!' So Astrid reached round, all puffed up and pleased, and pressed the alarm by my head and instantly there's this shrieking screech like drilling a hole through your eardrums and the flops all stop fighting and jump into line, and everyone gets up and rushes over to have a look at Brian. Everyone except me that is; I stayed sat where I was with one eye on the queue. 'Cause whatever gone on with Brian the Butcher, I didn't see how me missing my dinner was going to help no one at all.

Brian was laying flat on his back on the floor and his skin was so white it looked like marble – like a tomb in Ream's cathedral, said Michael, and Astrid sniffed and said how she wouldn't know. And Tina said they ought to loosen his collar. She didn't know much about first aid, but she did know they ought to loosen his collar. So Wesley pulled down the neck of Brian's sweatshirt and taken a look at his shirt underneath and the top button weren't done anyway – 'It's not done up,' said Middle-Class Michael – but Wesley undone another one just to be sure.

'He sweatin' man,' White Wesley said.

'Oh Lord!' said Rosetta. 'Think he's taken something?'

'They'll have to pump him out,' said Candid. 'Same as they done with me.'

Well I reckoned I'd heard enough by then, do you know what I'm saying, that's the trouble with dribblers, over-dosing all over the place, it done your fucking head in; so I gone and joined on the end of the queue, stood with my back to it all, and I stuck my fingers in my ears and shuffled along behind Jacko the Penguin, kept checking his wrist – he weren't wearing no watch – see how long till the hatch come down.

So all I'm saying is what happened next, I didn't actually *see* it, which I ain't got a problem repeating stuff, but I can't *swear* to it, that's the only thing, I mean not like I seen it myself.

With a single sweep of her manicured hand (I believe that alright), Poppy brushed everyone aside. And she knelt beside Brian and looked in his mouth to see if he'd swallowed his tongue, and she put her ear to his nose to check he was breathing, then what happened next depends who you listen to. Most people said Brian was breathing OK, so she taken his wrist (right, said Sue; left, said Michael) and felt for his pulse and started to count his heart rate. But Astrid said Brian weren't breathing at all. She said Poppy had gave him mouth-to-mouth, she'd *seen her do it*, she said. And when *that* didn't work she ripped off his sweatshirt, straddled him and started to pump his chest. Just like on *Casualty*, she said, and after a bit Brian come back to life and started to beep and everyone sighed with relief. But he couldn't of beeped, Rosetta said, there weren't no *monitor* to beep, and Astrid said he *did* because she heard it.

Tina said he might of beeped, but then again he might not, she couldn't remember. And she couldn't remember if Poppy had straddled him neither, but if Astrid said she did then she must of done. Poppy said the whole thing was bollocks and she couldn't believe the fuss they was making. All she done was ABC. And ABC was what she'd learned at Harbinger Krapwort Harbinger. Airways, breathing and something else, 'cause every floor got two first-aiders and she'd been made first-aider for her floor. Like Patients' Council, said Middle-Class Michael, but it sounded more like guiding to me, and Poppy said it weren't like neither it was just like first fucking aid. 'What *you* so uptight about?' said Astrid, really nasty. But there's me getting ahead of myself, 'cause she never said nothing, not at the time; it was only later when everything changed, which I ain't got up to there yet. That day the sun shone out Poppy's arse 'cause she'd saved Brian the Butcher's life.

Course everyone had their own explanation why Brian the Butcher fainted. Which seeing as he couldn't remember nothing, he weren't in no position to say and all he could do was sit in his chair and nod and say, 'Very much so.' Sue the Sticks said it was love at first sight, she'd seen it happen she said. Which being as she sat with her back to the door she *couldn't* of done unless she got eyes in her crutches. But that didn't stop her seeing him in her imagination and what Sue imagined and what Sue seen was one and the same, pretty much. So from that time on, she always sworn the moment he first set eyes on Poppy Brian the Butcher got blown off his feet by love. Literally, she said, blown off his feet, she'd seen it happen herself. And she said Brian should go on the breakfast TV. 'They always have stuff on like that,' she said. 'Give everyone a bit of something to hope for.' And she even offered to go on with him, like just as a witness to say she'd seen it happen.

Michael said Brian had had a premonition. Said he'd seen everything that was going to happen if they sold off Mental Health Services and it was such an awful terrible sight, he'd fainted clean away. And he told us all the things Brian seen and Brian's sat there nodding his head, but when I asked him later he couldn't remember none of it.

Course six months later people remembered, said maybe Brian *did* have a premonition, and they tried to make out they'd said so all along. It weren't no coincidence he fainted the morning Poppy arrived they said; there was even dribblers who'd have you believe Brian the Butcher was some sort of prophet. When all actually happened was

Brian come through seen the flops hadn't got their dinner yet. And he started to panic on account of that meant he must of stopped hand-washing early, and *that* meant the tower was about to fall over and seeing the flops kicking about on the floor he reckoned it already started. And that's when he fainted and fell to the floor like a tomb on the shit-coloured carpet.

Not that it mattered to me either way. By the time they got Brian back on his feet I was through in the canteen eating my fatty lamb stew. And I ain't saying it was nice exactly, but it weren't the worst I've tasted. And I felt pretty lucky to of squeezed through in time, the last before the hatch come down. And I felt kind of sorry for the others as well on account of they'd missed their dinner.

18. How everyone reckoned
the sun shone out Poppy's arse

That first day Poppy gone down alright. After she'd saved
Brian the Butcher's life, people give her the benefit. So
when she started slagging the doctors off, how she shat
better crap than they come out with, I ain't saying there
weren't a bristle gone round but people was prepared to
overlook it. On top of which she got novelty value; no one
met a dribbler like Poppy before, and when they finally got
their heads round the fact she meant what she said, *she didn't
want to be there*, they was that fucking jiggered, that stunned
to the core, it never occurred to them they should be
offended.

All afternoon they sat round her asking questions. How
many times she been sectioned? (She hadn't.) Where had
she been in before? (She hadn't never been nowhere.)
What meds was she taking? (She weren't taking meds and
she weren't *going* to take none neither.) What rate of MAD
money was she on? (MAD money? What the fuck's MAD
money?!) She never heard of MAD money? She never
heard of *MAD* money? *She never heard of MAD MONEY!!!!*
And so it gone on. And each time they asked her and each
time she answered, their shrieks of surprise got louder and
louder and louder. And the shrieks got so loud that the
dribblers down the line couldn't hear what Poppy was
saying. So Astrid told Michael and Michael told Verna and

Verna told Candid and so on all round the room. And you heard the shrieks like rippling through the flops.

But the more Poppy's answers got passed around, the more they got stretched out of shape. 'Cause everyone wanted to try them on, do you know what I'm saying, they couldn't resist it, and giving a little tug here and there, and not too concerned with drying them flat or nothing. So sometimes when they come back round they never even recognised the answers they'd passed on two minutes before, and they passed them again and they give them a good old yank as they handed them over. And once a rumour got that overstretched there weren't no way of shrinking it back into shape if you even wanted. Which I reckon that's how half the stuff 'bout Poppy Shakespeare started in the first place.

Some of the flops come over to look at Poppy. Clifton give her a poem he'd wrote on a napkin from the canteen. Something like, 'Poppy, red as your name. Your hair is like a glowing flame.' Which it weren't anyway, it was black/brunette, but he said he'd changed it 'cause of poetic licence. Fifth-Floor Elijah give her a blessing and Safid shown her this passport photo and asked her if she was his mother.

'You not got a question for Poppy, N?' Rosetta said, patting my arm.

'She's sulking,' said Astrid.

'Fuck off!' I said.

'Go on, man,' said Wesley. Do you know what I'm saying! It was like some fucking celebrity come to visit the Dorothy Fish!

'No it's *my* fault,' said Poppy. 'I was really rude. I'm

sorry.' She looked across at me but I made like I never seen.

It was when Poppy didn't show up next day the tide begun to turn. It weren't strictly logical maybe, but we'd sort of assumed she'd come in the gap where Pollyanna should of been. So when Astrid and Middle-Class Michael come in and seen the 'P' chair empty, it was like already we sensed there was something wrong. When Dawn turned up we was getting that edgy we forgotten to tell her our names, or where to sit or anything, so she walked up and down between the rows, looking around, like she'd lost the sugar down Kwik Save. But when Brian the Butcher finally come in, left his coat on his chair, had a quick look round, and gone off to wash his hands, that's when people begun to say how Poppy weren't going to show.

'She's not coming in,' said Astrid. 'What did I tell you!'

'Maybe she's lost,' whispered Tina.

'Lost!' said Astrid. 'She can't be lost! You can see the tower a hundred miles away!'

'She could have got lost on the Darkwoods,' Rosetta said. 'Even if she could see the tower.'

But Astrid snorted. 'She's not got lost!' she said.

'Poor Brian,' said Sue the Sticks. 'You see how he looked?'

'I know,' said everyone, 'cause everyone seen.

'It's cruel,' said Sue. 'That's what it is. Poor Brian! I knew he should of spoke to her yesterday. I said to him, I said "Grasp the nettle!" "Go for it, Brian!" I said. "You're only young once!"'

'He's not young, is he?' said Candid Headphones.

'He's younger than me,' said Sue the Sticks. 'Watch your mouth!'

I ain't saying I was over-concerned if Poppy come in or not. But the rest of them, they got that worked up, how she'd led Brian on, how she'd led them *all* on, how she'd took Pollyanna's place, cost her her life, then just chucked it away like an empty packet of fags.

'Pollyanna could of been sat there now,' said Astrid.

'Don't,' said Rosetta.

'Well she could,' said Astrid.

'I know,' said Rosetta. 'But that not Poppy's fault.'

'Whose is it then?!' said Astrid.

They got themselves that worked up about it, that when Poppy walked in at half-eleven, I reckon they was almost disappointed. She sat herself down in the empty 'P' chair, lit up a Bensons, crossed her legs and the toe of her boot switching left right left like the tail of an angry cat.

'We was wondering where you were,' Astrid said.

Poppy looked up and she glanced around and everyone looked away. She lit up a second fag and sucked it down.

'You found us alright?' Rosetta said.

'Can't miss us, really,' Astrid said.

'Something like that,' Poppy said, and she lit up another.

'Brian come through,' said Sue the Sticks. 'Think he was looking for you.'

'Do you still feel you shouldn't be here?' whispered Tina. But she gone bright red 'cause Poppy didn't answer.

The clock with no hands gone round and no one said nothing. Poppy's boot kept switching left right left.

'Where did you get your boots?' said Sue. 'They real or just imitation?

'I had some like that once,' she said. 'Well similar, different heel. They're nice,' she said.

'I give mine away in the end,' Sue said to Verna. Verna nodded. 'I give them to my niece,' she said. 'Don't know if she *wears* them.

'I couldn't no more with my leg,' she said. Sue the Sticks, she was Slasher Sue then, had a leg cut off when she jumped out a tenth-floor window. 'Not practical, do you know what I'm saying?

'Shame,' she said. 'They was nice boots as well. You'd never of known they was only imitation.'

'How often do you see the doctors?' asked Poppy, suddenly.

And everyone turned to her, like reflex, and I met her eye like just for a second before I looked back out the window.

'The doctors?' said Astrid. 'What do you want to see *them* for?'

'Does it matter?' Poppy said. 'I just asked how often you see them.'

Astrid snorted and turned away.

'Once a year,' Rosetta said. 'Once a year for our assessment.'

'But for other stuff,' said Poppy. 'How often?'

'What other stuff?' Rosetta said.

Astrid tutted and rolled her eyes.

'She wants to know how often we see the doctors,' Sue the Sticks said. 'Once a year,' she said to Poppy. 'We see them once a year for our annual assessment.'

'And what about in between?' said Poppy.

'What about *what* in between?' said Astrid and she bit her lip 'cause she hadn't meant to say nothing.

'We don't normally see them in between,' Rosetta said. 'Unless it's to change medication.'

'I'm not on medication,' said Poppy.

'Well you don't need to see them then, do you!' said Astrid.

'Shhh!' said Rosetta, shooking her head.

'Don't tell *me* to shhh,' said Astrid.

'But how do they know if you're better?' said Poppy. 'If they never see you, how can they tell?'

Middle-Class Michael been quiet up to then, like he'd wore hisself out the day before with keeping on giving his speech. But now he seen Poppy wanted an explanation. And if there's one thing Middle-Class Michael loved it was doing an explanation. So he started explaining about the assessments, how every year on your anniversary the doctors would call you in and decide if you'd got better or worse or stayed the same. And being Middle-Class Michael he didn't stop there, he has to go into every system they ever come up with ever for measuring madness. There was the Reichman Scale and the Blunkett Spectrum and this Chinese one I can't remember but Quok-ho said it meant something to do with gibbons. In the olden days, Middle-Class Michael said, they could tell just from the shape of your head, or by testing your humours, not humours ha-ha, but humours you got inside you. There was two different systems now, he said, an American one and one for everyone else. Then he started to list all the diagnoses, what symptoms you needed definite and what's like your bonus ball.

Which was all very well but about as much use as a book to be perfectly honest. I could of told Poppy simpler myself and a lot more practical, and I would if it weren't for the fact we weren't talking. If you'd got better they kicked you out and if you'd got worse you got sent upstairs, so the thing was to prove you'd stayed the same; but not *exactly* the same, not *stuck*, they liked to believe they was making a difference, so what you done was each symptom got better, you found something else got the same amount worse, and that way you made sure at the end, when they sent you out and totalled the columns, you made sure you come out balanced.

Most probably I changed more than I needed to. I drawn it out in my head like a table, the same like we done in Life Skills. And on one side I put all of last year's symptoms and on the other side all of this year's, and I marked them out of ten how bad they was. For any symptom I crossed out, I written a new one opposite – and some of the stuff I come up with you'd never believe it! Then I added all the numbers up and I fiddled them till they balanced, and if that sounds deceitful, you had to be, and besides I was good at it. I knew how to shade a symptom from one to ten, just like colour by numbers. And not bragging or nothing but I done it so well they had to invent diagnoses (Diabolus Syndrome, Azazel Disorder) on account of I gone through so many they run out.

To be honest, I didn't mind the annual assessments. It give me something to think about. I'd start planning my next one as soon as the door shut behind me. Then I'd sit for a year staring out of the window, shifting it up and down till it come out perfect. I planned it so hard, the assessment itself sometimes felt like an anticlimax. Like over before it begun sort of thing. When they come to the end of the doctors' questions, I'd still be waiting for them to go on and I'd drag out my answers to make it all last a bit longer. Sometimes they cut me off before I'd even finished.

The other dribblers weren't like that though. I ain't saying they was insecure, but there weren't nothing got them so para as the annual assessments. Wesley, he freaked out that bad when he seen Tony coming to fetch him, he leapt through the window, glass flying all over, and gone straight through the roof of this four-wheel drive what was parked in the car park below. And they still didn't let him off of it. 'Cause even as the fire brigade was trying to cut him out, all sawing away and Wesley up to his chest in the roof of the car, and Dr Clootie, whose car it was, stamping and screaming, and us lot all pushing and crowding the windows above, there was Tony crouched on the top of the Range Rover next to him, shouting across the doctors' questions, and Dr Azazel sat on the boot, shooking his head and trying to work out whether Wesley was mad or not.

'You ain't said about the mirrors,' said Sue.

'We don't *know* that,' said Middle-Class Michael.

'Well *I'll* tell her then,' said Sue the Sticks, but Michael got in first.

'There's a mirror on the wall in the assessment room.' About so big; he shown her. 'It's been suggested it might be one of those two-way mirrors with a viewing room behind it.'

'Like ID parades,' said Sue the Sticks.

'We don't have conclusive evidence,' said Michael. 'A smoking gun, so to speak.'

Poppy nodded but her eyes glazed over. I don't think she was even listening.

'It's stupid,' said Astrid. 'There ain't no room.'

'I heard them in there,' said Sue, 'and so did Candid.'

'And I smelled cigarette smoke,' said Wesley. 'And none of the doctors was smoking.'

'Amazing, Watson!' Zubin said.

'Fuck off!' said Wesley. 'I'm Wesley innit.'

'It's Holmes, anyway,' said Middle-Class Michael.

'You what?' said Zubin.

'It's "Amazing, Holmes!"'

Zubin give a tut. 'I was being ironic.'

'You've lost *me* anyway,' said Sue the Sticks, formerly known as Slasher Sue, before she give up self-harming. 'All I'm saying is we know there's a room and there must be a room 'cause Verna's seen them selling the tickets down Sniff Street Underground.'

'What!' we said, everyone except Poppy who looked like a sponge been that overfilled she couldn't take in no more.

'Verna seen them Saturday lunchtime,' said Sue. She looked around and nodded her head, like 'See what did I tell you!'

'Watson!' said Wesley. 'What did I fucking tell you!'

'Go on,' said Sue the Sticks. 'Tell 'em, Verna.'

Verna looked down and fingered this bump on her finger. 'Some of the junior doctors,' she said. 'They were selling these tickets. I don't know what they were for.'

'On Saturday lunchtime?' said Candid Headphones. '*I* was down there. I reckon I seen them too!'

'Go on,' said Sue.

'That's it,' said Verna. 'One pound a ticket, it was. Or six for a fiver.'

'It was probably a raffle,' said Middle-Class Michael.

'Exactly,' said Astrid; she was well pissed-off, 'cause she'd been down the Kwik-Kleen, hadn't seen them.

'Don't think so,' said Sue the Sticks. 'Listen to this!'

'I don't know for sure,' said Verna.

'Just tell them!' said Sue.

'Well one of them . . .' said Verna the Vomit.

'*Which* one?' said Rosetta.

'Dr Swazzle, I think,' said Verna. 'Or Dr Proctor.'

'They all look the same,' said Sue the Sticks.

'I heard him saying he could give them the best laugh in town,' Verna said.

'He said they got free drinks as well,' said Sue the Sticks, looking round. 'And if they give him a kiss he could get them a front-row seat.'

'All for a pound,' said Zubin. 'Ain't bad value.'

'I'm going to talk to the Patients' Council,' Middle-Class Michael said. 'This is a serious breach of patients' rights.'

'Well I wouldn't know about that,' said Sue. 'But it ain't what you'd call confidential.'

'They should charge more,' said Zubin. 'Fuck patients' rights. I'd *sell* my rights if they'd give me a cut.'

'Yeah man!' said Wesley and he sat there laughing at the thought of all the money pouring in. Then he remembered how Zubin had called him Watson. 'Tosser,' he said.

I ain't saying I thought it was true exactly, being no one like dribblers for cooking up paranoia, but the only thing was there wasn't no proof it wasn't. And the more I thought, the more I could see that room behind the mirror, and I seen it so clear and precise it was like I'd been there. Row after row of seats going up like a giant cinema, and ushers with torches showing in sniffs till every seat was full, and the sniffs all sat there chatting and laughing and snogging and stuffing their faces with popcorn, served in great fists by Sharon downstairs in the foyer. Then the screen gone up and everyone fell silent, and there was the window into the room and there was the doctors sat in a circle and Tony with his microphone. 'Come in, N!' he was saying.

So I felt pretty grateful when Verna and Sue offered to check things out. 'How you going to do that?' said Astrid. 'Buy yourselves a ticket?'

But Verna and Sue said they'd check all the doors with what they knew was behind them. And Middle-Class Michael said he'd give them a plan 'cause they got one down Patients' Council.

And after that it was dinner time so we lined up behind the flops. And even though we'd missed our dinner the day before and was practically starving, most of us, we all let Verna and Sue go first on account of they had to get going. 'Cause that's how dribblers is, magnaminious, but none of the flops wouldn't let them in at all.

19. How Poppy eaten a piece of humble pie

Dinner that day was fatty lamb curry, the same we'd had the day before with curry powder mixed in. Dinner on Tuesdays was always fatty lamb curry. When Canteen Coral give me mine, she said, 'Who's that new girl peas or carrots.'

'Peas,' I said. 'Oh, her; that's Poppy. I'm showing her round,' I said. And I looked back down the queue where Poppy was stood, in between Candid Headphones and White Wesley. Her arms was crossed and she leant on one hip like a piece of designer gear in a charity shop.

'And what's supposed to be wrong with "Poppy" peas or carrots,' said Canteen Coral, but she'd already moved on to Middle-Class Michael, who begun to explain how he only wanted peas.

I got my orange eventually, but Verna was doing for Sue the Sticks as well, 'cause Sue couldn't carry it. So I had to wait while she taken the first tray and then come back for the second and all the time my dinner was getting cold.

I was so busy downing my fatty lamb curry before it grown frost on top, do you know what I'm saying, and my head more or less on a level with the table, and my mouth like a great open cave as I shovelled it in, that I never even noticed Poppy come over.

'Do you mind if I sit here?' said this voice, and my head

jerked backwards to see where it come from and shown her a mouthful of curry.

I nodded; I couldn't do nothing else. It was full five minutes before I'd emptied my mouth enough to speak.

Poppy taken the seat across from me diagonal. 'I just need a bit of sane conversation,' she said. 'Do you know what I'm saying?!' And she smiled at me like she knew I was trapped; I couldn't come back at her till I'd chewed my mouthful.

'What a fucking morning!' said Poppy. 'These last two days; I can't get my head round it! I said to them yesterday, I said, "*You've* brought me here so why don't you tell me what's wrong?"'

'And do you know what they said to me?' she said.

I shaken my head; there weren't nothing else I could do.

'They said, "That's for *you* to tell us!"' she said. So what did you expect, I thought to myself.

'"No, mate," I said,' said Poppy. '"*You're* keeping me here. So how about *you* tell me why?" And do you know what that Tony said?' she said.

I grinned. I couldn't help it. It was just the thought of her calling Tony 'mate'. A small bit of lamb fallen out of my mouth and landed back on my plate. Poppy hadn't ate none of her dinner at all.

'He said,' she said, 'that that's what I was *here* for. "These things take time," he said. "You need to be patient." "I haven't *got* time," I said. "I've got a kid! Do you know what I'm saying! I've got to earn money. I can't be sat on my arse in here all day!" No disrespect,' she said. '"Well perhaps you'll have to *make* time," he said. "It's taken thirty-four years to develop your problems, you can't expect to solve them overnight." "But that's what I want you to tell me!" I said. "What *are* my problems exactly?!" "We can help you out with benefits advice," he said, and that was it. Jesus, N! – it *is* N isn't it? – I mean where do I go from here? That's what *I* want to know.'

I'd been chewing so hard my jaw was aching, felt like it been chewing elastic bands. To my right I seen Astrid and Tina sat down at the table next to us, 'stead of taking the one at the back like they always done. Astrid was straining so hard to hear, her ears was flapping like pair of great pink fans.

I nodded at Poppy like 'carry on'. She still hadn't touched her dinner.

'So this morning, right, I take Saffra to school, and then I go straight back home,' Poppy said. 'And I'm just ringing up the agency – I rang them on Friday as soon as I knew, but they didn't have anything in, same as always, which is how I wound up signing on, do you know what I'm saying! – so anyway, I'm on the phone and they're checking through to see what's come in, when the buzzer goes, and it keeps on going. So I'm like "Alright, mate! Calm down!" and I push the thing and all these fucking police come rushing up the stairs.'

She looked at me like, 'Do you know what I'm saying!' And I give her a nod and glanced to my right; Astrid was leant out halfway across the aisle.

'There was more of them outside,' said Poppy. 'This group in the road with *riot* shields. Do you know what I'm saying, N?' she said. 'My neighbours must have thought I'd murdered someone! So then they tell me I've got to go with them and I'm s'posed to be up here. "I'm not," I said.

"There's nothing wrong with me. Do I *look* like a nutter!"
No offence,' she said. 'And they said it wasn't up to them
and I needed to calm myself down. "If you refuse," they
said. "We'll have to section you." "Fuck off!" I said. "You
need to calm down," they said. "You're not making this
easy." And then they handcuffed me. Do you know what
I'm saying!'

I nodded and swallowed and felt it go down like a snake
just eaten a cow. 'Did they give you a jab up the arse?' I
said. My jaw felt like it run a marathon.

'What?' said Poppy.

'A jab up the arse,' I said. 'They usually do.' It didn't *look*
like they had, the way she was buzzing, but I weren't sure
Poppy be normal with anything. 'So you on a section?' I
said.

'I don't think so,' said Poppy. 'If I don't come they will
though; they'll put me on the wards.'

'Thing is,' I said. 'There's lots of people waiting for the
places. That's why they's funny about it.' And I told her
about the waiting list, how long it was, and all the people
on it. 'There's people,' I said, 'go on when they're born and
they's drawing their pensions before they've moved up
three places. There's people whose *grandparents* was on, and
their grandparents too, and they taken their place when they
passed and they still ain't here yet. I don't know if it's true,'
I said, 'but I heard if Jesus been put on the list like when he
was born – or even before, when Gabriel told Mary he was
coming – I heard if they'd put his name down then, he'd
still only be at three hundred and fifty-seven.'

'But I thought,' said Poppy. 'That bloke on the table . . .'

'Middle-Class Michael?' I said.

Poppy grinned. 'I thought he said it had only been going about twenty years or something.'

'I don't know,' I said. 'I'm just saying what I heard. And anyway,' I said. 'They would still of been waiting. Maybe that's why it got so long in the first place. They couldn't even *begin* moving up till twenty years ago. You going to eat your lamb?' I said.

'Think I'll leave it,' she said. And she pushed the tray away from her with a look on her face like a cat what sicked up his dinner. With anyone else I'd of helped myself, and I ain't saying my fork didn't start drifting over, but anyway I put it down; I weren't no Jacko the Penguin.

So then I explained how the waiting list was only the tip of the iceberg. Before that there was the pre-waiting list and before that you was just pre-list; your name got typed in a MAD computer and no one never heard of you again. Poppy begun laugh at that and I felt my face gone red. 'But it ain't like it's news to you,' I said. 'How long was *you* on the list, anyway?' Astrid was leant so far towards us, her great flabby arse was practically touching the floor.

'I wasn't *on* any list,' said Poppy.

'You must of been,' I said. 'Unless you come down through the wards, which you didn't.' She shaken her head. 'Or unless you got prioritised, but you'd still have to be on the list. Most probably you've been on it so long you've forgot you was even on it. Maybe your mum was on it,' I said.

'I don't think so,' said Poppy.

'Maybe they never told you your name was down. Either way,' I said. 'You must of been on it. There ain't no other explanation. And you must of got randomised,' I told her. '*Everyone's* randomised. They don't even let you in through the door without you been randomised.'

But Poppy said she'd never heard of randomising neither. So I had to explain about that as well, how they got to do it because of the law, to prove how the Abaddon worked. 'When you've got to the top of the list,' I said, 'they flick a coin so it's fifty-fifty: heads they admit you; tails, they don't. That's how they get their statistics, innit,' I said. 'So if more tails kill theirselves than heads, they know the Abaddon's working. And the other way round, they know they got something wrong.' And all the time I was telling her, I felt Astrid just to my right straining further towards us. So as I kept talking I dropped my voice and the more I dropped it the further Astrid leant over and Poppy seen what I was doing and she started to grin and she put up her hand so Astrid couldn't see she was laughing. 'They do it on the wards as well,' I whispered. 'It's sort of like science. That's what psychiatry is,' I was practically mouthing. 'It's all . . .' And just at that moment there come this enormous crash like a bomb exploded, and Astrid had leant that far she'd fell off of her chair, and she landed so hard on the floor she made like a crater and Tina had to push and pull and lever and lather to get her back on her feet. But me and Poppy, *we* couldn't help on account we was laughing too much. We laughed till we cried; we practically pissed ourselves laughing. And even after Astrid gone out, the worst hump you seen in your life and Tina fetched her a cup of tea and taken her arm and trotted along like a calf besides its heifer, we still couldn't stop; we laughed and laughed and laughed.

And after that, whatever I said, it seemed like the

funniest thing you ever heard. And I ain't saying I was nothing special or nothing but I must of got on a roll. 'Cause I tried to finish explaining Poppy about the randomising but I couldn't even finish my sentence before we was screaming again. 'We's just the *lucky* ones,' I said. 'We's just the *lucky* ones!'

And Poppy was laughing so much the tears was streaming down her face.

'We's just the *lucky* ones,' I said.

'Do you know what I'm saying!' said Poppy and we started again.

20. A bit about my childhood, you can skip if you ain't interested

When I was a kid, I got moved around more than a pass-the-fucking-parcel. I once tried to count all the places I been, and I couldn't remember half of their names, but I reckon it must of been well over fifty easy. Some of them I was a regular, like Mrs Dalrymple I gone to about twenty times, but only just for a couple of nights like emergency till they found me a long-term placement. Mrs Dalrymple had a bright red front door and you slept in this creaky bunk-bed. On the wall by the bed there was writing and that left by the kids gone before and sometimes she tried to scrub it off but you could still read the words if you looked at it close enough. I used to find stuff I'd wrote myself like messages from a younger me what didn't exist any more.

The longest I stayed anywhere was a year, which was when I was four till five 'cause they'd found me and Mum up near Ally Pally laying on the railway line. Mostly it was like three or four months, then they let her out and I gone back home for a bit till she lost it again. My favourite place was Sunshine House and as I got older they sent me there more and more. Sunshine House weren't too bad to be honest; you didn't have family dinners and shit, and no one to tell you to do your homework; you just sniffed glue and done what the fuck you wanted. But when I was younger, they used to try and place me. They placed me every which way they could think of, this way and that way and turn me around and how about over here, but wherever they placed me, they just couldn't get me to fit. It was like I was this jigsaw piece got into the wrong puzzle by mistake, and in the end they give up and stuck me in Sunshine House.

I ain't expecting sympathy, do you know what I'm saying; I couldn't give a shit. 'Cause it weren't just chance I didn't fit in, I *seen* to it I didn't. All them families wanted was to turn you into a sniff, and it didn't make no difference how nice they done it, you always known what was going on underneath. And I ain't saying nothing do you know what I'm saying but sniffs got to be the most arrogant people ever. I never met the sniff yet who didn't reckon *everyone* should be one – and I never met the dribbler neither willing to oblige. And even as a little kid, I known which team I played for, so as soon as they started their sniff stuff on me, and they give me presents or belted me one or whatever they reckoned worked best to win me over, that's when I told them just where they could stick it and pretty soon I gone back to Sunshine House.

Dribblers don't go in for none of that shit. They ain't trying to convert no one. Mostly they ain't even *noticing* no one; they's thinking about theirselves. The way dribblers see it there's dribblers enough already. There's hospitals, day centres, drop-ins and projects all packed full to bursting with dribblers. If anything, there's too many dribblers; there ain't enough care to go round. There's waiting lists, thousands of pages long, of dribblers sat waiting for places, and there's more lists of dribblers waiting to go on the lists. The way dribblers see it, there's dribblers enough already. And there ain't no need to go making any more.

I remember this one time my mum come to see me. I don't know how old I was, maybe eight, or how the fuck she'd got let out on leave, maybe she hadn't; maybe she'd give them the slip, she was clever like that. Anyway, it's Saturday and I'm sat in my room watching *Swap Shop*. And Mrs Dixon's hoovering 'cause that's all she ever done, hoovering, and I don't know where Mr Dixon is, out most probably 'cause the hoovering done his head in. Mrs Dixon's a stupid bitch; once she lost it and screamed at me, 'You're only here to help with the fucking mortgage!' There's this ring on the bell, not a ring exactly; the doorbell done chimes like Big Ben, and the hoovering stops and she goes to answer, all huffing and sighing on account she don't like her hoovering interrupted. 'Oh!' I hear her say, and I know. Before she's even finished the rest, like 'We weren't expecting you today,' I'm down those stairs with their new stair-carpet three at a time and wrapped in the arms of my mum. 'Why don't we have a nice cup of tea?' says Mrs Dixon, thinks everyone's as stupid as what she is. (Why don't we have a nice cup of tea while I call them to come and get you?) 'It's alright,' my mum says. 'I haven't got long. I thought I'd just take N out for a drive,' and she waves to this car, which I ain't never seen another car like it before or since. Golden it was, with huge tail fins and the mirrors stuck out like wings. It must of been about twenty-foot long unless I'm remembering wrong, 'cause one of its front wheels had mounted the kerb outside Mrs Dixon's front gate, while its back wheels was up on the pavement opposite. 'Perhaps I'd better just check,' says Mrs Dixon. 'Check what?' says Mum. 'Well, you know,' says Mrs Dixon, shatting her pants at the thought of her mortgage payments. As we driven off, Mum tooted the horn and we waved all the way till we disappeared round the corner.

21. How I offered Poppy
to show her Banker Bill

When Poppy and me gone back through the common room, you could tell Astrid told them we'd laughed, and most probably she'd exaggerated, made out it was All Our Fault, but we didn't give a fuck.

Poppy kept looking around like expecting something. She smoked a couple of fags and that but her mind didn't seem to be on them. She glanced up and down the line of dribblers, smoking their after-dinner fags, and she kept turning round and checking the doors; it was like she was waiting for something. The dopey dribblers was settling down to sleep for the afternoon. Gita blown her cushion up what had sagged a bit during the morning and stuck it around her neck and off like that. Harvey taken a little bit longer, but inside of three minutes he was gone too, snoring away with his chins sunk on to his chest. The flops begun to drift back down after their lunch-time meds and some of them still got butts left over and some of them didn't and just had to sit and watch.

And all the time Poppy kept looking around and fidgeting this way and that. 'So what do you lot *do* all day?' she suddenly said to me.

'How d'you mean what do we *do*?' I said. I could feel Astrid glaring at me.

'Well *I* don't know,' said Poppy. 'You must do *something!*'

'Depends what you mean, I suppose,' I said. 'You see your worker once a week. Sometimes there's groups, but most of them's cancelled usually.'

'What about weaving baskets,' said Poppy. 'Aren't we supposed to weave baskets?'

'Baskets?' I said.

'She's joking,' Rosetta said.

'I'm not!' said Poppy. 'I wouldn't mind weaving a basket. I'm not being funny but I *can't* just sit on my arse.'

No one said nothing.

'Don't see why not,' said Astrid. 'The rest of us have to.'

'Sit on *my* arse?' said Poppy. 'I *hope* not.' She was joking of course and I started to laugh but nobody else joined in.

'But don't you get bored,' Poppy said, 'just sat here all day?'

I glanced at Astrid; she rolled her eyes at Tina, like 'What did I tell you?'

'Perhaps you could go and ask Tony,' whispered Tina. 'The art room's locked, but they might have some materials.'

'Tony Balaclava!' said Poppy. 'Talk about the blind leading the blind!'

There was total silence. Poppy glanced round. She caught my eye and pulled a face like 'Oops!'

'What's that supposed to mean,' said Astrid and she give me a glare 'cause she seen Poppy's face. Do you know what I'm saying, like *I'm* fucking pulling her strings!

'Is from the Bible,' said Rosetta. 'Matthew, fifteen, I think. "If the blind lead the blind they both shall fall in the ditch."'

'I know what it *means*!' said Astrid Arsewipe. 'What I'm

saying is what's she *implying*?' And she added Rosetta's name to the list of people she got the hump with. And you might think with three names now on her list – Poppy and me and Rosetta – you might think the hump got divided in three, and it didn't feel so bad. But that weren't the way with Astrid at all; she didn't got no divide button. So instead of we each got a third of a hump, we each got a hump *times three*.

But Rosetta didn't care anyway; you seen she was running through Matthew fifteen in her head.

My mum always said you got to accept the cards you's dealt in life. There ain't no point ranting and raving, she said, you just got to play your hand. But a couple of times that afternoon, I got to admit, I found myself wishing they'd dealt me a different card. It weren't that I didn't get on with Poppy, it was more the others; they didn't know how to take her. And me being me, I felt responsible. Fact is it seemed pretty obvious, it weren't Poppy's fault she didn't know the rules, so when I managed to catch her eye for a second and no one weren't looking, I'd give her a wink just to show I was on her side. But the thing was it weren't no one *else's* fault neither, and I didn't want nobody thinking I weren't sympathetic, so when Poppy *weren't* looking I'd be shooking my head and rolling my eyes along with the rest of them. This one time I got me a bit confused and winked at Tina when I should of been shooking my head, and she frowned like she must of missed something so I had to make out I got something stuck in my eye.

Like I say, it weren't Poppy's *fault* exactly, but she weren't doing herself no favours. I never met no one so under-concerned about making the right impression. By the time Banker Bill come through with his stall, she done Dr Azazel ('Dr fucking Dazzle'), the common room ('Couldn't they *do* something with it?'), the dead plant ('That s'posed to brighten things up?'), Canteen Coral ('Looks more depressed than the patients, do you know what I'm saying?'); and when Wesley told her how *he* was depressed, Poppy driven him nearly to suicide by telling him he looked alright to her.

So at two twenty-five, when Bill come through with his little fold-up desk under one arm and his blackboard under the other, I seized my chance. 'I'm going to see Banker Bill,' I said. 'Anyone fancy coming?'

I didn't say Poppy's name out of tact but I give her a look and I reckon she got it 'cause she stood up right away. 'I don't mind if I do,' she said. 'If I sit here I *will* fucking lose it,' and she followed me down the queue what was already forming.

Banker Bill was second-floor, not Dorothy Fish at all, but he was a slippy sort of dribbler, could of carved his niche wherever he wound up. He carried his folding stool with him, so he'd always have somewhere to sit, and his blackboard and his fold-up desk and an end of white chalk in the pocket of his dusty brown jacket. Every Tuesday from half-two till four, whilst the staff was having their meeting with Dr Diabolus, Banker Bill would set up his little stall. He took out his chalk and wrote on his blackboard a list of what meds he was trading, and beside it two columns with prices for buying and selling. This is what it looked like:

	We Buy	We Sell
Minozine	1 butt	2 butts
Cerberum	2 butts	5 butts
Plurtuperidol	0.25 butts	1 butt
Phlegrapam	5 butts	20 butts

Rates are subject to change

There is an additional handling charge of 1 butt
per transaction or 10%, whichever is the greater

As me and Poppy gone down the queue, we passed Banker
Bill at his stall, with the blackboard leant against it and in
front of him four piles of meds, like chips on a roulette
table, and next to them the grey metal box, relocked after
every transaction, held his stash of fag butts.

Schizo Safid was stood in front of the table. He kept
reaching deep in the pockets of his combats and pulling out
handfuls of meds. Banker Bill weren't looking too happy
about it. He kept picking out tablets and holding them up
to the light, squinting his eyes like a jeweller inspecting a
diamond. And all the time Safid kept opening pockets and
scooping more tablets out of them.

'What's he *doing*?' said Poppy behind me, and I turned
round and seen she was stopped right in front of the table.

'Oh that's just Safid,' I said. 'He's always like that. Don't
show for ages then trades in the whole lot at once.'

'But what's he *doing*?' said Poppy, staring. Safid's combats
shown us the crack of his arse.

'How d'you mean?' I said.

'Well what's he *doing*?'

'He's trading, innit!'

'Trading?' said Poppy.

'Trading,' I said. 'You must of heard of trading. I'll show you,' I said, and I moved up a bit so Poppy could see the blackboard. The queue looped round again inside the first one, and then again and then again it looked like. 'Alright!' I said, as the flops begun harping. 'We ain't pushing in! I'm just showing Poppy round. Safid's on Plutuperidol,' I told her. 'But the thing is now he's give him so much, Banker Bill will have to change his rates. That's why they's all pissed off,' I said and they was as well, all steaming and stamping, like pay-day down Planet Kebab.

'So what does he do with it now?' said Poppy.

'Who, Bill?' I said.

'Does he chuck it away?' she said.

'Chuck it away? Of course not!' I said. 'What would the point of that be? No,' I said, 'he trades it back. That's how he makes his mark-up. Come on,' I said – she was still stood staring – 'we better keep going or we'll *never* find the end.'

Tony had put me through fast track for guiding 'cause he reckoned I had the skills in me innate, but after that first day I got to admit, I'd gone home a little bit doubtful. Now, as me and Poppy gone all down the queue, right round the room past the point where we started, then round again, inside the first line, and round again and round again like tracing the shell of a snail, I begun to think Tony might of been right after all. I ain't trying to make like I was a natural – that ain't for me to say – but the fact is to of seen me guiding, you'd never of thought it was only my second day. 'Cause other people thought so too; as we gone past the flops you couldn't help notice the looks they give me, all sort of shy and admiring, and some of them even started clapping – *spontaneous*, just started clapping – and I heard Fat Cath tell Curry Bob, who was stood alongside her one line in, clutching a handful of fag butts, I heard her tell him clear as mud, 'You'd think she been guiding since before she was even born!' Fact was I found stuff to say 'bout everything and everyone we gone past. I opened my mouth and out it come; I never even had to *think*. Sometimes that much stuff come out we had to stop, just so's I could finish before we moved on again. I told her about the flops we was passing and things they done when they lost it, I told her about the time Carmel got spooked and Fifth-Floor Elijah exercised her by reading the Bible backwards. I told her about when Max McSpiegel eaten six whole chapters of his history of the Abaddon, then forgotten he done it and tried to make out Safid stole them for Al Qaida. I talked about flops who'd never been talked about their whole lives before, and Poppy she listened to every word, like totally fucking gobsmacked and she kept saying things like 'You are kidding!' and 'No fucking way!' and 'Tell me you're having a laugh!' and sometimes I even made up a few bits just to make her say it, and they come so natural, I hardly even realised.

'So what's with Elliot?' Poppy asked. 'Why's he keep diving under his chair?'

'Elliot?' I said. 'Reckons there's snipers trying to shoot him. Never goes home,' I said. 'Reckons they's out in the bushes by the entrance. Hides in his locker till the flops had their supper then he comes and sleeps under the chairs.'

The way Poppy was I could tell she felt bad 'bout the day before and how rude she'd been, and how wrong as well, which I reckoned she should of done too, but I let it go.

We gone round that common room over a hundred times. Each time I seen my chair come round, I counted another lap, but after a while there was too many flops stood in between blocking my view. And soon I couldn't see nothing at all, just flops and flops and more flops, and they could of been queuing on the moon for all you could tell. As we worked our way in towards the middle, I kept on thinking we *must* be there, just another bend and we *must* be there, but we never was; the flops just kept on coming. 'How do they all fit in?' said Poppy. 'Good job they're not claustrophobic!'

'Dunno,' I said. 'They're used to it, I s'pose,' but I seen what she meant. I'd begun to think the spiral didn't *have* no middle, and the dribblers kept appearing out of nothing.

Poppy tapped me on the shoulder. 'Want one?' she said and she held out a pack of B&H.

'Alright,' I said.

'I'm trying to cut down,' she said. 'Do you know what I'm saying?' And she taken one herself and lit it, the first since we'd set out. This flop alongside us begun to drool, eyes trained on her fag like a hungry dog.

'For fuck's sake,' said Poppy. 'Here,' she said. 'Have one! I can't smoke with you doing that.'

He taken the fag and she lit it for him and he shuffled away without saying thank you or nothing.

'Careful,' I said. 'You'll start a riot if they think you's handing out fags!'

Poppy laughed. 'Let's take a breather,' she said. 'I'm getting dizzy.'

So we stood for a bit just smoking our fags and watching the flops shuffle slowly past on their way towards Banker Bill. Some had their butts out ready in their hands, and they clutched them so tight they gone soggy and spoiled and some held their tablets in palms that sweaty, when they got to the front they was ruined and turned to mush.

'That's the thing with flops,' I said. 'They never think ahead. Do you know what I'm saying! All this queuing,' I said, 'just a waste of time, if you ain't got nothing to trade at the end of it. There's no way Banker Bill will take that!' I said as this flop gone past with his tablets that mushy they squeezed out between his fingers. 'He's very strict,' I said, 'Banker Bill. If they ain't fit for trading, they ain't fit for trading and that's the end of it, no exceptions made. And he knows his stuff,' I said. 'There ain't no fooling him. You seen him with Safid holding them up to the light. And if he still ain't convinced, he'll take a quick lick, 'cause he knows the taste of every tablet ever been invented. One time,' I said, 'Curry Bob give him Moscazil, tried to make out it was Minozine on account of they look the same. Sussed him straight off,' I said. 'He got banned for three months.'

Poppy grinned. 'You're joking,' she said.

'I'm serious! You don't want to mess with Banker Bill,' I said. 'He keeps up to date as well,' I said. 'When he ain't trading meds he's reading the *National Fornicatory*.'

'He looked pretty sharp,' said Poppy.

'He is,' I said. 'Used to work in a bank,' I said. 'Used to *run* a bank, least that's what he says. Had a secretary for every day of the week. *And* a chauffeur,' I said. 'Least that's what he says, and a thousand employees or sometimes ten thousand or sometimes five hundred; depends on how he's feeling. Bit of a Candid Headphones,' I said and I give my chin a stroke like I seen people do.

Poppy laughed, like 'Tell me about it!'

'One time,' I said. 'He shown me this picture of a house. Like really posh, do you know what I'm saying, fountains and everything. It must of been worth ten million easy, probably more in London with house prices rising.'

Poppy looked a bit surprised. 'And that's where he lives?' she said.

'Not now,' I said. 'That's where he used to live. Now he lives on the Darkwoods,' I said. ''Cept he's been on the wards fifteen years. Anyway, this picture right – it was like a proper postcard – and on the back I seen it said *The Palace of Versize*, and I've heard of that, do you know what I'm saying. It's France or something innit?'

'Dunno,' said Poppy.

'It is,' I said. 'Or Spain, maybe. Somewhere foreign. I know it ain't in London.'

Poppy dropped her fag on the shit-coloured carpet and ground it out with a twist of her heel. 'Got to give up,' she said. 'I don't even *like* it. Makes me feel *sick*.' She pulled a face like someone about to chuck. 'It's alright at work; you can't smoke out on reception. You don't even miss it,' she said, 'when you can't. Just a couple at lunchtime. I don't smoke at home anyway.'

'Why not?' I said.

'Saffra,' she said, 'my daughter. Gets asthma. Not *bad*, but I wouldn't smoke in front of her anyway. I must have smoked about three packets yesterday,' she said. 'By the time I got home my throat felt like someone skinned it.'

I taken a drag off my free B&H but all I got was a taste of

burnt ash. I'd smoked it right down to the butt and it gone out.

As we walked along the queue, spiralling further and further into the middle, the flops we was passing spoke less and less and after a bit they weren't talking at all, nor listening neither, nor seen us even, I reckon. Just stood in line like shopping on a check-out, shuffling on in jerks towards the till.

'If I wanted legal advice,' said Poppy, 'do I have to pay for that? Do you know?'

'Why?' I said, grinning. 'What you done?'

'I haven't done anything,' Poppy said. 'I just want to see a solicitor.'

'Dunno,' I said and I felt my cheeks gone reddened.

'I'll just have to ring and ask,' said Poppy.

'Yeah,' I said.

'What's that thing that councillor man was talking about?' she said.

I shrugged. 'Don't remember,' I said.

'That patients' advice place.'

'Oh that,' I said. 'You mean Abaddon Patients' Rights. They're alright,' I said. 'They ain't solicitors though.'

Then she asked me all about APR and what they was for and how you could see them and if they was good or just a waste of time. And I told her they done people's MAD money mostly and sometimes housing and if you got a complaint. 'It's mostly flops go down there,' I said. 'On account of they can't stop harping.'

'But you think they'd be able to help?' said Poppy.

'Dunno,' I said. I seen Fag Ash Devine, so I slipped her two fags and she let us into the queue.

'Hi, Devine,' I said. 'Alright? This is Poppy.'

Devine nodded. 'You just starting?' she said. 'I wouldn't if I was you. Do you know how long they've had me here? Thirty-six years,' she said. 'Thirty-six years, and I don't feel any better.'

Fag Ash Devine was the most depressed dribbler you ever met in your life. She was even more depressed, people said, than Marta the Coffin before she topped herself, and Marta the Coffin was so depressed that hearses used to toot her as they gone past down the street. The reason Fag Ash Devine was depressed was she never taken her meds like she was s'posed to and the reason she never taken her meds was 'cause she palmed them instead and traded them in for butts with Banker Bill. She never done herself in though 'cause she always decided she'd smoke another butt before she did, and she'd got through thirty-six years like that, always just a butt away from death. Fag Ash Devine got every sort of illness you could think of. Her skin was the colour of Golden Virginia and when she breathed deep you seen the tar come bubbling out her ears.

'Nurses told me I had to cut down this morning,' said Fag Ash Devine. 'Nosy bastards. Weren't good for me, they said. "Show's how much *you* know," I said. "If I stopped for five minutes I'd have to kill myself. So why don't you tell me what's worse," I said, "killing myself or smoking."' She started to laugh; it sounded like a kettle boiling. ' "Just try it," they said, "just try . . ."' She bent over, wheezing as she tried to catch her breath. 'Fucking nurses think they know everything.'

Poppy pulled a face and mouthed something but I didn't get what she said.

'You won't want to hear *my* problems,' said Fag Ash Devine, and she weren't wrong neither but she told us all the same and she gone on telling us all the way back, round and round and round like a reel unwinding, till she got to the front of the queue. Then right in the middle of her sister's suicide − her brother and big sister being already dead, and her younger brother doing life in prison − Fag Ash Devine broke off mid-sentence and stepped up to Banker Bill's table.

'It's an omen,' Poppy whispered. 'I'm trying patches. I am *not* going to end up like that.'

Fag Ash Devine stood waiting impatient while Banker Bill gone through each tablet, holding them up like a jeweller. When he'd checked each one he placed it back on the table, marking it off on a paper in front of him. Two he rejected 'cause one had a chip and the other the 'M' was so worn you couldn't hardly see it. Then he counted the marks on his paper and counted the tablets, and counted them both again. All the time, Fag Ash Devine stood there watching, following every move of his small sharp hands and as he counted you seen her lips moving like she was counting as well. When he turned down the tablets she never said nothing; and her face shown no expression 'cept concentrating and I reckon she known they wouldn't pass but she slipped them in just in case. When Bill was finished he entered it all in this log beside her name and he written her out a little receipt and he turned it around and made her sign it before he give her the butts. Then off she gone with her fistful of butts without even saying goodbye, and after boring us braindead with all her fucking problems, which was Fag Ash Devine all over, up her own arse.

'So what can I do you for?' said Banker Bill, and I seen him give Poppy this look up and down and then up and down again.

'This is Poppy Shakespeare,' I said. 'Just started.' And he leapt up so quick his piles of tablets rattled like chattering teeth. 'Delighted to meet you,' said Banker Bill, and he held his hand out to Poppy across the table. 'Delighted to meet you. Welcome to the Abaddon.' And he leant right across and took Poppy's hand and shaken it up and down. 'We've a good selection today,' he said. 'Minozine, Cerberum, Plutuperidol, Phlegyapam', and he shown her each pile in turn. 'All checked and verified,' he said. 'You know what you're getting with me.' He beckoned Poppy, like confidential. 'Between you and me,' he said. 'You're best staying clear of those cowboys on the wards. I've heard them offer five Minozine a butt. *Five!* But what are you getting? There's no way that's decent Minozine, not at five tablets a butt; you get what you pay for. Look at these,' he said. 'Fresh in this morning. Not a mark on them, beautiful tablets these. Those cowboys on the wards,' he said, 'they'll give you anything, they don't care and you've got no comeback. Here you get a receipt.'

Poppy been stood there just staring at Banker Bill but as he taken a Minozine and held it out to show her, 'Beautiful!' he said. 'Look at her! Twenty-four carat she is!' he said.

Poppy looked at the small white tablet and started to smile. 'What's it for?' she said.

'Minozine?' said Banker Bill. 'Well I suppose she's an antidepressant. Stops you feeling things so much, just sort of dampens you down a bit. Try her,' he said.

'I'm alright,' said Poppy.

'No charge,' said Banker Bill. 'On the house. Just try her and see how she suits you.'

'I'm fine thanks,' said Poppy.

I thought Banker Bill looked a bit disappointed. He put the tablet carefully back on the pile. But suddenly he smiled. 'I know!' he said and he shaken his head. 'It's always the same with the ladies! You're worried about your figure,' he said. 'Always the same; I know, I know. Not that *you* need to worry,' he said. 'Slip of a thing like you. Have a cigarette,' he said (Banker Bill never smoked butts) and he held out his packet and Poppy took one and he even lit it for her with his little gold lighter and he never give me nothing.

'What *you* want,' said Banker Bill, 'is a Cerberum. A Cerberum,' he repeated, 'cause Poppy looked blank. Banker Bill slapped his small tight stomach. 'Tighten up the old spare tyre. Appetite suppressant.'

'Right,' said Poppy.

'Here she is,' said Banker Bill. He held out this yellow capsule between his finger and thumb. 'What a beauty!' he said. Me and Poppy squinted at it though I'd seen them enough before. Middle-Class Michael taken twenty a day. He got them off of Fat Florence in exchange for his Nutri-drinks.

I thought maybe Poppy was going to take it 'cause she looked pretty thoughtful, like doing sums in her head. 'No,' she said, eventually. 'I don't want to get into that.' Banker Bill frowned and I smiled to myself. I seen what she was doing.

Banker Bill put the capsule down. It left a yellow smudge

on his finger where the colouring come off. He taken a handkerchief out the pocket of his jacket and rubbed till it come clean. Then he taken a Plutuperidol and he sold it so forceful and so convincing I almost bought one myself and even though I had that much prescribed they had to deliver it special in a lorry. I never taken it anyway; it was bastard medication. It was meant to slow you down a bit and stop you acting mental but it gone completely over the top, seized up your jaw and locked up your knees so's your legs wouldn't bend in the middle. You could spot who was on it a mile off 'cause they shuffled about like frozen fucking penguins. No one never traded for Plutuperidol, or not unless they was after cheap meds to OD on but one time we give some to Pollyanna, dissolved so much in her coffee it thickened like soup, and she drunk it as well but it didn't work; least it slowed her down all wrong. She still spoke in rhyme and she still spoke non-stop, just slower and slurred so it sounded like talking through syrup.

Poppy said 'No' straight off to Plutuperidol.

'Alright,' said Banker Bill, 'cause he seen he was beat. 'Alright,' he said and he stroked his chin and he looked down at his Phlegyapam, like sadly, like he known he was going to lose one. 'Tell you what,' he said. 'I'll do you a deal. You buy one of these Phlegyapam; I'll throw in the others for nothing.'

Poppy just looked at him.

'I can't do better than that,' said Bill. 'It's four for the price of one. Just one Phlegyapam,' he said. 'And all the others free. I'll give you a receipt,' he said.

'What's it for?' said Poppy.

'Phlegyapam!' said Banker Bill. 'You've never heard of

Phlegyapam! Well!' he said, and I seen he was looking more hopeful. 'Funny sort of a drug, really. Some people like her; I'd go for the Minozine myself.'

Poppy looked at the board. 'It's expensive,' she said.

Banker Bill shrugged. 'Supply and demand. Like I say, some people like her; it's what you get used to I suppose.'

Poppy said nothing.

'Alright,' he said. 'Half-price, and the others for free.'

Poppy shaken her head.

Banker Bill stared. 'You won't do better,' he said. 'There's not a flop in the unit could match that for value. Come on,' he said. 'Ten butts; that's nothing. You're walking away with four tablets.'

I hadn't said nothing up until now 'cause I reckoned Poppy was doing alright by herself. But now I got worried she was letting her chance slip away. 'You don't have to swallow it,' I said. 'You can pull it apart and snort the powder. That's what I do anyway.'

'It's very kind of you,' said Poppy, 'but . . . Nah.' She shaken her head.

The queue had been waiting that long by now they was starting to get a bit restless. Some of the rappers begun jogging on the spot like the shit-coloured carpet was a treadmill moving beneath them. 'Get on with it!' called Big Nose Jase, worn a cardboard bedpan on his head like a cowboy's stetson. So then the others all joined in, 'Yeah come on! What's the hold-up!' Which is flops all over, never say nothing till someone else does then everyone jumps in together.

'Excuse me,' said Banker Bill to Poppy. 'Any more of that,' he called, 'and trading will be suspended.'

'There was instant silence. 'Yeah, shut up, Jase,' said Third-Floor Spence and he doffed the bedpan so it come down over his eyes.

'Alright,' said Banker Bill. 'You win.' He shaken his head. 'You win for sheer persistence.' He picked up a Phlegyapam and handed it over. 'Take her,' he said. 'Go on; just take her. Bad business,' he said. 'But there you go; I'm a softie.'

Poppy taken the capsule. I wanted to cheer. I was grinning all over my face.

'And what can I do you for?' said Banker Bill.

'I'm just showing Poppy around,' I said. I weren't buying nothing not after that cigarette thing.

'Well go on then,' said Banker Bill. 'Go on!' And he waved me away like that! I looked back to give him a dirty look but he never seen being squatted down changing the rates on his blackboard.

'Fuckin'ell!' I said to Poppy as we walked back towards our seats. 'Fuckin'ell! You know what you's doing!'

'Eh?' said Poppy. 'Oh!' she said. She still had the Phlegyapam in her hand, and you know what she done? She held it out, the bright pink capsule, like a precious jewel between her finger and thumb. 'Here,' she said.

'What's that?' I said. Her nails was like rubies.

'Take it,' she said and I held out my hand, like without even knowing, and she give it me just like that.

I stood there with my hand held out just staring at the bright pink capsule. My hand looked like it hadn't been washed for a week. 'For me?' I said.

'Well *I* don't want it,' Poppy said.

'You done all that for me?' I said.

'I thought at twenty butts a pill, they must be good for something,' Poppy said.

'Phlegyapam!' I said. 'They's fucking gold dust!'

Poppy smiled.

'I can't believe it,' I said. 'We can share it if you want,' I said. 'You can rub it into your gums if you don't fancy snorting.'

'It's alright,' said Poppy. 'I really don't want it. Take it; it's fine.

'Would you do something for me?' she said.

'Course!' I said. 'What else are friends for?'

'Will you show me this Abaddon Patients' Rights?'

'Oh that,' I said. 'It's only open Wednesday and Friday mornings.'

Poppy looked so disappointed, I felt like it was *my* fault the opening hours. 'I'll show you in the morning,' I said. 'I'll go with you if you want.'

'It's alright,' said Poppy.

'Are you sure you don't want to share this?' I said. She looked so upset I reckoned she might be regretting what she done.

'Actually,' said Poppy. 'Do you mind coming with me? It might be a good thing seeing as you know how it works.'

'Alright,' I said.

'You don't mind?' she said.

'Course not,' I said and I zipped the Phlegyapam safe inside my pocket.

22. Next morning outside Abaddon Patients' Rights

The way the ground floor was was like this: first you got the doors leading into the foyer, with Sharon in his cage and the farting sofa, then there was the sliding doors, and if you turned right, the staircase up to the Dorothy Fish and the common room like I told you, and if you gone on past the staircase, that's where the lifts was. By the lifts was a cupboard where Minimum Wage kept her cleaning stuff and put on her overall and gone for her breaks. I can't think of nothing else there was to the right.

If you gone through the sliding-doors and turned left, that's where you got APR, and aside of that and the line of chairs and a rack full of leaflets about all your rights, there was a door led into Sharon's cage with one of them number locks on and there was so many numbers the lock half-covered the door, and when Sharon come out to go to the toilet – got a number lock too, to stop people nicking the paper – it taken him half an hour to get back in his cage.

Next morning I was outside APR by twenty-five to nine. The ticket machine had ran out of tickets but I seen I was first anyway. I taken a chair and sat down to wait for Poppy. The chairs was orange plastic, linked together like school assembly. Mine had a crack in the front of the seat which opened as I sat back. I must of read the sign on the door about a thousand times; 'Abaddon Patients' Rights,' it said. 'Wednesday and Friday 9.30–12. *Please take a ticket!*' After a bit, I weren't reading no more, just staring at the letters and I stared so hard they stopped being letters and become just shapes and lines like a foreign language.

'What *you* got to complain about!' Fat Florence parked herself at the end of the line, the opposite end from me, and as she sat down I felt my end go up like a see-saw. Word was Fat Florence had used to be anorexic, which if she was she'd been making up for it since. She worn a big flowery dress which shown off her arms all covered in white scars like rashers of streaky bacon. Paolo taken the chair next to her, or half of it, the half that weren't overflowing Florence. 'You should try swapping places with us for a bit, then maybe you'd have a proper complaint . . .'

'Fuck off!' I said, but she carried on, so I shown her the back of my head.

It weren't long before Elijah shown up, and he took a seat in the middle and he carried this Kwik Save bag with him, stuffed full of papers, and propped it between his legs. After Elijah come Curry Bob and Clifton the Poet and Third-Floor Lemar and Carmel and Sanya, who weren't over-happy, 'cause I'd kept a seat for Poppy. Elijah and Curry Bob and Clifton and Lemar and Sanya was all doing MAD money appeals. You knew they was doing MAD money appeals 'cause they all had these carriers stuffed full to bursting with proof of how mad they was. Every few minutes one would panic they'd left out something they needed and they'd empty their bag on the floor and start going through it, and that would set the others off and they'd do the same and the piles was as high as your knees. Carmel weren't applying for MAD money; she had a complaint 'bout Dr Azazel. Carmel's complaint been building for fifteen years. No one knew what it was sparked it off, not even Carmel no more. Carmel's complaint was a great-grandma at least. It been married, had kids and the kids had had kids and half of them was divorced and remarried or living together or living alone and all the stepchildren, half-brothers and sisters, and foster kids too; her complaint had great nieces and their nephews had cousins and their cousins had more cousins four-times removed, and to find the complaint what started it all, do you know what I'm saying, was like trying to find Eve at the top of a family tree. Dr Azazel weren't nothing to the main complaint. He was something like a stepson of a step-step-step-half-brother. But one step at a time, said Carmel, and he was her job for today.

'So what you doing, Florence?' Sanya said. She got short dark hair and a ring pull through her nose.

Fat Florence jerked her head towards Paolo and lowered her voice to make sure we was all ears. 'He's making a formal complaint,' she said. 'About *you* know,' she said. 'New girl taken his place.'

'Oh,' said Sanya.

'Ain't right,' said Florence. 'No way it ain't right. Paolo's been waiting years for that place, new girl snatches it right from under his nose. Right from under his nose,' she said. 'But he's not going to sit there and take it, are you Paolo! Ain't right,' said Florence. 'No way it ain't right. I said to him "Paolo, *you* stand up for yourself!" So here we are,' Fat Florence said. 'And we ain't going nowhere till they done us a letter, and even if we have to stay sat here forever.'

'It doesn't work like that,' said Carmel.

'They never even *told* him,' said Florence. 'Just stood there while he packed up his things.'

'One step at a time,' said Carmel.

'Just stood there,' said Florence. 'And let him think he was going.'

'The same thing happened with us,' said Elijah, 'you know after Ebenezer, when they moved little Elliot down? It should have been Ethel,' Elijah said. 'And I should have moved down to four. The same thing happened.' But turned out it weren't the same thing at all, 'cause Poppy was new whereas Elliot been up on the seventh. And that made it totally different, said Florence, that made it so different there weren't nothing similar at all. So then everyone else tried to think up something had happened to them as bad as what happened to Paolo, but nothing they said weren't a quarter as bad; according to Florence, nothing come close to them slipping in Poppy right under Paolo's nose.

All the time they been debating and in between correcting them and telling them they was wrong and mistaken and didn't know nothing about it, Florence kept looking over and giving me daggers. But with so many people in the way, she had to lean right forward to do it proper, and that weren't so easy for someone like Florence; she give it a few attempts but fell back wheezing. So then she give it one final go and she given it everything she got and I reckon she knocked ten years off her life and bust a few blood vessels too, but she finally done it. She flopped herself forwards like someone been drowning flopped theirselves on to the bank and she stayed there, one elbow leant on each knee, gasping her breath back and giving me looks could kill.

Well I was just sat there laughing; I couldn't help it. I didn't give a shit what nobody thought, especially not Fat Florence. But then the others turned to look on account of she done it so blatant. And it weren't that I felt uncomfortable but I knew what they was thinking. 'Course some people,' Fat Florence said. She had to keep breaking off for breath and all you could hear was these wheezy gasps as her lungs, squashed flat between her chest and her stomach, tried to suck in air. 'Course some people . . . uuuh . . . uuuh . . . uuuh . . .' she said. 'No sense of . . . uuuh . . . uuuh . . . uuuh . . . loyalty. Right uuuh . . . uuuh . . . uuuh . . . and uuuh . . . wrong don't uuuh . . . come into it. Uuuuuuuhhhh . . .' And she started on about the war but I weren't even listening anyway. I reckoned I'd go and have a fag and wait for Poppy outside. Only thing was that as I stood up, the crack in my chair clamped shut on my tracksuit bottoms and it pulled them halfway down my arse before I could yank them out again, and I could of done without it to be honest.

I sat on the wall outside and smoked a fag. The wall was damp and I felt the cold come creeping through my tracksuit bottoms. It was clear and light after all the rain, and both ways you looked to the right and the left you seen straight down the hill, to the Darkwoods Estate, like a jungle all over the bottom, and beyond it the clear ring of Borderline Road, like one of them moats they have round castles, we been with Mr Pettifer, to keep the enemy out.

I'd been sat there twenty minutes easy. I'd seen Tina come in and Astrid and Middle-Class Michael. I'd seen them start out as specks at the bottom, nothing to choose between them, then as they come higher there'd be something about them, something about the way they walked, the way that one nodded his head with each step, the way that one worked his arms like flippers, and suddenly they crossed a line and there weren't no one else in the world they could be except them. As Brian the Butcher gone up and down, I kept myself busy trying to work out where he stopped being Brian and turned back to a speck, but it weren't so easy, not once you knew it was him.

I don't know how many specks I seen. Some turned into doctors and some into nurses and some into care assistants with Bibles reading to theirselves as they walked along. But none of the specks never turned into Poppy and I started to think she weren't going to show up and I strained my eyes with scouring the hill, right down to the junction with Borderline Road, where we'd said goodbye the night before and I'd watched her disappear into Sniff Street, dancing around the buses in her snakeskin heels.

I was stretching and straining my eyes so hard that when I suddenly heard her voice behind me – 'Sorry, N! Have you been waiting long?' – I jumped that high in the air with surprise I seen straight through the staff-room window, Rhona the Moaner slouched over her desk circling words in a wordsearch magazine. 'Saffra's teacher wanted to see me.' 'Saffra?' I said. 'My daughter,' she said. 'Oh, right,' I said. I'd forgot she had a kid.

Saffra was six years old then, like six and three quarters. Her birthday was January twenty-third, which made her just Aquarius, at least if you believe in that shit, which sometimes I do, depending. Poppy believed in it anyway. She got Saffra's star chart printed out and framed on her bedroom wall. This woman done it for twenty quid, but it was only like off a computer. Twenty quid, do you know what I'm saying! But Poppy fucking loved that kid, reckoned the sun shone right out Saffra's arse.

Saffra was *alright* and everything. She got shiny dark hair like her mum's 'cept tighter curls. Poppy used to go on 'bout how pretty she was and how clever and all of that stuff and most probably she was – though I reckon *anyone* would of been, the amount of attention she got. Poppy was always like helping her read and tucking her up in bed at night and making her tea all laid out nice – fish fingers and potato stars and beans. And I know she was only a kid and that, and I ain't saying nothing, but I reckon she knew which side her bread was buttered. This one time right, I seen her do it. Poppy and me was sat there chatting and Saffra was laying on the floor doing this picture – Poppy just give her the pens like a second before. So she done this house in pink and a tree besides it and a couple of squiggles meant to be birds. 'Look, Mummy! Pigeons! They're coming to get the bread.'

'Where's the bread?' says Poppy.

She rolled her eyes, really cocky she was. 'I haven't *drawed* it yet!' she goes.

'Well quick!' says Poppy. 'They look pretty hungry to me!'

So Saffra does a couple more squiggles in blue then jumps up to show her. And as she jumps up she catches her leg, like *nothing* – she hardly *touches* it – just a tiny tap, like *nothing*, on the edge of the table. I seen her do it, I seen her thinking, like 'Shall I, shan't I?' 'Yeah,' she reckons. And then she begins to cry. She starts sort of slow and shy, like looking at Poppy, but then as she sees she's got her, she turns up the volume, and inside of ten seconds she's screaming and crying like you'd think she'd had her fucking leg blown off.

'Oh!' says Poppy, straight up, arm round her shoulders. 'Show me. Where does it hurt?'

'Here,' says Saffra – it don't even hurt – and she pulls up the leg of her little designer jeans.

'Where?' says Poppy.

Saffra points.

'There?' says Poppy. Saffra nods, still crying.

'Oh,' says Poppy. 'That looks sore!' It don't – there ain't no mark or nothing. 'Shall I give it a kiss?' she goes and she does and Saffra looks down at her, pleased.

'Ointment,' says Saffra, as Poppy looks up.

'*Magic* ointment?' says Poppy. 'I'll have to see if I've got some in my bag.'

Saffra stands watching and waiting, one trouser up, and her little leg with its soft downy hair and not a scratch and her lip starts to tremble and honestly you got to hand it to her.

'I'm coming!' says Poppy. 'Just try and be brave!' And she gives me a look, like 'I won't be a sec . . .' but I make like I never seen her.

'Look what I've found!' she says, coming back and she hands her this little kid-size box of raisins. Saffra takes it. Then Poppy gets this tube of Savlon, ain't nothing magic *I* can see, and she squeezes out a tiny smear and rubs it in Saffra's leg – you can smell it, so strong it gets right in your eyes. 'There,' she says, and she pulls down her trouser leg. 'Does that feel a little bit better?'

Then Saffra sits on Poppy's lap, pushing the raisins into her mouth and giving me daggers and Poppy's arms all round her. 'Sorry,' says Poppy. 'Where were we, N?' But anyway, I'm getting ahead of myself.

Course Carmel and Sanya had nicked our seats like I knew they would all along.

'I was sat there,' I said. ''Scuse me!' I weren't going to let it go.

'I thought you'd gone,' said Sanya, but she didn't move.

Poppy leant against the wall besides the rack of leaflets on patients' rights.

'You're a fine one to talk!' Fat Florence said.

'Why's that?' I said.

'Why's that?' she said.

'Fuck off!' I said. 'I was only saying.'

'I saved you one,' I said to Poppy.

'I'm alright,' said Poppy.

'I thought you'd gone,' said Sanya, but she didn't move.

'You're a fine one to talk anyway,' Fat Florence said.

'Oh?' I said. 'Why's that?' I said.

And she couldn't even answer 'cause she knew she was wrong, so she just give a huff instead. And she give such a huff it was stronger than a gale or even a hurricane probably, and the piles of proof all taken off and blown around like washing in a drier gone mad, and Lemar and Sanya and Clifton the Poet, they run around in circles trying to catch it. And I kept on waving to Poppy and winking and pointing at Sanya's chair, but Poppy shook her head like it weren't worth the hassle and stayed where she was by the wall, and a piece of the proof fell out her hair and drifted down on to the floor.

'You know how long he's been waiting?' said Fat Flor-ence. And just in case there was anyone left who didn't, she told us again. And all the time she was telling us, Paolo's chin sunk further into his chest, then further still so his forehead was like in his lap and further till he looked like a curled-up woodlouse. She said how he'd come in at eighteen years old with the whole of his life before him, how he'd waited ten years on the seventh floor till a place come up on the sixth, and another ten years on the sixth for a place on the fifth and all the time taking his meds and being good and doing like the doctors told him. After fifteen years on the fifth, he moved down to the fourth and then to the third and finally to the second – which if you added up Fat Florence's maths ought to of made him a hundred easy when even with all the meds he was on, anyone could see he weren't twenty-five. And all those years and years on the wards, when all his schoolfriends was out getting jobs and marrying and having kids, Paolo laid on his plastic mattress and stared at the ceiling and dreamed of the Dorothy Fish. 'He sacrificed everything,' said Florence. 'Everything he had, he give up, and this is how they repay him.'

She had a look round to see how her speech gone down, but no one weren't listening. A fight broken out over one of the papers Clifton picked up off the floor. It weren't nothing much, just a small torn-off scrap with handwriting on like a bit of an old school report, but Third-Floor Lemar said it was proof and it come from *his* pile not Clifton's. And Clifton the Poet said bollocks, been his all along. In the end Elijah had to decide and he torn it in two and give one half to each. And Lemar's half looked bigger but Clifton's got more words on.

Appointments got seen first and emergencies after, but it seemed like everyone had an appointment aside of Fat Florence and us. Lemar gone in and then Fifth-Floor Elijah, who'd stuffed his bag with so many papers the handles give way and he had to carry it hugged to his chest like a baby. The reason we didn't have an appointment was it taken six months to get one and, though I seen no need for the hurry myself, I knew without asking, Poppy weren't willing to wait. Fact sat there in that waiting room as one by one the appointments gone in, I could feel how impatient Poppy was without even looking at her. I could feel her stood against the wall, willing each minute on to the next, could feel every time she looked down at her watch, could almost hear her say to herself, 'That *can't* of been less than a minute!' Even my toes felt it all by their selves and clenched up tight in my Nikes. 'It won't be long now,' I said to Poppy. 'Another three more then it's us . . .' And I kept on saying it just to make her feel better.

Only thing was though, the way the flops was, they never give a thought for no one else. The way they seen it, they'd waited six months and they wanted to get their money's worth. They knew they'd be waiting six months at least till they landed another appointment and the length of time some of them dragged it out, seemed like they was doing their best to make the one appointment last till the next one. They gone on so long and so thoughtless and selfish, I begun to feel almost embarrassed and I found myself making excuses and that like for kids who don't know no better.

'It's those MAD money appeals,' I said. 'They take for fucking ever.' And two seconds later: 'You seen the forms?'

I shown her. 'They're like three foot thick!' 'That was quick!' I said, as Elijah come out – he'd been in so long he looked all out of date and he talked like an old-fashioned film. 'See Poppy,' I said. 'We'll be through in no time!'

Poppy give me a smile. 'It's alright,' she said. 'It's not like we're missing much is it!'

I laughed out loud. 'Too right,' I said. 'We ain't missing much!' and I laughed some more. 'We ain't missing much!' I said.

'So what is this MAD money?' Poppy said. 'It's some sort of benefit, right?'

I looked at her. 'It is and it isn't,' I said.

'I mean it *is*,' I said, 'but it's more than that.'

'How do you mean?' she said.

So then I explained her all about MAD money. Well not *all* about it, obviously, 'cause if I'd done that, we'd still be there now, but I told her the twenty-seven rates, from High High High to Low Low Low and I told her how the madder you was, the higher the rate they give you.

'So how do they decide?' she said.

'Oh!' I said. 'They *know*,' I said. 'They got this special company, MAD Assessments it's called, specially for work-ing it out.' And I told her how they given you points according to everything wrong with you, then they added them up and that's how they worked out your rate.

'So let me get this right,' said Poppy. 'The madder you are, the more money you get?'

I nodded. 'Sort of,' I said. 'It ain't about the money, though.' And I tried to explain her what I meant but it weren't an easy thing to find the words for. I tried to explain how the money was only a part of it. 'The money ain't the *thing*,' I said, 'it's just like one way of seeing it. Same as a flower ain't nature,' I said. 'It's a *part* of nature, do you know what I'm saying, but it ain't actually nature itself . . . Or like Slasher Sue when they cut off her leg, her leg was hers but she weren't her leg; she was still Slasher Sue when it gone . . . Except for the fact that she weren't,' I said, 'cause I seen the hole before I'd finished the sentence. 'I mean she *was* but she *weren't*; she become Sue the Sticks. Maybe that ain't such a good example,' I said.

All the time I'd been talking to Poppy I could feel Fat Florence like a pig at the trough straining to get her snout in. And the moment I lifted my head for a sec, like just to take a breath, in come Florence, crashing in, how they didn't get *no* money on the wards, 'cause only day patients got money, and this weren't fair and that weren't fair and the other weren't fair neither, and none of it what Poppy wanted to know, but just an excuse for a harp which was Florence all over, and Poppy was leant against the wall, listening out of being polite and practically bored brain-dead.

'So why's everyone appealing?' she said, 'if you don't get any money?'

And Fat Florence taken the hump at that, thought Poppy was trying to make out they was thick and there weren't no point appealing your rate if you didn't get paid anyway. 'Why are they appealing!' she said. 'I'll tell you why they're appealing! Ain't *their* fault is it if they don't get paid. Might as well just write them off; they's only flops at the end of the day. Don't *deserve* no fucking respect!'

'It ain't about the money,' I said to Poppy as Florence gone on. 'It's more about what rate you get . . .'

'Why bother appealing! Fucking nerve . . .'

'But I thought they didn't *get* a rate,' said Poppy.

'She'll be wanting the shirt off our backs next, Paolo . . .'

'Yeah, they *do*,' I said. 'They get a *rate*; they just don't get *paid* for it.'

'Leave us with nothing! Take the lot . . .'

'Sounds complicated,' said Poppy.

But I hadn't told her the half of it, not the millionth part of it even. MAD money was like religion 'cept bigger. MAD money was every religion all added together and timesed by itself and bigger than that as well. Sniffs gone to college to study MAD money and come home knowing less than they did when they gone. People spent their whole lives studying just one single rate. I knew all about it 'cause years before, when I was still on the wards, this student come round doing research for a thesis he was writing on Middle High Middle. And not even *all* of Middle High Middle, he was focusing just on the second 'Middle' he said, 'for reasons of space'. Course nobody wanted to talk to him, being as they reckoned he must be a spy sent from MAD to lower their rates, but I was bored out my fucking mind and willing to take a chance on it, and besides I'd noticed a carton of Marlboro sticking out of his backpack.

'Guess what rate Astrid's on!' I said.

'Don't know,' said Poppy. 'I'm not sure I've quite got the system.'

'Middle Low Middle,' I said, and I laughed.

'Guess Verna the Vomit! Guess Candid Headphones!'

And that's how I got through the rest of the morning, doing my best to keep Poppy entertained. Fat Florence fallen asleep in the end, snoring away like a pot-bellied pig, with her chins piled up on her chest like a stack of pillows. And as she rolled forwards, Paolo uncurled, and he kept glancing sideways at Poppy and me, like wishing how he could join in.

23. What Poppy said

Abaddon Patients' Rights been a toilet before it got converted and even as a toilet your knees must of rammed the door. It weren't big enough for a dog to of laid down proper, or maybe a Yorkie, but I've never been into them yap dogs anyway. There was a table, no longer than Banker Bill's and half as wide on account it been sawed down the middle. They'd had to saw it to fit in the chairs – two orange chairs like the ones outside – and the half they'd sawed off been turned upside down and fixed to the wall for a shelf. If you's wondering how the table stood up with only two legs to hold it, there weren't nothing scientific about it, just so many papers rammed underneath the two legs it did have was six inches clear of the floor. On the wall behind where you sat was a notice-board, least that's what I reckon – you couldn't see 'cause of all the stuff pinned on top of it. There was notices pinned on notices pinned on notices pinned on notices; notices pinned up so thick they looked like an Argos duvet. The top layer had signs about MAD money rates and sections and who to complain to, though the names and addresses and stuff never been filled in. There was a sign for the project my bed come from, and another one 'bout training for work, half-covered by a sign for the Darkwoods drop-in. Like I say, underneath there was lots more signs, 'cept nobody couldn't read them; you just seen at the sides 'cause the papers bunched up so thick.

On the end wall Roberta had hung her bag from this pipe stuck out where the cistern used to be and it swung side to side like the pendulum of a clock and it kept it up all the time they was talking, and there's me stood by the notice-board and I got to keep dodging my head to the side case it give me a clout would of knocked me out for a fortnight.

It weren't so much that Roberta was slow, 'cause that's just the way she was. And it weren't her fault her scarves kept trailing down on the pad as she wrote, and she'd have to keep stopping to drape them back round and Poppy sat there revving away like a car in a Sniff Street gridlock. It weren't her fault she needed all Poppy's details, or she had to get her to spell out each word, repeating it back to make sure she'd got all the letters. But Poppy, I might of known her two days but long enough, do you know what I'm saying, 'Saffra,' she goes.

'Could you spell that for me?'

'S-A-double F-R-A,' she goes.

'S . . . A . . . F . . . F . . . R . . . A . . . That's two Fs, is it?' said Roberta. 'Not one?'

'Two Fs,' says Poppy.

'Two Fs,' said Roberta. 'Pretty name. I've never heard it before. And what's Saffra's date of birth?'

'6.12.98,' goes Poppy. 'Do you *need* all this?'

'6.12.98,' said Roberta, draping a scarf back round. 'Let's just get everything down, then we know where we are.'

Roberta was one of them dribblers I told you about,

fucked up her annual assessment. The best she could do was a voluntary job down Abaddon Patients' Rights, which though it weren't the same thing at all, at least it give her a foot in the door and she got to see the doctors sometimes coming in in the morning.

When she'd finished getting all of her details and checked them through and checked them through and checked them through, Roberta turned to Poppy. 'So you've just arrived at the Dorothy Fish,' she said, and she sighed like if only. 'Well first things first, let's find you a form,' and she bent right forward in her chair so her scarves trailed down to the floor, and started yanking out papers from under the table. 'That's Housing Benefit,' she said. 'That's a travel pass form . . . That's Social Fund . . . This looks more like it . . . Ah, but it's half-filled in.' Each time she rejected one she chucked it over her shoulder and they opened out and flapped round the room like birds. 'Now this *is* one,' said Roberta at last. 'Yes, just hold on! Can you lift up that corner there?' But Poppy's just sat there staring ahead like she's give up all hope of anything ever so it's me steps forward and lifts up the table and Roberta tugging with all her might. 'We're almost there . . . if I could just get a grip . . .' till finally it come away and she crashed back into her chair with the form. 'I always say there *is* method in the madness.'

The table now slanted like forty degrees, she'd pulled out that much from under it and as she spoke you seen her mug, two pens and a jar full of paper clips start edging their way to the front. 'Now,' said Roberta. 'MAD money. Have you applied before?'

'I'm not applying for MAD money,' said Poppy – quite arsey as well, least that's how it come over.

Well that thrown Roberta totally and it taken her half an hour at least to get a hold of the fact how Poppy didn't want to apply and it weren't that she was scared of applying or worried what rate she'd end up with, she just didn't want to and that was that. 'Well it's not for *me* to try and persuade you,' Roberta said. 'Far from it. But you are in a highly advantageous position being at the Dorothy Fish. Just think of all the people out there who haven't a hope . . . I'm not saying you *should* . . . But think about it won't you at least . . .' Smash! gone the mug, splashed my Nikes with coffee. 'The fact that you're here *proves* you're mentally ill. There are people who would give their right arm; there are people who *have* . . .' and she started to cry at the thought of the one-armed dribblers I s'pose which I've met one or two but you know what I'm saying ain't common. 'I'm sorry,' she said, and she blown her nose and all through Poppy never said nothing, just stared straight ahead like a coma.

'So how can I help?' Roberta said and still Poppy sat there staring ahead like come in planet Poppy, but then very slowly she started to talk like finding her way through a room in the dark, and then as her eyes begun to adjust the words started coming quicker and quicker till soon they was tumbling out so fast you couldn't hardly keep up with the story.

'Two weeks ago,' she said, 'I lost my job. Two weeks ago tomorrow, it was. Where are we? Wednesday. Yeah two weeks tomorrow. I can hardly believe it,' she said and she frowned; I'm like uh-oh she's off again. 'Two weeks ago tomorrow it was. I wasn't all that bothered, to be perfectly honest; I'd only been with them four or five months and I thought I'd just ring up MediaSavvy and get myself something else. They've got me loads of work in the past; it was them who got me Sniffsucker Sansome in fact and HKH where I met Saffra's dad, or maybe that was . . .'

'HKH?' Roberta said. You could see she was panicking, all of these names and her supposed to know everything; it cracked me up a bit.

'HKH?' said Poppy, frowning. 'Oh, sorry, HKH,' she said. 'Yes Harbinger Krapwort Harbinger. The ad agency!' she said. 'You know! They're huge! They do loads of stuff! You know that one for Femikalm, the one where the devil turns into an angel and starts playing the harp? Dud worked on that. And Shhhocolate! and Snugglers Nappies . . .' And she started listing all of these ads and all how Dud had worked on them and HKH this and HKH that and perked herself up no end she did, first time she'd smiled all morning.

'I've heard of them,' Roberta said, like bollocks you have, but it brought Poppy back like instant.

'So,' she said. 'I was going to try MediaSavvy, but I went for a drink with some of the girls and one of them's going travelling and one's off to college and I thought, I don't know, I suppose I just thought why not try something else? I mean I'm thirty-four now, Saffra's in school, do I want to spend the rest of my life sat out on reception? I'd been reading this thing in *Marie Claire*, this woman who'd been for life-coaching, and the life coach had asked her what she wanted and she suddenly realised she'd never *thought* about it before. So I started to ask myself what *I* wanted. I mean I know what I *want*, like a good life for Saffra, nice holidays, but beyond that. And I thought I could maybe try journalism, I've always fancied journalism, and half the stuff you read, to be perfectly honest, you can't believe someone's getting paid to write it!

'Anyway, I rang round all these helplines to try and find out about courses and stuff and funding too, 'cause I'm twelve grand in debt on my credit cards with a loan as well, I mean let's not even go there.

'So, in the end I got through to this helpline; I can't remember what it was called, just some sort of government training thing and they told me about this "initiative" − that's what they kept on calling it − and they said it was aimed at people like me who were looking at a change in career. "New Directions", that's what it was called. Have you heard of it?'

Roberta nodded. Like bollocks you have, I'm thinking.

'Well I went to this information day at the Kensington Holiday Inn. At least that's what they billed it as but it wasn't. I thought you'd just go round, pick up some leaflets, have a quick chat, maybe ask a few questions, but it wasn't like that at all. From the moment you walked in through the door, it was like you were being assessed. I mean, even the woman who gave me my ticket, I could see she was looking me up and down and ticking these boxes next to my name; I'm like what's that about, but anyway in I go. It was a really smart conference meeting room, all logos and banners saying "**NEW DIRECTIONS: investing in a NEW BRITAIN!**" There were maybe twenty little booths and a whole load of people sat waiting. I got chatting a bit to this girl next to me. She'd brought all these copies of her CV along, with all her qualifications and stuff and she's really focused and nervous about it, like all she's ever wanted is to get on New Directions − and there's *me* with my 2.5

GCSEs, and this bloke with huge ears next to her, kept eavesdropping, really smug.

'When your number got called you went up to a booth and sat down at a computer and you had to answer all these questions, like the usual sort of stuff it started with, like name, age, gender, education. I could see old Big Ears two seats down typing in his fifty-five degrees in astrophysics, but by this point I'm like what the hell. Then when you'd put all your details in, it asked you to wait while it processed them and I don't know how long it took, seemed like forever. Big Ears is drumming his desk like "Come on!" I couldn't see the girl, maybe she was behind, but suddenly it's "Congratulations! You are through to Level Two!"

'I didn't notice at first 'cause we were all sort of staggered, with everyone starting at different times but after a bit I realised the person sitting next to me had changed twice while I was sat there. Then Big Ears got up and tripped over his chair, and I *know* he sat down after me and I started to think, "Hang on, maybe I'm doing something *right!*" So I carried on working through level two. It was just more questions but slightly different. I mean, some of it was about interests and stuff and even what kind of music you're into, but then they had those complete the sequence, you know, with letters and numbers, and I've always been hopeless at stuff like that, and then situations and what would you do and all of these shapes, just like random shapes and you had to say what they all were. I was just putting anything down to be honest, you had to put something or it came up as "Error", but I didn't have a clue. I was feeling in my bag for my travel pass when the screen started flashing, "Congratulations! You are through to Level Three!"'

To be honest Poppy gone on a bit. I'm not being funny but you know what I'm saying, like all of the levels and how well she done and how surprised she was and shit, bit Verna the Vomit to tell you the truth; I'm like yeah and the point of the story? There was seven levels, that was the gist, and Poppy got through all of them and that's really all needed saying. And it weren't till she got to the end of the seventh, she had a look round and the room was practically empty.

'I hadn't noticed everyone going, I must have been really into it, the fact that I kept on getting through; I suppose it was kind of addictive. And the other thing I hadn't noticed or not at the time I mean, not until later, was how weird it was what they were asking. Just the questions I mean, they keep coming back, and I'm thinking I must of imagined it, but I'm certain I didn't, I'm *certain* I didn't. I mean they had a question on *masturbation*, like if I did and how often and stuff, I mean, I don't have a *problem* but do you know what I'm saying, what's *that* got to do with a course in Media Studies?'

Roberta nodded but she gone so red I practically pissed myself, I did, and forgot to dodge out the way of her bag so it clouted the side of my head.

'I wish I could remember them all,' said Poppy, ' 'cause it must be that; that's what I'm thinking. It must be one of the answers I gave, I mean, one of the ones I guessed at or something, or maybe I read the question wrong. I mean, if it had been a *person*, you know, but it was all just a,b,c or d, and none of them fitted. Jesus, it was a nightmare!'

'So what happened next?' said Roberta.

'Well by this point there were only five of us left. Me, that girl I'd met earlier, another girl a bit younger than us who wanted to be a beauty technician and these two blokes, just sort of normal blokes, one of them wanted to go to college, do IT I think, I'm not sure. So everyone finished and we all sort of sat there, staring at each other. Then Jess, the girl I'd met earlier, she went and asked them what was going on but they just said to wait, we'd get called. I suppose we just sat and chatted a bit. Everyone said they'd found it hard and how relieved they were to get through. It was kind of like *Pop Idol*, you know the auditions? I was half-expecting Ant and Dec to sneak in through the doors and ask how we were getting on. The only thing I kept thinking was, "Why *us*?" I mean, there wasn't any reason why *not* us, it's just I couldn't see why we stood out. I mean, I'm not being false modest, but *five* of us left out of maybe two hundred to start with? I even wondered if it was the other way round, and they'd kept us there because we *hadn't* got through, but that didn't make sense either.

'I hadn't noticed it before but over the far side of the room, they'd kind of screened a corner off behind these blue display boards. Well after a bit this man came out in a white coat, holding a clipboard and he called the IT bloke to come round and everyone's like, "What's happening?" Then eventually they came back out, shook hands, and the bloke went off. And then it was my turn. "Miss Shake-speare," he goes and the others all started wishing me luck. I was kind of half-laughing to be perfectly honest 'cause it just felt a bit unreal. Behind the boards they had this bed, covered in paper, like at the beauticians, and basically I had to sit on it while he checked my blood pressure and listened to my heart and shone a torch in my ears. "I just need a sample of blood," he said. "Nothing to be alarmed about." I'm like, "Go ahead, help yourself!" Then I had to get up and stand on the scales, and he measured how tall I was as well and he even got these callipers out, started pinching me all over the place for my Body Fat Percentage. Then that was it; he said they'd be in touch. And the last thing he did was to hand me this bottle. "If you wouldn't mind leaving a sample," he said. "There's a ladies' through in the foyer."

'I went home really excited about it. I know it sounds weird, I mean looking back, but at the time, I suppose I just sort of thought well they're not going to go to all that trouble just to turn me down. My friend Natalie was like, "You lucky cow!" 'cause she's desperate to go to college. I said, "Why don't you ring them up and ask. I mean if *I* can get on, do you know what I'm saying . . ." But she's already doing this foundation course in aromatherapy two nights a week, so she reckoned she'd leave it, see what happens with that. Well then two days later, I mean no time at all, I got this letter, here.' Poppy taken an envelope out. Royal Mail Special delivery; I seen the sticker on it. She got out the letter, bit tatty it was, smudged and begun to go through at the folds like she'd read it about a million times though you couldn't see why to be honest.

NEW DIRECTIONS: it said at the top. **investing in a NEW BRITAIN!**

Dear Miss Shakespeare
Thank you for your recent enquiry concerning the New
Directions programme. We would like to invite you to
attend an interview on:
Monday ■■ October ■■■■
at 9.05 a.m.
Your interview will be held at:
The Ridley Centre
8–12 Ridley Road
London N■ ■■■
It is very important that you attend. Failure to do so may
result in your application being disqualified.

'So this is Monday,' Poppy said. 'Two days ago, OK. I
dropped Saffra off then I just walked down. I know Ridley
Road, it's five minutes away. You know where the railway
bridge crosses Sniff Street, you turn left after that and it's
there. I was going through all this stuff in my head, trying to
remember about the tests and what I'd put, and why Media
Studies and all that sort of thing and I suppose I was
nervous, I *know* I was nervous but at the same time I
thought well it's only a course, and there's always MediaSavvy.

'It was when I got *in* there . . .' Poppy said.

I never even realised she was crying at first, most
probably on account of how I was stood up and her being
sat down and her head down as well; it was just when
Roberta passed her the tissues – toilet paper it was actually,
which I don't know where she got it from 'cause there
weren't never none in the toilets.

'Take your time,' Roberta said.

'I'm sorry,' said Poppy and she wiped her eyes, like upwards with the balls of her hands, run a finger under each one. 'It was when I got in there, everything changed. I knew immediately. Just a feeling; I wanted to turn and run but I told myself not to be stupid. There were two of them in there, a man and a woman, sat behind this table, then a second man, Simon, stood by the door; it was him called me in, really smirky and thin; I hated him from the start.'

'Take your time,' said Roberta again and Poppy wiped her eyes again; I'm not being funny but I'm starting to look at the door.

'I can't remember exactly,' said Poppy. 'I'm not sure how it began, but basically they said they'd looked at my tests and they had concerns about some of the answers I'd given. "I've got a few concerns myself," I said, just joking, to lighten the mood, but the woman nodded, really sympathetic. "I thought so," she goes. "That's very interesting." Then they said they'd got this psychologist in to assess everybody's answers and he'd singled out mine as showing evidence of a "severely disordered personality". They had the report right there on the table and the man – he had these huge bushy eyebrows – he kept looking down and reading bits, then glancing at me and nodding. Then the woman said they'd got a psychiatrist in and she'd diagnosed "a major psychotic disorder". I couldn't believe what I was hearing, I'm like staring at them: "You're saying I'm a *psycho*!" And she said that for someone in my state of mind doing Media Studies was out of the question, she said it could be really *dangerous*, and I needed treatment, the sooner the better, and they'd found me a place and . . .'

Poppy started crying. It weren't just a snivel this time,

neither, tears the size of footballs easy come SPLASH out her eyes and CRASH off the table, soaking Roberta and me to the skin with showers of hot salty spray. The toilet paper was turned to a pulp inside of a half a second so Roberta starts handing her fistfuls of forms and Poppy's like mopping away at her face and wringing them out and blowing her nose and it looks like somebody beaten her up, her face is so smudged with black ink.

'Then they tried to make out I was being defensive,' said Poppy. She taken a long deep breath, but it come out all jolty; she was shooking as well, like blasts of ECT. 'I said to them "You've made a mistake. You've got me mixed up with somebody else." But they'd got all my details, employment and stuff and they knew about Dud and me having split up. The woman, she's trying to be all sympathetic, you know, like "It's nothing to be ashamed of. It's just an illness like any other. No one's *accusing* you, Poppy; you're *ill*. Would you be reacting like this if we told you you had cancer?" And I'm just sort of staring back at her. I mean, I didn't know what to say. 'Cause whatever I said, I knew I'd sound like a bigot, and I'm *not* bigoted; it just isn't an issue. I mean, I don't have a *problem* with mental illness; it's just I'm not mentally ill!

'So I s'pose I said I'd think about it, but first I needed to get a job 'cause I had to think about Saffra as well and maybe I'd find a counsellor but I knew even as I was saying it . . . The way Eyebrows looked up at the man by the door, I just *knew*; I knew what was coming.

'She said it was Saffra they were worried about. She said if I didn't agree to treatment, I mean *full-time* treatment *five days a week*, they'd have to put me on the ward and Saffra would have to be cared for elsewhere and she said if it came to it they could "insist" but she hoped it wouldn't come to it.

'It just felt like a dream by this point, to be honest. Either that or I *had* gone mad. I thought maybe this is what going mad means. Maybe this is what happens. We went outside; there was an ambulance waiting. They all shook hands; I just stood there beside them. Eyebrows said something; I remember, 'cause that was the first time he'd spoken; he said they had to get over to Haringey, "No rest for the wicked."

'Of course as soon as the ambulance started moving, I knew it was all a mistake. Like one of those things you read about; I *knew* I hadn't gone mad. I tried to explain to this Simon bloke but he just sat there, pinching his lips and clutching his bag with my papers in. He said it wasn't up to him and I'd have to discuss it when I got there. And I'm like "Get *where*?" but he didn't say. Then the ambulance pulled up.'

The rest of what Poppy said weren't nothing new, 'cause it's all stuff I told you already. How she gone to see the doctors, said she didn't need to be there and the doctors said it weren't for her to judge. So she asked them to tell her *why* she was there and doctors said it weren't for them to say. And she had to be prepared to help herself and shit, and nobody couldn't do it for her. Which I never met a doctor yet who *didn't* say that; they all spout the same old bollocks.

The weirdest thing was the stuff she left *out*. Like she never said nothing about when we met and how she thought I was staff and that and how we laughed about it. And she never said I'd told her how to answer the doctors or all of the other things I done. Though she did say she reckoned she *would* of gone mad if it weren't for the fact she had me, which I s'pose was a sort of a compliment, though a back-handled one all the same.

'OK,' said Roberta, when Poppy had finished. 'So what would you like to complain about?' And Poppy said, 'Well, *everything*! I mean *all* of it!' But Roberta said that wouldn't work. 'You need to be specific,' she said. 'What is it you're unhappy about? The more specific, the better,' she said, else she wouldn't know where to address it. And she run off a list of all the things that people complained about, and how they was all of them specific, like something about the medication or something about something somebody said, or the food – there was lots about food, especially wanting to switch to halal 'cause it come in a separate plastic tray with a see-through lid you peeled off, meant Canteen Coral couldn't gob in it.

'But I don't need to *be* here,' Poppy said. 'That's what I'm trying to say.'

'I know,' said Roberta. 'I understand. I'm just suggesting we concentrate on what your needs are *now*.'

'But there's nothing *wrong* with me!' Poppy said.

'How are you finding your one-to-ones?'

'Jesus Christ!' said Poppy.

'Would you like to apply for a travel pass?'

Poppy was pounding her head with her fist.

'You're perfectly entitled to one.'

'Just SHUT UP!' shouted Poppy. And she got to her feet and kicked back her chair, ramming it into my legs. 'I'm sorry,' she said, though it weren't clear to who, and she turned and walked out of Patients' Rights, climbing over the mountain of forms that was blocking her way to the door.

24. How me and Poppy gone to see Mr Leech

Poppy didn't hang about. It can't of been more than two days later, we's all sat around like usual. 'I've rung every single solicitor in the Yellow Pages,' she said. 'I can't get anyone to give me an appointment.'

'Right,' I said. It weren't that I minded helping. I just would of rathered she didn't discuss it right in the middle of the common room.

'What d'you need a solicitor for?' said Astrid. 'You murdered someone?'

Poppy glanced across at her and blown out a stream of smoke. 'I will if I have to stay sat here much longer,' she said.

I knew, in time, they'd get used to Poppy, 'cause dribblers'll get used to *anything* in time – even after a week they was coming around, spent less time tutting and rolling their eyes and more discussing MAD money rates and meds and stuff like normal – but comments like that, do you know what I'm saying, even if they give me a snigger they weren't going to speed things up none.

'No one will even listen,' said Poppy. 'As soon as I mention the Abaddon, they all think I'm mentally ill.'

Astrid muttered under her breath.

'I'm sorry?' Poppy said.

'My brother's a lawyer,' said Middle-Class Michael.

'Works in the House of Commons. Fascinating job, drafting legislation. Fascinating! Every word . . .'

'You tried ringing Leech's?' Wesley said.

'If they're in the Yellow Pages,' said Poppy. But Leech's weren't in the Yellow Pages 'cause Leech's only done dribblers. And any dribbler didn't know Leech's, wasn't a dribbler to start with.

'They got me off of my section,' said Wesley and he said it like it been a great feat like George slain the dragon or something, when it only been twenty-eight days at the most and probably twenty-four hours. 'They got me off of my section,' said Wesley, '*and* my GBH.' So then all the others had to join in 'cause they wasn't about to be topped. And everything Leech's had done for them by proving they was sane or mad, or both, accorded to Candid Headphones, both at once in a single afternoon.

'*They* won't say you's mentally ill, not if you tell them not to. That's their job,' White Wesley said. 'They just say what you tell them. I know Mr Leech; he's alright,' he said. 'I can ring him . . .'

I mean, I'm not being funny, but if *you* was her guide, do you know what I'm saying, and I'm just going to say, when in comes Tony with Malvin Fowler start handing out envelopes. And the envelopes got our names printed on and everyone got one from Astrid to Zubin and Astrid she was all puffed up on account of she got hers first, when everyone knew they was just doing it alphabetic. Brian was outside washing his hands so Malvin left his on the seat of his chair and Dawn got hers on her chair as well 'cause she was off doing her tables, and Harvey tucked his under his chin like a bib and gone back to sleep.

Astrid opened her envelope first and she took out a small white card. And she tried to cup her hands around it to stop me and Michael from looking. But I seen anyway, it said:

Baseline Assessments ▮▮▮
Name: Astrid Arsewipe
Time: 9.30 am
Place: The Theatre
Please arrive at least 10 minutes early
and bring a urine sample.

And I thought that was pretty funny when she'd been so full of it. But when I got mine said exactly the same, except for mine was at 1.45. And everyone else's said the same too, except different names and different times. 'Baseline assessments?' said Sue the Sticks and she give it to Verna to check. Then we all sat, envelopes open in one hand, appointment cards in the other, staring at Tony. And when Malvin had finished handing them out, he gone back and stood beside him. And he stood with his mouth open, breathing so loud he was snoring worse than Omar. And he wedged his fat pink hands down the back of his trousers.

'It's nothing to worry about,' said Tony. 'The doctors just want to see you all . . .'

'What for?' said Astrid.

'Just listen,' said Malvin. His fingers wriggled inside of his trousers. 'Just listen and you might find out.'

'They want to hear how you're getting on,' said Tony. He weren't looking comfortable; he was stood with one foot on top of the other. 'They want to know if your treatment's helping . . .'

'Sorry?' said Poppy. 'What treatment's that?'

'And if there's anything more we can do.'

'It says "*assessments*" here,' said Sue. 'Doesn't it, Verna. Here, "*assessments*".'

'There's no need to worry,' Tony said. His feet was now crossed so his right foot was stood on the left-hand side of his left one. 'We're making some changes. From now on,' he said, 'the doctors will see you all once a month.'

'Check you're making progress,' said Fowler.

And out they gone to the sound of stamping slippers.

Everyone knew why assessments was changing from once a year to once a month; everyone said it was obvious why; the only thing was everyone disagreed. Michael said the whole thing stunk of Veronica Salmon all over. 'Evidence-based healthcare,' he said. 'That's the word of the moment!' And he gone off on one about privatisation and how the health service had to prove that hospitals made people better. 'Results, results, results,' he said, thumping his fist on the arm of his chair. 'This government's obsessed with results!' And he called a special meeting of the Patients' Council.

Verna and Sue the Sticks said bollocks, the reason weren't nothing to do with results, it was just 'cause they'd sold so many tickets they couldn't fit everyone in. And Sue said soon as her blisters healed they was going off searching again, and she shown us (again) where her hands was rubbed raw from walking so far on her crutches. They said this time they'd *find* the viewing room. They would of found it last time, they said, but the corridor was so long. And Zubin said what if there *wasn't* a room, but they said they got proof now there *must* be a room on account of the monthly assessments.

Rosetta, who weren't the same Rosetta since Pollyanna gone, she said they done it on account of what happened, 'cause they wanted to keep a closer check, make sure we was all OK. And she said it was proof of how caring they was and how good could come out of the worst things in life so long as you trusted in God. But Brian the Butcher didn't got trust, or if he did, do you know what I'm saying, he weren't relying on it. He upped his hand-washing six hours a day the moment he heard about it, whilst Tina kept trying to work out what she done and Elliot torn his card into strips and eaten them one by one.

The entrance to Leech's was this tiny doorway in between Café Diana and Borderline Cars. The only reason you knew it was there was this sandwich board they got out on the pavement pointing you up the stairs.

LEECH'S SOLICITORS
specialists in mental health representation
★FREE INITIAL CONSULTATION★
★WALK-IN SERVICE★
★Supported by the MAD LAW PURSE★

'You don't have to come, you know,' Poppy kept saying. 'I'll be fine by myself.' But I weren't going to *leave* her. There might of been *some* guides reckoned the job finished four-thirty sharp, but I weren't one of them and I said so as well, and Poppy smiled, and you seen she was pleased underneath.

I'd never been in Leech's before. I'd met solicitors of course – they was always sniffing around the wards, looking for flops to appeal their sections, and before that as well when I been in trouble, nothing too much, as a kid. Mr Moussaka, I remember, sat in the office at Sunshine House with his shiny black case on the floor by his chair. 'Well you're certainly keeping us busy, N . . .' and he give me a mint; he was alright, Mr Moussaka. But whenever I'd met them *they'd* come to *me*, now as me and Poppy gone up the stairs, I couldn't help wondering what it be like and whether they'd have glass offices and stuff like on the telly, and I couldn't really see it, over Café Diana, but I done up my puffa anyway to cover the marks on my sweatshirt, and I run a finger under each eye, though I weren't wearing nothing to smudge it.

Reception weren't nothing like *LA Law*, closest thing it reminded me of was the dentists my mum sometimes taken me to; Mr Smile, I think he was called, filled all of my teeth three times over. All it was was a landing with stairs going on up, the dirty blue carpet worn thin on the bend like the hair on an old dog's tail. The windows looked down on to Borderline Road and Planet Kebab opposite, through blue plastic letters transferred on to the glass.

A woman was sat behind this desk answering calls off of one of them phones, you know down the Social where the lights keep flashing non-stop. 'Leech's solicitors, how can I help yeeeeeew? Line's busy would you like to hold? Thank yeeeeeew! Leech's solicitors, how can I help yeeeeeew? Line's still busy would you still like to hold? Thank yeeeeeew!' Honestly like that forever, I ain't exaggerating; she never even drawn breath, hardly, lungs of a whale she must of had, and every time Poppy tried to break in, she'd hold up a finger and roll her eyes like 'I won't be a minute, honest.'

'And *I'm* the one out of a job!' goes Poppy and the woman looked up like sharp 'cause she heard. And I'm stood next to Poppy just giggling – I couldn't help it, the way she said it. 'Can I help you?' the woman goes, arsey as fuck. Then she nodded at me. 'Has she *got* an appointment?' she said.

'Who?' goes Poppy, like who do you *mean*? Though she knew 'cause she told me later.

The woman was stood with her wrist bent back, holding the phone like a cigarette in one of them old-fashioned films. She glanced at me, then she looked at Poppy again. 'And you are?' she said.

Well just as Poppy was saying who she was, who should come out of this door at the back but Rapper Rashid, you remember I said, who lived in the flat above me; and behind him this man with curly dark hair in a suit, cost a thousand pounds easy. And as soon as I seen them I turned away – I ain't sure why exactly – and I started reading this thing on the wall, a certificate or something it was, the wall was covered in them, and behind me Poppy was still going on how she wanted to see a solicitor and yes she knew it was mental health and no she wouldn't come back in a week and what was the use of a walk-in service you wasn't allowed to walk into. And I stayed turned round till I heard Rashid go past me and down the stairs, and when I turned back, the man in the suit was shooking Poppy's hand. 'Peter Leech,' he was saying. 'Come through.' And I didn't know what to do myself, like whether to stay or go or what, and I honestly thought she'd forgot I was there, but then Poppy looked back. 'Are you coming?' she said. 'Or do you have to head off?' And I walked across right in front of the desk, and if looks could kill, do you know what I'm saying. 'N's my consultant,' goes Poppy. You should of seen her!

Mr Leech was really nice, sat us down and offered us tea, and when Poppy said how she didn't want tea, on account she'd been drinking tea all day, 'cause that was all dribblers done drunk tea, he laughed and asked if she wanted anything else. 'Feel free to smoke,' said Mr Leech and he give us a cut-glass ashtray, and as soon as we'd stuck our fags in our mouths, he whipped out this lighter and give us a light, only I was so stunned I forgotten to suck and he had to give me another.

'So how can I help?' said Mr Leech. He opened the window behind his desk then sat hisself down, leant back in his chair and smiled like a warm cat stretching.

As Poppy told him her story he listened, and he made little notes on this pad on his knee, and he asked Poppy questions and wrote what she said. You could see right away how intelligent he was.

A couple of times I come in with stuff when Poppy forgotten to tell him, and I helped by explaining a few things as well, like how Tony asked me to be Poppy's guide, instead of Astrid, who'd been there longer, and how I'd advised her about the doctors and I watched the black pen with its shiny gold nib noting it down and I felt like I done alright.

When Poppy had finished, Mr Leech sat there just

shooking his head from side to side like he couldn't believe all the terrible things she gone through. 'It sounds absolutely appalling!' he said. 'I can hardly believe what I'm hearing!' And he run through a few of the details again and Poppy said yes, that was right, that's what happened, and Mr Leech shaken his head again, and not being funny but I couldn't help thinking it weren't *that* awful, was it! And I found myself wondering what he'd of said if I'd told him a bit of what *I* been through in my twenty-nine years – probably nothing at all on account of the words would of failed him.

'Legally,' said Mr Leech, 'we've a very strong case indeed.' And he gone on to list all the reasons why, which I can't remember none of them to tell the honest truth, and I couldn't of even two seconds after, being all so smart they gone straight through my ears leaving hardly a smudge in between. They was all acts and sections and presidents and fuck knows, all with a number and a date and a number and he never even had to look none of them up, and with all of them books in the glass case besides him, he didn't even need them, do you know what I'm saying, 'cause that was how clever he was.

'How come you know all *that*?' I says. Didn't mean to; I just come out with it and he smiled. 'How do you *remember*?' I says, 'cause I seen we was getting on alright. And each time he come up with something else, like another law or an act or whatever, I'd keep cracking up all over the place. 'Bet *you* was the smart kid at school!' I said. You could see how he weren't offended.

Poppy never looked at me. Sat downing all of his sections and acts like swigs from a can of Tennents. I ain't saying she *got* it no more than me, but she got it was good news anyway and every swig give her more and more hope till her eyes was all dreamy and drunk.

'So!' said Mr Leech, when he'd finished – the way he said it, like clapping his hands, it made you sit up in your seat. 'So!' he said. 'We need to get things moving.'

'Thank you!' said Poppy, like 'Thank God! At Last!' I'm like 'Alright; you ain't on Death Row!'

'First,' he said, 'it's tedious, I know, but we need to sort out the paperwork. I take it you receive MAD money . . .?

'Ah,' he said. 'Well that's the first thing. Unless you have savings you can access?'

'Don't even go there!' Poppy said. 'I'm twelve grand in debt; that's *apart* from my loan.'

'No other source of income?' he said.

But Poppy shaken her head.

'*I'm* on MAD money,' I said. 'On Middle High Middle, been on it for years.'

'I'm afraid that doesn't help us,' Mr Leech said.

'But I told you,' said Poppy. 'There's nothing the *matter*! Why would I be on *MAD* money!'

'I know,' Mr Leech said. 'You're perfectly right. It *doesn't* make sense, but there you are; that's just the way it works. You must be receiving MAD money in order to access the MAD Law Purse; that's how the system's funded. I'm afraid as things stand, I can't represent you, or not unless you can guarantee to meet the fees yourself, and – I don't believe in being less than direct – a case like this involves a great deal of work. Matters concerning mental health are notoriously hard to prove and tend to drag on indefinitely, though naturally . . .'

'But I thought you said I'd got a really strong case!' said Poppy.

'And you *have*,' he said. 'But it wouldn't be fair . . .'

'So what about No Win, No Fee?' she said.

But Mr Leech shaken his head. 'I'm sorry.' He was sat forward now. Arms crossed, with his elbows on the table. 'It's just the way we're funded,' he said.

'The stress!' Poppy said. 'I could sue them for thousands. I don't even want it; you can *have* it,' she said.

'It wouldn't be ethical,' he said. 'May I ask what your objection is to applying?'

'Forget it!' said Poppy. 'There's no fucking way!'

'I can help you,' I said. 'Get you Middle Low Middle . . . At *least*,' I said. 'Maybe Low Middle Low . . .'

'The rate doesn't matter,' said Mr Leech, but Poppy didn't say nothing.

'I know it's crazy,' said Mr Leech. 'You have to declare yourself mentally ill in order to prove you're *not* mentally ill, but there you are; I don't make the laws, I just have to work within them.'

'How much?' said Poppy.

Mr Leech frowned.

'How much would it cost?'

'Several thousand, at least. It depends; the whole question of burden of proof . . .'

'I'll find it somehow,' Poppy said. 'I'll borrow it. I'll sue their butts . . . I'm sorry,' she said.

'No problem.' Mr Leech smiled.

'You're sure you can get me out,' she said.

'You've a very strong case,' said Mr Leech and they shaken hands and he give her a card with his name on.

'Come on, N!' said Poppy and she'd opened the door before I was even stood up. It pissed me off slightly, to tell you the truth, 'cause I couldn't see what the rush was, and Mr Leech smiled like neither could he, and he shaken my hand and I gone out after her.

25. How none of Poppy's friends wouldn't borrow her the money

Poppy didn't hang about; as soon as she got home from seeing Mr Leech, she picked up the phone and rung everyone she could think of. First she rung her friend Natalie, the one she'd told me about before, the one who done aromas or whatever.

'Where have you been!' said Natalie. 'I've been leaving messages all week! Well, never mind that. Did you get a place on the course?'

So then Poppy had to tell her what happened and how she'd wound up at the Dorothy Fish instead of doing Media Studies.

'Shit!' said Natalie. 'Are you alright? You should of told me before!'

'I wasn't sure what you'd think,' said Poppy.

'Come on!' she said. 'This is me, Natalie, your *friend*, remember! Honestly, Poppy! I mean, I sometimes think I've a screw loose myself, well *several* actually. There but for the grace of God . . . It could happen to *any* of us. At least you're facing up to things. Most people just live their lives in denial. So what's it like? Are they helping you? Are they giving you stuff? Is it . . .'

'Like what?' said Poppy. 'What sort of stuff?'

'Well *I* don't know,' said Natalie. 'Prozac or something; *I* don't know!'

'THERE'S NOTHING WRONG WITH ME!' said Poppy.

'Oh,' said Natalie. 'Oh, OK. So what are you doing there then?'

'And what did you say?' I said to Poppy. She was telling me over fatty lamb stew in the canteen Monday lunch-time. And Poppy said how she'd gone through what happened again. All the stuff at the dole office, how they'd told her she was mentally ill and she had to have treatment compulsive, and if she didn't she'd go on the ward and if she gone on the ward then what would happen to Saffra?

'And when I'd finished,' Poppy said, 'there was like this huge pause on the phone. "I was wondering about Saffra," she said. "Wondering what?" I said. "Well maybe she could stay with me," she said. "Give you a bit of a break; it's not a problem." "I'm fine," I said. "Don't take this the wrong way," she said, "but you've got to think of Saffra." "And what's that s'posed to mean?" I said. "Well you *have* seemed pretty stressed," she goes. "To be honest, Poppy, ever since Dud left. Looking back, I guess I could see this coming." "You could?" I said. "Well it's hardly surprising," she said. "You've been under a lot of stress, Poppy. Single mum and losing your job and remember how upset you got, you know when you left your bag on the bus . . ." "I was *stressed*," I said. "I lost my keys. I had to get all the locks changed. I'm skint!" "Still," she said. "Natalie," I said, "I'm not being rude but I've had a long day." "You don't want to get overtired," she said. "And really," I said, "I just need a yes or no. Can you lend me the money or not?" I said. "I understand if you can't," I said, "but I just need to know." "I'm sorry,' she said. "You know I would but I can't; I just can't. It wouldn't be right," she said. "Who *is* this man anyway?" she said. "He's taking advantage of you, Poppy. You're vulnerable; he's just trying to make money. And even if he could get you out. To be honest, Poppy, you're barking up the wrong tree. You need the help; I'm just glad you're there. It's nothing to be ashamed of . . ." "Fuck off!" I said.'

I giggled just 'cause of the way she said it, but Poppy weren't laughing; she looked upset. As she talked she stabbed at her fatty lamb stew with her white plastic fork, kept bending. And she told me how she'd rung everyone, everyone she could think of. Her family, even American cousins, and all her friends, and all the people she'd been at school with and everyone she'd ever worked with and people she'd met on holiday; she'd gone through five address books. And listening to the list of people I felt a bit weird, do you know what I'm saying, just all the people she known. And I seen her having this massive party for all her friends and family and they'd easily fill up the whole canteen and most probably the Abaddon Tower as well, all the way to the top. And everyone laughing and talking about her and saying how great she was, and Americans too with American accents, and Poppy the centre of it all and here we was, do you know what I'm saying, sat having lunch together.

But it didn't sound like Poppy be planning a party anytime soon. Not one person had offered to lend her even so much as a fiver. In the end, she said, she stopped telling them what she needed it for 'cause the moment she did, the moment she mentioned the Dorothy Fish, turned out everyone seen it coming. 'But I haven't seen you for nearly ten years,' she said to one. 'What you talking about!' And they said how she'd always been highly strung, even at school she'd seemed slightly unstable, like the time when she'd slapped that boy round the face, what was his name, on account of he'd pinched her arse. But even though Poppy stopped telling people, the word got around why she needed the money, 'cause everybody rung everyone else, and they all agreed that to lend her the money, that was the easy option. And the caring most responsible thing was to all say no and hold their ground, so that's what everyone done. 'I even spoke to Dud,' she said. 'Someone had rung him, I don't know who. If I find out I'll fucking kill them. Said his parents had offered to look after Saffra. They'd like to help. "With what?!" I said. "We don't *need* any fucking help." "She *is* their granddaughter," he said. "Yeah," I said. "Yeah. So what are you saying?" His fucking parents, that's *all* I need.'

I'd been looking down at our plates as she talked; I'd finished mine ages ago and she hadn't ate nothing. 'Are you going . . .' I said, but then I looked up and I seen there was tears in Poppy's eyes. In fact they was spilling out of her eyes. She kept pushing them back with the palms of her hands so as not to smudge her mascara. 'You alright?' I said.

'I don't know what to do,' she said. 'I just don't know.'

'About the money?' I said.

'I spoke to my dad as well,' she said. 'I mean I didn't *tell* him obviously. I just said I needed to borrow some money.'

'And what did he say?' I said.

Poppy shrugged. 'I'm sure he would if it wasn't for Pam. She wants a new kitchen, do you know what I'm saying.

They only just *got* one three years ago. I said, "What, *another!*" . . . He said, "You know what she's like." I wish he'd just fucking stand *up* to her! And he asked what I needed it for, of course. I said to cover the mortgage while I'm doing my training. He said I thought you said you got this funding, and what about Dud? He's not stupid, my dad. "Forget it," I said. "I'll manage."

'So I'll just have to wait the month out,' she said. 'Three more weeks. I'll just have to do it. There's nothing else . . .'

"Cept MAD money,' I said.

But Poppy Shakespeare shaken her head. 'No way,' she said. 'There's no fucking way I'm applying.'

That afternoon in my one-to-one I s'pose I said something I shouldn't of. We'd sat in silence a bit like usual, and Tony had asked how I was like usual, and I'd said alright, like usual as well, and he'd said what does that mean and I'd said alright. Tony frowned like not sure what to say, like you seen him thinking it through, 'So how are you getting along with Poppy?' he said.

'Alright,' I said.

'Can you be a bit more specific?' he said.

'What do you want to know?' I said.

'Whatever you want to tell me,' he said.

I shrugged. 'We get on alright.'

Tony didn't say nothing to that. He folded his arms and crossed his legs. The toe of his shoe drawn circles in the air like the second hand of some invisible clock.

'Why have you changed the assessments?' I said. 'You only done me two weeks ago. What do you need to assessing me again for?'

His toe stopped moving at twelve o'clock so his foot was bent up in the air. 'Are you worried about it, N?' he said.

'No,' I said.

'There's no need to worry,' he said.

'I was only asking,' I said. 'I ain't worried. I ain't got no reason to worry, do you know what I'm saying. I don't care if they *do* kick me out; it don't make no difference to me . . . it's going to happen anyway, might as well be sooner as later.'

'What's going to happen, N?' said Tony. His foot relaxed and gone down to stop at six-thirty.

'Everyone I ever known,' I said. 'My mum, my nan. My dad,' I said, 'though I never met him, I still got his genetics. Mandy down Sunshine House,' I said. 'I *found* her, do you know what I'm saying. I fucking walked in and there she was . . .'

'It must have been very distressing,' said Tony.

I shrugged. 'Dunno,' I said.

'I'm just saying,' I said.

'I know,' said Tony. 'But what makes you think you're going to be discharged?'

'I never said I was,' I said.

'Good,' he said. 'Because let me assure you, your place is perfectly safe. No one is going to discharge you,' he said. 'Not until you're ready, I guarantee it.'

'You discharged Pollyanna,' I said.

'Pollyanna was different,' he said. 'I can't discuss Pollyanna.' It was weird like a cloud come over the room, like suddenly it felt like about to rain. Tony seemed to feel it too; he crossed his legs the other way and folded his thin arms tight across his chest.

'Sometimes,' he said, 'it's hard for clients to understand why we do things. But there always is a reason,' he said. 'I'm not saying we don't make mistakes of course; none of us is perfect. And obviously we're limited within the constraints of the system. It's not ideal, no one's saying that it is, but we always try to do what's best for our clients. The last thing we're going to do is discharge you. We're very concerned about you, N . . .'

'You're going to send me up to the wards,' I said, 'cause that's how it sounded. But Tony said they weren't doing that neither, they was keeping me right where I was.

'We'd hardly have made you a guide,' he said, 'if we were just about to get rid of you!' And when he put it like that, I seen what he meant and I couldn't help smiling a bit.

Then he asked me again about the guiding and how I reckoned Poppy was fitting in, and I told him I thought she fit in alright and *mostly* people was nice to her. And I didn't say who it was that weren't, but I seen him smile and I knew how he knew who I meant. Then I told him about how the guiding gone, and how me and Poppy become good friends and I told him what she said as well, how she would of gone mad if it wasn't for me, which I hoped didn't sound like boasting, but that's what she said.

I never told Tony how Poppy wanted to leave. Most probably I should of done, but I thought if I did, he'd think it was 'cause of my guiding. And seeing as how Poppy was pleased with my guiding, that would of been dishonest. So what I done was I actually told him how happy she was to be there. And I said a few other things as well; I can't remember exactly. How she had to *make out* how she wanted to leave, 'cause that was all part of her illness, but she'd been that worried about the assessments and how they was going to kick her out; she'd gone in the toilets at lunch-time and slashed her arms up. And I said some other stuff as well. Like I say I can't remember. And I felt a bit bad saying it, 'cause it weren't exactly the honest truth, but I reckoned it was lesser of two evils.

26. How Brian the Butcher was late for his break and I knew before he'd told us what had happened

Later that week or early the next one, I ain't sure exactly, Tina got discharged. This is how it happened.

We was all sat in the common room, all except Dawn who was making her tables, Brian who was outside washing his hands, and Tina who'd gone for her one-to-one with Rhona the Moaner, made Marta the Coffin look like a laugh a minute. From what I remember the talk was about the groups they was starting up. Social Skills and Self-Empowerment and Positive Thinking and Goal-Setting Group; everything 'cept Sit On Your Arse and Do Nothing; we wasn't impressed.

'It's like being sent back to school,' said Sue, reading through her timetable. 'Look at my Wednesday: Life Skills all morning, then Relaxation all afternoon. I'll hardly have time for a cigarette. Look!' she said and she held out the paper for Verna to take a look at it.

'What's this "Normality Group"?' said Middle-Class Michael.

'Normality?' said Astrid. 'Where?' Middle-Class Michael pointed. ' "Normality Group",' Astrid read. 'What's that?'

'I'll hardly have time for a cigarette,' said Sue.

'I don't know,' said Michael. 'What it says on the tin, I suppose. I don't like the sound of it.'

'Are you down for Social Group, N?' said Wesley.

I give a tut. 'It's confidential,' I said. But I looked anyway and I seen I was and I glanced across and seen Poppy was too. The groups you was in was highlighted in yellow marker pen.

'Got a light?' said Curry Bob, come slunking between the rows and everyone turned their timetables over, but he seen anyway and he told Schizo Safid and Schizo Safid told Big-Nose Jase and Big-Nose Jase told Fag Ash Devine and soon all the flops was pissing theirselves and jabbering with excitement 'cause if there's one thing really got them going it was bad stuff happening to dribblers, ain't nice I know but that's the way they was.

It weren't till we turned our timetables over, we seen what was wrote on the back. This is what it said:

NEW RULES FOR GROUPS AT THE DOROTHY FISH
The following rules were agreed by all present at the Community Meeting on Friday ■ Nov ■.

1. If clients wish to attend, groups are voluntary.

2. If clients do NOT wish to attend, groups are NOT voluntary.

3. Voluntarily or otherwise, clients must attend all their groups.

4. Clients who do NOT attend groups will NOT remain clients.

As we sat reading it over and over, all you could hear was the sniggers of the flops and beneath them the thundering rumble of Fat Florence laughing.

'Hang on,' said Sue, and she read it again. 'Do we have to go or not?'

'Depends,' said Zubin. 'Not if you want to, but if you don't want to, you do.'

'Come again,' said Sue.

'We got to go,' Rosetta said. 'That's what it boils down to.'

'Why can't it just say that then?' said Astrid.

'It does,' said Michael. 'That *is* what it says.'

'Maybe if you're *educated*,' said Astrid. 'Don't say that to *me*.'

Middle-Class Michael pulled at his nose and his ears turned the colour of Turkish shop strawberries.

'And anyway,' said Astrid, 'why didn't you *tell* us? I thought you was s'posed to go to these meetings, let us know what's going on.'

'It'll be in my notes,' said Middle-Class Michael. 'I don't remember,' he said.

'Not much good in your notes,' said Astrid. 'Ain't that right, Brian?' We all looked at Brian, and that's when everyone noticed he wasn't there.

'He's late for his break,' Rosetta said. So we looked at the clock and we seen it was true. Brian the Butcher was nearly three minutes late.

Now I ain't saying I'm psychic, but maybe I am, 'cause as we's all sat there puzzling, and wondering what could of happened, I suddenly got this really weird feeling. And it's like I knew what had happened already – and I *mean* knew as well, not suspected – and my stomach felt like it was turning itself inside out. And do you know what I'm saying, I weren't even surprised, it was like I been *waiting* for it, when the double swing-doors flew suddenly open and Brian the Butcher come bursting in and hurried across the common room and sat in his chair bolt upright with his hands in his lap.

'Is everything alright?' said Middle-Class Michael.

And Brian he give this quick look round and he rubbed his hands on his trousers, and behind him the double swing-doors still flapping, open and shut like the gills of a fish. 'Tina's been discharged,' he said.

27. How paranoia begun
to spread like wildfire

It was Tina going sent everyone over the edge. One dribbler discharged could of been a mistake, but *two* dribblers, do you know what I'm saying, paranoia run round that common room like lighter fuel in the hands of an arsonist, and with Astrid sat like a great pair of bellows belching air into the flames, it didn't take long till the walls and the ceiling and even the windows was so black with smoke you couldn't see nothing at all hardly, except for these little squiggles of light where Schizo Safid had sucked his finger and wrote his initials, SS, all over the glass.

Tina didn't kill herself. She gone home and slashed her arms up instead. Then she stuck them back together with steri-strips, 'stead of going up A&E get the job done proper, which was Tina all over, didn't like to cause trouble. The night they discharged her Astrid gone round but Tina wouldn't let her in. So Astrid looked through the letter-box but she couldn't see nothing 'cept her mac by the door and her see-through plastic hood on the peg besides it. So then she gone up to the walkway above and had a look over the side and through this gap at the top of the curtains she seen down into the sitting room, and there was Tina pressed flat to the wall like a cop in an action film, with her head to one side, not daring to breathe like someone tried to shoot her through the letter-box. 'You should of seen her arms!' said Astrid. 'Slashed to ribbons! Ribbons!' she said. 'I couldn't work out what it was,' she said. 'Thought she was wearing lace sleeves; it was all them steri-strips. It was awful,' she said and she started to cry. 'I'll never forget it, never,' she said.

Course Astrid being Astrid had to milk it for every last drop. Kept asking for extra time off of Tony on account she was so 'traumatised'. And she said she felt abandoned as well, 'cause Tina been like her best friend. And it brought up all the other people abandoned her in her life (like, yeah . . .) and she weren't never going to trust no one again and on and on till it done your head in and do you know what I'm saying we was *all* traumatised, and it was me used to walk up the hill with her every morning.

Astrid weren't traumatised anyway; she couldn't get traumatised if she tried, being about as sensitive as a fucking toilet seat. Astrid was just playing her cards, do you know what I'm saying. Making sure how she got a good hand with assessments coming up in two weeks' time.

Don't get me wrong. I ain't having a pop; I mean, everybody was doing it. The assessments was like a chrysalis. Weren't one single dribbler weren't checking hisself and checking his neighbours either side to see how he done compared. And it ain't nice I know, and I don't like to say it, but every time one of them spied something normal in somebody else, do you know what I'm saying, you seen how it perked them up a bit, and every time somebody done something mad like when Elliot tried to bleach hisself white so's the snipers wouldn't recognise him, you seen them all looking a bit kind of panicked on account of they knew they was going to have to out-top him.

It was like a fucking mad Olympics, dirty tricks and all. And I mean dirty too, do you know what I'm saying, weren't one single dribbler washed so much as his hands since we heard Tina been discharged, excepting of Brian the Butcher of course been washing so non-stop his knuckles worn through, like the knees on an old pair of jeans. And I'm not being funny but some of them, it weren't just not washing, it *couldn't* of been, they must of took extra measures I reckon, like pissing theirselves or rolling in shit, I mean that was how bad it got. White Wesley taken a whiff of his pits to see how he was progressing and he passed out right there in front of us from the sheer overpowering stench of hisself, while Astrid stunk so bad of gone-off fish the cats used to arch their backs and hiss as she walked through the Darkwoods each morning.

Elliot smelled stronger than anyone; he smelled like a swimming pool. He smelled so strong, Zubin had to wear goggles on account of his eyes started smarting, and one day as Michael was pinning his pass on, this sniff come in with a rolled-up towel, asked Sharon how much for a lane swim. 'And she wouldn't believe him,' Michael said. 'She thought he was trying to make fun of her. Of course it didn't help he was lifting weights at the time.'

By the second week Canteen Coral wouldn't serve us, said we put the flops off of their food. And they needed their food, she said, unlike us, up to our eyes in MAD money and never known the meaning of work, sat on our fat, flabby arses all day, and nothing wrong with us, 'side of being lazy, which if that weren't her words exactly, was her meaning plain as she'd spelled it out on paper.

Poppy didn't compete in the MAD Olympics, didn't do nothing at all to be honest, just sat there day after fucking day reading this book, with a tissue held to her nose. Every twenty minutes or so she'd reach in her bag and take out this bottle, a tiny brown bottle with a white screw-on cap and shake a few drops on her tissue.

'What's that?' I says to her.

'Lavender.'

'Thought lavender was purple,' I says.

'It's essential oil.'

'I was joking,' I says. 'I know what essential oil is.' So far she ain't even *looked* at me. Just drops the bottle back in her bag and turns a page of her book.

'Can *I* have a sniff?' I says to her.

She looks at me now. 'I'm sorry?' she says.

'Can I have a sniff of the bottle?' I says.

'Sure,' she says, and she gets it out and hands it over and goes back to reading her book.

'What's that you reading?' I says to her. I'm holding the bottle so close to my nose, the stopper's halfway up my nostril.

'What's that you reading?' I ask again.

'Same,' she says and she holds it up. *Assessment in Mental Health Nursing* it's called. Got a crystal ball on the cover.

'Ain't you finished yet?' I says.

'No,' she says.

'Is it interesting?'

'N,' she says. 'Sorry; it's just I'm trying to revise.'

I give a tut. 'I was only arsking!' I says.

★　　★　　★

If Poppy didn't want to talk no more, do you know what I'm saying, I weren't bothered. 'Cause when she did it was like change the fucking record anyway, to be honest. 'What do I do if I fail my assessment? What do I do *then*!' she'd say, like twenty times a day at least, if not two hundred and twenty. And every time she said it of course I'd think of that thing I said to Tony, start worrying case they asked her about it, and the more I thought, the more I reckoned there weren't no way they *wouldn't* ask, so what I done was I tried *not* to think and when Poppy started going on, I'd give a great yawn and roll my eyes like tell me something new.

The others couldn't be arsed with Poppy neither to tell you the truth. They was all too busy stunking theirselves and dreaming up new symptoms. When she come out with something extra offensive, like 'Jesus! Get me out of here or I *will* go mad! Sweet Jesus! *Please!*' they didn't know whether to be relieved or pissed off with her or both. You could see the confusion all over their faces, as they sat there trying to work it out, till they looked away and made like they hadn't heard.

It weren't like I minded but it did piss me off she seemed to think her getting discharged was so important when some of us our lives was at stake and she just didn't get it at all. This one thing she said, I mean I thought it was funny, but it just goes to show how far she'd got lost up her arse.

We's walking down the hill one night and right out of nowhere she turns round and says, 'You know, you should get your hair cut, N. You got really nice hair, just needs a few layers, do you know what I'm saying, bit of body.'

I didn't say nothing.

'I mean it,' she said. 'You have; you've got really nice hair. Don't be embarrassed,' she said. She laughed.

'I ain't *embarrassed*,' I said.

'You could try a few highlights as well,' she said. 'Just here, in the front.'

'Get off me!' I said.

'It would look really good,' she said. 'You ever *had* highlights?'

'Course!' I said.

'I know a really good place. Fact I'm going this weekend. You could come if you want.'

'Fuck's sake, Poppy!' I said. 'It's ASSESSMENTS! Jesus! Do you know what I'm saying!' And I shown her the back of my head, though I couldn't help smiling.

Then just two days before the assessments, Rosetta heard something she shouldn't of, and what she heard, do you know what I'm saying, had everyone give Poppy a second look.

28. How Rosetta heard something she shouldn't of, and what she heard had everyone give Poppy a second look

What happened was Verna and Sue the Sticks gone looking for proof again. Sue worn a pair of gardening gloves she bought out of Woolworths, 4.49, which I could of lifted for nothing as well but God helps them help theirselves. And this time they taken a key with them Rosetta borrowed off of Minimum Wage, opened every door, she said, 'cept the staff room got a Chubb lock. Course they come back full of the same old bullshit, everything they seen and done and all of it bollocks anyway, especially Verna; Sue weren't so bad on her own. They seen seven rooms just full of boxes they said, that's all they had in them boxes and boxes, all piled up on top of each other. And Verna used one of Sue's crutches to shift one, like hooking a sheep with a crook, and she brought it crashing down on to the floor, but all it had in it was thousands of forms, all exactly the same, just like thousands of forms, all covered with numbers in circles. And Verna said they was answer papers and the questions must of been somewhere else. 'You know,' she told us, '*exam* answer papers. Like GCSE,' she said. 'Multiple choice.' Which I didn't know neither to tell you the truth on account of I didn't *got* no GSEs, not like Verna the Vomit with her fifty grade As and her private school all stuffed up her arse, do you know what I'm saying, fuck her! So then they pulled down a load more boxes to try and find one with the questions but they never.

It was the last door though got everyone's para working overtime. It weren't there before, said Sue the Sticks, she'd swear on her life it weren't there before or not with the steel shutters anyway, 'cause they would of remembered that. The shutters was pulled right down and locked like the Turkish shop after ten. And the master key wouldn't open the lock; they tried, said Sue, they both of them tried, but you could see anyway it was a different sort of lock. Well while they was trying they heard this noise seemed to come from inside the room. Like a drumming, whirring, sort of a noise . . .

'You mean people?' we said.

'Not *people* exactly,' said Sue the Sticks.

'What then?' we said.

'I don't know,' said Sue. 'We weren't sure, was we Vern. But I didn't like the sound of it. I said to Verna, I said, "I'm going. I've heard enough," I said. "I'm going." "It's probably just Minimum Wage," she says. "Hoovering or something." "Hoovering!" I said. "Hoovering! Funny sort of hoovering! And I s'pose I'm a duchess as well," I said, "if that's hoovering!" I know what hoovering sounds like!'

But Verna still reckoned it could of been. It could of been a Dyson she said. And Sue said she wouldn't know about that, all *she* knew was it weren't hoovering. So in the end the only thing was to go and ask Minimum Wage.

At first Rosetta refused to go. 'She's done more than enough already,' she said. 'She's risked her job for helping us . . .'

'So give her a table,' Wesley said, but turned out she got

one already. 'So give her another one,' he said, but Rosetta said there weren't enough room 'cause the one she got had to stand up on end as it was.

'So what's the problem?' Astrid said. 'You's only asking if she's got a Dyson . . .'

'And if not, what that noise was,' said Sue. ''Cause it weren't hoovering. I know that much . . .'

'Perhaps I should ask her,' Michael said. 'On behalf of the Patients' Council.' But no one thought that was a good idea; Minimum Wage never taken to Middle-Class Michael.

Suddenly Poppy slapped her forehead. 'I know!' she said. 'It's obvious!' Everyone turned and stared like what's coming now.

'Duh!' she said, like ain't I stupid.

'What?' we said, couldn't help it.

'A cameraman!' she said. 'That's what it is! They've got a cameraman in there. They're making a dribbler *Big Brother*. Voting us out one a week,' she said. She looked up to the corner like taking the piss, do you know what I'm saying, like she's live on telly. 'Please vote for me,' she said. 'Please, please, please!'

'Is that supposed to be funny?' said Astrid.

'I'll take all my clothes off!' Poppy said. 'I'll sleep with Michael. Anything!' Michael's ears gone so fucking red, do you know what I'm saying, they lit up the whole room and the fag smoke swirling shades of pink like someone had swapped the light-bulbs.

'It *is* next door to the theatre,' said Sue.

'They got the mirrors,' Tadpole said. Tadpole taken Tina's place. I'll say about her in a minute.

'Fuck!' said Wesley. You seen him thinking. Pictured hisself on the front of the *Mirror*. 'Fuck!' He was smiling all over.

Suddenly Poppy started to laugh. 'You are live on Channel 4,' she said. 'Please refrain . . .' But she couldn't get it out on account she was laughing too much. 'Please . . .' she said. 'Please refrain . . .' she said, but each time she said it she cracked up again, till she was shooking and shooking and crying with laughter and all on her own and everyone sat looking. She taken a deep breath, held up a hand and give it another go. 'You are live on Channel 4,' she said. 'Please refrain . . .' she started to shake; it come out in snorts through her nose. 'You are live on Channel 4. Please refrain from swearing.'

Do you know what I'm saying, it weren't *that* funny. And I reckon she realised it weren't as well 'cause as soon as she said it she stopped laughing then like total anticlimax. And she run a finger under her eyes, and checked it and run it under again then she reached in her bag for her cigarettes and as she leant forward I seen these tears like welling against her lashes. And Rosetta must of seen it too 'cause she leant across give Poppy a rub on the arm.

'Alright,' said Rosetta, standing up. 'I'll talk to Minimum Wage. I'm not pushing, mind, I'll just ask her; that's all. If she doesn't want to tell me, that's her business. Lord knows!' she said. 'She's done more than enough already!'

Rosetta was gone for hours, it felt like. 'She's been discharged,' said Astrid, twice.

'Evicted,' said Zubin. He started to laugh.

'Oh don't,' said Sue. 'It's not funny!'

'I hope Trevor McDonald ain't watching,' said Tadpole. 'I don't want *him* knowing I'm in here. Start putting stuff in my head again. That's what happened last time,' she said. She was looking at Astrid. Astrid sniffed. 'Never leaves me alone,' said Tadpole. 'That's why I'm here, get some peace and quiet. If he finds out, that'll be it.' Tadpole was so fucking paranoid, made Elliot, hid underneath his chair, with his sweatshirt tied round under his eyes like a bleach-haired terrorist, made Elliot look like he'd just took a couple of sensible precautions.

They'd moved Tadpole down the day Tina gone; she'd been on the wards seven years. And all that time they'd had her on Plutuperidol – syrup, I think, or else injections, either way so's she couldn't palm it and trade it with Banker Bill. The Plutuperidol didn't work, 'cause it don't, just drugged her so comatosed, her brain weren't turning fast enough to remember her own name half the time, let alone the names of the people following her. The other thing was it pumped her up, quicker than a bicycle tyre. Soon she didn't got no neck at all; she was totally round, like a giant ball, 'cept for two skinny legs stuck out the bottom which is why we called her 'Tadpole'.

When Tadpole got to the Dorothy Fish she begun self-medicating, which means she stopped taking her medication, and inside of a day her neck come back, and inside of a week her waist come back, and inside of a month she was all skin and bone but she still kept her name like sentimental reasons. The paranoia was even quicker; her first full day at the Dorothy Fish, I seen her trying to twist round in her chair to check there weren't no one behind her, then the day after I was just saying about, when Rosetta gone down to see Minimum Wage, Trevor McDonald found out where Tadpole was hiding. 'Won't leave me alone for a second,' she said. 'I'll never get rid of him now.' 'So take your meds,' said Astrid Arsewipe; it was right before the assessments as well. Fuck, was she pissed off! But Tadpole said meds didn't make no difference. It weren't nothing to do with the meds, she said. What use was a tablet when he seen her on dribbler *Big Brother*?

'She's been discharged,' said Astrid, again, which is three times in total she said it. And my stomach gone all sort of cold for a second 'cause me and Rosetta, we got on alright, and one time she give me this flip-top bin – like she'd washed it all out and everything – when she painted her kitchen, and bought a new blue one to match. So when I seen Rosetta walk in, I says to myself, thank fuck for that, and I don't mind admitting I did, I felt quite relieved.

'So?' we said.

But she shaken her head. 'She wasn't there,' she said.

'And it took you half an hour to work *that* out?' said Astrid, who still got the hump with Rosetta, on account of Rosetta had rubbed Poppy's arm when Poppy started crying about the *Big Brother* thing, which Astrid reckoned was aimed at her, or something like that; it all of it come out later.

'No,' said Rosetta. 'Something else.' And that was when she told us.

'I knocked a long time,' Rosetta said. 'But she didn't open the door. So in the end I tried the handle and it opened just like that. I was thinking I'd leave a note saying I called but I couldn't find anything to write on. So I started rummaging through my bag; I suppose I must have let go of the door – I did, I remember it slamming behind me – and just as I found an old envelope that's when I heard these voices outside the cupboard. Lord knows, I'm not one for listening to private conversation, so I stuffed my fingers in my ears and even started singing a song to myself but it didn't do much good; they were so close you couldn't miss a word of it.

' "Well there's not a great deal one can do," says the first voice. Sounded like an educated man, a scholar or something, the way he was talking. "I understand your concerns, indeed I *share* them; it's terribly difficult. But sadly that's the way things are; one always has to work within certain parameters . . ."

' "No, I realise that," says the second voice; it's Tony Balaclava! "I realise that, Derek, I wasn't suggesting . . ." ' ('Derek?' said Michael. 'Derek *Diabolus!*' 'Shhh!' we said. 'Go on!')

' "And clearly if one could have avoided that unfortunate . . . Pollyanna, was it? Tragic business." I'm listening now; got my ear pressed tight to the door! "But you see where they're coming from," he says. "As a doctor, of course, one thinks only of one's patients, but as a taxpayer I do recognise we can't just keep pouring money in . . ."

' "Well, no . . ." says Tony.

' "One needs evidence that the treatment is effective, quantifiable results, otherwise it's very hard to justify extra funding. If A, then B, that sort of thing. But we have to *prove* it, QED. As a scientist, I must say, I rather relish the challenge."

' "Of course," says Tony. "You're right, of course. I just wondered whether in Tina's case . . ."

' "It's rather like when my wife goes to Waitrose." It's the first man talking again. "She wants to choose what goes in her trolley; she wants to see what she's paying for. She doesn't just hand over her purse and let them fill it for her."

' "No," says Tony. "No, I'm sure . . ."

' "And it's really no different with health services. We need to offer our customers . . ."

' "The patients?" says Tony.

' "Well, yes, the patients . . . but it's the government really, isn't it, or the taxpayer at the end of the day; he's the one footing the bill. We need to offer him something tangible, something he can put in his trolley, if A then B, QED. He wants to know where his money's going. What is he *getting* for it; that's the question!"

' "Quite," says Tony. "It's just, with Tina . . ."

' "I'm not suggesting it's straightforward, Tony. I'm well aware, as a psychiatrist, of the problems in obtaining concrete data. It's hardly as though one can measure the tumour, or not in any obvious sense, I mean; where does one place the ruler, you see?"

' "I do," says Tony.

' "And that being so, how does one prove in facts and figures the efficacy of one treatment over another? But I always insist – and there *will* be those who seek to demote us, make no mistake – I always insist psychiatry is a *science* first and foremost. I'm not talking about psychology or social work; that's all very well. But psychiatry is a science, pure science; I always say, in its purest form one doesn't need patients at all."

' "I'm not sure . . ." says Tony.

' "I know, I know . . . I know what you're trying to say.

Compromise is inevitable when it comes to *applying* one's science in a clinical setting. But I have to say that as a clinician, I rather applaud what Veronica's doing, in certain respects at least. We have to work within the system; I'm all for taking a principled stand, but the argument's far from straightforward. If they shut us down where's the good in that?" '

'They shutting us down!' White Wesley said, and it run round the room like dominoes. But Rosetta said Tony wouldn't never allow it, not in a million years she said. 'Don't worry about that, Tony lives for this place. He's not going to let *that* happen. But we've got to help him as well,' she said. 'We must do all we can; we're the cause of his trouble, none of us getting better.'

'So it's *our* fault is it now,' said Astrid. 'It's *our* fault if we're mentally ill . . .'

Rosetta ignored her. 'He said something else.'

'Who?' we said. 'Dr Diabolus?'

'Just beggars belief,' said Middle-Class Michael. 'This is precisely what we've been . . .'

'Tony,' Rosetta said.

'What!' we said. 'What did he say, Rosetta?'

But she shaken her head. 'I'm not sure,' she said. 'It's private, I'm not sure I ought to tell.' She was looking at Poppy. 'He talked about you.'

'About *me*?' said Poppy. 'What *about* me?'

'I'll tell you later,' Rosetta said.

'No,' said Poppy. 'Tell me now. *I* don't care, do you know what I'm saying. I'm really not bothered if everyone knows,' which everyone nodded agreement at that, being about the most sanest thing Poppy said since she'd arrived.

But Rosetta leant forward and beckoned Poppy and Poppy leant forward so they's head to head, over the stacks of empty cups, and saucers swirling tea and soggy fag butts. And Rosetta whispered in Poppy's ear, which even though I was listening so hard I sprained my fucking eardrum, I still couldn't make out what it was she said, sounded like 'Tony Warrior Cop', like a fucking Nintendo Gameboy.

'He what?!' said Poppy. 'Do you know what I'm saying!' Rosetta whispered something again.

'Well what do they expect!' said Poppy. 'Of course I'm fucking stressed!' she said. 'I wouldn't *be* stressed if they let me out! Jesus!' she said; she gone red in the face. I thought she was going to start crying again and she lit up a fag and smoked it so fast the ash come spraying off of the end and all down the front of her see-through black top, hardly what you'd call practical clothes for a psychiatric loony bin chock-full of perverts and fuck knows what, but there you go that was Poppy.

'Maybe I shouldn't have said,' said Rosetta.

'Said *what?*' said everyone. 'What did you *hear?*'

Poppy threw her butt at a cup; it fizzed as it gone in.

'Goldfish!' said Zubin.

'They're worried I'm not coping,' said Poppy. 'They're worried I'm cracking up, alright? The stress of being mentally ill is starting to make me mentally ill. I'm here 'cause I'm mad and I'm mad 'cause I'm here.' She tapped her head. 'D'you geddit?'

No one said nothing for maybe a minute. Poppy lit up another. She was sat bent forward with her elbow on her knee, one hand shading her eyes like a baseball cap, while the other worked the cigarette up and down in a cloud of

B&H. I ain't sure what it was she expected, but if she was hoping for sympathy, do you know what I'm saying, you'd of felt for her more if she'd give you a good hard slap round the face then complained how she'd hurt her hand. There was this sudden dazzling splinter of light seemed to shatter the whole fucking common room, then three claps of thunder like suicide bombs and the panic alarm begun screeching as the lights gone out.

When the lights come back on, I couldn't work out for a second what had happened. The carpet turned into this giant chessboard with the flops lined up down the sides like prawns; you got a shit-coloured square then a white-coloured square then a shit-coloured square then a white-coloured square. I thought I was fucking seeing things for a second, I honestly did. Then I glanced up, do you know what I'm saying and there's all these wires poking out of the ceiling between the round plastic lights. And what it is right, it's the tiles fallen down where the lights ain't holding them on. 'Cause one landed right on Astrid's head, till she shaken it off and it slid down beside her chair. 'I could of been killed,' she said as Tony run in and Dr Neutral behind him. 'Surprised it didn't smash my head in.'

'Hardly,' said Michael. 'It's polystyrene.' He picked up the tile and give it a tap, made a hollow sound; I sniggered, couldn't help it.

'Don't you tell *me* what I felt,' said Astrid. '*You* ain't the one with the fractured skull. I'd like to see . . .'

Tony cleared his throat. 'Everyone! Can you pay attention please!' Then he told us we all had to go downstairs, like a fire practice, he said. 'Cause they had to make sure if the room was safe and he clicked his knuckles in turn as he spoke, and it sounded like pulling crackers.

So then we's all stood in the car park for about five hours, do you know what I'm saying, 'cept for Elliot, that is, stayed under his chair, which they never even noticed.

'You forgotten the gravity anyway,' said Astrid, weren't like one to give up. 'You got to add on the gravity. Ten miles of gravity, that's what they say. Felt more like a paving slab,' she said, which even if it did, which it didn't, she wouldn't of felt nothing anyway, fucking bull-terrier jaws she got and bull-terrier skull to go with them.

Middle-Class Michael didn't reply. He was stood squinting up at the common-room windows, trying to make out what was going on inside.

'He won't be told,' said Astrid to Sue. 'They're all the same, men. Can't bear to be told . . . My husband was the same,' she said.

'You heard from him?' said Sue the Sticks.

'Two years, man!' White Wesley said. 'My brother got longer for jacking a car!'

Poppy was over by the barrier, redoing her make-up in the mirror of this four-wheel drive. 'Don't look stressed to me,' said Astrid. 'I seen *Tony Balaclava* look worse than that! I seen more signs of mentally ill in the check-out down Sniff Street Tesco!

'You can't of heard right, Rosetta,' she said. 'Worried she ain't coping! What's *she* got to cope with anyway! That's what I want to know.' And everyone agreed with her, except for Rosetta who known what she heard how Tony was worried Poppy was cracking up.

'What I don't get,' said Sue the Sticks, 'is what all this has to do with hoovering.'

'Alright, Poppy?' I said. Didn't answer. She was bent to the wing mirror doing round her eyes, soft grey pencil, smudging out at the corners.

'We used to collect them down Sunshine House,' I said to her.

She turned her head slightly. 'Sorry?' she said.

'Wing mirrors,' I said. 'We used to collect them.'

'Right,' she said and gone back to her make-up, like turning her head to check from different angles. Sharon was stood by the entrance, watching, huge arms folded across his chest, his business thrust forward and his legs spread so wide you could of drove a bus in between them.

'I ain't never thought of that,' I said. 'I wonder what happened to them.

'Most probably Nasser the Nose,' I said. 'Most probably helped hisself when I left.

'Made out they was his,' I said.

'I bet that's what he done as well!

'Do you know what I'm saying, Poppy?' I said. 'I bet that's what he fucking done. Taken my mirrors then tried to make out how they'd been his all along.

'I should track him down, ask for them back,' I said. 'D'you reckon?' I said. 'Do you reckon I should?

'Fucking pisses me off,' I said. 'Now I've remembered about it.

'What's up with you, anyway?' I said.

'I'm fine,' said Poppy.

'I was only asking.'

'I know,' she said. 'I know; I'm fine.' She was finished doing her make-up now, zipped it back in her bag and turned to face me. Bit overdone to tell you the truth but there you go, that's me, subtle.

'I was only checking,' I said. 'That's all. No need to bite my head off.'

She smiled. You could see it like crack at the corners. 'It's just what Rosetta said,' she said. 'About them being worried I'm losing it. What if they don't let me out of here! I don't know what I'm going to do . . .'

'At least they's concerned about you,' I said.

She looked at me.

'Well they are!' I said. 'At least you know they's *worrying*!' It pissed me off to be perfectly honest, the fact she couldn't see it, the look she give me like *I'm* being slow when it was me said to Tony Balaclava 'bout her slashing her arms in the first place! 'If I was you, I'd be grateful,' I said. 'Not being funny, Poppy,' I said, 'but I would. If I was you, I'd be counting my lucky chickens!'

29. How the dribblers gone on about fetching the sangers till it done me and Poppy's heads in

Assessment day and Poppy shown up with her long flowing hair cut off in a bob. 'I thought I'd go chic,' she said. She'd had her nails done too and she worn this jacket, like the smartest thing you seen in your life and there's everyone else in scabby old tracksuit bottoms.

The assessments begun half-nine with Astrid and finished half-four with Zubin. I was first on in the afternoon and Middle-Class Michael was last in the morning and everyone else fitted somewhere in between. At nine-twenty Astrid got up out her chair and everyone said good luck. All except Poppy who was going through her notes with a highlighter pen what was pink at the one end and fluorescent yellow the other. Her books was all piled on the table between us: *Madness Made Easy*, *Psychiatry for Idiots*, *Assessment in Mental Health Nursing*. Every few minutes she'd pick one up, flick through it to find the page she was after, and check to make sure she hadn't missed nothing. 'If you highlight *everything*, Poppy,' I said, 'there ain't no point, innit!' and everyone laughed and I reckoned I been pretty funny as well, but I needn't of bothered; they was strung so tight they'd of laughed at anything.

'Where's Rosetta?' said Sue the Sticks, who'd forgot to put her false leg on. ('Can you believe it, Vern!' she said. 'I'd forget my own head if it wasn't screwed on!') 'Where can she have got to?' she said. 'She's *always* here by twenty past nine . . .'

'She rung me last night,' White Wesley said. He got sunglasses on and worn underpants outside of his tracksuit bottoms. 'She was worrying, man.'

'Aren't we all?' said Astrid. 'She should just be glad she's not in first!' And she stalked out with her nose in the air 'cause Rosetta stolen what ought to of been her moment.

What cracked me up was two minutes later when Brian the Butcher come crawling in, after climbing the hill like seventy times to make sure we all got through. As he opened the double swing-doors, this huge pink seal snuck out of the toilets and hurried across the landing. Which if you ever seen a panicked seal trying to hurry, flubbering past with a bear behind him and David Attingborough doing the comments, you'll know why I was pissing myself at the sight of Astrid Arsewipe. Especially, that is, when I seen the lipstick, bright pink lipstick to match with her sweatshirt; after stunking it up like a tank of dead fish, with the cats keeling over and dying in the gutter, she'd snuck off and put on her lipstick (perfume too, must of swum in the stuff; you seen the flops drowning one by one as the wave crashed over the common room) 'cause she couldn't have Tony thinking she was disgusting.

Twelve o'clock me and Poppy gone round the Gate-house to fetch the sangers. Every day since Canteen Coral wouldn't serve us, we'd took it in turns to go round the Gatehouse fetch sangers for everyone else. It weren't worth the hassle to be totally honest what with everyone getting so arsey. Like, if you brought them ham instead of tuna or egg instead of cheese or something, or even if you just forgot who was white or brown, or no salad cream. And the money always got fucked up as well, like everything cost one ninety-five, or two twenty-five or one pound fifty – egg was the cheapest – and some people wanted crisps and some didn't and some said 'Get us ten Superkings, will you?' but I drawn the line at that.

I reckoned we should all get our own, to be honest, and I said so as well. 'It's only next door,' I said. 'Ain't worth the hassle.'

'You never thought it was such a hassle,' said Astrid Arsewipe, 'when *I* was fetching them yesterday. When you wanted five packets of cheese and onion, you reckoned there weren't nothing to it,' she said, which was lying as well 'cause I'd only asked for three.

'Fuck off!' I said. 'Get your own!' I said. So then they *all* ganged up. And Astrid sat there preening herself like an overfed duck up Paradise Park and just 'cause she done her assessment first, which was alphabetic, and she known what they said and she wouldn't tell nobody neither.

'Come on,' said Poppy. 'Let's just go and get them. If I don't get some air soon I'm going to pass out,' which I thought that was fucking funny as well, right on the Nasser the Nose. And Astrid the worst hump you seen in your life, like red in the face, do you know what I'm saying, and everyone trying to make out how they wasn't laughing.

The Gatehouse was pretty much empty for once on account all the flops was so shameless and gagging for news of our assessments, they was sat all along the corridor checking each dribbler as they come out, trying to tell from their face if they been discharged or not. They was so fucking desperate they missed their dinner rather than give up their places, all except Curry Bob that is, sat in the Gatehouse drowning his sorrows: Candid Headphones gone through with flying colours. 'Fucking dribblers,' he said. 'No offence. I knew she wouldn't be going anyway. I said to Gunga Din, I said, "Forget it, mate! They ain't going nowhere. It's all a fucking sham," I said. "First this Poppy Shakespeare shows up. No offence," he said. "Ain't your fault is it, but how long's Paolo been on the wards! Just 'cause you got a nice pair of legs. No offence. I don't trust them fucking quacks; never did but now I *know* I don't." I said to Gunga Din, I said, "You're better off having a drink with me. Got to be realistic," I said. "That Gita ain't stupid." She's through, I suppose?' I nodded. 'Fucking sham!' he said and he shaken his head and gone back to his pint.

I give the order to Gatehouse Pete three times. The first and the second was different, he said. So I done it a third time and that was different as well. 'Fuck it,' I said. 'Just do what you want. Do *you* remember?' I said to Poppy, but Poppy said she didn't remember and she hadn't been listening anyway.

Pete laughed. He was alright, Pete, as long as you knew how to take him. 'D-day today, girls,' he said. 'How you feeling? Look at you!' he said to Poppy. 'Very nice. Why don't *you* dress like that,' he said to me. 'Bit more feminine.'

'Fuck off!' I said.

'I was only joking!' He wiped his knife on this blue-and-white tea towel he'd stuffed in his jeans for an apron. 'Now,' he said. 'Decision time! Shall we go for salad cream with both ham, neither or one?'

Me and Poppy eaten our sangers sat at the table under the TV screen. We still had eighteen minutes to go before Sharon had said he'd *have* to report it if Poppy weren't back, and she wanted to make the most of them. 'It's good to get out of there!' she said, picking the cheese out her sandwich and leaving the bread. 'Just a bit of normality, N, do you know what I'm saying! Sorry,' she said. 'I know it's different . . .'

'No,' I said. 'No, I agree with you! Jesus, Poppy, they was doing my head in! Especially Astrid, do you know what I'm saying. Stupid cow! *Michael* don't fetch the sangers and neither does Dawn *or* Sue, they's exempt, so how come *we* got to fetch them then? Just 'cause she done her fucking assessment, it pisses me off, do you know what I'm saying. One rule for some and some rule for others, or whatever. Are you eating your bread?'

They was showing the news on the telly and Poppy was pissing me off a bit 'cause she kept on glancing up at it while I was talking. 'Anything interesting?' I said.

'Just the news,' she said.

'Oh right,' I said. I picked up her cling film and unwrapped four buttered brown triangles.

'It's all this league-table shit,' she said. 'They're measuring everything! You know my little girl, Saffra?' she said.

'Of course I do,' I'm like what do you think!

'She's got exams this summer,' she said. 'Six years old, do you know what I'm saying! The other night she was really upset.'

'Oh dear,' I said. 'Poor Saffra!' I said.

' "What's the matter, sweetheart," ' I said. 'I could see there was something like eating her. And it turns out she's worried about her exams! Six years old, do you know what I'm saying! Something her teacher had said, you know, I was fucking livid, I nearly gone up there, but the thing is *they're* under pressure as well; I mean it doesn't excuse it, do you know what I'm saying, but if they fail their inspection or come low in the league, they can close them down, that's what Natalie said, and there's Saffra thinking it will all be her fault 'cause she can't remember her four-times table! I mean not that they'd close them down anyway; they're a really good school, like top twenty per cent, but *she* doesn't know that at six years old. She's all stressed out, bless her; six years old! It's not right is it, N? It can't be! At six? I didn't have a care in the world! It's her teacher; she's just scared of losing her job. Mind you,' says Poppy, 'I can't say I blame her. Not after *my* experience . . .

'I told Dud about it. D'you know what he said? Maybe it wasn't such a bad thing. "They're just concerned about standards," he said. "We want her to get into Uni, don't we?" "Dud!" I said. "She's *six years old*! And what's wrong with *not* going, anyway? *I* never went to college," I said. "Yeah, but they've got targets now," he said. "Seventy-five per cent," he said. "Three quarters of kids, they want, going to Uni." "Why?" I said. "Because *that's the target*," he said, like I'm thick. "You're just being neurotic." Neurotic! Do you . . . One sec,' said Poppy and turned back to look at the telly.

It weren't that I didn't feel sorry for Saffra, getting all stressed about her exams, but if that's all she got to worry her, do you know what I'm saying, not having a go, but to tell you the truth, I'd of give her a good fucking slap.

'Who *is* this Veronica Salmon?' said Poppy. 'What the fuck does a Mad Tsar do?'

'Dunno,' I said.

She glanced at me, then back at the telly and started to laugh. 'What does she think she's wearing!' she said. I looked up, couldn't help it. 'A tartan trouser suit!' she said. 'Jesus, N! No fucking wonder!'

30. How I walked past the 'Urine Samples' sign without even noticing and I had to go back and hand it in and what happened when I did

I weren't even nervous about my assessment. I knew I'd be OK. I knew if Astrid had got through no problem and Candid Headphones and Elliot and Dawn, there weren't no way they could discharge *me*, even if Tony hadn't of said how worried and concerned they all was, which he had anyway, that same one-to-one when I'd said about Poppy's arms, which I wished I hadn't.

The flops lined the corridor right down both sides, propped against walls or the doors or each other, like sacks of rice down the Turkish shop. I had to keep stepping over their legs, which was so close together I tiptoed it mostly, and Fag Ash Devine said I trod on her hand, which even if I did, do you know what I'm saying, you couldn't fucking see it, being so brown from tobacco it camouflaged into the carpet; but the flops started harping anyway and hurling their slippers, like any excuse, and everyone I stepped over so careful; next time, I thought, I won't bother.

Second-Floor Nancy was sat halfway down, holding hands with Nuthouse Neela. Neela got a joss-stick stuck in her ear, a picture of an elephant hung round her neck and a splodge of red on her forehead looked like ketchup. 'I won't take it *personal*,' Nancy said as I stepped across her veiny white legs; her flesh-coloured pop socks was down round her ankles. 'Just do what you have to do, love,' she said.

'I will,' I said.

'Not *your* fault,' she said. 'Not *her* fault, is it, Neela, love! We're all on the same side here,' she said. 'We ain't going to take it *personal.*

'Just do what you have to do,' she said, and she carried on calling after me, 'We ain't going to take it *personal.* Not her fault, is it, Neela, love!' all the way down the corridor.

'She's off her cake,' said Big-Nose Jase. He got huge great DMs on, the size of two cars so you had to do a Chris fucking Bonington to haul yourself up and over.

'Don't want to move down,' said Clifton the Poet. 'Second-Floor Syndrome: that's what it is.'

'Like when Taz glued hisself to his bed,' said Jase.

'Forgot it had wheels!' said Third-Floor Lemar.

'So they just wheeled him into the lift!' said Jase. Him and Lemar was cracking up.

'Fucking idiot!' said Lemar.

'Still got half a mattress stuck to his back,' said Clifton the Poet. He was grinning as well.

'Just do what you have to do,' shouted Second-Floor Nancy.

There was a sign on the door of the theatre said:

BASELINE ASSESSMENTS ███
Wait here until you are called.
Thankyou

But underneath there was another sign, handwrote in green marker pen:

HAVE YOU HANDED
IN YOUR
URINE SAMPLE?
If not, please do so NOW

So I taken the bottle out of my pack (Aqua Pura, Turkish shop) and knocked on the door of the theatre. It was Tony answered, holding a plate of sangers. When he seen it was me he glanced down at his watch. 'We're not quite ready yet, N,' he said. 'Could you wait out here for a minute?'

'Alright!' I said. 'I'm just handing this in.' And I held out the Aqua Pura. Just a couple of inches, there was, in the bottom, had a bit of a scum sort of thing on the surface, 'cause I'd tried to dissolved in some Plutuperidol, make my levels up closer to what they should be. Tony frowned. 'Like it says!' I said, and I tapped the sign with the bottle to show him; you could hear it sloshing about.

Tony cleared his throat. 'Ah, right,' he said. 'Well that goes down there,' and he pointed back down the corridor. Behind him, I seen Dr Azazel sipping a glass of wine, and someone was laughing, Dr Clootie, I think. 'You'll see the sign,' said Tony and shut the door.

So back I gone, climbing over the legs, with the bottle in my hand and a thousand flops all staring. And there it was, maybe six doors down, opposite Clifton the Poet.

URINE
SAMPLES

But wrote so small you'd of needed a telescope not to just walk straight past. 'Gis a swig,' said Big-Nose Jase and the flops all started pissing theirselves, which is flops all over, immature, but anyway I just knocked on the door and gone in.

It weren't no bigger than a cupboard inside, like a meds room up on the wards. Dr Neutral was sat on this stool by the counter which run down one wall. He worn a white coat, like out of *ER*, and black rectangular glasses. All over the counter was bottles and funnels and jars and a rack full of test-tubes. Seeing me, he said, 'Come in,' which I had, then looked down at this list on the top in front of him. I seen Middle-Class Michael one above me then a row of numbers in boxes. His clean, blunt finger run down through the names. 'N, isn't it?' he said, and taken the bottle.

'One second,' he said, as I turned to go out. 'I just need to check we've got enough.' And he taken this jug with like measurements on and unscrewed the top off the Aqua Pura. He frowned; I seen he was on to the scum. 'Did you wash this out?' he said.

'It's water,' I said. Do you know what I'm saying!

'I mean after you drank the water,' he said.

'I didn't drink the water,' I said.

'Right,' he said. 'So . . .'

'Why'd I want to drink bottled? I got it fresh in the tap,' I said.

'Some people just prefer the taste.' He held the bottle up to the light. Flakes of Plutuperidol stuck to the surface like fish food.

'Really?!' I said, like playing it thick. 'But I thought it

weren't *s'posed* to taste,' I said and I frowned like I didn't get it at all, like 'Ain't the world confusing when you's totally thick like me.' 'Cause that's how you got to be with doctors; you got to flatter them. And especially when you's getting assessed; if you don't want to end up out on your arse, you got to convince them their years of college and swatting non-stop from the age of three, it's all payed off 'cause it's turned them into the Brains of fucking Britain! And the best way of doing it is come over so stupid, it makes them feel smart compared. Like if they don't know what day it is, *you* don't know what *year* it is; and if they don't know what year it is, *you* don't know what *century* it is, and that makes them feel a bit better. Course some dribblers find it more easier than others, like not being funny but Astrid Arsewipe, do you know what I'm saying, they just had to *look* at her.

'I never drink bottled,' I said, which I don't, being as I never drink water at all, prefer Pepsi Max or Fanta. 'Don't trust it,' I said. 'Could be poisoned,' I said.

There was this knock at the door. Dr Neutral was pouring. His hand give a jerk and he slopped some on to the counter. 'Come in!' he said, like a bit pissed off and this woman I never seen before come walking in with a plate of sangers and a glass of wine balanced beside them.

'I thought . . .' she said. 'Ugh! It smells like a stable! I thought you might like some sandwiches.' She smiled. You could see she fancied him. 'But maybe not,' she said.

Dr Neutral smiled. 'You get used to it. Thanks,' he said, and he put down the bottle and taken the plate. 'Smoked salmon!' he said. 'Yum yum.'

'You all on your own in here?' said the woman. She

weren't even pretty but she reckoned she was. She got blonde hair tied back in a pony-tail and this badge on her jacket said, 'Beverly Perfect, Phlegyas Pharmaceuticals'.

'If he's on his own,' I said to her. 'Then what am I, a piece of shit, walked in on his shoe off the pavement?' 'Cept I didn't, but I wished I did anyway.

'So what are you doing, exactly?' she said.

'Just labelling,' said Dr Neutral. 'Measuring and labelling, then packing them up for collection. They all have to go to ten different places. You know how it is,' he said. 'No one trusts anyone else to do it properly.'

'Sounds fun,' said Beverly Perfect and she laughed this stupid laugh.

'That's fine, N,' Dr Neutral said. He was bent down checking it come to the line. 'That's fine. If you wait by the theatre, they'll call you in a few minutes.'

Beverly Perfect stepped out of the way, pressing her arse up against the counter so's I could get past to the door. I give her a look but she made like she never seen.

31. About my assessment and how it weren't at all what I been expecting but I done my best to use the resources God give me

Like I say, I weren't worried about my assessment but when I seen them all sat there behind that table, even *I* felt my stomach done a few forward rolls, and then a few more, and then over and over, like a fucking gymnastic, do you know what I'm saying? Like that Nadia Commonitch, who was Russian, 'cause I watched her with my mum.

So there's me on this little plastic chair and there's them in a row behind this enormous table. Bang in the middle, opposite me, there's Dr Diabolus' throne. Dr Azazel's sat one side and Dr Clootie the other. Sat next to Dr Azazel there's Tony and sat next to Dr Clootie there's Fowler, keeps eyeing Dr Clootie's tits. Rhona's on her own down the end, at this little desk covered in papers. She keeps on sighing and shooking her head and going through her papers and glancing at Tony and shooking her head again. Aside of Rhona and Malvin Fowler, everyone else is all of them looking at me. They's looking at my scabby old tracksuit bottoms I got inside out so this label on my leg says 'KEEP AWAY FROM FIRE Made in China'. They's looking at my sweatshirt with the crap down the front and snot all over the cuffs. They's looking at my hair – ninety-nine per cent fat, as my mum used to say – and the fag ash under my eyes. And even though they don't say a word, I reckon I'm doing alright.

But nothing prepares me for what happens next. I seen this man on telly once; he'd won like fifty Olympic gold medals, and every time he won one, he said, it taken like a month to sink in, and even then it still felt like a dream. Which I couldn't of put it better myself.

I mean even just the one of them, that would of been, do you know what I'm saying, but *all four of them*; I couldn't believe it, still *wouldn't* believe it, to tell you the truth, if it weren't wrote down for all to see in *The History of the Abaddon*, a history, which it will be Professor McSpiegel said, just as soon as he gets 'official confirmation'. All four of them they held up their cards, that's Tony and Fowler and Dr Azazel – and Dr Clootie as well, all four – they held up their cards and give me four perfect 6s. I stared. I couldn't take it in. '6.0, 6.0, 6.0, 6.0.' Just shapes; I couldn't see the numbers. Then suddenly there's this roll of drums and they start playing the National Anthem, and this Union Jack comes rolling down and the crowd cheers so loud I get real tears in my eyes.

After that, the rest is a bit of a blur. Rhona read out this list of statements ('I see things other people can't see'; 'People are plotting against me' – the usual) and after she'd read each one out you got one of five choices how you could respond. You could strongly agree, moderate agree, neither agree nor disagree, moderate disagree or disagree strongly. There weren't nothing else you could do, just one of them five. If you didn't reply, they marked you down as 'neither agree nor disagree'; it weren't like you got no bonus or nothing, which sometimes you do for 'non-cooperation'.

Every time you give a response, they held up the cards again. I got 6s mostly, a few 5.9s and a 5.8, like fair enough, do you know what I'm saying; I ain't greedy. But I couldn't help noticing Dr Clootie always give me less. And after a bit it pissed me off, like I'm doing my best, do you know what I'm saying, and every time, she's marking me down. I mean this one statement, it gone something like, 'I find it hard to make decisions' and as soon as she said it, I seen the trap straight off: if I said I strongly agreed they could say I was lying on account I just made one, and if I said I disagreed they could say there weren't nothing the matter. So in the end I gone number 3, neither agree nor disagree, and Dr Clootie, she give me a 5.65! 'Up yours!' I thought. 'Up your tight Scottish arse!' and I just ignored her after that, never even looked at her card, like 'it don't make no difference to me *what* you think', 'cause I knew it was just female jealousy and not proper marking 'cause that's what some women are like.

It's got to be said, I been better assessed. I ain't saying they wasn't accurate, as far as they gone, that is. But that was it: they didn't go far *enough*. Like all the stuff they *didn't* ask; they hardly scraped the surface. I mean all the stuff I could of said: stuff what happened when I was a kid, stuff would of give them tears in their eyes at how sad it was and how brave I been and they never even asked. I could of told them stuff goes on in my head like every day, you'd never believe, like every minute of every day, would of got me four 6s straight off. But the moment I opened my mouth to speak, like one single word more than what I was s'posed to, Rhona the Moaner would hold up her hand. 'Just answer the question please, N!' And she'd read out the five different choices again. '1. Strongly agree; 2. Moderately agree . . .' and so on in this monotone voice, 5.9 suicidal, easy.

32. How Rosetta gone
and done a Captain Oats

Poppy was next but one after me, with Omar in between. I ain't said much about Omar yet 'cause there ain't much to say to be honest. He sat down the end between Candid and Faith and opposite Unity. Zubin called Omar 'Omar Bombing' because of Northern Ireland. But Verna the Vomit said that was tasteless 'cause people died and lost their legs and you didn't ought to joke about stuff like that and Sue said, *who* lost their legs, *who's* joking? And Zubin said Omar Bombing don't mind. Do you Omar Bombing? And Omar just shrugged like whatever they said, it didn't make no difference to him.

Nothing mattered to Omar Bombing on account he was too depressed to care or else he was eating his pic 'n' mix, else sleeping, or all three at once. One time I seen him down Borderline Woolies, walking round and round the stand, grabbing huge fistfuls of chocolate eclairs and mini Mars and jelly snakes and piling them into his basket. He'd heaped his basket up so high they slid off and on to the floor, most of them, but I don't reckon Omar even noticed, just carried on, like in some sort of trance, cramming his hand into tub after tub 'stead of using the scoop like you's s'posed to. These two shop assistants was stood there watching and one of them started giggling and the other one nudged her like 'Shut the fuck up!' before he come over and hacked them to pieces, then grilled the steaks I shouldn't wonder, community care do you know what I'm saying, on one of those instant barbecues they was selling, three for £5.

Fact Omar was pretty much a pacific; he only ever done one thing I know of and that didn't hurt no one anyway, aside of hisself, or his big toe to be precise. What happened was Omar Bombing's dad died, drunk so much his liver exploded or something like that; he was hazy on the details. Omar hadn't seen his dad since he got took into care as a kid, and he'd never mentioned him neither, not once; fact we never even realised he even got one. When he heard his dad died, Omar never said nothing, just slumped in his chair, eating pic 'n' mix and breathing so loud it sounded like he was snoring. First we knew was when he shown up one morning pegging along on crutches, and his foot bandaged up the size of a polyfoam pillow. 'What's up with Omar Bombing?' said Zubin. 'Don't call him that,' said Verna the Vomit. 'It isn't funny; people died. Children lost their legs . . .' 'What's that?' said Sue the Sticks. '*Who* lost his legs? Omar hasn't lost his legs. You ain't lost *your* legs have you, Omar? What you done? You hurt your foot?' So Omar told her, yes he had, he'd broke his big toe kicking his father's gravestone. And he told us it felt good as well, he'd never felt so good, he said, and you seen him, he was all buzzed up and the next day too and the day after that but then it worn off and he slumped in his chair like normal.

So Poppy was next after Omar Bombing and she come out the toilets just as I was going past. She looked like a fucking film star, no kidding, in her high-heeled shoes and her perfect legs, all freshly made up with her hair in a razor-

sharp bob. And suddenly this shouting starts up, then I seen
Fat Florence with a traffic cone held to her mouth like a
giant loud hailer. 'One, two, three, four! What do we
want?' And all the 'Ps are supposed to join in but instead
they just stand there mouthing the words, hiding behind
their banners and stuff and looking down at their slippers.
'What do we want!' Fat Florence yells. 'One, two, three,
four! What do we want?' but they's mumbling so low you
can't hardly hear, and Fifth-Floor Praveen blows his whistle
a bit but so feeble it hardly squeaks. 'One, two, three, four!
What do we want? Move down a floor! Five, six, seven,
eight! Ps want action; Ps won't wait! One, two, three,
four! What do we want?' 'Ps want action!' whispers Paolo
and she elbows him so hard you can hear his ribs cracking,
while Pepsi swings this football rattle so limp it don't even
click.

So Fat Florence give up and just shouted herself, over
and over again. And she made up more of them as well,
'Fee, fi, fum, fo! Poppy Shakespeare has to go!' which stuck
in my head for the rest of the day on account it was so
fucking stupid.

'Alright?' I said as Poppy gone past, and she said something, 'cept I didn't hear what, but it sounded like 'Wish
me luck.'

'Where can she be?' said Middle-Class Michael. Rosetta
still hadn't come in. 'I wonder if somebody ought to
phone? She hasn't got long now; she's next after Quok.'

'Stop hassling, man,' White Wesley said. 'She coming
innit. She told me she coming.'

'I'm not *hassling*,' said Middle-Class Michael (he got the

hump on account of two 5.5s). 'I'm not *hassling*; I'm merely concerned.'

'You two!' said Verna. 'Oh my God!' She was staring over Brian's chair. The dribblers sat with their backs to the door twisted round to have a look what she seen.

'Rosetta!' said Sue. 'What you *done* to yourself?'

White Wesley said nothing but he looked like he seen his own ghost.

Rosetta come round to her chair and sat down, smoothing out her skirt so's it didn't crumple. 'Afternoon,' she said, and she smiled at us like nothing weren't different at all.

'What you *done* to yourself!' said Sue the Sticks.

'It's assessments!' said Astrid. She sounded suspicious but Rosetta just smiled and nodded.

'What she *done* to herself?' said Sue the Sticks.

'Don't know,' said Verna, picking a bit at this patch of vomit, dried on the sleeve of her sweatshirt.

'The outfit, man!' White Wesley said. 'What's with the outfit!' He stared at Rosetta like blinking his eyes to see if she'd disappear.

'Lord!' said Rosetta and she shaken her head, but she smiled to herself as well. 'Can't a woman take a little trouble now and then without all this fussing and questions!'

'Suit yourself!' said Astrid Arsewipe and she looked at me and rolled her eyes but I shown her the back of my head.

I'm not being funny, but Rosetta looked beautiful. She got this green scarf tied round her head like a turban, shown off the rich brown skin of her face, not dusty no more but so shiny and polished you seen yourself reflected like in a mirror. Her eyelids was painted in blue and gold all the way up to her eyebrows, and clamped on her ears was these massive gold clip-ons the size of a pair of light-bulbs. Round her neck she got more gold too; on top of the necklace from Pollyanna, this thick gold chain, I mean every link at least an inch side to side. I ain't sure it was 22 carat, do you know what I'm saying, I mean sat there beside her you could see these bits where the gold had rubbed off and it looked sort of grey underneath, but it didn't notice. Her dress was the same sort of thing as her scarf but long and flowing right down to the floor and the great wide sleeves half-covered her hands so you couldn't see the fag burns hardly at all, just the gold rings on every finger. Like I say, she did; she looked really good, but more carnival to tell you the truth than Dorothy Fish assessment.

It weren't like we didn't try telling her. But nothing you said made no difference. She just sat with her hands clasped, calm and smiling, listening to Wesley, with tears in his eyes, saying how she been like a mother to him and he'd kill hisself if she got discharged. 'Please man,' he said. 'Ditch the jewellery at least! For me,' he said. 'For Pollyanna. You'll never get through looking like that! You're throwing your life . . .' but he had to stop on account of he started crying. Rosetta leant over and patted his hand but she didn't take off her jewellery.

Quok-ho gone out and we sat and waited. The only sound was the creak of chairs as dribblers shifted this way and that avoiding each other's gaze.

Rosetta stood up.

Good luck,' we said. My cheeks was burning.

'I may be some time,' Rosetta said, and, without looking back, she walked out the double swing-doors.

★　　★　　★

We all agreed how it weren't our fault, 'cause it weren't, but we still felt shit. 'It's not like we didn't say!' said Sue. 'Thought she knew better,' Astrid said. 'She was trying to get through on the ethnic bit.' 'What ethnic bit is that?' said Zubin. 'Yeah,' said Sue. 'What ethnic bit?' 'The ethnic quota,' Astrid said. 'That's right, innit Michael?' Michael said nothing. 'The ethnic quota,' Astrid said. 'Black people stand a better chance.' 'Ten *times* better,' Michael said. 'I never heard of that!' said Sue. '*You* heard of that, Vern?' 'Ten times!' said Astrid. 'That's not really what . . .' said Middle-Class Michael. 'I'm only saying! Why do *you* think she did it?' said Astrid. 'Fuck off!' said Zubin.

Poppy was really upset 'cause they'd told her she got to stay another six months. 'You seem to have issues with trust,' they said. 'We can't help until you start talking to us. We're not mind readers . . .' 'Well that's bollocks for starters!' I said when she told me. 'Tony is! He knows what you's thinking before you thought it. This one time, right, there was Marta the Coffin . . .' 'I just can't stand it,' Poppy said, and she started crying. 'I can't go on. I can't get through another day. I really can't. I'll go out of my mind.' 'Come on!' I said. 'It could be worse. At least we got each other,' I said. 'Look on the bright side! Think of Rosetta. Most probably top herself now,' I said, but she wouldn't be comforted.

33. How me and Poppy done mirroring and it was, it was really weird

When we come in next morning, Rafik had already moved down. He was sat in the 'R' chair so full of hisself he was spilling out his own ears. 'Pleased with yourself, are you?' says Tadpole. 'Rosetta ain't halfway down the hill! Show a bit of respect!' she said. And she shaken her head at me and tutted. 'Flops!' she said. 'We'd be better off without them.'

Poppy weren't in yet; she still weren't in by ten o'clock, when Communication started with Rhona the Moaner. 'Has anyone seen Poppy Shakespeare?' she said and we all said no we hadn't, so Malvin Fowler gone off to look, tugging one fat pink hand out his trousers to open the door and letting it slam behind him.

Me and Middle-Class Michael and Brian and Gita and Harvey and Rhona the Moaner was sat round in a circle in the games room. 'Last week,' says Rhona, 'we were looking at ways we sometimes use to communicate without saying precisely what we mean. Does anyone remember?' she said.

'Hinting,' says Michael. 'Insinuation.'

'Which is hinting isn't it, more or less,' says Rhona the Moaner. I smirked, couldn't help it. 'Thank you, Michael. Anyone else?' She smiled round us all. Brian the Butcher looked down; I could hear him going through his sevens. Gita kept turning her magazine. 'Anyone?' says Rhona.

Harvey snorted and woke hisself up, then shut his eyes again. Middle-Class Michael started to twitch, sounded like a packet of crisps, on account he was sat on a Woolworth's bag, said the chairs was unhygenic. 'One second, Michael,' says Rhona the Moaner. 'Anyone else? OK, well let's move on.'

Normally I *would* of spoke, made the groups go quicker I reckoned. Before you knew it you was back outside with a fag in your hand and a cup of tea and last one done for the week. But I got a bit of a headache that morning on account of the six cans of Tennents I'd drunk the night before, say well done for my perfect 6s.

'OK,' says Rhona, smiling around. They didn't half perk her up, them groups; you never seen her so cheerful. 'OK,' she says. 'Well I thought today we'd try a bit of non-verbal communication.'

Then we had to clear the chairs to the side and get into pairs together. So guess who winds up with Rhona the Moaner? Billy fucking No Mates, that's who. And she makes me go and stand opposite her, like to show them all what to do. And we're doing this thing called 'mirroring', so she starts doing circles and stuff with her hands and lifting her feet up and I'm s'posed to do it back. 'That's right,' she says. 'That's right, N. Good! That's right, point your toe . . . Now *your* turn!' she goes, and all I can think of is waving my hands, so I wave at her and she waves back and I wave some more and she waves some more and I feel like a total toolhead. 'Well done!' says Rhona. 'That's excellent, N! Now, everyone, decide who's leading and who's going to be the mirror. OK? Are we ready? Three minutes. No talking. Begin.'

And that's when Malvin and Poppy come in. I ain't saying she'd been on top form exactly when I'd left her the night before. I mean, I knew she was upset about the assessments. But the way she looked now, do you know what I'm saying. Her face was as pale as a puffball mushroom, her eyelids so swollen, there was barely two slits for her bloodshot eyes to see out of. 'Jesus!' I thought. 'Something *terrible* must of happened.'

'Poppy!' says Rhona. 'You're just in time!' And she paired us off just like that. I mean, not even 'Are you alright?' or nothing; could be dying, could be *dead* for all they care, so long as they ticked you off. First it was me had to mirror Poppy. She didn't move. Just stood there all limp and dropping down from her shoulders. I'll tell you what she reminded me of: one of Mum's plants she'd forgot to water, just before it died.

'You alright?' I whispered.

'No talking!' said Rhona.

Poppy shrugged. I shrugged back at her. She folded her arms. I folded my arms.

'What?' I mouthed. She shaken her head. I shaken my head.

'That's lovely!' said Rhona the Moaner.

All I could think of was Saffra was dead. That was the only thing I could think of. Saffra been run over. And if she weren't dead she was dying anyway. Or maybe she got leukaemia and she needed a bone-marrow transplant. And what if I was the only match and I give her some and I saved her life and it turned out Poppy was really rich and she said she could give me anything, anything in the whole wide world, but I'd just shrug and say, 'S'alright; don't worry about it!' . . .

Behind Poppy, Michael and Brian the Butcher was turning their hands like over and back, over and back, over and back. They done it so perfect you couldn't tell who was the mirror. 'Lovely!' said Rhona.

Then it was my turn. I give her a grin, but Poppy didn't grin back. I frowned. She didn't frown back neither. I couldn't even tell if she was looking at me on account of her eyes was too swollen. 'Poppy!' I hissed.

'No talking!' said Rhona.

I waved. Didn't wave. I tutted – weren't *talking*, but Rhona still gone 'Shhh!' So then I give up and just folded my arms, and I felt a bit pissed off, to be honest. I mean, *I'd* copied *her*, do you know what I'm saying. And I'd give her my marrow for nothing as well! So I changed my mind. I wouldn't say no. But I'd charge her; that's what I'd do, fucking charge her. Like so much a pound, do you know what I'm saying? I'd have to think about how much. I weren't sure what people would pay for good marrow. Quite a bit though, *quite* a bit. The way she gone on about that kid. But what about meds? What if that meant you couldn't? Well, I'd come off my meds then, wouldn't I? But what if the meds meant you couldn't *ever*? So I wouldn't *tell* them; how would they *know*? And that's when I noticed Poppy had folded her arms.

I thought it was a coincidence, but just to see, I unfolded my arms and, straight off, Poppy done the same. I shrugged; she shrugged. I scratched my head. She scratched her head, exactly identical. I turned around; she turned around; it was really weird how it felt like. I frowned; she frowned. Do you know what I'm saying! And she done it so perfect, so exactly together, it was like she knew before I done it. And

I ain't being funny but it got to the point where I didn't know who was mirroring who. I weren't even thinking no more, just moving; and Poppy the same, we was both just moving, like wheels on a bike, both exactly together, spinning all over the room.

'That's lovely!' said Rhona. We flown up in the air. We circled around the panic alarm. We ducked and we dived and we dived and we ducked. Fowler tried to catch us but we flown through his fingers. We was two wings of one butterfly. We flown out the window and off round the tower. Round and around and around the tower, higher and higher, we flown in the autumn sunshine.

34. How Poppy asked me to help her out and I done it 'cause I was her friend

We was stood in the toilets next to the sinks. Poppy kept splashing her face with cold water, checking the mirror, then splashing again. When she'd finished, she rubbed it dry with a blue paper towel. 'I look like shit,' she said.

'I called in at Leech's this morning,' she said. 'I need you to help me, N.' Then she told me what Mr Leech told her, how they'd changed the legislation. 'All fucking night I've been trawling the Net. Three loans, I've got, five new credit cards and practically nothing left in the flat that isn't for sale on eBay. And now he tells me, N, *now* he tells me, he can't represent me anyway 'cause they've changed the legislation.'

'Keep it down can'tcha!' shouted Fran. I give her fuck off. 'How d'you mean?' I said.

So Poppy explained me what he'd said, something 'bout mental-health lawyers being swamped with all of these sniffs started trying to pay and was stopping the dribblers getting the help, didn't make much sense to be honest. 'So now I've got to be registered mentally ill to see a mental-health lawyer,' she said. 'And I can't be registered mentally ill unless I'm receiving MAD money.'

'Can't you try a different lawyer?' I said. I didn't really get it to tell you the truth. I didn't see why sniffs should see dribblers' lawyers neither.

'But that's just it,' she said. 'I can't! I must have tried

every lawyer in London; they all say exactly the same. "You need a mental-health specialist. We don't deal with mental-health issues here." "But that's what I'm saying to you!" I go. "I'm not mentally ill. That's what I'm saying!" "I'm sorry," they go, "I'm afraid we can't help." And then they hang up, mostly,' she said.

Fran turned her radio on up to blasting

'Or else they *are* mental-health specialists, in which case they say they can't help me either.'

"Cause you's not on The Register?' I said.

'Exactly,' said Poppy.

'Makes sense,' I said. 'I'm not being funny but you know what I'm saying. If they just let *anyone* in,' I said. 'They got to make sure you's a genuine case.'

'But I'm not,' said Poppy. 'That's the point!'

'So that's the problem then, innit!' I said.

'N,' she said. 'Listen. Will you help me apply for MAD money?'

That Saturday half-eleven exactly, I left my flat for Poppy's. She'd wrote me the address down on the back of a Benson's foil wrapper and I walked along with it clutched in my hand like a little gold ticket, case anyone stopped me, asked where I thought I was going:

Poppy
Flat 6
43 Selby Street
7607 4432
opposite the old folks home
ring if you get lost!

'It's in the A-Z,' she'd said so I lifted one down the newsagent's. It was so fucking old the cover gone yellow and the corners bent back like a Jack Russell's ears, but that's Borderline Road for you; shite.

I seen Tina, come out the Turkish shop, with her coat belted in so tight at the waist it was like there weren't nothing inside. And I shouted to her, 'Hi, Tina! Alright?' and she looked so panicked it was like she didn't know me, just bolted out into the road – without looking – then I seen her over by Planet Kebab, running along with her arms by her sides and her bag in her hand, to make like she was walking.

By the time I reached Sniff Street, it was almost quarter to twelve. Poppy never give me a time, just said to come for dinner. And I'd made myself wait in till half-eleven 'cause I didn't want to be early, but now I got worried I'd end up being late and the dinner be sat on the table going cold, roast chicken, roast taters and peas, I reckoned, and gravy in a jug. Café Diana done dinner from eleven; by half-twelve they was out of meat and you'd got to make do a chicken kiev, with a cold yorkshire pud and a dollop of apple sauce.

I started to run, just like jog on and off, but the forms in my backpack crashed up and down, smashing into my back with every step, and by the time I reached Argos I had to stop, take off my pack and perch on the bench in the bus-stop for a breather. There's like four sniffs already sat on the bench and four hundred more stood waiting. If the sniffs on the bench just shoved up a bit, there's room for at least four more on the end, do you know what I'm saying, easy. And this one woman right, with her fifteen bags, she's practically laying flat along it. 'Oi!' I gone. 'Shift up a bit!' and she give a great huff, started moving her bags, like I've asked for the world, do you know what I'm saying. I'm telling you: Astrid's sniff sister.

I taken a look in my A-Z. There was *five* Rowan Walks in the list at the back but none of them weren't my one. Course I didn't know that till I'd looked them all up, which every time I turned a page – ain't *my* fault I got elbows, is it! – Astrid starts huffing and giving me daggers, and even the sniff on my other side, this black sniff with a kid on her lap and a fold-up pushchair and half of Kwik Save in carrier bags hanging off of it, she shifts her arse three foot down the bench, do you know what I'm saying, like pardon me for breathing.

So then I looked up Borderline Road, and I found that alright with Sniff Street running into it. But what they'd done was they'd cut it off. You know Borderline Road gone round in a circle, like a moat all around the Dark-woods? Well they didn't show none of that at all; all they shown was the bottom bit just under the top of the page. There was a little blue box, said 77 and triangle, meant to go to page 77. But when you gone to page 77, there was Borderline Road at the bottom, like just the very top of the circle before it got cut off. And the box said go to page 48, and page 48 was where you just come from but the Darkwoods weren't there neither. And it was like they'd missed a whole page out, the page where the Darkwoods ought to of been and Rowan Walk and the Abaddon, but none of it weren't there.

Maps ain't much use anyway; unless you know the scale, which I never. I mean if Sniff Street's maybe six inches long from Borderline Junction down, that could be a fifteen-minute walk and it could be the other side of the world. I mean, literally; I seen fucking Australia closer than that in the atlas at school, which like how you supposed to know?

I lit up a fag, 'Do you mind?' says Astrid. 'No,' I said. And I would of stayed just to piss her off, except I was worried about the time, so I made sure I give her a faceful as I left.

You didn't even need a map anyway, it was all like Poppy had said, right down to the three Rumanians stood on the corner selling fags, the school, the newsagent's opposite, and after that you gone left. They was smart houses, none of that council shit, some of them only got one bell, and the cars was like new with parking badges and baby seats inside. This woman was unloading Tesco's bags out the boot of one of the cars and this little kid like helping her. 'Keep it upright, Sam!' she gone. 'Keep it upright; that's Charlie's cake.' And I'm waiting for him to fall flat on his face but he never, just vanished inside.

'Who is it?' come Poppy's voice.

'N,' I said, and I give two Vs to this old bloke sat in the home opposite, been staring at me for the full five minutes it taken Poppy to answer the door; he give me a finger back.

'N?' she goes. 'Oh. OK! Come up.' Then the door gone buzz. 'Just push,' she said. So I pushed. 'Third floor,' she said.

There was a pile of post on the floor by the door and a bike and a baby's pushchair. It was dark, just light enough to see on account of this glass above the front door, and it smelt of damp; not at all like what I'd expected. The stairs seemed to go on for fucking ever. By the time I got to the third-floor landing, my legs felt like lumps of the dead meat they give you Sundays down Sunshine House; blue-grey it was and stunk so bad stray dogs used to come in and try and roll on the table.

Poppy was stood in the open doorway, grey jogging bums, bare midriff, painted toenails. 'N!' she said. 'Are you alright?' I got the feeling I'd fucked up somewhere along.

'I come as quick as I could,' I said. 'Ain't next door, do you know what I'm saying. And this backpack weighs a fucking tonne!'

Poppy frowned.

'Here. Lift it!' I said.

She taken it from me. 'Christ!' she said.

'*And* I run all the way from the Darkwoods.

'Sweating like a pig,' I said. I could feel my sweatshirt clung to my back.

'N,' she said. 'Sorry, but . . .'

'What?' I said. And that was when I twigged.

'You forgotten, innit!'

'No,' she said.

'MAD money forms! You forgot all about it! You asked me to come round and fill them in.'

'I hadn't forgotten,' said Poppy. 'It's just . . .'

'So you going to invite me in?' I said. 'Or d'you want me to do them out here on the landing?'

'Sorry,' said Poppy. She smiled. 'Come in.'

'Can't believe you forgot!' I said, stepping past her into the hall. 'You'll be making tables next,' I said. 'You and Dawn. How many she done you?'

'I've lost count,' said Poppy. 'Seven, I think. Saffra! I thought you were staying in bed.'

I looked round behind me where Poppy was talking. This little kid stood in the door of a room staring back at me.

'Hello,' she said.

'Alright?' I said. Not rude or nothing but I ain't really into kids.

'Are you N?' she said.

'I s'pose,' I said.

'Either you are or you aren't,' she said.

I shrugged. 'Whatever.'

'You're early,' she said.

'Saffra,' said Poppy, 'just go back to bed. I tell you what, if you go back to bed, N will bring you a mug of hot lemon.'

'Will you?' said Saffra.

'Now,' Poppy said, and she gone.

The kitchen was just like Saffra everywhere. There was pictures she'd painted all over the walls and her trainers lain all over the floor and her little puffa jacket on the back of a chair and her backpack spilling all over the table, do you know what I'm saying, it weren't hard to see who was boss.

'She was s'posed to be going to Dud's this weekend,' said Poppy, 'but she's got a sore throat . . .' She was squeezing a lemon into a mug, a mug with a snake on in the shape of an 'S', or I might of made that up. 'She's a bit upset at the moment,' she said. 'All this business with me; kids pick things up.' She spooned some honey into the mug and stood stirring in the hot water. 'The other night she woke up,' she said, 'came into my room and I was crying.

'I hate her to see me upset,' she said. She give me the mug. 'I'm sorry,' she said. 'Would you mind?'

As I carried it down to Saffra's room, I taken a sip; it was warm and sweet. When I looked up, Saffra was watching me from the doorway.

Me and Poppy sat at the kitchen table. 'Jesus!' she said. 'All that!' she said.

'That's just part one,' I said.

'So how many parts *are* there?' she said.

'Seven,' I said and one by one I loaded them on to the table.

'"MAD Money Application Part One: Information about yourself". That's just your name and your details and stuff. "Part Two: Information about your illness". That's where you fill in what you got, like all your diagnoses and stuff and what medication you's taking. "Part Three: Why you reckon you's been hard done by . . .", "Part Four. . . . any worse than anyone else", "Part Five: Why that means you deserve taxpayers' money", "Part Six: What that implies about you", "Part Seven: Any further information, specifically why it is you can't just pull yourself together".

'That's the lot,' I said. 'One to seven.'

'Jesus!' said Poppy. She stared at the pile. The table groaned like a weightlifter, its legs bulged outwards under the strain.

'It repeats itself a bit,' I said.

'Jesus!' said Poppy.

'Here,' I said. 'You can use my lucky biro.'

'Thanks,' said Poppy.

'I done all my forms with this,' I said. 'Should of run out years ago. There ain't even no ink left. Look!

'Look!' I said, unscrewing the end to show her the empty tube inside. Poppy looked. 'No ink!' I said. 'Been like that for ages,' I said. I give it a kiss and handed it over. 'Middle High Middle,' I said. 'Every time.'

'I'd be happy with anything,' said Poppy.

'Shoot for the sky,' I said.

I ain't saying nothing but without me helping, Poppy hadn't got a *clue*.

'Hang about!' I said. 'What you doing?'

'I'm just filling in my name,' she said.

'Not like that,' I said. 'You're not!'

'Eh?' she said.

'You got to scrawl it.'

'It says BLOCK CAPITALS,' she said.

'Fuck what it says,' I said. 'Just scrawl it. You's s'posed to be mentally ill,' I said.

'Alright,' said Poppy and she done it small.

'Try with your other hand,' I said.

'They need to be able to read it,' she said.

'Trust me, Poppy,' I said. 'I know what I'm doing.'

By the time we reached the end of Part One, she was starting to get the feel of it. I ain't saying she was dribbling exactly but she weren't doing a bad impression. Some of her lines gone up in the air, crossing over the line above and wandering out of the box and into the margin. Others sunk down, like all shrunk and depressed and shrivelled away to nothing. When she wrote the address of the Dorothy Fish, like the *full* address, do you know what I'm saying: The Dorothy Fish Psychiatric Day Hospital, The Abaddon Unit, Abaddon Hill . . . it started off climbing out of the box, then suddenly seemed to lose its nerve, around the middle of 'psychiatric', and swung down sharp, down the side of the box, bending back on itself just before the bottom, so the first 'Abaddon' was wrote upside down, before climbing back upwards, up 'Abaddon Hill', to curl back inside the first line. 'London' was so small you couldn't hardly read it, and the postcode just looked like a smudge in the middle of the box.

'You don't want to make it too neat,' I said. 'It looks a bit . . . do you know what I'm saying?'

'What?' said Poppy.

'Like you thought about it,' I said. 'It'll do. But maybe if you cross some words out and like write in the margin with arrows and stuff. And your handwriting too, you got better at it . . .'

'I'm supposed to be mentally ill,' said Poppy. 'Not mentally retarded.'

'Same difference,' I said. 'S'far as they's concerned.'

'But *you* don't write like this,' said Poppy. 'I've seen your writing. Your writing's alright.'

'Not on my MAD forms it ain't,' I said. 'My last one you couldn't read it at all. It was a waste to be honest 'cause some of my answers, not bragging or nothing but d'you know what I'm saying, and you couldn't even read them. I never signed it neither,' I said. 'You know where you sign it?' I shown her the box. 'Done a fingerprint in my own blood,' I said.

'I don't want to overdo it!' said Poppy.

'You ain't, Poppy! Trust me,' I said. 'You ain't! You'll be lucky with Low Low Low at this rate. They don't just hand it out,' I said. 'You got to dribble for it!'

Poppy smiled this strange sort of smile and signed the form. 'Alright,' she said. 'Part Two.'

I'm not being funny but the fact of it was that Poppy had said come for dinner, and since I arrived, 'side of Saffra's hot lemon, I hadn't seen so much as a cold sip of water do you know what I'm saying and my stomach was starting to grumble. I didn't like to *say* nothing on account of it looked so bad and brought up, but when I seen the sunshine clock on the wall hit a quarter past one and she *still* ain't said nothing, I reckoned I *got* to drop a hint 'cause else I was going to pass out.

'Diagnosis,' said Poppy. 'You may state more than one.'

I laughed. 'Like you's going to leave it at one! Alright, let me think about it.

'Feel a bit light-headed,' I said. I glanced up at the sunshine clock. 'Ain't eaten nothing today,' I said.

She didn't say nothing.

'Depression,' I said.

'Depression's *accurate*,' said Poppy.

'It's easier than psychosis,' I said. 'Don't want to run before you can walk. And self-harm as well and an eating disorder, panic attacks . . .'

'Hang on,' said Poppy.

'Personality!' I said. 'You definitely got one of those. Everybody's got one of those! Borderline mostly . . . D'you hear my stomach! . . . Just means you're a pain in the arse,' I said.

'Is that one word or two?' said Poppy frowning.

'Pain in the arse?' I said. 'Four; *I* make it.'

'Borderline,' she said.

'Dunno!' I said. 'Jesus, Poppy. I'm fucking bloody *starving!*'

So after that she finally caught on, come over all sorry. 'It's alright,' I said. 'Thought I was going to pass out there a minute.'

'I'm sorry!' she said. 'I've been *so* distracted. I haven't even offered you a cup of tea! *And* you're helping me out,' she said.

She stood up. 'I'll put the kettle on.'

'Good job I didn't faint,' I said. 'Imagine that! If I'd of fainted!'

'What would you like to eat?' she said. 'Look! I've got loads!' She opened this cupboard. Full, it was; packed full to bursting with Penguins and peanuts and packets of crisps. 'Help yourself,' she said. 'What would you like? I get it all in for doing Saffra's packed lunch. We'll eat a bit later if that's alright. I think she must have gone to sleep. Make the most of it!'

I stared at the cupboard. 'I don't know,' I said. I didn't; my mind gone numb. So she brought over armfuls of peanuts and crisps, 'Cheese and onion. You see? I remember.' And Penguins as well, all laid out nice on a sparkly plastic plate.

'I got this metabolism,' I said, as she emptied the peanuts into a bowl and I finished a packet of crisps. 'Just got to eat regular,' I said, ' 'cause otherwise I feel faint if I don't. Must burn it off really fast,' I said.

Poppy smiled. 'Shall I make you some tea? Or *I* know. How about a beer?' And she opened the fridge, fuck-off huge one it was, as tall as the ceiling practically, and more beer and wine inside than a Darkwoods offie.

'Good job Swiller Steve ain't here!' I said.

'Here you are,' said Poppy. And she give me a beer and a glass as well, and she opened it for me.

'This is alright!' I said.

'I'm *not* putting down that I foul the bed,' said Poppy. 'I'm sorry; I can't.'

'Hold your horses,' I said. 'Just listen.' I taken a sip of my beer. 'This ain't about what *you* want,' I said. 'What *you* want don't come into it. You got to give them what *they* want to hear. Lot of dribblers make that mistake . . .'

'But why would they want to hear *that*?' said Poppy. 'Can't you be mentally ill without "incontinence of the bowel"?' She grinned.

'Alright then, put what you want!' I said.

'I'm sorry,' she said.

I taken a handful of peanuts.

'Please, N,' she said. 'Go on, explain.'

I shaken my head. 'You's missing the point,' I said. 'This form ain't got nothing to do with mental illness. This is about giving sniffs what they want. It's like an exchange,' I said. 'You tell them what they want to hear and they give you the MAD money.'

'No such thing as a free lunch,' said Poppy.

'It ain't what dribblers are like that matters; it's what they want to *think* we's like . . .'

'But why?' said Poppy. 'That's the bit I don't get. Why do they want us to *be* like that? I mean shitting the bed, and all that stuff.' I looked at her. 'I'm serious!' she said.

'Well,' I said. I thought a bit. 'Well 'cause that's what we's *for*,' I said. 'Makes them feel better about theirselves, if we's dribbling all over the place. They can look at us, think "Thank God, *I'm* not like that!" It's a public service is what it is. You got to have dribblers, else you wouldn't have sniffs.'

'So what are sniffs for then?' said Poppy.

'To pay our benefits,' I said. 'And they want their money's worth.'

Poppy grinned. 'So this is their pound of flesh . . .' she said. 'You're not stupid, are you!'

'Whatever,' I said, and I polished off the rest of my beer.

In the end we settled on pissing the bed. Pissing she could just about cope with, said Poppy, but shitting the bed, no way. 'I think I need a beer myself,' she said as she fetched me another. 'Or shall we open a bottle of wine? Do you fancy wine or beer?' she said. 'Ain't bothered,' I said, so she opened the wine. White it was, didn't taste of much, but it done the job, do you know what I'm saying. By the time we reached the end of Part Three, Poppy weren't the same woman who'd printed her name so careful on the opening page. 'I can't believe I'm writing this!' she'd say, but we was laughing about it. 'How did it come to this!' she'd say.

'It's a public service!' we'd shout both together. It become like a catch-phrase, like who said it first. I never laughed so much in my life.

Saffra come through, must of heard us laughing. Made out she was starving to death, so Poppy done her fish fingers. I don't remember much after that but I know Saffra watched a video while we finished off the rest of the form. And I know it taken for-fucking-ever, but we was laughing so much, we didn't even *want* to finish. And I'd still say that now, do you know what I'm saying; we had such a good time, the two of us, it was worth it, almost, despite of the consequentials.

35. How Middle-Class Michael done this speech and everyone switched off

You always known when Middle-Class Michael got an announcement to make. He couldn't settle until he'd said it, and he couldn't say it until he'd picked his moment. So he sat there twitching and glancing around, and checking his watch, and glancing around and clearing his throat, and checking his watch and glancing around, till we's all of us like 'For fuck sake, Michael, stop twitching and just fucking say it!'

'I received a letter this morning,' he said. He cleared his throat. 'Perhaps I should wait for Brian.'

'Just fucking get on with it!' we said. Weren't like we give a shit either way, but you know what I'm saying, he'd hooked us now.

'All right,' he says and laying his briefcase flat on his lap, he undone the clasps and taken out this letter. 'It might be simplest if I read it to you.' The flops all gone silent, like straining to listen, hoping for more bad news.

Middle-Class Michael put on his glasses. He only worn glasses for Patients' Council and reading and counting his peas. He stood up. 'I can't see!' said Candid Headphones.

'So turn your headphones down!' said Sue.

'I can *hear*,' said Candid. 'I can't *see*, I said!'

'Well I don't know how,' said Sue, 'with that racket. Surprised you can hear anything with that racket. Think

245

what you're doing to your ears,' she said. 'It's giving *me* a headache!'

Middle-Class Michael gone up the end, stood facing us all with the dead plant behind him. A crisp brown leaf dropped on to his shoulder and he whisked it away with his hand. 'It's from Dave Franks up in Barnet,' he said. 'You may have heard of him already. He used to chair Friern Patients' Council?' He paused. We hadn't. Do you know what I'm saying, hardly Dave fucking Beckham, was he? 'Well,' says Middle-Class Michael. 'No matter. The point is he's set up a pressure group.'

'A what?' said Sue

'A pressure group,' said Verna the Vomit.

'Shush!' said Astrid.

'I've heard of a pressure cooker!' said Sue and we all cracked up, 'cept for Astrid who tutted. Candid turned her headphones down, but slowly so Sue didn't notice.

'He's set up this pressure group,' said Michael, 'to campaign against the privatisation of our mental-health services. This is what he writes,' he said and he started to read it out. And maybe on account it weren't *his*, and he didn't got the same feel for it, as he done like for one of his own, he read it in this flat sort of voice, 'stead of punching the air like he normally done, and getting the flops excited, just read it straight through like a set of instructions, like a 'Patient Information Leaflet' he'd found in his packet of meds.

Dear All, [*it gone*]

Let's get this clear. A massive transformation is under way in how our government deals with the mentally ill. You won't have heard much in the media, but the fact is sweeping changes are planned – some have already taken place. We need to act **NOW** to prevent a catastrophe!

This government has told lie after lie, promising us our health service would never be considered for privatisation, whilst at the same time appointing a Minister for Madness, responsible for overseeing nothing less than *the wholesale sell-off of all mental-health services*. The truth is the government has landed itself in a mess. Having pledged to reduce hospital waiting times by fifteen minutes before the next election, it now finds it lacks the resources to do so without raising taxes (big vote-winner, that one) or increasing Public Sector Borrowing [*Here Middle-Class Michael spotted the chance for one of his explanations, and fuck did he go off on one, all what that was and what it meant and why it weren't a smart move and shit, which I would go into except for I can't on account of I switched off anyway soon as my first few brain cells keeled over and died of fucking boredom!*], a move certain to raise eyebrows in the City.

But now it seems ministers have hit on a win-win solution. By selling off mental-health services, not only can they raise some quick cash (negative spending, they call it!), they also stand to save still more by increasing the efficiency of psychiatric treatment. Companies will compete with each other to discharge the most patients in the shortest time for the lowest overheads. Already our very own Mad Tsar, a former number two at the

Ministry for Transport, has introduced a whole raft of measures designed to make madness more lucrative and attractive to investors. And already investors are sniffing around. Guess who? You got it! – the pharmaceuticals companies.

Not content with bribing the medics (remember the Porsches for pills fiasco!) the giant pharma companies now want a share in the mentally ill themselves. But we will show them, **OUR MINDS ARE NOT FOR SALE!!!**

You may have noticed in your hospital a sudden upsurge in discharge figures; what you may not have realised is that this is happening *right across the country*! In a bid to increase their asking price, the government is getting down to some last-minute home improvements. 'Failing' hospitals everywhere have been threatened with closure unless they come up with 'quantifiable evidence' (whatever that means!) to prove the effectiveness of their treatment programmes. Underfunded hospitals, invariably in the poorest areas, are now being forced to *fiddle their figures* by discharging sick patients, or lose funding altogether!

And what's more, this is just the beginning; things are going to get worse! Once the pharma companies take over, not only will they get their syringes into a captive client-base, but they also stand to make millions more from 'performance-related bonuses'. Performance-related? Yes, you got it! For every patient the doctors deem 'cured' – the doctors being employed by the pharma companies – the government stumps up fifty quid to be spent on (that's right!) yet more cream for the fat cats!

Brilliant, isn't it! Even better, after three months enjoying life outside, those who survive can be readmitted and (get this!) cured all over again, guaranteeing an endless supply of extra thick double. (Who's supposed to be mad here?)

There's no doubt about it: the government's plans constitute the biggest outrage to be inflicted on the mentally ill since the Nazis gassed more than 70,000 psychiatric patients after doctors declared that their lives were 'not worth living'. We cannot afford to be complacent. *We have to act and act now!*

LOBBY VERONICA SALMON AT THE PHARMA FAIR!

The Minds Not For Sale Campaign is calling for a mass lobby of the Pharma Fair on the day Veronica Salmon comes to open it. The Mad Tsar is directly responsible for implementing the government's plans. A good vocal lobby will remind her that our minds are not for sale!

Tuesday ▮▮ November ▮▮▮ from 8.30 a.m.
ExCel centre, London Docklands
(Prince Regent Docklands Light Railway Station)
For further details see the Minds Not For Sale
website www.mindsnot4sale.org.uk

CONTACT YOUR LOCAL MEDIA!
Ask them how their readers/listeners feel about axe-wielding psychopaths being released untreated into the community. (That ought to get us some coverage!) **Check the website for further guidelines.**

OUR MINDS ARE NOT FOR SALE – MARCH!
Details to be announced.

Finally, we need volunteers to come and help us prepare for the lobby, building props and making costumes and banners. Saturday and Sunday ▮▮ October. The Styx Drop-in Centre (Nearest tube – High Barnet, Northern line) from 9.30 a.m. – 4.30 p.m. See you there!
Madly,
Dave

'So,' says Michael. 'What are we going to do?'

Well the truth of it was aside of Zubin, weren't one single dribbler been following further than the middle of paragraph two. I mean, I don't know who this Dave bloke was, with his campaign and all the rest of it, and I ain't saying he weren't intelligent, got more words in him than the dictionary from the sounds of it, and good for him, but *he didn't got a clue how to write a letter.* He lost the flops as soon as he mentioned the government, those he hadn't lost already, with your average flop got the focusing powers of an ADHD goldfish, been clinically proven. The next time he mentioned the government, half the day dribblers switched off, and the third time seen to the rest of them, do you know what I'm saying, like fuses tripping, off, off, off and all the lights gone out.

Zubin must of been wired up separate; by the end of the letter his eyes was shining brighter than 1,000-watt bulbs. 'Who *is* this Dave?' he said to Michael. 'You met him have you?' And Michael said, 'Yes, of course I've met him. Several times.' At the MAD symposium he'd met him, the same place he'd met that woman called Poppy, the one who'd enjoyed his speech so much and said he'd of made a politician. ('You're wasted on the Dorothy Fish,' he said she said. Like up your arse.) 'He sounds alright!' said Zubin. 'Sound! I'd like to meet him. Funny as well.' Michael shrugged, 'He's a nice enough guy. Bit casual perhaps, but he knows his stuff . . .' 'I'd like to meet him,' Zubin said. He chuckled. 'I like where he's coming from.' 'Perhaps not cut out for the mainstream,' said Michael and he coughed and pulled at his nose.

36. How Poppy finally heard about her MAD money claim

Poppy been at the Abaddon two months now. The second assessments come and gone and with them Harvey and Candid Headphones; nothing Brian could do to save them despite of upping his hand-washing to seventeen hours a day to get everyone through. It been more than a month since we posted the form, but still not a word from MAD money. 'You got to be patient,' I said to Poppy. 'They got to *read* it first,' I said. 'That's going to take them a month at least, and then they got to weigh everything up. It's complicated deciding the rate, they can't just do it like that,' I said. 'Takes time and skill to be accurate; they got to get it right.

'When they give me my Middle High Middle,' I told her, 'I heard so quick no one couldn't believe it. But that was exceptional, *everyone* said. It takes at *least* a month normally. It must of been 'cause of my history,' I said. 'Do you know what I'm saying?' Poppy nodded.

We was getting on really well, me and Poppy. Every night four-thirty exactly, we'd get up to leave and walk down the hill together. All the others would still be sat there, waiting for Tony or Malvin or Rhona to come and throw them out. 'Off home?' Sue the Sticks would say. 'Well, see you tomorrow, girls.' And Astrid would sit there muttering how it was alright if you got a home to go to.

I ain't saying it weren't a bit of a wrench to always be leaving so early, but there weren't no persuading Poppy to stay for one second more than she had to. '*You* don't have to come,' she said, the one time I suggested an extra five minutes. 'Stay if you want to, N,' she said, but I knew she was only being polite; our walks down the hill was the best bit of the day. That's when she used to tell me stuff, without dribblers everywhere listening in; she used to tell me all sorts of stuff, personal too, do you know what I'm saying, stuff she didn't want nobody else to hear. She told me all about her and Dud, and how they split up, like all the details, and how Saffra seen him every other weekend. She asked me if *I* had a boyfriend too, and I told her I didn't, not at the moment, and she said that was best 'cause men was a waste of time. We used to talk about dribblers too and we'd laugh about how mad they was, not nasty or nothing, just having a laugh, and we'd go through them all and we seen eye to eye on practically everyone. The only bit I didn't like was getting to the Darkwoods turning. And sometimes I'd stop at the corner shop for a couple of cans to drink when I got home.

One Friday she says to me out of the blue, she says, 'What you doing this weekend?' 'Dunno,' I says. 'I ain't decided.' 'Saffra's going to Dud's,' she says. 'I don't really feel like being on my own. Do you fancy going to the cinema?' So we gone, had popcorn and everything. Best night of my life.

Six weeks and two days it was, to the day, when the letter finally come:

mma

mad money
assessments

An Executive Agency of The Ministry
for the Advancement of the Deranged

INVESTING IN PEOPLE
MAD is part of the Department of Health

Your reference is ▆▆▆▆▆▆▆

Please tell us this number if you
need to get in touch with us

MAD MONEY ASSESSMENTS
ACKAMARACKA HOUSE
ACKAMARACKA PLACE
CHESTER-LE-STREET
DH3 3XR

Phone 0845 6287354
TEXTPHONE for deaf/hard of
hearing 0845 7835623

Date 2 Nov ▆▆▆▆▆

Dear Miss Shakespeare

ABOUT YOUR CLAIM

This letter is about your claim for MAD money. After careful
consideration of your claim, the adjudication officer has decided that
you are not entitled to MAD money.

How this decision was made

This decision has been based on the information you provided on
your form. Your referees may also have been contacted.

What to do if you think this decision is wrong

If you think this decision is wrong, you must write to us WITHIN ONE

Now go to the next page

Miss Poppy Shakespeare REF: ▇▇▇▇▇▇

MONTH of the date on this letter. You can ask us to look at the decision again or appeal against the decision. To help you decide if the decision is wrong you can ask us for an explanation first. If you ask us for an explanation, the month will be extended by the time it takes us to send it. If you ask us to look at the decision again and we decide not to change it, we will write and give you a month to appeal. If you appeal and we don't change the decision, we will write to you and give you another month to respond to this decision. You can ask us to look at the decision again or appeal against the decision. To help you decide if the decision is wrong you can ask us for an explanation first. If you ask us for an explanation, the month will be extended by the time it takes us to send it. If you ask us to look at the decision again and we decide not to change it, we will write and give you a month to appeal. If you appeal and we don't change the decision, we will write to you and give you another month to respond to this decision. You can ask us to look at the decision again or appeal against the decision. To help you decide if the decision is wrong you can ask us for an explanation first. If you ask us for an explanation, the month will be extended by the time it takes us to send it. If you ask us to look at the decision again and we decide not to change it, we will write and give you a month to appeal. If you appeal and we don't change the decision, we will write to you and give you another month to respond to this decision. You can ask us to look at the decision again or appeal against the decision. Appeals must be signed by you, giving your reasons and the decision you are appealing against.

Help and advice

Please get in touch with us if you

☐ do not understand anything in this letter

Now go to the next page

Miss Poppy Shakespeare

☐ want to know more about MAD money

Our phone number and address are at the top of this letter.

To make sure you receive a good standard of service your call may be recorded.

If you have any comments about our standard of service, please write to the Customer Services Manager at the above address.

Please keep this letter safe.
It is proof that you are NOT entitled to MAD money.

There are no more pages

'Wankers!' I said when I finished reading. We was sat side by side on the stairs.

'Can you fucking believe it!' Poppy said.

'Wouldn't know mad if it jumped up and bit them!' I said. 'Weren't nothing wrong with that form.'

'What am I going to do now?' she said.

'Weren't nothing wrong with that form,' I said. 'I know that much. Ain't *my* fault they's wankers. Can't blame *me*, innit, Poppy,' I said. She was sat leant forward hugging her knees. She shaken her head. I couldn't see her face.

' 'Cause I give it my best shot, Poppy,' I said. 'It's like I say, it's a lottery. But not even Low Low Low,' I said. 'Thought you'd get Low Low *Middle*, at least, if not *Middle* Low Middle, to be honest,' I said. 'You get Low Low Low just for *being* here,' I said. 'It's an insult's what it is!

'Wankers!' I said. 'Innit, Poppy!' I said. I looked at her and that's when I seen she was crying. 'You alright?' I said.

'Shit, Poppy!' I said. 'I ain't *saying* nothing. If it been down to me I'd of give you the lot. Low High Middle I'd of give you at *least*, if not Middle High Low,' I said. 'I would.

'And money well spent as well,' I said, but she didn't reply, just sat leant forward, hugging her knees and crying.

'I'm on Middle High Middle *myself*,' I said. 'That's only one up from Middle High Low.' She still didn't say nothing. 'Be like that then!' I felt like saying but I never 'cause I knew she was upset.

'Nah,' I said. 'Poppy, you taken me wrong. I weren't saying you only *deserved* Low Low Middle. It's just like I know how tight they are, and it ain't like you got a long record is it? Not being funny, but you know what I'm

257

saying, *I* been a dribbler since before I was born. Been fostered out fifty-three times,' I said. 'Self-harming since the age of two. Tried to *top* myself at fourteen,' I said. 'Been sectioned more times than you've wiped your arse. You see what I'm saying! I ain't having a go. But – you *ain't* been sectioned, have you, Poppy?' She shaken her head. 'See stuff like that bumps up your score,' I said. 'All I'm saying is to get a good rate . . .'

'But I don't care!' said Poppy. 'I don't care, N! I don't care *what* fucking rate they give me so long as I get on the register.'

'I know,' I said. 'That's what I'm saying!

'Be nice though, wouldn't it!' I said. 'Middle High Low. Be *nice*, wouldn't it!'

'I just don't know what to do!' she said. 'I've been banking on it. I've been holding out. That's the only thing's kept me going,' she said. 'Just get on The Register, get a lawyer . . .'

'It's like I say it's a lottery.' I give her a pat on the shoulder.

'I just don't know what to do!' she said. 'I really don't. I *really* don't. Honestly, N, I'm going to pieces. I just can't cope with this any more. I really can't. I mean, I *really* can't. I'm going to go to fucking pieces . . .' She was crying so much it poured down the stairs like the waterfall up Paradise Park, flooding the lobby enough for a duck to swim on. 'Look,' she gone and she pulled up her sleeve. On her inside arm just above her elbow was three round blisters like small water-filled balloons.

'When d'you do it?' I said. She shaken her head. 'You should pop them,' I said. 'That's what I do with mine. Pop them and peel the top off,' I said. 'Lets them scab up. That's best,' I said.

'I just don't know what to do,' she said.

'Leave it with me,' I said. 'I'll think of something.'

37. How Poppy had to prove
she was a dribbler

'Poppy,' I says to her next day. We was stood in the dinner queue. 'I been thinking all night and all morning as well and I reckon I sussed why it is they turned you down.'

'Go on,' says Poppy.

'Well,' I said. 'Alright there, Astrid?' She was up ahead at the counter taking her chops off of Canteen Coral, and when I waved she spun back round, so quick she let a hold of her plate and it flown across the canteen like a frisbee up Paradise Park. Thought for a sec it was aiming to lop the head off of Jacko the Penguin, who was stood by the tray racks picking his way through the dirty plates for his afters, but without even turning he held up his hand, caught it, still spinning, half an inch from his ear, and tipped the whole lot into his mouth like a dog snatched a sausage, down in one, before anyone could stop him.

'It's your proof, Poppy; that's what it is,' I said. 'You need a diagnosis.' And I told her how I'd reasoned it out and I thought she'd be pleased, do you know what I'm saying but all she said was, 'Right, OK.'

'What's the matter with you?' I said but she didn't say nothing, just shaken her head.

'Peas or carrots,' said Canteen Coral.

'Peas,' I said. 'No, carrots.' But she give me peas anyway,

wiping her nose on the palm of her hand as she handed me my plate.

Poppy slammed her tray on the table so hard my tray jumped an inch in the air and upset my orange all over my crackers I been saving to squidge the butter so it come through in worms. 'Have mine,' she said. 'That ain't the point,' I said, but she made me take them. 'How come *they* all get it no problem?!' she said.

'What's that?' I said.

'Do you know what I'm saying,' she said. '*Everyone* gets it! Astrid's on High Middle Middle,' she said. 'Wesley's on Low High Low, for fuck sake. Even Verna's on Low Middle Middle . . .'

'Low Middle *Low*,' I said. 'Last I heard.'

'And what the fuck's *wrong* with them?' she said.

'Shhh!' I said. 'Keep your voice down!' I said.

'What the fuck's *wrong* with them!' she said. 'So Verna chucks up her lunch. Big deal! So does half of London,' she said. 'Natalie's been bulimic for years. She doesn't get *paid* for it,' she said. 'And what's wrong with Wesley, do you know what I'm saying! What's stopping *him* from getting a job? No wonder he's depressed,' she said. 'Sat in that common room, smoking all day. He needs to get out . . .'

'He's got problems,' I said.

'*I've* got problems. We've *all* got problems. It's whether you make a career out of them. Don't get me wrong,' she said. 'Wesley's alright. Or he would be alright, do you know what I'm saying, if they hadn't pensioned him off at sixteen. There's a thousand Wesleys out there,' she said. 'And Sue the Sticks. I mean, what's wrong with *her* . . .'

And she gone round everyone in turn, how they wasn't really mad at all, and they didn't need to come to the Dorothy Fish and they didn't need MAD money neither, she said, be better off going to work like the sniffs, and after a bit I switched off to be honest, sat looking out of the window instead, at the huge mass of London spread out below, and I tried to imagine a thousand Wesleys somewhere inside all them houses and streets but it started to do my head in. 'I know she's got problems,' Poppy said. 'It's just how does this help? That's all I'm saying . . .' It was a bright-blue day, like cold and clear. It crossed my mind it be nice down Paradise Park.

'It just fucks me off, that's all,' said Poppy. 'I've had *my* shit to deal with as well . . . Do you know what I'm saying, N?!' she said. 'N?' she said. 'Are you listening, N! I've had *my* shit to deal with as well . . .'

'No good comparing, Poppy,' I said. 'My mum said comparing just makes you depressed. You can always find somebody madder than you. That's what she used to say,' I said. I grinned suddenly. 'She was funny, my mum.'

'N,' said Poppy. She grabbed my hand. 'I've *got* to get this MAD money.'

'I know,' I said. 'That's what I'm saying. That's why you need more proof.

'You free this Saturday night?' I said.

'Dunno,' she said. 'I could be. Why?'

'You free?' I said.

'Alright,' she shrugged. 'Saffra's going to the fireworks with Dud.'

'Seven o'clock by the entrance,' I said.

'At the weekend!' she said. 'Can't we go somewhere else?'

'You want bread you go to the butcher's,' I said, which I'd meant to say 'baker's' but I left it; it sounded alright.

38. Why I like fireworks and stuff like that you can skip if you can't be arsed

If there's one thing I reckon makes life worth living apart from dogs and Angel Delight and that first swig of Tennents with the sun in your face on a bench up Paradise Park, if there's one other thing it's fireworks every time. I gone with my mum up Ally Pally one year when I was really small and I sat on her shoulders and watched it all, and the biggest rockets you seen in your life, like this whoosh and then darkness and everyone waited . . . then BANG and the sky lit up like a dome, like we's all inside this enormous dome like St Paul's or something, instead of the night just going on forever. It was like someone cupped his hands around and my mum's face, tilted back to the sky, reflected the light and . . . I can't describe it but that was one of my happiest moments ever.

Fireworks on the Darkwoods always starts round mid-September and it doesn't end till February and even then it don't really end; there's always a group of teenage dribblers letting off crackers and bangers and shit on that little patch of muddy grass, about the size of a MAD money giro, where Rowan Walk runs into Elder Rise. Nasser the Nose done fireworks as well; he used to fire rockets out the toilet window, only opened half an inch – all the Sunshine House windows only opened half an inch – and try and get people going past. Once I was walking back from school with

264

Mandy, the one who topped herself, and we seen one coming along the pavement, like straight towards us along the pavement about a foot in the air. It was like one of them torpedoes or something, like *The African Queen*, 'cept bigger and faster, more of a cruise fucking missile. We jumped to the side and it veered straight for us. So we jumped again and it veered again and the third time we jumped it gone ZAP! in my shin, and I didn't dare look, thought it blasted my leg off, that's how much it fucking hurt. Then Mandy starts laughing. 'Sod off!' I gone but I had a look down and I seen the rocket stucking straight out of my shin like right angles. It was still alive, made this fizzing sound and all you could smell was like burning flesh and Mandy's stood there pissing herself. 'Sod off!' I gone and I started to walk with the rocket still stuck out my leg. 'Why don't you pull it out!' goes Mand. 'I ain't fucking touching it,' I said. 'They'll have to call an ambulance.' And I should of had an operation most probably, 'cept it fallen out as I gone up the steps and they never believed me in the office and even though I shown them the hole, like right through my fucking leg practically. 'You can have a bit of Savlon if you want,' they gone. 'Savlon!' I said. 'You taking the piss?' 'Suit yourself!' they said and shrugged and gone back to chatting like they normally did, like we weren't even there, do you know what I'm saying, never give a fucking pig-shit about us, and I ain't told nobody this before but right until that hole healed up I kept sort of hoping it might go sceptic and I even tried to help it along like rubbing in bits of dirt and shit but it weren't having none of it.

39. How me and Poppy gone up the tower looking for proof

That Saturday me and Poppy met outside the tower. The queue for the fireworks gone twice round the car park and halfway down Abaddon Hill but Wesley had saved us a couple of places right at the front; he'd been sat there since Friday, him and Swiller Steve and Chip and a mountain of empty beer cans. 'Here they are!' White Wesley said as me and Poppy stepped into the light of the entrance. 'Alright girls?' he said. 'Look at you!' 'Look at what?' I said. 'Dig da outfit!' he said. 'You got make-up on?' 'Fuck off!' I said and everyone laughed. Chip give me a wink but I made like I hadn't seen.

Behind us the queue had all started up harping. 'Oi, you! Wait your turn like the rest of us! Can't you see there's a queue, or what!'

'Do you think we should go to the back?' said Poppy. 'Why?' I said. 'Well . . .' she said. 'No fucking way!' I said. 'Darkwoods dribblers, innit!' I said. 'Always blaming somebody else. They could of slept out if they wanted,' I said. 'It's first come first served,' I said, 'cause it was and besides of which I couldn't walk no further in my heels.

At seven exactly, not a second before, Sharon unlocked the doors. He held up five fingers. 'Five at a time.' And he counted us off as we gone in the lobby. Wesley then Swiller Steve then Chip, then me, then Poppy and locked the

doors behind us. We all had to write in the visitors' book
with the name of what flop we was visiting. 'Put Mitchell
the Meds,' I said to Poppy. 'I'll put Mitchell the Meds as
well. I always visit Mitchell,' I said. 'Or Lee if Mitchell's
taken. They's only allowed two visitors each. Look,' I said
and I turned back a page and shown her my name from the
year before, then the year before that as well. 'Year before
that it was Lee,' I said. 'Fucking Margery barged her way in.
Year before *that* it was Mitchell,' I said.

'Get on with it!' growled Security Sharon. He ripped the
corner off a foil sachet with his teeth and sucked the drink
out.

The lift was piled full of carrier bags. 'What da fuck?' White
Wesley said. Then the bags begun to rustle and shift and
first a foot appeared then a hand round the side and then the
face of Professor Max McSpiegel. 'Is this the seventh floor?'
he said. 'Oh dear,' he said. 'I keep going down. I'm trying
to get up to the seventh,' he said. 'But this script has got a
life of its own. The bags keep pressing against the buttons.'

'We ain't gonna fit in dere,' said Wesley. Sounded like
Dizzee fucking Rascal. 'We'll have to wait for de other lift,
innit.'

'Perhaps if we piled them up some more,' McSpiegel said
and he picked one up what had fell out the side and piled it
on top of the others. But as soon as he done it another fell
out exactly the same and when he picked that up another
fell out and there weren't no holding them back.

'We'll have to wait for de other lift, innit,' White Wesley
said, pushing the button again. But there weren't no way I
was missing the fireworks standing around for a lift never

come, so me and Poppy squeezed down the side, legs spread, arms wide to make like a fence and Professor McSpiegel stacked them behind, do you know what I'm saying; you could feel them all pushing but we never shifted an inch. Then Max McSpiegel stood at the front with his arms stretched side to side. And Chip chucked the last few over his head and pressed number seven. 'See you up there,' he said and he give me a wink as the doors shut.

It must of been 'cause of the bags I reckon but the lift gone so slow, do you know what I'm saying and in jerks as well like Middle-Class Michael was hauling us up on a pulley. Every time the lift give a jerk, one of the bags jabbed into your back or against your leg or so hard in your neck it felt like it lopped your head off. 'What you got *in* them?' Poppy said.

'Ah!' said Professor McSpiegel.

'It's his book,' I said, 'innit, Poppy,' I said. 'His *History of the Abaddon*; that's what it is.'

'Ah!' said McSpiegel. 'But which chapter? That's the question.'

'Seeing as how we've helped you,' I said, ignoring him, 'cause once he got going . . . 'Seeing as how we've helped you,' I said. 'Maybe you could help us an' all.'

'Delighted,' said Max McSpiegel.

'Me and Poppy are looking for proof.'

'Ah!' said Professor McSpiegel. 'Proof!'

'We got to prove she's mad,' I said.

'Mad,' said Professor McSpiegel. 'I see.'

'It's not that I don't *know* about madness,' I said. 'Do you know what I'm saying. I know all there is to know,' I said. 'I been a dribbler since before I was born. My mum was a dribbler and her mum as well and all the way back to Adam and Eve and the Garden of Eden and . . .'

'The thing is,' said Poppy.

'The thing is,' I said. 'It's proving it. I never *had* to prove it,' I said. ' 'Cause it's true, do you know what I'm saying. Everyone always known I was mad since before I was even born,' I said.

'But *I'm* not mentally ill,' said Poppy. 'I just need to *prove* I'm mentally ill to get me a lawyer to prove I'm not . . .'

'Poppy,' I said and I give her a nudge. Two carrier bags come toppling out like over between our shoulders. 'He don't need to know all that,' I said. 'All she's saying, Professor, is . . . Well put it like this, Professor,' I said. 'How do you prove you's mad?'

'How does one prove one's mad,' said McSpiegel. 'Hm!' he said; he'd of stroked his chin if he didn't got his arms stretched either side to hold up the carrier bags. 'Hm!' he said. 'Presupposing of course, one accepts proof itself as a viable concept . . .'

'What?' I said.

'Presupposing . . .' he said. 'I mean, can one prove *anything*?' he said.

'Ain't got no choice,' I said. 'We got to.'

'Ah!' said Professor McSpiegel. 'You see. Reality's one thing. The truth quite another. Proof, if proof exists at all, might be seen as the bridge in between them,' he said. 'But is such a construct feasible?'

'Fuckin'ell!' I whispered to Poppy. 'No wonder his book's so long.'

'I'm not being funny, Professor,' I said, 'but all we's

asking, do you know what I'm saying, is how to prove you's mad, just like . . .'

'Precisely,' said Max McSpiegel.

'Supposing you *had* to,' Poppy said.

'Ah,' said McSpiegel. 'But *can* one be compelled to perform the impossible? Alright,' he said. 'For the sake of argument, let us suppose that rather than proof, which may lie beyond our reach, we are striving instead for the *appearance* of proof. A sort of Platonism . . .' he said.

'For fuck sake,' I gone and I turned my head like sideways to look at Poppy. But Poppy was turned to Professor McSpiegel so all I got was the back of her head and a great wodge of papers jabbing my cheek.

'According to Plato,' goes Max McSpiegel, 'what surrounds us is not reality but the *appearance* of reality, not the truth itself but a *reflection* of the truth. Imagine,' he goes, 'that this lift is a cave, and we're all chained together . . .'

'Might as well be,' I said. Poppy still didn't turn round.

'And imagine it's dark, maybe just a small fire throwing shadows on to the walls. We've never been outside the cave, so what are in fact merely shadows, reflections, we take for reality. But suppose one of us escapes . . .'

'Hang on!' goes Poppy. 'I heard of that! One of the men escapes from the cave and . . .'

'Alright,' I said. 'I'll tell you what. Why don't *I* just get out and leave you to it. Seeing as you's so fucking smart,' I said. 'Can't see what you need *my* help for.' Poppy turned at that; I could feel her turn but I never looked, just folded my arms, which I shouldn't of neither, could of been killed – started a fucking avalanche, bags come tumbling down both sides, crashing and smashing and tearing theirselves . . .

'Might as well just get out,' I said, when they'd finished and all gone silent. I couldn't get out 'cause the lift was still going, but anyway that weren't the point. I *say* it was going; the higher we gone, the slower and jerkier it got. Like a couple of inches and stop for a breather then half an inch, then a couple of inches; reckoned Middle-Class Michael might keel over and die of a heart attack any second.

It taken the nurses best part of an hour to fucking let us in. Poppy was helping Professor McSpiegel, carry his bags one by one out the lift and pile them up on the landing. I stood with my back to them pressing the buzzer again and again and again and again and hammering on the glass and swearing. I seen that Caina go past three times but she never even looked, do you know what I'm saying. I mean, they's getting fucking *paid*!

'They may be reflections,' I heard Poppy say. 'But they're heavy enough! My arms are aching.'

Professor McSpiegel give a laugh, not a proper laugh, just like 'Hoh, hoh, hoh!' I nearly fucking puked.

When Ptolomea answered the door, she said 'Yes?' I said, 'We come to see Mitchell.' 'Alright,' she said and she pressed the release then stood there, arms folded, chewing. 'Two visitors per patient,' she said. 'Yeah?' I said. 'Me and her!' I said. She scowled as I shown her the pass. Anything, she'd of give, *anything* to have it said something different. But there it was, **VISIT APROVED** in red letters. She stared so hard she gone permanent cross-eyed, trying to rejig it, make it say **FUCK OFF**.

★   ★   ★

'Do you know which room Mitchell's in?' said Poppy as we gone down the corridor.

'Shall I ask?' she said, 'cause I never said nothing.

'N?' she said.

'Oh, sorry!' I said. 'You speaking to me now?!' I said.

'I'm sorry?' said Poppy.

'Forget it,' I said.

'Look, N,' she said. 'Oh for fuck sake!' she said. And she give a great huff, proper strop!

We was outside the dorm but I couldn't go in, could I, not with us not talking. So I made like I was reading this notice sellotaped up on the wall. 'Abaddon Patients' Rights,' it said. 'Roberta visits the seventh floor on the third Friday morning of every fourth month and the second Wednesday of every third month except when the twenty-first falls on a Sunday . . .'

'N,' she said.

'Get off me!' I said. We stood there ten minutes in silence.

'Look . . .' she said.

'Alright!' I said. 'I'm only doing it for you,' I said.

'I know,' she said. 'I know. I'm sorry.'

'What you having a go at *me* for? I'm trying to help you out,' I said. 'Get you some proof, do you know what I'm saying.'

'You've been really helpful,' Poppy said.

'And my feet are killing me!' I said.

She patted my arm. 'Come on,' she said. I could swear I heard her sigh.

The other lift must of done twenty trips in the time it taken us thanks to Max McSpiegel. The men's dorm was full to overflowing with Darkwoods dribblers pushing and shoving and crowding the windows and stood on the lockers and hung from the rails round each bed, like dirty washing. Every few seconds one fell to the floor, sworn a bit, rubbed his hands on his jeans, then jumped back up again.

I couldn't see Wesley nowhere at first, then I spotted him. Him, Steve and Chip, in a row on top of the wardrobes. Wesley was writing his name in the air again and again with a sparkler he'd bought off these two Rumanians going round.

'Come on up!' they called.

'You joking?!' we said.

'Nah!' They reached down. 'Come on! We'll give you a haul.'

'Haul yourself!' said Poppy. 'I may have put on, but I don't weigh *that* much!' And she can't of done neither; my whole life before and let alone my whole life since, I never seen nothing so nimble and swift as the way Poppy Shakespeare jumped up on that wardrobe – not Nadia Commonitch I mean, neither; not nobody, not nothing.

'Come on, N!' shouts Poppy. 'Come up!' *She* got a sparkler now as well. Like whose idea *was* this!

'I'll help you up, N,' says Chip, jumping down, almost landed on top of Angelorna, squeezing herself through the crush of bodies to hand out apples and parking.

'No way!' I said. 'I ain't going up there!'

'Come on!' they said.

'I ain't!' I said. 'I'll sprain my ankle.' But in the end I didn't got no choice the way they all gone on. Chip give me a leg up and Wesley pulled and Poppy got hold of my arm and pulled and 'Christ!' I said. 'Good job *Astrid* ain't coming up here!'

After the fireworks – 'They're amazing!' said Poppy. 'I've never seen them before from above! Aren't they incredible, N!' she said. 'It's like looking down on fountains or something. That must be Primrose Hill,' she said. 'And Highbury . . . And Ally Pally, down there . . . This was such a good idea, N!' I shrugged. 'I *said* they was good,' I said. After the fireworks we stayed on the wardrobes, chatting and eating our parking . . . 'So come on!' said Poppy; we'd been drinking a bit – three quarters of vodka in cartons of orange. 'So come on! How do you prove you're mad?'

'*You're* the one going to the Dorothy Fish!' said Swiller Steve, taken the hump a bit. '*You're* the one going, what you asking *us* for?'

I was waiting for Poppy to come back at him, and when she never, I give her a look. And that's when I seen she got tears in her eyes. I'm like what?, do you know what I'm saying! You never seen nobody swing so fast, not even Pollyanna before she got stuck. Two seconds ago she's all laughing and joking and loving the fireworks, flying she was, and now CRASH! like you'd ripped her wings off.

'She's alright, man,' White Wesley said. 'She's new. Still finding her feet, no offence. How do you prove you're mad?' he said. 'Well you do mad things, innit,' he said. 'Innit, Poppy!'

But Poppy didn't answer; she was crying now, proper tears. I'm like, Jesus! Do you know what I'm saying! It must of been what Swiller Steve said 'cause there weren't nothing else it *could* of been, but, it weren't hardly *nothing* what Swiller Steve said. Darkwoods dribblers was always sniping. 'For fuck sake Poppy, get a grip on yourself!' I'm thinking.

'You alright?' said Chip. You could see he didn't get it neither; none of us didn't. Swiller Steve sat looking down at the top of the wardrobe.

'I'm sorry,' said Poppy.

'Here,' Wesley said, and he give her a bottle of Mellizone. 'Have one of these, take the edge off,' he said. I ain't saying nothing but I swear she taken two if not three 'cause I seen her.

After that visiting time was over. Ptolomea come in, stood propping the door wide open with her big fat arse. We had to queue half an hour for the lift and the whole time I never said nothing. And I never said nothing all the way down the hill and when we got to the turning I never said nothing, just 'See you on Monday,' that's all I said. I never said nothing about her crying, not once, and I done it deliberate.

40. How Poppy come along
pretty remarkable good

I'm not being funny but Poppy come along good. Fact she come along pretty remarkable good if you think of how normal she started. Course she had a good teacher, ain't saying it don't help, but right from the start she was adding in stuff of her own like off of her bat. I might of suggested sorting her clothes out, ditching the hipster jeans for a start, and the snakeskin boots, do you know what I'm saying, just like basic dribbling the end of the day, but it was her started gnawing her nails non-stop, like a gerbil gnawing the bars of his cage, and when there weren't no nails left she gnawed at the skin and fucking disgusting it was as well. 'Give it a rest,' I'd say. 'Jesus, Poppy! You's putting me off of my fatty lamb stew!' And she'd stop right away like I'd give it a kick, the cage not the gerbil, do you know what I'm saying, like Mandy's gerbil down Sunshine House, used to gnaw half the night but I ain't going there 'cause I got to get on with the story. Then inside of two seconds she'd start up again. 'Poppy!' I'd say and she'd look at me startled; she never even realised, it seemed like sometimes. 'Sorry,' she'd mutter and wander off, smoke a fag out in the common room with her tracksuit bums slipped halfway down her arse, never ate nothing neither, aside of her fingers, that is.

Course two steps forward, one step back, do you know what I'm saying; weren't plain sailing. Sometimes it seemed like she'd lost her nerve. 'What the fuck am I *doing*, N?' she'd say. 'Look at me! What the fuck's going on! I wouldn't of got out of *bed* like this two months ago! I mean, look at my hair!' And she'd stand and stare at herself in the mirror, hair hung down like a spaniel's ears, and this look on her face, like 'What is *that* I've trod in!' . . . 'You just ain't used to it, Poppy,' I'd say. 'That's all it is. Do you know what I'm saying. It's 'cause you been living like a sniff all your life; you can't see nothing just how it is. I'm not being funny,' I'd say to her, 'but you don't even look that bad, to be honest. You might scrape Low Low Middle,' I said. 'I'm just saying my opinion,' I said. 'You might scrape Low Low Middle,' I said . . . 'I look like a *psychopath!*' she said. 'You don't,' I said. 'That's what I'm saying. You got to take your sniff specs off. Take your sniff specs off!' I said. She taken them off. 'You see,' I said. 'You look practically normal now,' I said. She frowned. 'I bloody well hope not!' she said. 'You going to be out there all day!' shouted Fran. I give her 'Fuck off!' 'You get used to it,' I said.

That's all I said – I mean, not even *that*, to be honest, just give her a bit of support. And I weren't no different from anyone else. They was all like, 'Remember when you come in! Stiff as a pole you was, stiff as a pole. Ain't that right, Vern, stiff as a pole. You look *much* better now. You'll get your money! Taken Michael three attempts!'

'That was to increase the rate,' said Michael. 'They didn't turn me down; they applied the wrong rate. They admitted their error in the end. It was quite a different . . .'

'Whatever!' said Sue. 'All I'm saying, Poppy, is you'll get there. I was like you when I first come.'

'No you weren't!' says like everyone.

'I was,' said Sue. 'I was just like Poppy. Couldn't show what I was feeling inside. That's why I used to slash my arms up. Always dressed stylish over the top. Nice little jacket, boots, you know! But inside . . . Remember how angry you was! Blowing off all over the place!'

'She was *awful* to me!' says Astrid Arsewipe. 'I was scared to open my mouth! I was!'

'Brian seen through it,' said Sue the Sticks. 'Right from the start he said to me, "There's a sweet girl in there, Sue!" That's what he said. "There's a sweet girl in there!" '

'*I* seen it,' said Wesley.

'She ain't saying you didn't, is she!' said Astrid, got the hump with Wesley for something. I can't remember what.

It was Poppy decided her next assessment, 'stead of trying to get let out, she'd aim for a decent reference. I warned her: 'You got to be careful,' I said. 'They's weird that way, doctors. You tell them you's mad; that's just when they'll make up their minds you been cured.' 'Well, good,' she says. 'I'm trying to get out. That'll save me from going through the hassle of Leech's.' 'I'm just saying,' I said. 'You got to be careful.' It weren't like I didn't warn her.

But that's just the way Poppy Shakespeare was; once she'd made up her mind, do you know what I'm saying . . . Assessment day morning, in she comes, looked like a ghost she was that fucking pale and rings round her eyes like Marta the Coffin would kill for. 'No need to overdo it,' said Astrid, give her a nervous once over.

Astrid then Brian then Candid then Dawn, one by one they all gone off and one by one they all come back. 'I feel sick,' said Tadpole. 'I do; I feel sick.' Gita kept turning her magazine. 'What's up with Rhona?' said Candid Head-phones.

'What do you mean what's up with her?' said Sue the Sticks, bit grumpy as well. It was nerves; she weren't normally like that.

'She smiled at me,' says Candid Headphones. 'Rhona the Moaner smiled at me.'

'Bollocks!' said Verna. 'You're so full of crap!'

'Suit yourself!' says Candid and turned her Walkman back up to blasting.

'I thought she seemed friendlier,' said Michael. 'Last Communication Group. We might have to instigate a change of name . . .'

'She never smiled at *me*,' said Astrid.

'Must be getting it,' Wesley said.

And Omar said something, but you couldn't hear what, on account all the pick 'n' mix tumbling about in his mouth.

I wouldn't call it smiling exactly, the look what Rhona give me. But it's true there was something going on and I ain't just saying that benefit of hindsight. I know because I said at the time, I said to Omar as he gone in, I said, 'Is it me, or what's with Rhona?' and you can ask him as well 'cause I'm pretty sure he'd remember.

Poppy thought Rhona was really pissed off. 'With you?' I said. 'Not with me,' she said. 'I don't know,' she said. 'Do you know what I'm saying, though?' 'Yeah,' I said. 'Maybe.'

We was walking down Abaddon Hill that night. It was

so fucking dark you couldn't hardly see nothing. Down at the bottom, Borderline Road was like the lights round the shore, do you know what I'm saying, like when me, Mum and Shirley gone out in a boat and I seen a seagull snatch a bit of fish.

' 'Bout time they done something about these lampposts,' I said to Poppy. ' 'Fore someone gets killed. It's the whole of the Darkwoods as well,' I said. 'Must be on the same wiring or something . . . That's what Tony said,' I said.

'I know,' Poppy said. 'You said.'

'They's just upset 'cause of Wesley and Verna,' I said. 'It ain't 'cause of nothing you done . . . Just looking for someone to blame,' I said. 'Fucking dribblers! Do you know what I'm saying! I said to them, I said, "Don't pick on Poppy. Ain't *her* fault, is it, they got discharged." '

'When did you say that?' said Poppy.

'You must of been out in the toilets,' I said. 'I said, "Maybe it's time they kicked *you* out, Astrid. Ain't done you much good has it, being here so long!" ' I seen Poppy smile as she taken a drag. 'Can't hardly believe I said it!' I said. 'Can you imagine!'

'No,' said Poppy.

' "Maybe it's time they kicked *you* out, Astrid!" Fuckin 'ell!' I said.

'The thing is,' said Poppy. 'What if they're right?'

'Astrid?!' I said. 'But I stuck up for you!'

'Not Astrid,' said Poppy. 'The doctors and Tony and . . . What if I *am* going mad?' she said. 'Then it all starts to make sense, doesn't it? Maybe they're just trying to help me,' she said. 'Maybe I'm so mad I don't *know* I'm mad. Do you think so, N? Do you think I could be?'

'Don't ask *me*,' I said. 'I'm mad *myself*.'

'It's like I'm in no man's land,' she said. 'I don't know where I belong any more. It was Saffra's parents' evening last night. I couldn't go in, do you know what I'm saying. We got to the school; I just couldn't go in. Saffra's like "Come on, Mum!" but I couldn't. I couldn't even go through the gate. I just *couldn't*; I can't describe it, N. I couldn't face seeing everyone; that was part of it, but it was more than that. It was like I was almost *paralysed*. I *was* paralysed; I couldn't move. I'm just stood there with Saffra tugging my arm and I honestly thought, I'm serious, N, I honestly thought for a second at least, they'd have to call an ambulance. I mean, what would I have *said* when they came! "I can't move. I'm sorry; I just can't move. I can't go in and I can't go back." Can you imagine! But that's how it felt.'

'So what happened?' I said.

'Well I sort of snapped out of it,' Poppy said. 'We just went back home. It was awful, though. 'Cause they're all arriving, like *everyone*, and Saffra's in tears and I'm trying to like pull her. "I can't help it, Saffra, can I!" I said. "I can't fucking help it if I don't feel well!" I swore!' said Poppy. 'I *never* swear. Not at *Saffra*, *never*, not *ever*, not *once*. It was awful, and everyone's going past, and you can see what they're thinking, I mean, not that I care, but do you know what I'm saying, you can tell they all know. And I can't blame them either, I'd have been just the same. Well I don't know though actually, I *would* have said *something*. But then maybe I wouldn't; you just can't tell. I mean, I've known Kate since antenatal class. Talk about a neurotic mother! Used to ring me up fifteen times a day. "Do you *really* think he's eating enough?" . . . "Kate," I said. "Chill! If he's hungry, he'll eat." I *know* she saw me; she looked so embarrassed. They all did, N, it was like I'd pissed myself.'

41. How me and Poppy got more and more closer and told each other stuff

With every week passed me and Poppy got more and more closer. I gone round her flat like *all* the time, become like a second home pretty much, especially at weekends with Saffra round Dud's. She even give me my own set of keys, least she lent me them once when I gone to the shop and I never give them back. She give me *loads* of fucking stuff as well. 'I just want *rid* of it,' she'd say. Like *everything*, her hair straighteners, ten pairs of shoes (they pinched, but still), her juicer she'd never even used, a digital camera, a stack of CDs; *everything*. 'I just want *rid* of it!' Between that and the stuff she'd sold on eBay to pay for Mr Leech, there weren't hardly nothing left in the flat, except for Saffra's toys of course; she didn't get rid of those. She emptied her wardrobes out as well, three bin-liners full, for Oxfam she said. 'I just want *rid* of it, N, to be honest.' 'You don't want to waste it on Oxfam!' I said. 'That's good stuff in there!' and I taken them home, three bin-liners, one each day.

I met Dud as well, just the one time I met him, when he brought Saffra back one Sunday night. We'd been lain on the sofa all day watching vids and drinking and smoking and chatting and stuff, really nice, when the buzzer gone. 'Shit!' says Poppy. 'What time is it? Fuck! Oh my God, N! Quick! No, you stay in here. Just open the windows!' And she rushed out the room.

Well then I heard the buzzer again and Poppy shouting into the phone. 'Alright, alright! Come on up.' And even while they was climbing the stairs I could still hear her crashing around in the kitchen and I opened the windows like she said and I had a look out but I couldn't see nothing 'cept the old people staring opposite and this flashy red car what was parked in the street below. Then I heard her open the door. 'Saffra! Oh, darling! Give Mummy a hug. Did you have a nice time!' Then this man starts talking, really posh, I mean *really* posh, make Middle-Class Michael sound practically common. 'Poppy. Look Poppy, we need to talk. This can't go on.' 'Not now,' says Poppy. 'Not now, alright, Dud; I'll give you a call.' 'Yes, now!' says Dud. 'I'm not going till we've talked. You *say* you'll call . . .' 'I will, Dud. I will. I know . . . Fuck off! You can't just barge in my fuck . . .' and suddenly the door burst open and this man come in, seen me, and stopped. Fact he pulled hisself up so sharp and short it was like he'd slammed into a wall.

He was fucking good-looking, that's the first thing I thought. I'd of fancied him, I honestly would, if it weren't for Poppy was my friend and stuff, which even if they *wasn't* together no more it was still like hands off 'cause that's me. But I did wish I wasn't still in my pyjamas, MAD ones as well, what I'd nicked off the ward, and I wished it especially when Poppy come through and I seen she was wearing a sweatshirt and jeans, must of rushed through and changed when he buzzed. It was weird seeing her stood there next to Dud. I don't know what it was exactly; he weren't dressed smart – just a jumper and jeans, which if anything *Poppy's* was smarter, and he hadn't shaved neither and his shoes was all scuffed – but something about him, I don't know; it's just Poppy looked different stood along-side. Shabby almost; the whole flat looked shabby in fact.

'This is N,' said Poppy.

And I nodded. 'Alright?'

But for all he was posh he didn't got no manners. A pig got better manners than him. Do you know what I'm saying, no 'Alright?' or nothing, just turned away, 'Jesus, Poppy!' he said, like I weren't even there at all. Poppy made like I weren't there as well but she said sorry later on account she been stressed. I might of forgot I was there myself, if it weren't for that Saffra stood holding her hand and glowering at me like I'd murdered her fucking mother.

If there's one thing used to drive Poppy mad, it was every time she got a letter saying why she'd failed her appeal. They always said the same, more or less. 'This is a letter about your appeal against our decision not to change our decision not to award you MAD money. You asked us for an explanation why we made this decision. This decision was based on the information you provided in your appeal. Your referees may also have been contacted. If you think this decision is wrong, you must write to us WITHIN ONE MONTH . . .'

'What do they want me to do?!' she'd go. 'Jesus Christ, N! What more do they want!' And the thing is I didn't know what to say, to be perfectly honest; I honestly didn't. 'You just got to keep on appealing,' I said. 'That's some-thing at least. You can keep on appealing.' She's like, 'What fucking good . . .' 'Alright, Poppy!' I said. 'Don't have a go at *me*!' I said. 'I'm just saying, that's all. You can keep on appealing. It ain't *my* fault,' I said. 'Jesus Christ!' But the thing is although Poppy always said sorry and how she was just stressed and stuff like that and it *weren't* my fault and I *knew* it weren't, I couldn't help feeling like underneath maybe she reckoned it was. It weren't like I give half a fuck if she *did* to tell you the truth, I mean what can you do. I done my best, do you know what I'm saying, but the fact is I wanted to help her out 'cause that's just the way I am.

'You rung them up, Poppy?' I says to her. 'They got this number, you can ring them up.'

'Have I rung them up!' she said. 'Only like fifteen hundred times. Do you know what I'm saying, N, you can't get through!'

'You got to keep trying, Poppy,' I said. 'I'm not being funny but most probably they're busy. You just got to keep on trying,' I said.

'*You* try!' she said.

'I will,' I said.

'I've spent fucking hours trying to get through!' she said.

'If you give me the letter, I'll do it,' I said.

'I'm not kidding, N. I mean *hours*, I've spent.'

'Alright!' I said. 'So just give me the letter; I'll do it.'

Well I didn't got no choice after that, I fucking *had* to get through. And I didn't got no phone, just to make life easy. I used to have one till they taken it off me. 'You haven't paid your bill,' they said. 'I ain't made no *calls*,' I said. 'I been in fucking hospital.' 'You still need to pay your bill,' they said, 'for having the facility. You *could* have made calls.' 'I *couldn't*,' I said. 'I told you, I been in hospital.' Tony offered to sort it out – to be fair to him, that's one thing he done. 'Ah, fuck it!' I said. 'Let them take it. I can't be arsed.' And I didn't miss it neither to be honest with you. You's better off not having a phone than having a phone don't ring. The only time my phone ever rung was the phone people ringing me up to complain I hadn't paid my bill. I used to lift the receiver and listen, just to make sure I still got a tone.

Would of come in handy though, having a phone 'stead of going down the phone box every time I rung up the MAD Assessments. I must of called them a million times, every morning on my way up the hill and every night on my way back down, when I didn't go round the Gatehouse with Poppy or else back to her flat which I did half the time, then I'd have to say, 'Go on, I'll catch you up. I just got to ring my friend a minute.' 'You can ring them from mine,' she'd say. 'Nah,' I'd say. 'You're alright. You go on ahead.' And she'd smile to herself – don't know what she thought! Must of thought I was having an *affair* or something! – and carry on down Sniff Street. Then I'd sneak the letter out my tracksuit pocket and dial the number and wait. I must of spent easy a thousand pounds, all my fucking MAD money! But then one day this dribbler was waiting outside, Indian he was, with a chestful of medals, and he seen me putting the money in and when I come out he said, 'What are you doing! You need to get a phone card. What are you doing!' And he give me one just like that, for nothing. 'I see you every day,' he said. 'I call my brother in Hyderabad. Freephone British Gas,' he said, and he stamped his foot and done me a salute.

Whenever you rung the MMA, it was always the same voice answered. 'Thank you for calling MAD Money Appeals Ltd. We are sorry but all our operators are busy at the moment taking calls from other clients. Your call is being held in a queuing system and we estimate will be answered in approximately (*pause*) TEN (*pause*) minutes.' Then they give you this music to listen while you waited and it weren't so much that I minded the music; I mean, take it or leave it, do you know what I'm saying, I ain't got a problem with classical, but when you're stood there watching your card going down, or feeding in pound coins every two seconds, ain't exactly the most relaxing time for taking in highbrow culture.

After five minutes she come back to you, told you you got another five minutes then stuck on the music again. After two and a half she was back again and again after one and a quarter. After that she was counting in seconds. 'Thirty-seven point FIVE seconds.' 'Eighteen point seven FIVE seconds.' 'Nine point three seven FIVE seconds.' 'Four point six eight seven FIVE seconds.' With a quick blast of music between each one. 'Two point three four three seven FIVE seconds.' And every time like faster and faster and higher and higher like Donald Duck, like my mum done with records when I was a kid, used to play them the wrong speed on purpose to crack me up.

The longer you waited, the longer you thought, if I give up now, do you know what I'm saying, you've just wasted the money then, innit. You couldn't even tell what she was saying no more; it all merged together in a single shriek, 'Aiiiiiiiiiiiiiiiiiiiiiiiiiiiiiiiiii', with no beginning or end or nothing till you hung up the phone or your card run out like three months' benefit later.

So when someone picked up, do you know what I'm saying, it just thrown me a bit on account of I weren't expecting it. I didn't even wait, like two rings and I'm through. 'MAD Money Appeals,' she said – I almost dropped the fucking phone. 'This is Trish speaking. How can I help you?'

'Oh?' I said. 'Right.' 'Can I help you?' she said. 'Oh,' I said. 'Right. Gis a sec,' I said. I taken a deep breath and with my free hand I unzipped my pocket and got out the letter. One time they answer I ain't fucking ready. 'I'm calling,' I said. 'I'm ca . . . I'm ca . . . I'm . . . I'm . . . I'm . . . Ma . . . Ma . . . Mad money claim,' I said. 'OK,' she said. 'Do you happen to have your National Insurance number?' 'My what?' I said. 'Hang . . . ang . . . ang . . . Jussa sec.' I scrunched up the paper besides the receiver like I'm desperately searching through mountains of crap. 'Just your address will do fine,' she said. 'Nah,' I said. 'S'OK. Hang . . . ang . . . jussa sec . . .' Then I read her the number from off of the letter. 'OK,' she said. 'Alright,' she said. 'Come on!' she said. 'I'm sorry, it's this computer; it takes forever.' 'I'm . . . I'm . . . I . . . I'm nnnervous of phones.' 'Come on!' she said. 'You never know who . . . who . . . who . . . who's lllistening, do you?' 'Ah!' she said. 'Alright, here we are.' 'I'm pppp . . . pa . . . pa . . . pa . . . paranoid,' I said. 'Oh my God!' she said.

'Poppy!' she said. 'I don't believe this! Poppy Shake-speare? Is that you!' 'Yeah,' I said. 'Um . . . um . . . yeah . . . yeah . . . yeah, it is!' Alright, girl, I'm thinking. Alright, girl, keep cool . . . 'It's me!' she said. 'Trish! You know, Kilkenny Trish?' I almost hung up then and there, I did. 'Kilkenny Trish from Harbinger Krapwort Harbinger!' Fuck, shit, bugger, I'm thinking. 'So how are you, Poppy?' says Kilkenny Trish. 'Ay-oh,' I said. 'Yeeooo knayoh!'

Gone all la-di-da. Don't know why, it just happened, born actress or something. 'Are you alright, Poppy?' she said. 'How's Saffra?' 'Little daaaaahrling!' I said. 'She's a lahv!' 'And how's Dud?' she said. 'Or shouldn't I ask?' 'Ay-oh,' I said. 'Yeeooo knayoh!' 'I do!' She laughed. I laughed. I'm like what the fuck. 'You know I lost my job,' she said. 'I'm back in Kilkenny now staying with my parents.' 'Ay-oh deeahh!' I said. 'Semply awwwful for yeoo!' 'You sound really different. Are you *alright?*' she said.

So then of course I had to get back to why I'd rung up in the first place. 'Cause she'd thrown me a bit do you know what I'm saying, all that la-di-da business, forgot where I was and now I was worried I'd gone and blown it by coming over too normal. So I give it full throttle, do you know what I'm saying, all about how mental I was, all that slashing my arms up and puking and shit, and how Al Qaida put a bug in my brain and was playing my thoughts live to the Taliban and they wanted to turn me into a suicide bomber. And I told her how there was like seven of me. ' "Multiple personalities", that's what they call it,' I said to her. 'All different, they are, and they talk different too. And some of them sound almost normal,' I said. 'But they're the most maddest of all.'

I got to admit I thought Poppy be pleased when I told her about what had happened. I run up the hill to the Abaddon, and I sat there and waited, weren't even half-nine, like puffing and sweating and wheezing away and all buzzed up do you know what I'm saying to tell her how slippy I'd been. But the thing is with Poppy you just couldn't tell. She was so fucking moody, I'm not being funny, she was worse than Astrid, she honestly was, and sometimes it did piss me off a bit, like especially when I'd gone out of my way to help her, do you know what I'm saying, and all I got back was a slap in the face. I used to think why fucking bother.

'Trish!' she said. 'You're joking, aren't you?'

'Said she used to work with you,' I said.

'I know she used to *work* with me! She was a two-faced bitch, as well,' she said. 'I swear to God she slept with Dud.'

'I told her how mad you was,' I said. 'You should of heard me!' I grinned, couldn't help it.

'I'll never get out of here,' she said.

'Course you will!' I said. 'If you want to.'

'What's that s'posed to mean, "If I *want*"?!' she said.

'If you *want*,' I said. Do you see what I'm saying; couldn't win!

Poppy kept on about coming round mine. It weren't that I had a problem with having her round, do you know what I'm saying, it's just aside of police and social workers and the man come to put in the pay as you go, and the man took the phone, who I told you about, and the men from the Lease of Life Furniture Project and about twenty doctors and ambulance men, which weren't none of them sociable visits exactly, I weren't used to having company.

I'd give my flat a bit of a *Changing Places* over the past few months. I'd done the sitting-room walls this pale lilac colour I found in the Woolworths down by Sniff Street Tescos. I never even realised how close it was to the colour of Poppy's kitchen. Or not till I'd started anyway, which I couldn't hardly undo it, could I! I'm like 'Hang about, girl. Ain't you seen this before?' So next night when I gone round I taken a bit, just like dabbed on my inside arm. And when she gone to the toilet I had a quick check. I'm telling you; it could of come from the same fucking tin. Then of course there was all the stuff she'd give me. Like wherever you looked it was all her stuff. Not that there weren't nothing *wrong* with it, you just couldn't help wondering what she'd think, like if I was copying her or whatever. I don't even know what I'm saying to be honest but I can't describe it no clearer.

The night before she come I done this thing, like imagining I was her in my head and I even gone out in the hallway and that, like shutting the door and then walking in to see what she'd think first impression.

I don't think she noticed to tell you the truth, 'cause either way she said nothing. Just sat at the table drinking her wine, as I stood in the kitchen stirring the pasta, testing bits to check how it was doing.

'Half an *hour* should be enough, innit,' I said.

'I should think so,' Poppy said.

'I got to make sure it's cooked!' I said. The pasta come from the Turkish shop. I'd lifted it straightforward enough but cooking the stuff was something else; the instructions was all in Turkish. 'Don't want to send you home sick,' I said. 'You won't come back, will you, if I send you home sick!'

'I'm sure I'll be fine,' she said.

'Here,' I said. 'Here, have a top-up,' I said. 'I'll give it another ten minutes just to be safe.'

I needn't of worried; the pasta was good. Poppy said so herself, it was really good. I done it with tuna and salad cream. 'I can do you some more, if you want,' I said. 'It was lovely,' she said. 'But I'm fine, honestly.' 'Don't want to send you home hungry,' I said. Poppy smiled. 'It was great, but I'm fine.'

'Ain't had no one for dinner in ages,' I said. 'You get out of the habit a bit,' I said.

'I know what you mean,' she said. 'Jesus, do I! I haven't seen a friend in months!

'An *old* friend, I mean,' she said.

'Can I go to the loo?' she said.

'Don't have to ask,' I said. 'Through that door, on the right.'

She was out there for ever. I gone through the kitchen, done the washing-up.

Then I heard her calling. 'N! Is this you?'

'Is what me?' I shouted.

'The picture,' she said.

'What picture,' I said.

'Through here,' she said.

She'd picked up the photo off my bedside table and was stood there looking at it.

'Is it you?' she said.

'It's my mum,' I said.

'The kid,' she said.

'Yeah,' I said. 'Yeah, that's me.'

'Oh look how she's holding you!' she said.

'Is that chocolate?' she said.

'Dunno,' I said.

'Oh look!' she said, laughing. 'It's all over your face!'

She looked at me. 'Oh, N!' she said. 'Come here!' she said, and she give me a hug. 'I'm so sorry,' she said.

'What for?' I said.

She got tears in her eyes. 'Oh, N!' she said.

'S'not *your* fault, is it!' I said.

When we gone back through, Poppy sat on the sofa. We drunk another bottle of wine. 'What are you doing over Christmas?' said Poppy. The Dorothy Fish always closed Christmas Day, and Boxing as well and Good Friday and Easter. And every bank holiday on top. Seemed like they shut more days than they fucking opened. 'Dud's taking Saffra skiing,' she said. 'Or his parents are; they've booked a chalet. His sister and her husband are going with their little boy, Sholto, same age as Saffra. He goes to Dulwich College,' she said. 'Can you imagine? At *seven!*'

'Fuckin'ell!' I said.

'Last year we went to my dad's,' she said. 'I said to Natalie, "Never again!" Pam's like "Make yourselves at home. There's tea and coffee in the corner cupboard." I'm like "Oh, thanks, Pam!" Do you know what I'm saying! I've lived in that house all my fucking life, not that you'd recognise it now. That's the first thing she did was clear everything out, like *everything*; they hired a skip, furniture, carpets, curtains, the lot. Like one of those TV makeover shows, *Changing Places*, do you know what I'm saying! Like my whole fucking childhood, everything gone, every trace of my mum . . .'

I don't know if Poppy'd got a bit pissed or what. The words come spilling out like they'd overfilled her.

'I just want Saffra to know her grandad,' she said. 'Do you know what I'm saying. But he won't stand up to Pam at all. She's painted the sitting room apricot. He's allergic to fucking apricots! Before that it was lemon and before that pink; she changes it every year. Must be fifteen layers on top of Mum now; she'd paint me and Saff out as well if she could.

'That's why I came to London. I was only sixteen. My mum hadn't even been dead a year. It was all so quick. One minute she's working, then she goes to the doctor and three months later she's dead, do you know what I'm saying! Me and Dad are like, 'What happened? Where did she go?' and Pam saw her chance and stepped into the gap; by the time Dad came to she was there. Every picture of Mum disappeared. She even got rid of the cat. 'She gets asthma,' my Dad said. 'From photos?' I said. He's like, 'Don't put me in the middle, Poppy.' 'You *are* in the middle,' I said. 'Face facts. *I* didn't ask her to move in, did I?' 'She's insecure,' he said. 'Give her time.' I think what it was he was scared of being left on his own.

'Sorry,' she said. 'I didn't mean to go on.'

'S'alright,' I said.

'It's just Christmas,' she said. 'Brings it all up, doesn't it?' she said.

'Dunno,' I said.

'What about *you*?' she said. 'What happened with *your* Mum? I mean I know . . .'

'Jumped in front of a train,' I said.

You could tell she was shocked.

'Mill Hill East,' I said.

'How old were you?'

'Twelve.'

'Jesus Christ!' she said.

'Yeah,' I said. 'Know what I'm saying!'

★   ★   ★

In the end Poppy spent Christmas round mine. We just drunk and watched telly and Poppy rung Saffra. It weren't nothing special, but like I said to her after, 'You know some ways, Poppy, that's the best Christmas Day I've had.'

42. How Tony Balaclava
washed his hands

By February Poppy was doing so good, it would of needed a very expert doctor to tell she was putting it on. She taken to boiling the skin off her arms, pouring the water straight out the kettle, dreamily moving the stream up and down, like watering plants, as the skin slid away in sheets. She was pulling her hair out by then as well, not just the odd strand, like huge fucking clumps. Parts of her scalp shown through totally bald like the coat of a mangy dog. You wouldn't of known 'cause she covered it up with this knitted black hat pulled down over her ears and her hair, what was left of it, hidden, pushed up inside. I never even realised myself she was doing it till I walked in her bedroom one time I was round (I'd gone in to borrow some make-up or something) and I found her in front of the chest of drawers, got this mirror on top you could turn different angles, just stood there with her hat in her hand staring at her reflection. She never noticed I'd come in at first, just stood there gazing back at herself, not happy or sad or surprised or nothing, just totally blank like it weren't her at all, like looking at a poster. *I* was quite shocked, do you know what I'm saying. 'Steady on, Poppy!' I said to her. 'You'll be Middle High Middle if you go on like this. Or Middle High Low at any rate. No need to overdo it!' I said. I was joking her but she didn't even smile, jumped a foot in the air and her hat back on quicker than it took to say 'Steady'.

'But I've only got until April,' she said. 'My six months is up in April, N. What if I'm still not on MAD money then? What if they kick me out?' she said. 'There are no guarantees; they got rid of *Brian!*'

'I know,' I said, 'Poppy. I know,' I said. 'But you got to think positive,' I said. 'Look at it this way, Poppy,' I said. 'There ain't hardly nobody left,' I said. 'If you hung in this far, must be doing *something* right!'

It was true there weren't hardly anyone left who'd been there from the beginning. Banker Bill sat in Brian's chair, Professor McSpiegel taken over from Michael – though Michael taken it pretty well. 'No hard feelings,' he said as he left and shaken McSpiegel's hand. Some weren't even *second*-floor flops. Curry *Bob* sat in Candid's chair; Clifton the Poet been and gone and was already back on the seventh. The only originals still left was me, Astrid, Dawn and Sue the Sticks, formerly known as Slasher Sue before she give up self-harming. Omar survived eating pic 'n' mix, used to wind Astrid up something chronic, and Elliot made it through as well, though you wouldn't of known 'cause he stayed in his locker; only opened the door for Poppy, who give him her dinner every day save her having to throw it up.

'Poppy reckons she's going in April,' I said in my one-to-one. 'She ain't though, is she, Tony?' I said.

'I can't discuss Poppy with you,' he said.

'I'm just saying,' I said. 'She ain't ready; that's all.'

'I thought she *wanted* to leave,' he said.

'Well she does,' I said. 'But like not till she's ready. We *all* want to leave when we're ready,' I said. 'But she *ain't* is she, Tony; she's really unwell. I don't like to think if you kicked her out . . .'

Tony didn't answer. He looked like shit. He looked like his skin gone grey in the wash. The rings round his eyes was so dark they looked bruised.

'We *all* want to leave when we're ready,' I said. Do you know what I'm saying, like Shut the Fuck Up!

Suddenly Tony rung this bell; it was a small brass bell on the floor by his chair. I'd never even noticed it was there till he rung it. 'Tingalingaling' and instantly, I mean *instantly* like she must of been waiting, in come that Beverly Perfect woman, carrying this silver bowl with a white towel over her arm. She bent down holding out the bowl, bowing her head so her pony-tail stuck up in the air like a yorkshire terrier's topknot. And I seen the bowl was full of water and Tony started washing his hands and he washed them really careful and thorough like a Brian the Butcher job. Then he taken the towel and wiped them dry and draped it back over her arm. And Beverly Perfect stood up straight and turned and was gone as quick as she come, so you'd almost of thought nothing happened at all if it weren't for the splashes on the carpet.

43. How Tony give us a piece of good news and Middle-Class Michael called a crisis meeting

Assessments was changed from once a month to once a fortnight to once a week. We sat in the common room clutching our chairs like sailors clutching the wreck of our ship, never known when the next wave was coming.

Rosetta got sectioned back on the seventh. They herded her down with the flops for her dinner. She worn a MAD nightdress flapped open up the back, shown us her off-white knickers. 'How you doing, Rosetta?' we'd say and she'd shuffle across to say 'hello' and we'd give her fags, even *Astrid* give her fags.

'Wesley came to see me,' she said. 'Lord knows! He's struggling! "Why did they discharge you?" I said. "'Cause you're well enough to leave! No good weeping and wailing about it; that will just make you feel even worse. You're a good boy," I told him. "Got your whole life ahead. Don't be a fool! You sort yourself!" Lord knows, though! He looked terrible. Not eating, not sleeping, all that business. He'll be back in here before long.' Then one of the seventh-floor nurses would spot her and come and fetch her back into the queue like a cow wandered off from the herd.

Sue the Sticks still seen Verna sometimes. 'But it's just so hard,' she said. 'What do you *say*? I mean, here's me getting all this support and Verna's got nothing. Ain't *right* is it? "Least you got your Scrabble, Vern," I said. I mean, what *else* could I say? But she ain't even doing *that* no more. Lost the urge, that's how she put it. "So what *do* you do?" I says to her. And you know what she said? "I bake cakes," she said. I promised I wouldn't say but I got to. "What sort of cakes do you bake?" I said. "Chocolate, Carrot and Lemon Drizzle." Just like that, no hesitation. And you know what she told me? Every morning, *every* morning, 'cept Sunday when it's closed, she's off down Sniff Street, five-thirty sharp. And you know that twenty-four-hour Tesco, right down the bottom?' 'No,' we said. 'Well, there *is* one,' said Sue. 'She walks right down there, miles it must be, and she buys all her ingredients, then she carries them all the way back. You know eggs and flour, muscovado sugar, caster sugar, lemons, cocoa – heavy, you know; must hurt her hands. Then as soon as she's home it's straight in the kitchen and weighing and measuring and mixing them up; the chocolate then the carrot then the lemon drizzle, always that order, one straight after the other. While they're baking she goes for a run. Up Paradise Park and four times round, twenty-eight minutes exactly. Then she turns them out and leaves them to cool, while she washes the tins and the mixing bowl and the scales and the grater and the jug and stuff, really slow, like taking her time 'cause she can't do nothing till nine. At nine exactly she does the toppings, chocolate fudge with all curls of chocolate and the carrot cake icing with walnuts all round and when she's finished she clears up again, bags the leftover ingredients and takes them out to the rubbish.

'At half-nine, she says, she's allowed a slice. She can choose which cake to take it from but she tells herself after she's ate that slice, she's not allowed nothing more for seven hours. Inside of ten minutes all three cakes have gone and inside of twenty she's chucked them back up and inside of a half hour she's heading back down to Tesco's. Four times a day, she's doing it,' said Sue. 'Can you imagine? Four times a day! Two grand she told me she owes on her card. "Visa!" I said. "What you doing with a Visa?" "Dunno," she said. "They just give it to me." "You got to stop," I says to her. "Cut down at least, maybe three cakes a day." But it's the only thing gets her through, she says. What sort of a life is that!'

Not much of a life is what we reckoned, and the more we heard about the dribblers who'd left the more desperate we was to stay. No one weren't taking no chances now; we madded it up so concerted and thorough the wards looked like Sniff Street compared. Omar overdone it in fact, took all his clothes off in Relaxation, done like this headstand against the wall and sung the National Anthem. He would of gone upstairs Rhona said, if he hadn't recovered hisself so quick and decided her not to tell Tony. He would of gone up and Owen come down that was how close he come to it.

Fat Florence was s'posed to have Faith's empty chair, next to Omar Bombing, but she said she weren't moving so much as a muscle till Second-Floor Paolo been given his rightful and nobody else shouldn't neither. And she sat there besides him day after day, arms folded like huge wings across her chest, staring daggers at Poppy. But it didn't make no difference how evil she looked, weren't nothing compared to the view behind: the whole of London spread out like a giant warning.

So there we all are one afternoon, what's left of us, and the flops down the sides – disgusting they was to be perfectly honest, even Jacko the Penguin said they made him feel sick, and he'd *been* a flop till the week before. 'Like vultures,' said Tadpole, 'that's what they are!' 'No self-respect!' said Curry Bob. 'Waiting to pick our bones,' said Tadpole, when suddenly there's this rolling of drums, like *seriously*, a rolling of drums, like 'Prrrrrrrrrrrrrrrrrrr! Prrrrrrrrrrrrrrrrrrr! Prrrrrrrrrrrrrrrrrrrrrrrrrrrrrrrrrrrrrrrrrrrrrrrrrrrrr!' and the double swing-doors swing open wide and three flops jump up start blasting three golden trumpets. Then in comes this man in a dark grey suit, shiny shoes, shirt, tie, everything, and he ain't so much walking as bouncing towards us, like the shit-coloured carpet got springs under-neath, and he's beaming all over and rubbing his hands and looking so general pleased with hisself that the flops, who ain't got separate minds of their own, just pick up the mood like plants pick up weather, they all start up clapping and cheering and whooping till he holds up his hands and they all fall silent 'cept Schizo Safid who does this wolf-whistle. 'Thank you, Safid!' the man says, laughing. And it ain't till then, it ain't till he *speaks*, and even then, do you know what I'm saying, it ain't till then I got to admit what my eyes have been seeing but my brain won't believe, that this Kellogg's Cornflakes Sunshine Man is Tony Balaclava.

The flops all start clapping and cheering again and he raises his arms in a giant 'V'; his hair's different too, not a purdy no more, like all short up the sides and all smooth on the top. 'Everyone!' he goes. 'Everyone! We've just had some wonderful news!

'I've just this second come off the phone to the Ministry for Madness! [*loud cheers*], I'm thrilled, I'm delighted; above all I'm honoured, to be able to tell you the Dorothy Fish has been shortlisted for Beacon of Excellence status! [*cheers, whoops, whistles, stamping of feet*] Allow me to read you something!' he said, and he reached a hand in the pocket of his suit, pulled out this leaflet, scanned it a sec then held up a finger. 'Here we are!' he said. ' "To be awarded Beacon of Excellence status [*cheers, whoops, whistles, stamping of feet*] . . . To be awarded Beacon of Excellence status [*cheers, whoops, whistles; Tony held up a finger*], an institution must consistently offer a standard of service of *such a level as to serve as a guide and inspiration to others in the same field.* A Beacon of Excellence [*cheers, whoops, whistles*] . . . A Beacon of Excellence denotes that the said institution has achieved *a 'good' or 'very good' service rating* in *each of the five key target areas* of mental-healthcare delivery. [*By this time the flops was like hugging each other. Fat Cath sat back gazing at Tony, fanning herself with a blue paper towel as the tears streamed down from her eyes.*] Beacons of Excellence enjoy a degree of autonomy. Freed from direct line management by the Ministry for Madness, they are able to vary staff pay and conditions . . ." In other words,' says Tony, slipping the leaflet back in his pocket. 'In other words, thanks to all of *you*, every single one of you here, the Dorothy Fish has been singled out as one of the highest performing day hospitals in the country! [*whoop, whoop, whistle*], I'm proud of the service we offer here, I'm proud of my team, their commitment and vision, but most of all I'm proud of our service users! [*He started to clap, like slow and deliberate, turning each side, and behind him as well and the flops was going crazy all screaming and stamping and Fag Ash Devine thrown a pair of her knickers*] Come on!' shouted Tony. 'Applaud yourselves! [*and slowly us dribblers begun to join in*] Don't clap me; clap each other!' he shouted. 'Go on! *Tell* each other, "Well done!" [*'Well done,' we's all muttering, 'Well done, well done' – under our breath, do you know what I'm saying, never felt like such a fucking arse in my life, but I s'pose with everyone like doing it you stopped being embarrassed after a bit and soon we was shouting across to each other. 'Well done, N!' shouts Sue the Sticks. 'Well done, Astrid! Well done, Tadpole!' 'Well done you,' shouts Tadpole back. 'Well done, Poppy! Well done, N!' Poppy didn't answer, but I done for us both. 'Well done, Sue the Sticks!' I said. 'Well done, Tadpole! Well done, Professor!' I did, I give Max McSpiegel 'Well done!' And then, and then Astrid turns to me and she holds out her arms, she's got tears in her eyes. 'Oh well done, N!' she says. 'Well done. Oh N, come here,' she says. 'Well done!' and she smothers me up in this massive pink hug. Do you know what I'm saying, proper bury the hatchet time!*]'

But Tony weren't the only one with a piece of news up his sleeve. When we come out the Abaddon that night, who should me and Poppy run into but Middle-Class Michael sat on the wall by the entrance. 'Michael!' I said. 'You heard the news! We got Beacon of Excellence innit now!' '*Short* listed,' he said. 'I know. You've still the final inspection to come . . .' 'Alright,' I said, 'Michael! Nit-picking!' 'We're calling a meeting tonight,' he said. 'Dark-woods drop-in. Seven o'clock. It's absolutely essential you

come. *Both* of you,' he said, looking at Poppy. I seen his
eyes jolt like he sat on a pin. 'What's it about?' I said. 'Be
there!' he said. 'It's a crisis. I can't tell you now, but just
make sure you're there.'

44. How I shown them the back of my head, every single one of them

I weren't even going to go to the meeting, was I, anyway. Poppy weren't going. 'I can't!' she said. 'What do you mean you can't?' I said. 'I can't,' she said, 'I'm meeting Dud.' '*Dud!*' I said. 'What you meeting *Dud* for?' 'I don't know,' she said. 'He wants to talk . . . About Saffra,' she said. 'Oh, right,' I said. 'And what Dud wants, Dud gets,' I said. 'Don't, N!' she said. 'Please. Please, don't!'

To be honest, I was a bit pissed off. It weren't like I wanted to go to the meeting, I could think of plenty of stuff I'd rather than spending all evening sat in a room with the same bunch of dribblers I'd spent all fucking day with. But Poppy, she never done *nothing* no more, do you know what I'm saying; she was getting as bad as what *they* was. I'm like 'Why don't we go into town tonight? We could go to a club, get a Chinese or something.' But Poppy just stares at me, like '*Town?*' like I'm saying let's go to the fucking moon; I'm like, 'Alright, let's get a DVD, if you ain't in the mood for going out.' Do you know what I'm saying, like bent over *backwards*, but she don't feel 'up' to a DVD, so I'm 'Alright, what *do* you feel like doing?' and she's 'Maybe I'll just get an early night.' And not just the once, I mean the *whole fucking time.* I'm like, 'Lighten up!' do you know what I'm saying, 'You ain't in a concentration camp!' I mean I never *said* that, but I *felt* like it. 'You ain't dying of cancer; do you know what I'm saying!' I'm like pull yourself together!

I made myself pasta with pesto sauce and when I'd ate it I sat on the sofa, smoked three whole packs of B&H straight, and tried to work out when Poppy had got so boring. And I'm not being funny but it seemed like years, it seemed like fucking *centuries* ago we gone to the cinema that first time, shared a bucket of popcorn, best night of my life; now she weren't no different from the rest of them, like all she fucking cared about was getting through her next assessment. And then I suppose I just decided I might as well *go* to the meeting, like nothing to lose, do you know what I'm saying; it weren't like she give me a whole lot of choice side of staying sat in on my own.

I was late. As I gone down the steps to the drop-in, I seen through the windows everyone already there. Michael up one end, stood on a crate, and this whole crowd of dribblers like squeezed on to sofas and sat on the floor and perched on the tables, and crammed in five deep at the back. There was Dawn, sat next to Robert the Cab, and Wesley and Chip and Swiller Steve; and then I seen Astrid; she never seen me, she was sat half-turned away from the window, gazing up at Middle-Class Michael, licking her lips and lapping up every word, but there was something about the way she was, I couldn't of said no more than that, it was like some sort of a stunk she give off, do you know what I'm saying, I *knew* I was in the shit. Then Verna right, ain't seen her in months, she suddenly looks up and clocks me. And she says something and everyone turns, and suddenly everyone's staring at me, the whole fucking lot of them staring at me, the whole fucking lot of them lit up inside and staring outside at me.

'Uh, oh, girl!' I says to myself but I walked past and rung the buzzer, ain't no scuttler.

It was Jike on. She answered the door, 'We haven't seen *you* for a bit,' she said. Dawn's tables was all piled up in the hall, stacked both sides, as high as the ceiling; you walked down a tunnel between them. 'Can I get you a cup of tea?' she said. You could tell she knew. 'I'm fine,' I said. I gone past her into the sitting room.

You never heard nothing so deafening loud as the silence of all of them dribblers. I could hear my own tea churning round in my stomach; the taste of pesto come back in my mouth as they parted to let me walk through. 'Alright everyone?' I said, 'Alright Rosetta.' There she was, must of come down to the Darkwoods special, still in her Abaddon nightie. 'Alright Candid Headphones,' I said; she'd even turned her music off. 'Alright Tadpole. Alright Brian. You done your checking,' I said. I was only being friendly, but no one said nothing. Weren't like I give a shit, know what I'm saying, but you couldn't help feeling edgy. 'Zubin!' I said, 'cause I suddenly seen him, stood by the notice-board. Got this red-and-white scarf tied round his head. 'Didn't recognise you!' I said. 'Thought you was a *pirate*, stood there!' Not one of them laughed. 'So where's the treasure?' I said.

Weren't nowhere to sit, so I just got to stand there. Everyone staring. Total fucking silence.

'N,' said Middle-Class Michael. He coughed and pulled at his nose and his ears gone red.

'Ain't *her* fault!' said Sue the Sticks suddenly. 'Ain't *N's* fault, is it, Verna!' she said but everyone told her to shush. I don't know why 'cause I weren't upset, but I felt these tears well up in my eyes and for one awful moment I thought I was going to start crying.

'You haven't brought Poppy?' Michael said.

'Ain't her fucking keeper,' I said, least I would of. I couldn't; just stood there.

'It ain't though, is it?' said Sue the Sticks. 'How was *she* s'posed to know? None of *us* realised, did we?'

'She's right,' said Rosetta.

Astrid tutted.

'I'm not *sure*,' said Verna. 'I thought there was *something*.'

'It was obvious!' said Astrid. 'I knew it. The way she waltzed in with her nose in the air. I said to myself, "Steer clear of that!" It's just a pity . . .'

'Hold on!' said Rosetta. 'You really *can't* blame *N*!'

But Astrid Arsewipe said she could, and what was more than that she would, and what was more than either of them she weren't about to be told what to do by a fucking flop thanks very much! Which gone down about how you might expect and inside of around two seconds flat, the whole room's scrapping and hurling crap, slippers and trainers and mugs of tea – a Big Mac Happy Meal flown past my nose – being about half for and half against whatever it was they was scrapping about: me, I suppose, at the end of the day, not that none of them couldn't remember.

The weird thing was the longer I stood there, the more I just didn't give a shit. I don't want to sound ungrateful or nothing, fact sometimes that worries me a bit, like Rosetta and Sue, do you know what I'm saying, but the fact of it was that the longer I stood there, and Middle-Class Michael coughing and stamping – 'This is *no* way to conduct a meeting. I must ask you to *control* yourselves' – I felt the tears dried up from my eyes and then suddenly, it was only a moment, it was like I risen above them all, and I mean that literal, 'risen above'. My feet, they stayed where they was, by the crate, splintered it was now from Michael's stamping, but the rest of me, it was like I grown, like all in an instant as tall as the sky and I'm looking down and I can't hardly see them, like ants scrapping over a couple of crumbs and taller until I can't see them at all and the whole of the Darkwoods the size of my fist, and the tower, one finger, 'Up yours!' in the middle.

Then just as quick I'm back down to myself, normal size, in my trainers, and Michael's explaining all about Poppy and everyone's quiet, 'cept a tatty old slipper, a Coke can and two MAD money forms, still flying back and forth till they's evens.

Looking back, I fucked some things up. Maybe I fucked a lot of things up. My whole life even, except for the parts what hadn't already been fucked up for me before I was even born. But if there's one thing I'm proud of, still to this day, if there's one thing I want them to play at the end, do you know what I'm saying, like my *Big Brother* highlights, it's when I walked out of that drop-in. I turned round. Never said one single word. I waited till Michael had finished his bit, then I turned round and shown him the back of my head. I could feel them all waiting, like holding their breath, and I walked, didn't look, just walked straight out the door, and I shown them *all* the back of my head, and I turned and I walked down the tunnel of tables, heard Jike behind me: 'N,' she said.

And I shown *her* the back of my head and all, then I opened the door and gone out.

By the time I reached Poppy's it must of been midnight, or maybe even later. I know it was after one when the ambulance come.

In between, I'd been walking about, not going no-where special, just walking about. I maybe gone in a couple of pubs, but mostly I just kept walking. Eventually I wound up on Borderline Road and I kept walking on and on. It was cold. I walked fast. Started raining a bit. I remember the feel of the wet on my face and the street lights reflecting off the shiny pavement. And all the time just this one single word, I kept on repeating it over and over, turning it round and around in my mouth, like chewing gum, till it lost all flavour, over and over and round and around, till it didn't got no meaning, just a series of sounds, and I kept on repeating it, 'Normal. Normal. Normal.'

An hour gone by, maybe two, even three; I was just at the bottom of Abaddon Hill where it crosses Borderline Road and turns into Sniff Street. 'Fuckin'ell girl!' I says to myself, like snapping out of a trance. 'How many times you crossed over this junction! You must of walked round that hill seventy times! Do you know what I'm saying!' I said to myself. 'I *thought* you was getting shorter!' And I laughed; I did. I laughed so loud, that gum I'd been chewing shot out of my mouth, done this massive arc over Borderline Road and stuck to the window of Leech's. Which if you don't believe me, you can still see it now; if you stand and look up outside Café Diana at the blue plastic letters transferred on the glass, first 'O' of 'SOLICITORS', bang in the middle: bull's-eye.

Then without even really thinking about it, instead of crossing Abaddon Hill I done a left, over Borderline Road, and set off down Sniff Street for Poppy's. I don't know if all of that going round and round, it done something weird or what – like winding up one of them Happy Meal toys – but all of a sudden I'm wanting to skip and I can't see no reason why *not* to start skipping, so I do, and I'm laughing and skipping along and I ain't even out of breath, know what I'm saying, and I run a bit too, and my body feels light and I know I could run round the world.

It was hours before Poppy answered the buzzer and when she did she dropped the phone, then she clattered around for another hour picking it up.

'Whoothhaa?' she said.

'It's me,' I said.

'Whoothmee?' she said.

'It's me!' I said. 'Open the door.'

Now anyone who knows me, have to say I was easy going. But if there's one thing fucking winds me up it's dribblers overdosing. Ain't saying I never done it myself, ain't saying I'm perfect neither, but there I am with my wine in the one hand, my Phileas Fogg's in the other (twenty-four hour shop, no questions asked), bounding up the stairs three at a time, 'Poppy!' I'm shouting. 'Listen to this!' Someone hammered on a wall but I give them fuck off, weren't nothing couldn't dampen my spirits. 'Poppy! It's all OK! It's fine! You're normal, Poppy; you ain't mad at all. I got proof!' I shouted. 'Open the door!' I'd reached her landing but she hadn't come out. 'I got wine,' I shouted. 'I'm leaving as well! I'm going to be a receptionist. We can work together! Open the door!' Then slowly she opened the door.

It weren't even hardly an overdose what Poppy had took, do you know what I'm saying. Fifteen Plutuperidol. She'd bought them off Banker Bill. But it was still enough to write off the celebrations.

'Dithuun mean id, N,' she said. 'Pleasth dhon be aaangry. I dithuuun mean id!'

'But there ain't nothing *wrong* with you!' I said. 'That's the whole fucking point! You was right all along!'

Poppy frowned at me, gone slightly cross-eyed. 'Whawhathaa?' she said.

'You's *normal*,' I said. 'That's *why* they picked you. They needed somebody normal,' I said. 'They been measuring us lot against you,' I said.

'Whafffor?' she said. 'Whaddyoutalkingabou?'

'I'm saying there ain't nothing *wrong* with you!' I was shouting by now, you just couldn't get through, like talking to someone who didn't speak English. 'Middle-Class Michael can *prove* it,' I said. 'They been using you like a fucking bench!'

'Dithuunn mean id, N,' she said. Her knees give way and she slid down on to the floor.

45. How 17 March was a sad day for anyone, cares about truth and justice

Next day when I gone up the Dorothy Fish, I never even made it as far as the first-floor common room. You could hear the shouting from down in the lobby. 'Sounds like the shit's hit the fan,' said Sharon, and he winked at me as he give me my pass. I couldn't believe he done it.

But as soon as I gone through the sliding doors I caught the force full in my face. You never heard shouting so loud in your life! It whirled round your ears like a fucking tornado; it whirled around Abaddon Patients' Rights, whirled all the leaflets out of the racks, whirled them around and around in the air so I had to keep batting them off with my arms to force my way through to the stairs. All up the stairs it got louder and louder till everything was vibrating with sound and the stairs shooking so bad beneath my feet, I thought they was going to collapse. It weren't till I got to the first-floor landing, I started to make out the separate words 'cause even though it was still fucking loud, it weren't like the same distorted.

'Compromise!' it gone. 'Compromise! There's nothing else *left* to compromise!'

Someone said something; you couldn't hear what.

'But Tony, that's the whole damn point!' Jesus! I thought, that's Rhona the Moaner. Wonder what's ruffled *her* feathers! 'She could have been *killed*! What's happened to you!'

Tony said something else; I'd of give my MAD money to know what it was he said.

'No, Tony! No! This has all gone too far!'

Tony said something else.

'The *Beacon*!' she screamed. 'You think I give a *shit* about the *Beacon*?! You know what you can do with your *Beacon*; you can stick it up your sad little arse!'

Then suddenly she's storming down the corridor towards me. You never seen no one so mad in your life! I swear to God; her eyes was balls of fire.

Fowler stuck his head out the staffroom doorway. 'Get off of your moral high horse!' he yelled.

And you know what she done, that Rhona the Moaner! Without even looking back, she give him two Vs up high in the air, and she kept them up too, all the way down the stairs, which I know 'cause I seen from the landing.

'What's so funny?' shouts Malvin Fowler. I made like I never heard him. 'Oi!' he gone. 'N! Wipe that smirk off your face, and down here; Tony wants you.'

For three weeks after they kicked me out, all I done was lain in bed. Didn't eat, didn't smoke, didn't take my meds even, just lain on my side underneath the duvet and stared at the clock on the table beside my pillow. The furthest I gone was through to the bathroom, taken a drink out the tap, then I'd fit myself back in the hollow I'd left, like climbing back into my polystyrene packing.

Hours I lain there, watching each minute come and go on the clock. Sometimes there seemed like so many of them I couldn't believe I'd get through. I set myself landmarks like 5.45; if I could make it to 5.45 that meant it was only forty-five minutes until it would be 6.30. I got through whole days, whole nights like that. It was like I was waiting for something but I didn't know what.

That first afternoon I thought I was waiting for Poppy, but when she knocked on the door, 17.03, my body wouldn't move. 'N,' she called, 'open the door; it's me!' It was like I was froze, just my eyes staring out, like holes in the ice on a pond. 'Come on, N; I know you're in there!' 17.03 seemed to last forever but eventually it become 17.04. 'N, everyone's really upset you've gone . . . They all saying it's *my* fault . . . N *please* let me in!' But I couldn't; I just couldn't move. 17.05, 17.06. At 17.12 Poppy gone.

All night I lain there watching the minutes. I ain't saying I was hoping exactly. I weren't feeling nothing, just stared at the clock, but when 9.30 come and she hadn't been back, I felt something then, like a sort of a panic, like all of the minutes I got to get through until 17.03.

She was early that night, more like twenty to five, must of run from the Dorothy Fish. 'I've brought you some cigarettes,' she said. 'N, please let me in. I need to talk . . . I don't know what to think anymore, N. Tony says it isn't true. He says if there's nothing wrong with me, then why did I take an overdose? I don't know what to do, N. Please! I haven't got anywhere else to go . . . I'm sorry. I'm really sorry, N.' She was crying. I lain there, stared at the clock. 'N, I'm worried about you. Are you OK? Just say something, please. Let me know you're alright . . .'

I felt bad, I did, just laying there, but I couldn't do

nothing about it. A couple of tears rolled out my eyes into the pillow.

'I've got to go. Dud's bringing Saffra round. I'll come back tomorrow. Please N, don't . . .' There was a patter as something hit the floor. 16.53 and she was gone.

At 19.26 I got up, opened the hall door and there it was, a pack of Bensons, stood on one end, under the letter-box.

At 21.03 I gone back. The packet was still there.

It was still there at 22.12 as well.

At 23.10 I picked it up and taken it back to bed. Didn't smoke them or nothing, didn't open them even, just lain there holding them tight in my hand till the cellophane felt damp against my palm.

9.30 was the deadline; I give her till 9.34. When she still hadn't come, I gone through the hall and picked up my backpack, still on the floor where I'd dumped it when I got home. I knew my biro was in there somewhere but with so much other crap as well, I had to lug it back through to the bedroom and sit on my bed to go through it. You'd never believe how much crap there was, you had to dig down through the layers like mining. Top layer was mainly make-up and shit – twelve different tubes of lip gloss I counted, from Violet Candy to Midnight Shimmer – then underneath that come *Marie Claire* and this book I'd picked up round Poppy's one time called *Bridget Jones' Diary*; we seen the film, it was alright, a bit far-fetched. Then a mass of crumpled MAD money giros, a letter from MAD to Poppy saying how she'd failed her appeal and a couple of copies of *Abaddon Patients' News*. There was a sheet of paper with typing on too which I couldn't work out where it come from: 'Irrespective of claims to the contrary which have been made by a number of prominent historians, most notably Schatten (*Zeitschrift für Psychiatrische Geschichte* 30/31 1973 S.241–282), the Abaddon's introduction of the Whirling Chair for the treatment of melancholia predates its arrival at Bethlem by more than a month . . .' then I noticed a number at the bottom of the page like 11,248, and I smiled despite of how low I was, remembering how we got stuck in the lift, me and Poppy, with Max McSpiegel; somehow or other a page of his book must of wound up inside of my backpack. My lucky biro was right at the bottom in a pile of empty meds bottles.

I written on the back of the MAD money letter:

I'M ALLRIGHT
GO AWAY

Then I read it a few times, thought for a bit and added, 'Thanks for the fags' underneath. I glued it to the door so's the writing shown through the glass and gone back to bed.

When she come that night 16.48, Poppy didn't even knock. She just called through the letter-box. 'Alright N, I'll leave you if that's what you want.' And then she gone. 'Fuck off then,' I said out loud. 'Yeah, that's right, just fuck off like everyone else!' and I picked up the photo of me and my mum and lobbed it across the room so hard it gouged a great chunk out the top of the wall near the ceiling.

The banging seemed to come right inside; it was like someone hammered on my coffin. I thought they'd come to section me. I knew they was coming. They *got* to be coming. I was a danger to myself if not to nobody else. I'd of killed myself already except for I couldn't be arsed.

'N, it's Poppy. I've *got* to talk to you . . . N, please, if you're there; it's really important. It's Saffra, N; I'm fucking desperate!' The letter-box flapped shut. I didn't move.

I never seen the note at first, there was so much crap by the door. A hundred pizza menus easy, Chinese and Indian twenty-five each, six minicab cards, two *Council News*, two MAD money giros. It was kind of a shock to realise how long I must of been laying in bed. Then I noticed this envelope: Poppy Shakespeare, Flat 6, 43 Selby Street, and I thought, like this is how fucked I was, I thought, 'That's weird. What's the chances of that!' I mean, I used to get stuff for Rapper Rashid, do you know what I'm saying, and him for me, fact everyone in Rowan Walk got everyone else's post all the time, which being as they was mainly just take-away menus it didn't make much difference. But this was a proper coincidence. I mean, Poppy lived maybe a mile away, unless there was *another* Poppy Shakespeare, but she'd still have to live at the same address . . . I picked it up to have a look and that's when I seen the writing on the back:

N, I HAVE TO SPEAK TO YOU! I REALLY NEED YOU TO HELP ME PLEASE!!!!! WILL COME BACK TOM (SAT). IT'S VERY IMPORTANT!!!!! PLEASE LET ME IN.
    POPPY x
    PS HOPE YOU'RE OK

When she come I was waiting. Been waiting for hours. Sat on the floor of the hall since 5.03. I could see her through the frosted glass of the door, bits of paper still stuck to it where I'd pulled the letter off, could see the shape of her head in the hat as I sat on the floor looking up.

I opened the door before she knocked. 'N!' she said and she give me a hug. 'I'm sorry,' she said. We was hugging and crying. 'You look awful,' she said. I felt it again: my mum wrapped around me, warm and strong, the softness of her jumper against my cheek, the smell of her, the sense of home. 'I'm never leaving you ever again,' which we both of us believed it for a moment.

The knock on the glass brought me back where I was, still sat there on the floor of the hall, the cold radiator dugging into my spine. 'N,' said Poppy. 'Are you there? It's me.'

I remember being surprised I didn't move.

'N? Are you there?' She knew I was there. 'N, please let me in. Please! I need your help. Dud wants custody of Saffra, N. I've had a letter from his solicitor. He says it's bad for her living with me. It's his parents; I fucking know it is. He says I can't take care of her. Do you think that's true? Do you think I can't? Maybe I can't, N; what do you think? Do you think she'd be better without me, N? Please talk to me!' She started to cry. 'I'm sorry, N.' She was crying really bad. The words come out all juddery. 'I jjjust dddon't know what the fuck to ddoooo.'

You couldn't make out half of what she was saying; she was so upset she could hardly breathe. Saffra's teacher was really worried. Saffra'd begun self-harming herself. I caught like a line of it here and there as I gradually realised I weren't going to move, which I know it sounds bad but I honestly *couldn't*. I'd of stood more chance being paralysed, least I could of blown through a straw.

Eventually she calmed down enough that the words come through again. Then she stopped crying completely, some ways that was worse; her voice sounded hollow and empty.

'Tony says I need to see the MAD inspector. She's coming to the assessments on Friday. He says if I can convince her I'm fine, they're happy to discharge me. There's no way they can take Saffra then. But what I'm worried about is those MAD money forms. What if she knows about them, N? What if she's read all that stuff we wrote? What if she thinks it's true, what then?

'Please, N, please will you say it was you! I'll tell them you were helping me out. I'll say I was desperate. I was; it's true. You'll do it, won't you? You'll help me? N?

'It's his parents; I fucking know it is. They've always wanted me out the way. I wouldn't be surprised if it was them all along. Do you know what I'm saying, they've got the money. It's all who you know at the end of the day. They had me admitted so they'd get Saffra. They planned it. They've been bugging my flat. There's nothing fucking wrong with me. It's a set-up, N; they're all in on it; Tony, Diabolus, everyone.

'There's nothing wrong with me, is there, N? You told me I'm normal; that's the reason I'm there.

'You don't think I'm bad for Saffra, N?'

I could see her hands against the glass. Her palms was pressed white against the glass. 'Do you think she'd be better without me, N?

'N? Do you think I'm losing it?'

As she turned away, I felt it again: that terrible sense of endless nothing. The TV room at Sunshine House, the magnolia walls smeared with scrubbed-out graffitti, where they told me my mum was dead.

I got up. I banged on the glass. 'Wait!' I shouted. For a second I thought she was still stood there. But all it was was my own reflection looked back at me.

46. How I done my best to be a good friend, despite of everything

It taken me hours to get ready. It was 6 a.m. when I run the bath. I soaked for a bit, just to loosen the dirt then starting from the tips of my toes I lathered upwards inch by inch. My toes, then my feet, then my legs to the knee, then I stood up and finished the rest of me, slow and methodic inch by inch, taking care not to leave no spaces. From the tips of my toes to behind my ears, front and back, was a bottle of Dove, which just goes to show how much weight I'd lost; two and a half I'd of took before, easy, fact I'd lifted three down the Turkish shop just to be sure. When I'd finished, I shaved my legs; I'd lifted the razor as well, old habits die hard. Then I washed my hair with a mug in the sink as the steel-grey scum of a month in bed gurgled out down the bathtub plug hole. After that I had another bath and I washed my hair again and after a third bath there weren't nothing left, not a mark on me from top to toe, aside of my scars what wouldn't come off if I scrubbed for the rest of forever.

I'd lost so much weight, when I tried to get dressed my clothes was falling off of me. Even the new clothes I'd bought with Poppy; that denim skirt I'd been planning to wear, it looked like I'd borrowed it off of Fat fucking Florence. It weren't just the fact I hadn't ate for three weeks; I hadn't took no meds. And especially the Plutuperidol, puffs you up something chronic, remember Tadpole. I'd been on anti-psychotics *all my life*, do you know what I'm saying, taken Parazine along with my mother's breast milk so I s'pose it weren't surprising when you took out the stopper to find half of me disappeared. The skinny me – I was almost *skinny!* – it didn't even *look* nothing like the old N and it weren't going to share no clothes with her. So I tried on a couple of things of Poppy's, them clothes I'd rescued from Oxfam, and they fitted like I'd bought them new, only the skirt left a button undone; and the top was a little bit tight across you-know-where. By the time I'd straightened my hair with the irons and wet it again and done it again and wet it again and done it *again* and it *still* got a kink but that might of been intended, it was 07:58. I put on my make-up like Poppy had shown me, a layer of foundation worked on with a sponge, then Touche Eclat smeared under your eyes and another layer of foundation on top – Poppy never said that, but I reckoned it looked better. I used eye-shadow, pencil, mascara and curlers, liquid gold the eye-shadow was, it come in a tube and cost so much I reckon it got real gold in. Poppy said make-up should always look subtle, which meant you could hardly see it at all; I said 'I ain't spending six months' MAD money on something you can't even see.' Truth is since I'd begun wearing make-up my confidence gone up and I reckoned I had a bit of a flair, not bragging I mean, I just knew what looked good, or what looked good on *me*. And not being funny, do you know what I'm saying, but Poppy weren't hardly best placed to comment, fact I'd have to say something one of these days, like just as a friend, once we'd got her discharged – and Saffra back home, if that's what she wanted. 'Poppy,' I'd say, 'I'm not being funny, but you should make a bit more of yourself.' I given my cheekbones a dusting of pink, proper cheekbones now I got, and finished my lips with three layers of Violet Candy. I could of worked on a make-up counter to look at me, which ain't big-headed; I'm just saying how I looked. And it was Poppy I done it for anyway, I needed to look my best; ain't much point having a dribbler turn up to tell everyone you's normal.

As soon as you walked in the Dorothy Fish, you could tell they was doing an inspection. The notice-boards on the first-floor landing was covered in bright-coloured posters and leaflets with all of these groups you could do and shit and all of these trips you could sign up for, like ten-pin bowling and the Science Museum and the Dorothy Fish Day Out to BRIGHTON!!! It made you want to puke. There was even a notice how Tony Balaclava was running the London Marathon to raise funds for MIND. 'COME AND CHEER HIM ON!' it said, like we's one big happy family, like any dribbler in his right mind show his face within ten miles of the race or even watch it on telly case Tony seen him, reckoned he must of gone normal. It weren't even nine yet; the common room was empty. The shit-coloured carpet been scrubbed so hard reckon Minimum Wage scrubbed her fingers off. It weren't even shit-coloured properly no more, just a dishwater grey like she'd scrubbed all the colour out of it. There was a new pot plant where the dead one been what Paolo had curled hisself under that day, when Pollyanna gone and the whole thing started.

I didn't hang about in the common room. To be honest,

I started to feel a bit weird. Not like I got second thoughts or nothing but you know what I'm saying, I could of slipped back so easy, just sat in the 'N' chair, smoked a quick fag, feet on the table and before you knew it another thirteen years had gone by; it was like that the Dorothy Fish. I gone in the toilets, gleaming they was, paper and everything. 'Alright, Fran,' I said, but she give me 'Fuck off!', 'Fuck off yourself,' I said. 'Stupid cow!' And again it felt like slipping back. Like Cinderella sworn at the ball. 'You'd better hope Poppy's up first, girl,' I says, ' 'Cause you ain't going to last till midnight.'

As I come out the toilets what should I see but the great fat arse of Malvin Fowler, squeezed into a light grey suit and heading off down the corridor. I watched as he gone past the staff room, the art room, the room where they held the one-to-ones; when he stopped outside Dawn's wood workshop I thought he was going to go in, but it must be his ear was itching him 'cause he stuck in a finger and wagged it about, checking the end, then wiping it clean on his trousers before going on.

When he got to the door of the theatre I seen him stop again, and this time he taken something out the pocket of his jacket. I couldn't work out what it was at first; it was square and flat, 'bout the size of a visitor's pass. He held it up in front of his face, started smoothing his hair this way and that, tilting his head to see if he'd covered his bald patch. Then he checked his teeth, quick glance up his nose, a final once-over and slipped it back in his pocket. I held it until he gone inside, then I practically pissed myself laughing. 'Come on Poppy,' I says out loud. 'Get a move on, you's missing the party.'

I hung around for fucking ever but Poppy never shown up. And neither did nobody else, come to that, not a flop not a dribbler, nobody; I started to get a feeling something weren't right.

I couldn't of told you why it was I set off down the corridor, or why my heart was thumping so loud, or how come I found the door so easy when Verna and Sue been looking for months. A seventh sense I s'pose is what you'd call it.

They's all sat around of this great shiny table. Fifteen of them maybe, all in suits and each with a little plastic sign tell everyone who they is. There's Dr Diabolus sat at the head and Azazel and Clootie, one either side, and this woman I never seen before with a mole on her chin and three black whiskers sprouted out of it. All down the middle there's jugs of water and little stacks of glasses. And the lights from the ceiling bounce off of the water and ripple all over the table.

The reason the water's rippling is Tony Balaclava. Tony's sat with his back to me but I can see his face reflecting off of the table. He's reeling off this list of figures: 'Self-harm down 600%; paranoia 850%.' And every time he says a number he bangs on the table with his small tight fist, like an auctioneer's hammer. The woman with the mole sits nodding her head and the doctors all sit nodding their heads and everyone's like nodding their heads and rippling into each other. 'Since the introduction of our control, day-patient discharge rates have increased by 2450%, even allowing for seasonal variation.'

'Most impressive,' the woman says.

'The most tentative projection . . .'

'Excuse me?' I jumped round. Beverly Perfect was stood in the doorway, holding a tray of sangers. 'I'm not sure you're s'posed to be in here.'

'Says who?' I says.

She looks at me. Ain't nothing rippling 'bout Beverly Perfect.

'Are you a patient?'

'Do I *look* like a dribbler?'

'I'll have to ask you to leave,' she says.

'I want to see Poppy. Where is she?' I says.

It was something about the look on her face. I seen it before. Twenty years before nearly. The TV room at Sunshine House. 'I'm sorry,' she said. 'I'm afraid . . .'

'No!' I shouted. 'No she ain't! She can't of done! There's nothing the fucking matter with her!' The shouting must of brought everyone out 'cause suddenly there's Tony and Malvin pushing their way in the viewing room and somebody's grabbing my legs from behind and Dr Azazel's got hold of my wrist. I can see the woman, the one with the mole, watching me from the doorway.

'You can't believe them!' I said to her. 'You can't! They never helped nobody! They set it up from the start,' I said, 'cause I got it now, I finally got it, the whole fucking twisted picture. 'That's why they made me her guide,' I said. 'That's why they picked me to show her around; they knew it would do her head in! And all for their fucking targets!' I shouted. 'All for the Beacon of Excellence . . .'

'I'm afraid N's not very well,' said Tony.

I couldn't see the woman no more, had me pinned face down on the floor. But I managed to turn my head to the

329

side to have the last word, like my mum used to say, 'You always got to have the last word!' 'Let's just get one thing straight,' I shouted. 'I Am NOT a Dribbler! There is Nothing Whatever Wrong with my Head!' before they jabbed me up the arse.

47. How I remembered
and how it done my head in

This ain't *The Wizard* of fucking *Oz* and *I* ain't Judy
Garland, but when I woke up I *did*, I honestly thought it
was all just a crazy dream. Fact the first thing I done was I
leapt out of bed on account of the clock shown 10.22 and
I thought I was late for Poppy. But the moment I stood
up I felt so dizzy I had to grab hold of the radiator to stop
myself falling over. My arse hurt as well and my legs was
so stiff had to shuffle about like a penguin or something
holding the wall with one wing. 'Something ain't right,
girl,' I says to myself as I sat on the toilet pissing pure
tranquilliser. 'They slipped me some drugs,' I says to
myself. 'They don't want me going up there, that's
why! They's scared of what I got to say! Well I ain't
letting Poppy down now!' But as I got up I nearly fainted
again, had to grab a hold of the sink this time else I *would*
of passed out, smashed my head on the bath, most
probably broken my neck as well; they don't think of
that when they give you a jab up the arse. And that's
when I seen my face in the mirror. I thought the mirror
was shattered at first, run my fingers over the glass to
check. But it weren't the mirror was cracked it was me.
My face was all criss-crossed and shattered with lines
where the dried-up foundation cracked through.

And then I remembered, not slowly but sudden like a

huge fucking wave come crashing in and taken the whole world with it.

It weren't like I hadn't been there before. I mean, everyone I ever known, like my dad before I was even born, my nan – my other nan too most probably, reckon I must have *had* one – then my mum when I was twelve years old, no goodbye or nothing, do you know what I'm saying and even Mandy down Sunshine House who I had to go and *find* her. But with Poppy, I'd only known her six months, and it don't make no sense and I ain't saying it does, and she weren't like flesh and blood or nothing but I reckon that hit me harder than *anyone*. Well, saying that, I don't want to do my mum down, but Poppy was different, do you know what I'm saying: Poppy weren't *s'posed* to do it; there weren't nothing wrong with her.

Them first few days, I don't mind admitting, I found myself pretty confused. I thought about it all the time, and the more I thought, the more it done my head in. It got to the point where I didn't know nothing. I weren't even sure if she was dead or alive or if she'd ever existed to start with. Even all of her stuff in my flat it didn't seem real no more. Like I'd walk in the sitting room half-expecting the lot to of just disappeared.

But the one thing I carried everywhere, solid, cutting into my hand, the one thing convinced me I couldn't of dreamt her, and that was the keys to her flat, the ones she give me.

The first time I gone round I only stayed like a minute. All the way there I was shitting myself, kept wanting to turn back but something made me go on. It was night-time but a light was on as I gone past Saffra's school. I could see in this classroom, a wall full of pictures on coloured sugar paper. I suddenly wondered where Saffra was. What if nobody told her, I thought. What if she's sat in the flat on her own? It can't have been more than a week gone by but I seen her turned into skin and bone like one of them little African kids you get on Comic Relief.

As I put my key in the lock downstairs, it made such a racket I thought I'd woke up the whole house. I stood there holding the open door, like caught in the act, not daring to move. The entrance light shone in from outside, lit up a pile of old papers and post laying on the floor by the wall. 'The Occupier, 43 Selby Street . . .' I kicked it aside and the next one as well. Then before I know it I'm squatted down, one arm stretched behind me holding the door, while my other hand's rifling its way through the mail, Thames Water envelopes, credit-card deals, faster and faster, more and more panicked till all of a sudden there she is: 'Miss Poppy Shakespeare', black on white, and it jolts me so bad I fall off of my balance, the door slams behind as my arse hits the floor, and I'm froze stock still on the cold hall tiles, heart thumping, clutching the envelope, a 0% finance offer from Lombard Direct.

After all that, the flat was a bit of a come-down. I don't know what I expected to find but it weren't there that first visit. All it was was a bunch of empty rooms. A couple of coats hung up in the hall, the sitting room bare except for the sofa and the TV with the video blinking beneath it. I don't know if someone been in and cleaned up but everything looked all dusted and hoovered made it seem even more emptier. The fridge been switched off and the door held open with a neatly folded tea towel. On the drainer two mugs stood upside down with the cafetière besides them.

I tried to imagine her washing up before she gone and done it. I couldn't believe she gone and done it. I couldn't believe I was stood in her flat and Poppy was dead, do you know what I'm saying. I just couldn't get my head round it. It didn't make no sense.

When I left I was certain I wouldn't be going back. I had a quick glance in Saffra's room just to check she weren't laying there starving or nothing but it all been packed up, or most of it. There was still a few clothes stacked up on the shelves, her blue school sweatshirt draped over the chair. As I shut the front door I got this urge to drop the keys back through. Like over and done, do you know what I'm saying; I ain't even sure why I didn't but I never.

The next night I gone back, and the next night too, and the night after *that* and all. I become like a burglar laying in all day, waiting till everyone gone to bed. You could *hear* it almost, 10 p.m., all over the Darkwoods the sound of pills, popping out of blister packs, rattling out of bottles as everyone downed their meds. Half an hour later out I gone, hurrying down to Borderline Road, hood up and head down, past flat after flat of snoring drugged-out dribblers. I couldn't of said why I kept going back. It felt weird to be honest, like pervy almost; I didn't want no one to know. Sometimes as I was walking down Sniff Street – I always walked, never taken the bus – I'd suddenly stop, feel my face turn red, like really boiling red-hot red, and I'd stand there for several seconds unable to move.

I think what it was, I was looking for something; I didn't
know what, do you know what I'm saying, and most
probably it weren't even *in* Poppy's flat, but I didn't got
nowhere else, so I had to keep trying. My third, or maybe
my fourth night there, I was sat on the bed in Saffra's room,
not nosing or nothing, just like sat on the bed, when I
noticed these couple of exercise books on the little shelf
next to her desk. There was other books too, like reading
books and a book about *Animal Hospital*, 'Love Grandma
and Grampy' it said inside, but the exercise books was what
caught my eye. They was blue and yellow, Maths and
English, Saffra Shakespeare, Ruby Class, Year Two. And
they weren't hardly started – fact the Maths *weren't* started
and the English was only like five pages in, two pages of
spelling and a bit of a story, like once upon a time sort of
thing, weren't much of a writer to tell you the honest truth.

Seeing them books made me think of Mr Pettifer. And
I'd almost forgot Mr Pettifer but now I remembered him
really clear and my fox poem too and my highly commended and what he'd said, not bragging I mean, just like
what he said: 'There's a poet in you, N.' And I taken the
books and a pencil as well, gone back through the kitchen
and sat myself down at the table, same table as where I'm sat
writing this, same table where me and Poppy was sat when
we filled out the MAD money forms. And not thinking or
nothing, do you know what I'm saying, I just started to
write it all down. And never stopped neither, not even
once, or only to grab like a couple of Penguins or have a
look round find other stuff to write on.

48. How the last piece fallen into place

General speaking, if you want to live, jumping in front of a train ain't your easiest option. According to the *Sniff Street Gazette*, most people die straight off. A few survive with 'severed limbs'. Only Poppy come through without a scratch.

The article was on the front page: SNIFF STREET WOMAN RESCUED UNDER TRAIN! There was a photo of these two men got her out, stood with their arms crossed on the station platform, smiling 'cause they'd give them a bravery award. Witnesses said she just jumped in front, 'like diving into a swimming pool'. Nobody couldn't believe she'd survived. Course it didn't actually give Poppy's name specific.

I stood reading it in the newsagent's. 'Are you *buying* that?' the woman said. I'm like, 'Alright! Who rattled *your* cage.' But I paid anyway just to get out the shop and I sat on the wall of the school opposite like staring until the words moved around on the page. It was weird, I didn't feel jealous or nothing. Like every dribbler's *dream* you'd of thought. High High High by return of post for the rest of forever, no need to fill out a form. But the honest truth was I didn't want none of it. I didn't want none of the Abaddon. All I felt was the last piece fell into place. Or almost the last; there was one thing left, one more thing I still got to do before I could write 'The End'.

It weren't nothing like I'd remembered it. The hill weren't hardly a hill at all, just a bit of a slope, what a ball wouldn't know to roll down it. Either side was an ugly great housing estate, row after row of brown brick flats, stacked three storeys high with walkways between them, stunking of piss and stale beer. I ain't saying I didn't *recognise* it, of course I did, ain't fucking *stupid*. But it weren't the Darkwoods . . . At least it was, but it *weren't* if you know what I'm saying. I'm like 'Jesus!' all the way up the street, like 'Jesus, N, where you been!' 'Cause it weren't how it *was* was freaking me out, it was how it been *before*.

The Abaddon Mental Health Centre was this red brick building, halfway along the street. Seven floors; I know 'cause I counted. Seven rows of windows. Then it stopped like someone just chopped it off, flat roof and cloudy sky. I stood there and I give it a look, like a *look*, do you know what I'm saying. 'Fucking wankers!' I said out loud. This couple of flops was sat out on the wall, sharing a can of Tennent's. 'Not you,' I said, but they weren't even listening anyway. 'Fucking wankers!' I said again. It was like, I don't know, it was like I been conned. Like the tower and all that; I ain't saying it makes sense, but you know what I mean, I'd give it thirteen years of my life and it was all just a big fucking con.

The sign by the entrance was new alright. 'The Abaddon Mental Health Centre' it said, and right underneath, where you couldn't hardly miss it, this picture of a lighthouse, or that's what it looked like, and '*Beacon of Excellence 2005*'.

'Visiting's two till six,' says Sharon. He was alright, I s'pose, nothing special.

'It's five to,' I said but he didn't say nothing, just shrugged and gone back to his mag.

I stood there, arms folded, leant on one hip. I'd been dreading it to tell you the truth, but now I was here, I needed to see her; I needed to get it over.

'Alright, seventh floor,' he said.

'Thanks,' I said and I smiled like thanks for nothing.

The lift stunk of fag smoke and months of no washing. I tried holding my breath but it gone so slow, like half an hour practically every floor, by the time it reached the seventh my eyes was popping out their sockets.

First person I seen was Sue the Sticks, sat in the TV room with a crowd of flops.

'N!' she called.

'Shit,' I thought. 'Alright?' I said. 'I never seen you there.'

'You got a spare fag, N?' she said.

I give her a pack. 'You *sure*?' she said.

'Go on,' I said.

'You *sure*?' she said. 'I don't want to take advantage.

'You just come in this morning?' she said.

'Ain't *in*,' I said. 'I'm visiting!'

'Oh,' she said. 'Oh! I thought you was in! I thought there's N back in again! Didn't I Mohammed; that's what I thought!' Mohammed grunted, whoever he was, fat flop sat watching the telly.

'You alright though, N?' said Sue the Sticks. 'You coping? You getting the help you need?'

'I'm fine,' I said.

'You *look* alright. I thought that when you come in, I thought, she *looks* alright, but you just can't tell. That's one thing I've learned, you just can't tell. Not any more you can't anyway. You heard about Poppy?'

'What?' I said.

'You ain't offended are you, N? I didn't mean there weren't nothing wrong with you. The opposite, that's what I meant to say . . .'

'What about Poppy!' I said.

'Oh!' she said. 'Well what they've found out is: Poppy weren't never right in the head to begin with! She got this flaw in her psychic, they said. Didn't show up when they done the testing. Most probably born with it, they said, and all her life she'd been covering it up, trying to survive by pretending she was normal. It weren't till she got to the Dorothy Fish and started to get the support she needed, she could finally admit to herself there was anything wrong.

'She's told me all about it,' said Sue. ' "Just think if I hadn't of come!" she said. "Don't bear thinking about," I says to her. *Thirty-three* diagnoses, N, and they's finding more every ward round!'

'So how come they missed it then?' I said. 'How come it never shown up in the tests?'

'Just one of them things, I suppose,' said Sue. 'Something with the computers they think.'

'A bug,' said Mohammed.

'That's it. That's the word. Middle-Class Michael's furious, writing letters all over the place, threatening to sue; you know what he's like. "Leave it Michael," I says.

"Let it go. Every cloud got a lining," I says. "If it weren't for the whatsit . . ."'

'The bug,' said Mohammed.

'If it weren't for the bug then they'd never of found her at all.'

It was the same room we'd come to see the fireworks. The old men's dorm, must of swapped them around. Poppy was laying on a bed at the end, elbows bent, hands under her head, staring up at the ceiling. A nurse was sat in a chair by her feet, swigging at a can of Diet Lilt as she rung round words in a wordsearch magazine.

'Alright, Poppy?' I said. 'I brought you some fags.'

She turned and looked. Her eyes was blurred.

'I brought you three packs but I give one to Sue. I can go out and get you some more if you want, if you's running low. Ain't a problem,' I said. The nurse didn't move so I had to climb around her.

'Least you got a window bed,' I said. There was six beds in the room altogether, three along each side. Opposite Poppy someone was snoring, bedding pulled right up over her head like a seal trapped under the covers.

'Least you got a window bed,' I said. 'Wish they'd turn their fucking radio's down.' Three different stations was playing at once from three different bedside lockers.

'Ain't nobody even listening,' I said. 'Do you know what I'm saying! Don't it do your head in . . .?

'I can get you out of here,' I said. 'I'll go and see Leech first thing Monday,' I said. 'You's on MAD money now, innit, Poppy,' I said. 'You *must* be on MAD money now,' I said. 'We got to get you out of here.' I was crying. I never fucking cry. 'This place'll do your head in,' I said.

Her face was like all pale and puffed. She was looking at me like she didn't get it.

'I'll get you out of here, Poppy,' I said.

'You want to get out, don't you, Poppy,' I said.

'Least you got a window bed,' I said.

'You can see right the way round the world,' she said. 'When it's clear.'

Acknowledgements

I would like to thank my parents, Liz and Graham Allan, for their tremendous support and encouragement.

Tash Aw, Bobby Baker, Leala Padmanabhan, Ben Rice, and Kate Weinberg all read the manuscript at various stages and gave generous and insightful feedback. Many thanks.

Thanks also to Clare Alexander and to Alexandra Pringle, Emily Sweet and all at Bloomsbury.

And to Juliet Allan, Gail Block, Helen Jowett, Kirstin Nicholson, Joanna Price, Jessica Rimmington and Andrew Whittuck.

And, of course, to Bernadette.

And a Palmerston steak for Billie.

A Note on the Author

Clare Allan was the winner of the first Orange/
Harpers short-story prize. She lives in London.
This is her first novel.

A Note on the Type

The text of this book is set in Bembo. This type was first used in 1495 by the Venetian printer Aldus Manutius for Cardinal Bembo's *De Aetna*, and was cut for Manutius by Francesco Griffo. It was one of the types used by Claude Garamond (1480–1561) as a model for his Romain de L'Université, and so it was the forerunner of what became standard European type for the following two centuries. Its modern form follows the original types and was designed for Monotype in 1929.